THE SPECTRE CYCLE

The Dray Prescot Series

THE SPECTRE CYCLE

Kenneth Bulmer

writing as
Alan Burt Akers

Published by
Bladud Books

First published in 2015 by Bladud Books

Originally published separately in German by Heyne Verlag in 1996-7.

Published separately by Mushroom eBooks as:
Shadows over Kregen (2014)
Murder on Kregen (2014)
Turmoil on Kregen (2014)

This paperback omnibus edition published in 2015 by Bladud Books, an imprint of Mushroom Publishing, Bath, BA1 4EB, United Kingdom

www.bladudbooks.com

ISBN 978-1-84319-929-8

Contents

Shadows over Kregen

A note on Dray Prescot

Lit by the ruby and emerald fires of Antares, the planet Kregen, four hundred light years from Earth, is a world cruel yet beautiful, terrible yet alluring. There any woman or man may achieve what the heart desires, if they plan and persevere with all the spirit within them. To this world of opportunity Dray Prescot has been brought by the Star Lords to serve their mysterious purposes.

Dray Prescot is a man above middle height, with brown hair and level brown eyes, brooding and dominating, with enormously broad shoulders and powerful physique. There is about him an abrasive honesty and an indomitable courage. He moves like a savage hunting cat, silent and deadly. Reared in the harsh conditions of Nelson's Navy, his character is far more complex than he reveals. Because he possesses the yrium, a super charisma, he has been chosen by the Star Lords to bring all the lands of Paz together, as the so-called Emperor of All Paz. They must resist the deadly Shanks who raid from over the curve of the world.

Delia and Dray Prescot have abdicated the throne of Vallia and now seek to make the dream of a united Paz come true. Fate, though, has other headlong adventures for them under the streaming mingled lights of the Suns of Scorpio.

Alan Burt Akers

One

Rumors of the activities of slavers had brought us flying to Djasra Island and now as we sat our mounts and looked through a thin screen of trees onto the beach we saw that rumor had not lied.

"By the Veiled Froyvil, my old dom! We can't have this!"

My blade comrade Seg's strong handsome face glowered with loathing upon the scene on the beach where coffles of men, women and children shuffled in their chains down to the waiting boats. Offshore, three fat-bellied argenters rode at anchor with furled sails, already low in the water from their ghastly freight.

"We shall," said my blade comrade Inch, freeing his long-handled axe, "have to teach a lesson here as well as freeing the people."

There was no way I could disagree with that sentiment. Yet—there were but a score of us and the slavers down there numbered at least fifty. The Suns of Scorpio blazed in molten ruby and jade overhead, the scents of flowers filled the bright air with heady perfumes, birds sang and cavorted, and we chosen brethren of the Kroveres of Iztar must ride down and risk all to follow the precepts of our self-imposed duty.

"Benighted Whiptails!" quoth Nath Javed, quietening the zorca between his knees. "Hack 'n' Slay 'em all!"

For, yes, indeed, the slavers were Katakis, as unpleasant a race of diffs as you'd ever wish to cross swords with on a wet and murky night.

The captured people down there were ordinary normal folk, farmers mostly, earning an honest living from the land. And now these Opaz-forsaken Katakis had swooped and swept them up in iron chains. Already the dismal moaning floated mournfully into the bright suns-shine of the morning. Oh, yes, by Vox, twenty against fifty or a hundred or even more—we Kroveres of Iztar knew well what was required of us.

No use lollygagging about then. Beyond the screen of trees the beach trended away in a slope that began steeply enough and evened out as the sand was washed by the waves. This was going to be a full-blooded charge, a whoop and holler helter-skelter, by Krun!

The smells of oiled leather and steel, the warm friendly animal scent of the zorcas, surrounded us. Sober reflection showed me instantly that this was not a holler and a whoop attack. Oh, no.

Seg unslung his Great Lohvian Longbow. "When you reach the bottom of the slope." He selected a shaft with finicky precision.

Feeling the pressures of the moment, I said: "What d'you think? Four? Five? A talen apiece?"

"Done, my old dom, and you'll be poorer tonight. Ha!"

I lifted in my stirrups and looked left and right. The lads were as bonny a bunch as you could hope to meet. Naturally, Korero the Shield drew a sword and pushed the two shields higher, and started to speak. I interrupted him with a: "And mind you don't get killed."

In a line we moved forward between the trees. A little breeze kicked up sandy dust from the crest as we passed. I said one more word. "Silence!" Then, free of the trees and with the beach ahead, we rode carefully down the slope. At the foot I sensed the tensing up, the gathering together, of the lads. Side by side, comrades in arms, we charged.

Spiral horns thrusting onward, polished hooves kicking sand, all the passionate animate beauty of the zorcas expressed itself as sublime poetry in that headlong charge. Lance heads with their brave scarlet and yellow pennons fluttering lowered into a wicked hedge. Onwards we rushed over the beach, nearer and nearer the damned Whiptails.

Clearly, just like an image seen through a telescope, circumscribed, I saw a Kataki lifting his heavy whip to bring the lash down across the naked back of a woman stumbling to her knees under her chains. Abruptly, the Kataki stood up, stiff, rigid. The whip dropped from his hand. He turned like a marionette, and fell face-first into the sand. From his back sprouted the long Lohvian arrow.

The first one to Seg, then.

There is no archer in all of Kregen—or all of Earth, come to that—who can compare with the incomparable Seg Segutorio. A second Kataki spun around with the smashing force of the shaft through his neck above the corselet rim. Two down. By this time the slavers, preoccupied with their favorite pastime of hitting poor people with whips, sluggishly became aware of our presence. A third Whiptail dropped and this wight let out a screech. Three to Seg.

Now our straining zorcas fleeting over the sand dragged shouts of alarm from the slavers. Katakis began to run and draw weapons and try to form some kind of defense. Katakis—so-called Jibrfarils—do have courage of a dark variety and we did not think they would just run away. They'd fight, particularly when they saw how few we were, and even more particularly in defense of their human spoils.

We hit a bunch of them as they scrambled to form up and the lances struck and swung and withdrew. The bright pennons now stained a darker red.

My lance did not break, although some did, and I went bald-headed for the next rast of a Whiptail as he flailed a sword above his miserable head. Almost he deflected the small keen lance head. The steel went in, anyway, and this time the lance snapped. I threw the stump at the next Kataki and whipped out my Krozair Longsword.

He went down screeching and an arrow snicked off my saddle and caromed away with a most unpleasant sound. In the next instant in the hubbub I spotted the shooter who was busily nocking the next shaft. Before I could urge faithful Baldik across I saw that was unnecessary so I swung the zorca the other way. A Lohvian shaft with the red fletchings from the Zim-korf had done the fellow's business for him.

Thinking that was number four to Seg I realized it was five as the zorca nimbly avoided a sprawled Whiptail with one of Seg's messages through his eye.

One more and I'd be paying out gold to my comrade.

And, by Krun, that'd please me mightily!

The fight had settled into a scrambling, slashing, up and down affair now. The screeching sound of blade on blade rasped the nerves. The Katakis had recovered from their initial surprise under the silence and ferocity of our attack. Now we had a battle royal on our hands.

Swirling the Krozair blade in a cunning underhand I hoicked a damned Whiptail up and over and so dispatched him down to the Ice Floes of Sicce. Recovering and looking the other way I saw a zorca standing still with head down and reins dangling. By his front hooves a man lay prostrate. His insignia were red and yellow. A welling sadness suffused through me, sadness and anger and futile remorse.

That was young Nath Arumsted ti Volsover, a new and enthusiastic member of the Kroveres of Iztar. Rather, that had been young Nath.

Three more Whiptails went down to their personal hells before I had myself fully under control. I shook blood drops from the Krozair brand. I breathed in gulps, the smell of the sea and the stink of blood coiling like a miasma. All the time the people who had been doomed to be slaves were screaming and caterwauling away in a most distressing fashion.

One or two of them tried to help, using chains or what weapons they could pick up from fallen Jibrfarils. The suddenness of our onslaught had served us well. Now we had the long slog as numbers began to tell. If more people joined us—but then, ordinary folk, even on Kregen, which is barbaric enough, Opaz knows, aren't in the habit of snatching up swords and fighting. Although, mind you, sometimes it does seem as though battles and combats flower all the hours Opaz gives to the world.

A swift glance back to the dune crest showed a hurtling figure already at the foot of the slope and haring across the sand towards us. Good old Seg!

A fleeting glimpse of an incredibly tall fellow swinging a long-handled axe in lethal circles showed Inch was in action. Good old Inch! And, as was to be expected, the battering yells of: "Hack 'n' Slay!" reverberated over the clangor of the combat. Good old Nath Javed, known as Old Hack 'n' Slay.

All the brothers of the KRVI were in violent action, smiting the ungodly. The pathetic coffles of slaves lay in their chains, their eyes like curdled milk, shaking. All save those hardy few who lapped a bight of iron around a Whiptail's throat, risking the lethal stab of the blade strapped to his tail.

I looked around for the next antagonist. Seg reined up, sword in fist.

"Any left?"

Other brothers were looking about, weapons bloodied. The slaves keened their dolorous dirge. The only Katakis we could see lay sprawled on the sand in their own blood.

I thought, but did not voice the thought, that perhaps the rightness of our purpose had conferred a victory beyond normal expectations. Certainly, we had won this battle. We had suffered two dead, Nath Arumsted, and Ornol the Firm. Sundry cuts and bruises adorned our skins; yet we still possessed our hides. Opaz be thanked!

Seg hitched his zorca around. "The boats."

"Aye."

Across the gap of water the three argenters were setting sail. The canvas came down and was sheeted home smartly enough; yet my old sailorman's eye detected an odd hesitancy in the operation. Strange.

The boats in which the slaves had been transferred to the fat-bellied merchant ships lay hauled up along the shore. We'd never catch the slave ships if we pulled out. The brisk little breeze would see to that.

"Damned Whiptails," said Inch, methodically cleaning his axe. "Don't even bother to see if any of their friends are alive."

"Oh, I expect they've had a spyglass trained on us," Rolan Ledwidge said, starting to turn his zorca about. Rolan, a spry, useful old barnacle, had served many seasons in the Vallian Navy. "They may be Opaz confounded slavers. They ain't stupid, no, by Corg!"

"Aye." Seg turned his zorca. "Best get back to the flier."

Before we returned to our voller we freed some of the slaves with keys discovered upon the bloodied bodies of Katakis. The rest of the people, overjoyed, thankful, would be released in turn.

Proper arrangements for our dead would be made later. Now we had pressing business to conclude.

The voller nestled safely among trees where we'd landed. Rollo the Runner, who was, by Krun! not so young any more, had remained aboard to maintain contact. Mind you, as a Wizard of Loh, he still was not totally happy about going into lupu and scrying out. When he heard our report, he nodded in his fresh determined way and told us that he'd go into lupu at once. His preparations included spinning about, contemplation, the concentration of all his energies, so that he could reach out through that weird other dimension frequented by mages. Everybody politely took no notice of Rollo as he brought all his faculties into a single piercing thrust of thaumaturgical power. A line of sweat glistened on his smooth forehead.

Yes, I did look covertly at him, just to make sure.

Presently he returned to the mundane world. He'd got through and the main body was on its way.

Although a natural sense of urgency gripped me, I knew we had plenty of time. Those plump argenters with their square sails and bluff bows could never outsail fliers. The problem would be to deal with the damned Katakis without harming the innocent folk.

Katakis are an unpleasant lot, to be sure. Their thick black hair is habitually oiled and curled. Their faces are a snarl of low brow, flaring nostrils, jagged snaggly teeth in a wide cruel mouth, and eyes as narrow and cold as the Ice Caves of Gundarlo. The steel blades strapped to their long whip-like tails make them dangerous foes.

Opaz-forsaken slavers!

Now we brothers of the KRVI are a hard-bitten bunch. We've seen, if not all, then most of it. We understand the pressures on men and women. But do not run away with the notion that we do not care, that we do not react to situations. The horrific scenes on the beach had not left us unaffected. Callousness had not overcome all human feeling. All the same, we had a task set to our hands and until that task was fulfilled and seen to be fulfilled there was no room to shake and quiver and feel sick.

As the voller soared into the bright air of Kregen, guided by the piloting skills of young Oby—who, again, by Vox, was no longer a youngster!—we could not rest until our duty was accomplished.

Somberly, I reflected that the miserable maggot-begotten Katakis might hurl the slaves over into the sea. The chains would quickly drag them down. That tactic to escape pursuit had been well-known on Earth when slavers to the Americas were being chased by the Royal Navy. Even Whiptails, who were notorious for not wishing to give up their merchandise, might do that dreadful thing.

We'd have to be ready for that and have airboats on standby to lower down to the water and snatch up the poor wretches before they sank.

Inch's acid comment about the Whiptails not bothering to see if any of their comrades were still alive made me think on, as they say. The slavers must, as Rolan Ledwidge said, have watched us through a telescope. So they'd see how few we were. Still they hadn't come roaring ashore brandishing weapons. With the ships laden down they were prepared to leave the last of their merchandise on the beach.

From these facts and the clumsy although reasonably rapid fashion in which they'd got under way I deduced that they were short-handed. Possibly our small force actually would outnumber the crew of each individual vessel.

By Zair! That was a mighty fine thought!

The invigorating air of Kregen blustered past as the voller sped on. The streaming mingled rays of the Suns of Scorpio shone down splendidly in a riot of reds and greens. We flew on, soaring above the countryside at no great altitude heading for the coast.

The voller's speed would carry us swiftly to our destination; but in the time we'd taken to ride from the beach back to the flier the three argenters, despite their sluggish sailing qualities, had dropped the coast astern and were now well out to sea.

"Keep her low, Oby." His face intent, his hands on the controls sure, Oby nodded, and in the same instant we spotted our quarry he dropped us down again out of sight.

Three ships and one voller did not add up, did not balance. We would just have to wait for the main body to reach us.

Now this did not square with my impatience. We all could visualize the conditions of horror in which the slaves were held cramped and chained below decks. The quicker we could start the quicker they'd be freed.

Yet if my optimistic deductions about the strength of the crews proved correct the two we didn't attack could deal with their cargos before we could finish the first and get stuck into them.

Really and truly I ought not to have been surprised by the suddenness and completeness of our victory over the slavers. Truth to tell, the Brotherhood of the Kroveres of Iztar was not idly named. The Order owed allegiance to Zena Iztar, that mysterious supernatural woman of awe-inspiring powers. She bestowed ability upon us over and above that of normal men when we were engaged on the duties of the Order. Yes, we were bound by notions of honor and chivalry. We championed the weak against the strong. But our achievements for the Brotherhood could only be reached through the mystic support of Zena Iztar.

Each member of the Order could use the honor title of Ver, particular to the Brotherhood. We carried the memories of our martyrs as bright guiding lights. The first martyr for the KRVI, Dredd Pyvorr, had died on the tiny island of Nikzm, off the coast of my home island stromnate of Valka. That island was now called Drayzm, and Seg had remarked in all seriousness that we of the Order could call ourselves the Kroveres of Drayzm.

Needless to say, I shrugged that off, more than a trifle embarrassed.

After all, Seg Segutorio was the Grand Archbold of the KRVI.

As I thus ruminated these unsettling thoughts, Oby kept the voller discreetly low, occasionally lifting and dropping to continue our observation of the damned Katakis.

And—that brought to my attention the unwelcome fact that I'd given the orders, both to Oby to fly low and to the others. My blade comrade Seg was the Grand Archbold. As a comrade and true friend he'd let me have my head in my old intemperate way. This, also, was a result of the charisma, rather, the super charisma foisted off on me by a hardhearted fate, this so-called yrium that curses and blesses.

I favored Seg with a wary glance. His dark mop of hair emphasized the handsomeness of his face. His fey blue eyes, usually so merry, now stared bleakly ahead. Seven-feet tall Inch shuffled up at our backs to stare out over our heads. I felt a chill, as of a sudden blast from the Snowfields of Sandora-feyl.

Speaking carefully, each word pronounced with the utmost precision, I suggested we might drop a third of our strength upon each of the argenters.

A great meanness of spirit descended upon me at what I almost added; thankfully, I snapped my old black-fanged winespout shut in time.

For I'd almost gone on to say that Seg was the Grand Archbold of the Order and should make the decision.

The enormity of that betrayal of friendship made me brace up, I can tell you! By the barnacle on Beng Thrax's backside! What a miserable specimen of humanity I must be even to contemplate such cowardly and dastardly an act!

Seg said: "So let's do it."

"Aye," said Inch.

A muted chorus of approval and agreement rose from the brothers clustered for'ard on the deck.

Below us the sea glittered blue, above us the Suns of Scorpio slanted across a high blue sky. Yes, this was a bright bonny day on which to die.

Flags snapped against their staffs as the little breeze played with the bright colors. There were two flags there whose owners now lay sprawled in their own blood back on the beach awaiting a decent interment. Brave flags, a brave day, a brave time to go down through the encircling mists to the Ice Floes of Sicce.

This enterprise was strictly harebrained. Any emperor and leader of armies ought to be most reluctant to split his forces except in the most urgent circumstances. That, the general feeling agreed, was the case here.

Rollo would stay to fly the airboat, whose name was *Pink Lily*. There is no accounting for taste in these matters. I gripped the rail, staring ahead over that blue glittering sea. On Kregen eighteen divided by three comes to six, just as it does on this Earth.

Six of us to drop onto each deck where we would encounter—how many Katakis? Seg was always one for a little wager in the most fraught of circumstances. So I put forward the opinion that we might face odds of three to one, at which Seg immediately fired up and declared roundly that there'd only be two to one. Gold was wagered.

Then—with a curve to his lips indicating joy in my approaching discomfiture—Seg said: "As the Grand Archbold I shall, naturally—"

"What!" I exclaimed. "You're pulling rank!"

"Oh, aye, my old dom. So that's settled."

Do not forget, Seg Segutorio was the Emperor of Pandahem, which really existed. I was supposed to be the Emperor of All Paz, which remained more of a dream than a reality.

Inch would take his five men down onto the first argenter. Then I'd assault the second and Seg would attack last. This meant, as even the most simple swod with a spear in the ranks could see, that the Katakis would be ready and waiting to hit him as he touched down.

Fret though I might over my comrade, I could do nothing in honor to change that decision.

"Ready?"

page number footer
9

"Aye, ready."

With that, Rollo, who'd taken over from Oby at the controls, swung *Pink Lily* round ready for the mad dash low over the sea. We popped up and a screeching yell erupted at our backs.

We turned sharply to look back. Engar Valmin stood tall, left arm pointing rigidly back, sword in fist, yelling: "They're here!"

Here they came, like a handful of flung pebbles, hurtling on over the heave of the sea, their flags streaming in their onrush. Thank Zair! I said to myself. The main body had arrived to save us from an all too probable fate.

Among the fliers soared two vast skyships, many-decked and tiered, bristling with weapons. The suns struck sparks of fire from their flanks. They looked absolutely marvelous.

Not all the warriors crowding those decks were members of the KRVI. There were elements of the bodyguards owing allegiance to Seg and Inch, and others of the brotherhood's guard formations. The guards of my own Emperor's Sword Watch and Emperor's Yellow Jackets, stout fellows all, would be craning overside to get a first glimpse of their quarry. Oh, yes, by Vox! I felt a warm glow of pleasure at that gorgeous sight, I can tell you!

Looking ahead again we could see the argenters lolloping along with the spray bursting around their plump sides. Not long now, and we'd be pouncing upon them, stooping with steel in our fists.

Black specks appeared in the sky beyond the ships.

Staring up as the spots drew closer and grew larger and took on recognizable outlines, I felt an enormous weight fall upon my shoulders. A sense of despair shocked all through me.

Those fliers up there with their sleek black hulls and squared-off upperworks, brightly-painted, had voyaged from the other side of Kregen. They were here over the curve of the world to slay and pillage and burn. They came from Schan. They were the scourge of every living person in Paz.

Someone said the word, the dread name.

"Shanks!"

Two

"Shanks!"

The very name itself was enough to drive terror into the hearts of the simple folk of Paz. And, by Krun, truth to tell many a grizzled veteran who had fought in the wars and bore his scars would far prefer to fight any other foes than the Shanks. The Fish-heads from over the curve of the world were by many degrees far, far worse than even the Katakis.

The converging forces looked to be evenly matched. Any commander of sense would like to go into action against the Shanks with odds in his or her favor of two to one at the very least.

The brilliance of Zim and Genodras still smiled in streaming ruby and jade radiance across the sea. The clouds drifted, high and white and fluffy. Gulls pivoted on cranked wings and screeched their cries. The world of Kregen still existed as it had only moments before.

Yet now I felt a chill as though the Ice Floes of Sicce reached out to seize me up in their frozen embrace.

"Look at those three!" snapped Seg. Instantly I was brought up short, facing the prospect ahead and to a Herrelldrin Hell with all morbid thoughts.

All but three of the Fish-heads' vollers sped straight on over the argenters, heading directly for our main force, dark and powerful and ominous. The three airboats dropped down. They were obviously of a different design from the others, bulkier, and with a lot of cargo space between decks.

By the slime-filled nostrils and dangling putrescent eyeballs of Makki Grodno! I saw at once what they were and what they intended.

They were slave vollers. The evil plan was laid bare. The Katakis rounded up the slaves for the Shanks who kept off the coast to avoid detection. Now they were dropping down to load their holds with the miserable folk taken up by the Whiptails.

"Now I owe you gold." Seg looked savage. That fierce expression was not because he'd lost our little wager. No, he, like us all, saw the diabolical scheme and what it meant.

Moving with deliberateness, I looked back. The force of airboats drove on as though broomed by a hurricane. The two skyships made directly for the main body of Shanks. Aboard that little armada were men and women who understood politics, warfare—and the fishfaces. As that thought crossed my mind three fast vollers swooped down in a long slanting rush towards the three slave argenters.

"Your gold's safe, Seg." I spoke, I confess, with a kind of grunt. "Praise Opaz it be so."

Swiveling around to face front I gave Seg a hard stare. Now Seg Segutorio as the Grand Archbold of the Kroveres ran the Order without questions from me. He took advice and then made up his own mind. The two forces of airboats drew closer together. Time was running out. Now it was up to Seg to make the decision.

Easy enough for me, by Krun, to decide what I'd do. The advent of our main body had changed everything. My utter faith in my blade comrade was never in question. After all, he was Seg Segutorio, in my opinion the best archer of two worlds.

He spoke with a hard metallic snap to his voice.

"The Brotherhood is saved. The Katakis with their damned Shank customers overhead won't dispose of their merchandize now. We go down on the furthest argenter. Our lads coming on can take the other two. There will be, as Zena Iztar is my witness, enough time." To Rollo: "Take her down!"

So down we plunged, hurtling through thin air, plummeting full on our target. Good old Seg Segutorio!

Air screamed past. The flags stood out stiff as best starched linen. The slave ship bloated in size. The glitter of the sea, the heave of the waves, the white scuds breaking, all roared up to us in a welter of scattered impressions.

With the speed of our descent the ship appeared to leap up at us. A quick glance back showed me that Seg's appreciation of the tactical situation was askew by a small point; but that point a matter of honest human emotion. Seg had said our three vollers would go for the other two slave argenters. The men and women aboard those airboats knew the people who were aboard *Pink Lily*. As I expected, two fliers went hell for leather for the other two sailing ships. One dropped down swiftly in our wake.

Oh, yes, by Zair! Those grim warriors of ours were not about to let their friends and commanders go into action unsupported.

Seg nodded briskly. "Yes, I expected that."

Inch laughed. "By the flags, Alten Schongar commands."

"A fine fellow." Nath Javed delivered himself of the verdict with relish. "He can Hack 'n' Slay with the best." Then, because he was who he was, he added: "Indubitably!"

In that all-embracing glance back and up I saw the rolling banks of clouds boiling in to cover the sky. The dun gray masses cast a pall on all the bright sea in our wake. Ominous, unhealthy, they spread a chill into the brilliance of the Kregish afternoon.

A last fleeting glance upwards before we struck showed the three Shank slave vollers hovering. Clearly, they were uncertain with the swift Pazzian airboats lunging into the attack. Bad cess to 'em!

In a whirlwind of erupting action *Pink Lily* smashed heavily down onto the fat deck of the argenter bringing down the mainmast in a rending welter of splintering timbers and lashing rigging. We went over the sides as leems leap on their prey by the waterholes. The Shanks faced us. Oh, yes, those Fish-heads from around the curve of the world have courage. They fight. Now we had to overcome them without thought or pity. That was the duty laid on us, the Brothers of the Kroveres of Iztar.

The argenter bore on, slowing as the drag of the mainmast tangled in its web of rigging overside slewed her. The deck felt hard underfoot. Under the gloom of the stormclouds there was no gallant glitter of blades. The steel looked gray, honed to penetrate guts and lop heads. The Shanks screeched: "Ishtish! Ishtish!"

A single savage bellow of: "Iztar!" and we were into them.

There were, indeed, more of them than us. That we expected.

The Fish-heads know how to fight. Normally their name is enough to make fellows who do not have the steel up their backbone run off. The misfortune of this bunch was to come up against the bonny lads with me. Screams burst up. Blood spurted. Swords thrust in the short lethal jabs of close combat. Shank tridents darted for our stomachs or throats and were met and parried on good Vallian steel.

All the time above the staccato sounds of combat there rose the long dreadful moans of the slaves chained below decks.

If anything, that dolorous sound drove our blades into quicker action, our muscles into more ferocious onslaught. The battle swayed across the cumbered deck. We held them; but for the moment could not make headway against their numbers. Very well, then! By the Blade of Kurin! If there were more than us we would have to cut them down and so reduce the imbalance.

Cold, impersonal words for strife and blood and death!

Death spread his dark wings above that blood-stained deck. Death's companion, Destruction, plied her gory trade with every slash of blade. We struggled and the gloom about us deepened. The glory of the Suns of Scorpio dwindled and died in the encroaching storm clouds.

Spots of rain began to hiss onto the deck. Footing became treacherous. A neat backhanded slash aimed at the scaly head of a fishface thrusting his trident at me missed as I slipped. The argenter's motions in the sea, checked by the mainmast overside, were unpredictable. Recovering by the expedient of ducking away I managed to deflect the trident.

A sword sliced in above my head and the Shank screeched and toppled away.

"Here's another, my old dom."

No need for me to gasp out a thankyou to Seg; we'd done this before, and, by Vox, we'd do it again. I took the newcomer with a straight pass as Seg switched around to chop another.

No need, either, for us to prattle on about "Warm work!"

The combat was warm, and would grow hotter.

The ship surged sluggishly and again I nearly lost my balance. Me, an old Sailorman! With more than a trifle of irritation I took the next Shank, chopped him, glared around for some more.

The darkness swooped as the thunderclouds rolled above. Rain thickened into a gray sheet, bouncing off the deck. Water ran down our faces. Lurid lightning split the sky. Thunder drenched everything in noise.

The vollers flying up there must be having a ball, by Krun!

The Pazzian voller coming down to our assistance showed as a mere shadowed blot against the dimness. She bore in, her bows touched the foremast, brought that down in a welter of confusion, and she crunched full onto the forecastle. Warriors leaped out, the steel naked in their hands, roaring unheard in the din.

Now we'd have the damned fishfaced reivers!

The fight edged towards the ship's stern. We were now pressing our enemies back with a relentless wall of steel. Just about then the rigging holding the mainmast to the vessel's side chafed clean through. Unable to see the mast surging away among the waves, I could feel the instant change in the way the ship gyrated. A number of men staggered and fell. The Shanks let out their screeching: "Ishtish Ishtish" audible above the uproar of the gale.

The deck went up and down like a roller coaster. The ship twisted herself in the sea gyrating like one of those abandoned dancing girls of the desert tribes of Dordre-Um, hostile to strangers. My left fist fastened on the rail and for a moment I, like everyone else, clung on for dear life.

Those poor unfortunate slaves chained below must be going through hell right now. The Kataki slavers were bad enough; the Fish-heads who had dropped down to take over were far far worse—and now the slaves were being thrown about like apples in a barrel rolling downhill over bumpy cobbles. Still, feel for them though we did, we knew that it would be disastrous to free them and bring them up on deck. The chaos that would cause didn't bear thinking of.

In the ranks of our foes, Katakis had fallen with commendable regularity and their Shank customers were not now likely to rejoin their confounded slave voller. All in all, this little fracas could be going a lot worse.

Now we had to hold on, clear the rest of the slavers out, ride through the gale, and then jury-rig the argenter enough to sail her back.

This was late afternoon of a Kregan day when the Suns of Scorpio should be beaming their ruby and emerald rays to turn the sea into a fairyland of glitter and color. Instead the pall lay dark and dense and the rain lashed viciously in long battering streaks and the lightning crackled and the thunder roared.

In one lacerating lightning flash it was just possible to catch a fleeting glimpse of dark forms leaping into the sea off the poop. The Shanks were abandoning the vessel!

"Good riddance!" said Seg, breathing hard through his nose.

"Aye." Old Hack 'n' Slay grasped the rail with one massive fist. "Indubitably."

We were experienced enough in warfare to be thankful when our enemies ran off, or, in this case, jumped into the sea when there was no need to chase after them.

Others of our people, those from the voller, ardent in their detestation of Kataki and Shank alike, determined to carry on the fight to the bitter end. Half a dozen of them ran and staggered aft.

Seg let rip a: "By the Veiled Froyvil!" and started after them. Between lightning strokes he vanished into the gloom.

Shouting with extreme venom, I bellowed into Nath Javed's ear: "D'you go down and see to the slaves, Nath!" Without giving him time to expostulate, I hared off after Seg, sliding and lurching across the deck. Water broke green and white in a lightning flash, foaming over the bulwarks. For an instant waist deep in the swirl I thought I was done for, washed overboard. But the level sank, a desperate grasp at the rail and I hauled myself on after Seg.

Even in that instant of cursing the idiots who so tempted fate, I spared a wry thought for poor old Hack 'n' Slay. Still, there was no doubt he would obey, mumbling away to himself in baffled fury. What the huddled slaves would think of his enormous frame, black with water, girded for war, suddenly appearing before them like a spectre devil from Cottmer's Caverns I didn't care to dwell on. Forcing myself on I followed Seg as fast as I could.

Not all the Fish-heads were jumping overboard.

The shards of lightning piercing the darkness flashed more frequently. The thunder melded into one continuous uproar. In that stark illumination the Shanks battled our impetuous folk.

The deck gave a tremendous heave as a giant wave hit the ship. Skidding with flailing arms I was pitched headlong into the starboard door under the poop. My head rang with the impact, and I saw enough stars to populate the heavens.

A savage grasp of the ladder and an even more savage wrench around set my foot on the second rung. Up I went in no mood to be polite. If the situation was not so fraught the scene on the poop would have been farcical.

Pazzian and Shank staggered about like loons, trying to strike their opponents. Swords went swishing about Fish-heads and tridents stabbed into the deck. "By Makki Grodno's diseased left nostril and fungus-infested armpits!" I said to myself. "What a bunch of clowns!"

That macabre scene luridly illuminated by the strokes of blue fire presented a conundrum. A flicker of motion in the corner of my eye swung me about and in the next flash I saw that however bizarre the scene was, it must be left to sort itself out. There was work to my hands, here and now, over by the poop rail.

The lightning sizzled less frequently and the intervening stretches of dimness lengthened. I must be quick. Damned quick!

I had seen what I'd seen and I knew what I'd seen. The brief flare of electrical discharge showed me two men—a Kataki and a Shank—ferociously attacking a Pazzian. By the slim lissomness of the figure, by its shape, that Pazzian was a girl, a young girl warrior desperately battling for her life.

"Sink me!" I snarled, hurling myself forward, sword in fist. "I'm not having this!"

The lunge of the ship skittled me off a direct run and the general dimness hampered a clean thrust—but! But, all the same, my brand skewered into the Kataki as his wicked bladed tail swished around in a slanting cut at the Jikai Vuvushi's head.

Right fist gripping the sword stuck through the Whiptail I brought my left hand up, wrapped my fingers around the fellow's tail and hauled back. In the contortions of the vessel the two anchorages on the Kataki maintained my balance, the six inches of daggered steel strapped to the end of his tail missed the girl and he toppled back. His screech broke clearly above the clamor of the gale.

The ungainly motions of the vessel, the Kataki's twist as he went back, together with the urgent need to grab onto the rail, tore the hilt of the sword out of my hand which in the next instant fastened on the poop rail. I swung about. Letting go of the tail I crashed heavily into the rail. A bolt of light showed me the girl's back a pace away as she swirled her sword facing the Shank.

The Fish-head had lost his trident and now wielded a sword with a double-curved blade, a nasty looking object. The Jikai Vuvushi's thraxter, a straight cut and thrust weapon, glanced off her foeman's steel and I saw that in a twinkling of an eye that double curved length of death would transfix her. A single leap, a savage heave back with my arm wrapped round a slim waist, and she toppled away to slide across the deck into the darkness.

The Shank let out a hissing I could hear and so sharp and fierce had been his attack he smashed into me, body to body, the double-curved sword going past my side—as I then thought.

Locked together we struggled. Locked together as the ship rolled we went over the side together. As a single item we plunged into the hostile sea. Black waves enveloped us. The argenter vanished. Washed away, we struggled for life in an empty sea. In that fraught moment, from somewhere, I heard—did I hear or was it merely a fevered figment of imagination?—a shrill voice call: "He's fallen in the water!"

Three

Black as the cloak of Notor Zan, the water pressed in all about us. Down we sank. The water was not cold, warmed by the twin suns during the day;

but the coldness of finality awaited me if I did not do two things remarkably quickly.

Able to hold my breath under water for an extraordinarily long time I fancied I could accomplish the two items on the agenda and still have air enough to last me back to the surface.

One obvious task was to shed my armor. That was not the first priority though, no, by Krun! This pesky Shank clinging to me like a leech had to be dislodged. He'd lost his sword and now he attempted to draw the dagger strapped to his thigh with one hand whilst the other dug into my windpipe.

Putting my own hand up I wrapped my fingers around his throat. He was a damned Fishman, wasn't he? He ought to be able to swim like a fish, then. I squeezed—I squeezed with the hard determination that I'd do for him before he did for me.

We were both struggling about with thrashing legs in the constricting confines of the sea. My other fist fastened on his wrist forcing the dagger away from its intended destination—my guts.

The name of Makki Grodno floated across my consciousness. Fool! This unpleasant experience had thoroughly addled my brain. What tomfoolery did I think I was up to? I, Dray Prescot, was acting like the biggest onker of all time.

On the instant I whipped my fist away from the Shank's throat and, with all the savagery my muscles could command, drove a straight arm jab into his stomach.

I didn't want to stop him from breathing! No, by Krun, I wanted to let him breathe as much as he damned-well liked. I wanted him to breathe all right—breathe water!

He jerked like a fish landed on the bank, which in a way he was, and a string of bubbles broke from his mouth, going straight up. He tried to shut that nasty fish mouth of his, so I gave him another jab. A froth of bubbles exploded past his fangs and gyrated upwards.

Now I know the Star Lords must have given me this useful gift of being able to see well in dim conditions, for I'd experienced the handiness of that before. At first I'd not really believed. But events had more or less forced me into acceptance.

All the same, here we were under the water, with a black cloud-filled sky above, and I could see enough to check his dagger and see his stomach to hit him. I felt a tingling about my body. I looked down at myself. I did not feel shock, only startlement.

Thin threads of light writhed all over my body, forming a constantly-moving net. The dream-like effect of this web was heightened by the color of the wriggling lines, a sickly green-tinged blue. As I watched, feeling the tingling like a mild electric current, the web began to expand.

My fingers were still wrapped around the Shank's dagger-hand. The bubbles from his fishy mouth thinned and slackened. He was quite clearly done for. Even in these moments of supernatural peril I felt my hate for him drifting away. I cannot say I felt true sympathy, but I suppose any human being must feel a tinge of sorrow when Death reaps his grisly harvest. Not so much sorrow for the Shank victim but general sorrow that Life has lost another to Death. I always feel that, keenly.

The blue-green writhing threads forming the net expanded in a globe about me, the spaces between the lines remaining less than a hand's breadth apart, the numbers of lines constantly increasing.

The threads crept along my extended arm where I still held the Fishhead. They curved over my wrist, my knuckles, clustered around the Shank's hand. I felt nothing apart from the pleasant tingling. I was still holding the Fishman's hand. But the threads of lambent light amputated that hand as cleanly as a bacon slicer. Cut through at the wrist, the Fishhead's arm was no longer held by me. The body was pushed away. The webbed globe thrust it away into the dark sea that encompassed the globe of light.

There I hung suspended in the center. The tingling over my body persisted even though the wriggling threads of fire had gone to form the protective globe. This was about ten paces in diameter. There was no water inside. By this time I knew I could not hold my breath much longer.

Unless the interior of this occult globe was a vacuum, as it might damnwell be, by Vox!—there had to be air. Breathable air or not, vacuum or not, whatever chanced, I had to open my mouth.

A huge gulp—air! Sweet, clean, lovely Kregish air!

When anyone is fortunate enough to live on Kregen under the twin suns of Antares, magical mysteries form part of daily experience. That may be an exaggeration, I suppose, for perhaps not every single day witnesses its miracle. But, by Vox, it's not too far from the truth! So I sucked in the blessed air thankfully.

This whole eerie experience could be the doing of any number of human mages, or supernatural beings. I wondered with a curiosity I found to my surprise was not particularly strong, if this globe could be the handiwork of the Star Lords.

Well, whatever was to happen, would happen. Selah!

As to that, of course, The Star Lords brought me to Kregen from Earth, the planet of my birth four hundred light years off, and flung me about the world willy-nilly to do their bidding. They might perhaps regard me as far more useful to their plans than I had been; I was not weak enough to imagine they cared any more for my hide than they ever had.

Of two things I was keenly aware.

One, I needed a good square Kregan meal inside me.

Two, I needed a good Kregan draught to quench my thirst.

A moment's sober reflection convinced me that those two requirements were not selfish, not weak. On Kregen six or eight regular meals are the norm. If whoever—or whatever, by Zair!—had brought me here to save my life then she, he or it ought to be aware I needed to be fed.

So this brought me round to worrying about the fate of my comrades left up there fighting Katakis and Shanks in bloody combat. Whenever I am in battle with my comrades I tremble for their safety. The fact is when I know they are fighting and I am not shoulder to shoulder with them I shudder for their welfare a thousand-fold.

These fragmented thoughts made me fret and fume away—totally uselessly. By the nit-laden hair and sagging bosom of the Divine Madam of Belschutz! If the supernatural wonders who'd snatched me here didn't make an appearance soon, I'd—I'd what?

"By the Black Chunkrah!" I snarled. "Get a move on! Bratch!"

The wriggling lines of blue-green fire forming the encompassing globe continued. We sank down. In the illuminated area just beyond the capsule of air fishes glimmered and swarmed. Eyes, red, yellow, purple, glowed hungrily. Vast shapes moved on the periphery of vision. Giant jaws, edged with razor teeth, gaped.

"Well, you onkers," I said to these fishy monsters. "You haven't a chance in a Herrelldrin Hell of biting through here!"

That pettiness made me feel a trifle better. The severed hand still clutching the dagger tended to enhance gloom, resentment, baffled fury. The grisly thing drifted about within the globe, like an Earthly astronaut in free fall. That thought gave me little comfort, I can tell you, by Krun!

Although I could turn and swivel my body, I could not move away from the center of the sphere of blue-green fire. I hung there like a plumb bob. The hand and dagger drifted about randomly. The moment they came within reach I gave 'em a hefty kick. As a consequence I span about like a manic Catherine wheel.

A vivid flare of light suffused the globe. I clapped my eyes shut instantly; but I'd caught a glimpse of the fist wrapped around the dagger flying into the network of writhing fire.

Both were consumed in that intolerable flare. Eyes streaming, I left them closed. After all, there was precious little left to see at the moment.

The obvious conclusion was not that I ought not to leave the center for fear of being burned up; but that if I could do so the fiery net would not harm me. Why should it?

Something was doing this to me—I was beginning to believe it to be a something and not a someone—and until it chose to reveal itself I was stuck, hanging as it were in limbo. Down and down we drifted. The fishes faded away above. Only blackness pressed against those eerie writhings of fire.

We touched bottom. An old sailorman does not forget that sensation. Conscious that the sphere was rolling along the sea bed I failed to determine the direction. Not long now then, I said to myself. And, by Gaji's Bowels, that was too long!

Tendrils scraped along the front and sides of the sphere. Seaweed! Long fronds of weed, dangling from above, slipping and sliding away as we passed through. The weeds came in all shapes and sizes from long thick fleshy leaves to delicate fern-like fronds. The seaweed closed in abaft, so we rolled along surrounded.

After an indeterminate time the glowing sphere rolled clear of the final fronds of seaweed. The light revealed a cavern where bleached white deformed growths flowered in ledge and crevice. I stared about ready to shout insults in my usual style.

The wriggling strands of fire began to fade.

Slowly the net lost its radiance, the writhings slowed down, the blue-green lambency dulled to a shriveled brown.

The globe crumbled to dust.

I gulped what I imagined to be the last of the air.

Directly ahead a sharp green light burst forth, shining in a slanting cone upon a rectangle of shells. The shells I could make out covered a door set in a grotesque archway. A musty, decaying smell infected my nostrils, and I grimaced.

My body, of its own will, snapped up, straight and erect. Now folk may be used to magic and all the weird devices of mages upon Kregen under Antares. Do not for a single moment imagine that I did not feel terror. Oh, yes, I, Dray Prescot, Lord of Strombor and Krozair of Zy, experienced that demoralizing dread of the unknown.

I took another breath of that foul air. So the seaweed tunnel had brought the globe of fire from water to air. The green light beat lambently upon the shell-covered door. Absolute silence enveloped the cavern.

I opened my mouth to shout. Some bravado-like nonsense, yelled out without thought; that should suffice. My mouth snapped shut.

A voice spoke like steel slicing silk.

"What are you waiting for, Dray Prescot, Emperor of Emperors, Emperor of All Paz? Go through the door!"

To myself I snarled: "You sarcastic bastard!"

Roughly I shoved the door open and stepped through.

Four

The shell-covered door crashed open abruptly, so brutal had been my shove, and smashed back on its hinges. Some of the shells fell off. They made a pleasant little tinkling in the echo of the door's opening. The stinking fish smell wafted away. Two steps into a pallid green light and the fish stench vanished completely to be replaced by the perfumes of flowers.

A rapid glance around revealed an octagonal chamber four of whose walls were covered with shells, and four with varieties of wooden flowers sculpted and painted quite attractively. That little critical appreciation of flower-arranging in these eerie circumstances made me perk up. By Vox, yes!

Weird disembodied voices speaking from thin air were no novelty to a fellow who went adventuring on Kregen. This was one favorite method to talk to me used by the Star Lords. If all these goings-on were the work of the Everoinye then I had the disastrous feeling that I knew just which one of the pack was in charge. That stopped my improving feelings in their tracks.

My thoughts were about to twine around a Makki-Grodno concept when the voice spoke again.

"Close the door, onker!"

Now I did not really believe the Everoinye could read my inmost thoughts. Their skill, I fancied, lay in reading body-language. Quite probably also they had the knack of, as it were, tapping into a person's aura and by some super-empathy understanding their more superficial thoughts. Whatever the truth, they so often spoke just as I was about to. This, they no doubt planned, would throw me off balance in our conversations.

So, I went back and kicked the door shut.

Some more shells fell off.

The instant the door slammed closed the whole room gave a lurch as though we were at sea in a gale. The floor pressed up against my feet.

Letting my knees bend a trifle I swallowed down. Even on Kregen lifts are used here and there. This one, though, was no bucket or willow basket on a rope and pulley. The thing quite possibly ran on sorcery. The wizards of Kregen would consider that a much more sensible solution.

One particular problem I'd not allowed into my conscious thinking had been stuffed away, not to be contemplated. Now I could take it out and look at it and know the problem did not exist.

As the lift rose the air pressure remained constant.

Underwater diving on Earth had taught me the rules of pressure. So, now, I guessed the seaweed tunnel had formed a kind of airlock, like a membrane at the interface of water and air. There was no need to worry that I'd been under pressure and this rapid rise would give me the bends. Thank Opaz! Then, grimly, I rephrased that. No, oh no! Thank the Star Lords!

The rise seemed to me very rapid, although, of course, I'd no idea of the actual speed. The ascent continued long enough for me to surmise I'd gone up a long way. My breathing remained steady. Good Kregen hunger and thirst had to be ignored.

The octagonal lift stopped. The shell door opened.

Waiting quite deliberately I stayed where I was. I wanted to hear that damned acidic voice again—to make sure.

"Step out, Dray Prescot, onker of onkers."

Yes. Confound it all! There could now be no doubt whatsoever. The owner of that cutting voice was Ahrinye, perhaps the youngest of the Star Lords by a million years or so. He wanted to run me, as he inelegantly phrased it. He wanted to employ me to the fullest of my mortal abilities, and run me past them, too. So far, thank Zair, the other Everoinye had managed to keep his rebellion against them in check. For how much longer?

Obediently I stepped out of the lift into the entrance to a corridor. A chair stood directly before me. The chair was fashioned from metal, with spidery legs and slatted seat and back.

"Sit down!"

I sat.

Immediately, with a loud hissing, the chair started off along the corridor. The walls of a dun ochre color blurred past.

I sat back, crossed my legs, and waited, stony-faced.

No other moving chairs passed. The temperature remained constant and pleasant. The perfume of flowers hung in the air. I mention these observations to illustrate the way I attempted to control my emotions. Apart from hunger and thirst, I acknowledge that fear twined around rage in my feelings.

The chair hissed past a screen of hanging vegetation and slid to a halt just inside a small oval shaped room. The walls were hung with ivy. There were no furnishings.

"Out!"

So, out of the chair I got and the thing hissed and whistled back from whence it had come. I stood there, waiting. By this time exasperation was bubbling uppermost in my reactions. Despite my attempts at self-control I found myself gripping the hilt of the drexer scabbarded to its own belt. My Krozair brand was gone, stuck through some damned and hell-bent Kataki. I could hope that Seg and Inch had retrieved the sword before chucking the Whiptail overboard.

A tiny zephyr brushed my cheek and was gone.

From somewhere, from the air, from everywhere about me, a sound like the breeze through trees began. This particular sound held that quality of people talking in an adjacent room, half-heard.

So, being Dray Prescot and being in a perilous situation, I bellowed out: "So where's a little something to eat and drink, then?"

The distant rumble of voices stopped instantly. The thin scratching voice of Ahrinye said: "Very well. We do not want you damaged, mortal."

Mortal! I said to myself, with an inward snort. That wasn't the style of the Star Lords. That was self-important, bombastic Ahrinye, for sure.

A single-legged round table rose up from the floor. The table carried a flagon and a jug and a plate. On the plate reposed bread and cheese and onions. That was fare for an oar-slave, if he was lucky enough to be fed. It was also very good and welcome in a tavern after a long day's march.

Without more ado, as they say in Clishdrin, I took up the jug, poured the ale—not wine!—and quaffed it off.

Then—ah, then! I passed the back of my hand across my lips and said the immortal words: "By Mother Zinzu the Blessed, I needed that!"

The hollow murmur of voices began again and I could make out that Ahrinye was talking to someone—or something—called Razinye. Not all the conversation could be fully understood. The definite impression was gained that Razinye was reluctant to join in some scheme and Ahrinye was pressurizing him. "They are all dotards," he said, "not fit to run these important affairs."

That was his view of the other Everoinye. Now he had a recruit to his plans. I ate some bread and cheese and listened.

Razinye wanted absolute proof—of what I didn't catch.

"Show me you have chosen the right tool. Then I will join you. There are, after all, many weapons available."

"Not like this one."

"Yes, yes, I am aware of the reports. But it remains to be proven."

Emptying the jug, I filled it again from the flagon. Both vessels were handsomely made in some soft metal resembling hammered pewter. The rim felt cool against my mouth. The bread and cheese and onion went down satisfyingly enough. The two Star Lords carried on their half-heard conversation.

At length Ahrinye, his acrid voice positively corrosive, said: "Very well. Watch!"

A noise scuffled at my back, so I turned around to look.

Immediately, I swallowed the last of the bread, swigged off the ale, placed the jug back on the table, and drew my sword.

The thing slobbering towards me was a true monster from nightmare, no doubt about that. It crawled on a number of scaly legs, its four jaws gaped into a cross of yellow fangs, dripping slime, a clump of tendrils waved like undersea fronds seeking to draw me into those fangs, and its hide glistened greenish gray.

Eyeing the thing, I began to work out the best way of dealing with it. That I felt sorry for it goes without saying. This shint Ahrinye just hauled out anything to do his dirty work without a single thought for their welfare.

The voice that belonged to Razinye made a sound that can only be described as: 'Tut, tut!'

"What?" demanded Ahrinye.

"The Scompeto is hardly what I had in mind. Here."

A blue radiance grew about this monstrous Scompeto. A halo of light formed about it. It shrank. It dwindled to the size of a cat and then—puff!—vanished.

I let out my breath. My next act, carried out with stupid bravado, was to sheathe the sword. With even more onkerish behavior, I took up the flagon and jug, poured more ale, and so stood there, jug in fist, glowering.

A four-legged rectangular table grew into existence by the near wall. The surface was covered with symbols, letters and numbers. From the opposite wall, at a point just above my head, a pipe jutted. Water began to flow from the pipe. Its splashing would normally have been quite pleasant. Right now, though, by Krun, it carried only menace and the promise of final termination for one foolhardy adventurer called Dray Prescot.

Razinye called in a mocking voice: "Solve the puzzle on the table and the water will cease to flow."

I stared down on the table. The puzzle looked hopeless. With that gentle splashing sound in my ears, I glared at the problem. All the time as I stood like a loon the water rose up about my legs. Soon it would close over my head.

Five

Sloshing water away I went over to the door. Even though the chair that had brought me here was gone, I fancied I could still walk out. The door was locked. Well, I expected that, didn't I? The panels were thick. I thumped a couple of them and the solid thunk told me I wouldn't break through this side of reasonable.

A sound drifted on the air, a very definite snigger.

Those two Opaz-benighted Everoinye were enjoying this, bad cess to 'em and may their extremities drop off.

Back at the enigmatic table a fresh look at the combination of symbols suggested Jikaida might be involved. The pre-eminent board game of Kregen was hardly likely to be overlooked by beings facing thousands of years of life. Another swig of the ale did not bring enlightenment any closer.

If I climbed on the table it might float—or might not—but then when the water reached the ceiling I'd be done for anyway.

Water gurgled from the pipe. The flow was not forceful, rather it poured out with a relentless inevitability, very menacing.

"Well, Emperor of Emperors? Get on with it!"

"Sarcasm is an extraordinarily low form of wit." If I was going to die then I wasn't prepared to die with a still tongue in my head. Oh, no, by Krun! I'd tell these couple of cramphs what I thought of them and their murderous tricks.

Body language must have spoken again, and no doubt my emotions were boiling up a sizeable aura about me, for Ahrinye snapped out in a pettish fashion: "You are ungrateful, Dray Prescot! You have no thanks for the repair to the damage from the ankster."

A quick glance down my side showed a few dried blood streaks on my leg. I frowned. So that damned double-curved Shank sword had not missed me, as I'd thought. In the hectic events I'd not heeded the wound. This is not uncommon on a battlefield. The ankster, the double-curved blade, had bitten me and Ahrinye had patched me up.

"I did not know," I said, trying not to sound too surly. "Of course I give you thanks for that. But not for this."

"The water rises. The puzzle awaits."

So, perforce, with the water rising over my thighs, I studied the problem more carefully. I began to see a possible answer; but it rapidly became clear I'd need more time. The water would creep up to the ceiling before I was finished—then I would be finished.

Another swig of ale and a blinding image of Delia struck clean through my brain. There she was, glorious, glorious! Her wonderful brown hair with those outrageous auburn tints adding a new luster swung back in a plain silver band. She was binding up young Inky's leg where he'd tripped and gashed himself. He was not crying, although I remembered the cut had been painful. Carefully my gorgeous Delia wrapped the yellow bandage around his leg. I saw this vision in a flash that pierced me to the core.

The sash I was wearing was, naturally, in the brave old scarlet. I finished off the ale. The drink took on an altogether more marvelous taste. With a softly breathed: "Delia!" I went to work.

The soft metal of the jug squashed easily. I checked the diameter and squeezed and forced the pewter into about the right shape. The red sash wrapped about it tightly. With my construct in my hand I crossed to the water-gurgling pipe. The force I used was, I own, savage. That, I felt, was necessary. Slap bang into the pipe rammed the emergency plug. Viciously I stuffed the plug up.

Water spurted about me in a fan, and then stopped. Only a few drips fell to splash into the water. I stepped back.

"You cheat, Dray Prescot!"

"Yeh?"

The voices of the two Everoinye blended and faded. The time needed to solve the problem could be anything; all I knew was that I must get a move on and not waste this reprieve.

The Star Lords appeared to have taken themselves off. Very little sound echoed in the room, the drip from the pipe, and my own frustrated exclamations as I wrestled with the damned puzzle.

Eventually I got the hang of the thing. It was a problem in Jikaida, an end-game situation. The notations were in code, which made it more difficult. I did not recognize the position, had I done so I would have been quicker without doubt.

Then—and this is not to be marveled at—I found myself admiring the elegance of the Jikaidast's solution. With the final notation decrypted and written down a loud gurgling permeated the room. For an instant I imagined my emergency plug had been washed out. The truth came very refreshingly. The water was subsiding, was running away, was glugging and gurgling down a hidden drain.

Thank Opaz! But, far more wonderfully, thank Delia!

Unfortunately all the ale had been drunk. Still, I hoisted a mental draught in honor of Beng Dikkane, the patron saint of all the ale drinkers of Paz.

The door was no longer locked. The ochre passage did not look inviting. Now, assuming I would be allowed to walk down the corridor, use the elevator, find my way through the airlock of seaweed, why, then, how would that benefit me?

Yes, by the time I'd traversed the seaweed I'd be breathing air at the pressure of the ocean at that depth. There would be no magical globe of green-glowing filaments to protect me at a normal one Kregan atmosphere. So I'd have to take a deep breath, and hold it, as I floated up. Even if I could hold my breath for the length of time that would take, without staging stops to get rid of the nitrogen bubbles in my bloodstream, I'd be a useless cramped object crippled with the bends. No way, by Vox!

Well, then, there had to be another way.

So far during the time I'd been brought here—wherever here might be—only what one can call mechanical means had been employed. No thaumaturgical powers of the Star Lords had seen their Giant Blue Scorpion snatch me up and deposit me somewhere else on Kregen. Certainly, the seaweed interface partook of the magical, no denying that. But, until the Blue Scorpion or any other of the Everoinye's arsenal of wizardly tricks materialized, I was treading mundane turf.

So, there was another way out. So, I must find it. As they say on Kregen, Queyd-Arn-Tung, no more need be said.

As I thus prowled around looking for another way out, I found myself wondering what those two unhanged rogues of Star Lords were up to.

If Ahrinye managed to get his way over the other Everoinye then he would run me into the ground. I had a shrewd inkling what he wanted me to do, although apart from the obvious his motives remained shrouded in the typical obscurity of Star Lord thinking.

If I add that I did not wish to contemplate what Ahrinye was requiring, then that must be perfectly understandable.

The corridor just went straight on to where the chair had started from the lift. So I went methodically about the oval room looking for another door.

The scarlet sash could be pulled free of the plug and I waved it about a bit. It would dry in time.

My long experience in locating secret doors and passages hidden between walls served me well. The oval shape of the room was, in fact, more of an egg shape. At the blunt end that small but so often betraying distortion of the wall line indicated a possibility.

A diligent search at last uncovered the answer. Taking a deep breath and squaring my shoulders, I pressed the wall.

An oval door revolved on a central axis with the slightest of grating sounds to betray its existence.

A puff of stale air billowed out.

This was it, then. The blackness before me was not absolute. Many small flickering lights appeared to be dancing about in the distance. Gravel covered the floor. My footsteps crunched. Now this I dislike, habitually moving as silently as possible.

Going further on I came upon the cause of the many little flickers of light. A crystal wall studded with many small facets, set at an angle, reflected the light from whatever originated it around the right angled bend.

Moving as silently as possible I walked around the corner.

A maze of crystal columns and surfaces splashed light everywhere. My distorted reflection jumped at me from hundreds of mirrors. The glittering uncertainty of this place held a weird beauty. No sound apart from my movements disturbed the flash and glitter sparkling everywhere about me. The perfume of blossoms twined tantalizingly on the air, in one part thinning to a mere trace, in another growing overpoweringly pungent.

Oh, yes. On Earth this glittering crystal cavern would be described as magical. On Kregen magical means magical. There was no sorcery involved in the crystal, the rock, the lights. This spectacle represented one of the wonders of nature, the results of aeons of time and the slow movements of the very earth itself.

Whilst I was quite enchanted by this faery grotto, I had to find a way through and out of it, and that, by Krun, was not going to be easy.

Despite that resolve and my usual determination to bash on regardless, I had to resist the strongest temptation to hold my breath in this resplendent display of nature's magnificence—what a foolish notion! There should have been a cutting reference to Makki Grodno on my lips, and I should have gone barging on.

So it was with some slight feelings of sacrilege I checked to see how easily the crystal nicked under the edge of my blade.

The glittery stuff sharded without problem. I added to the facets already there; only mine were shaped with meaning. If I happened to wander back this way I'd know I'd already passed along before.

With that decided I set off into the forest of sparkling columns. They were probably not stalactites and stalagmites joined evenly over thousands of seasons, although just what type of Kregan crystal they might be I couldn't guess. Going from the first mark in as straight a line as possible, I chipped signs as I went along.

Using the blade of my sword, slightly offset from my eye to avoid the hilt, I could adjust the angle of two signs so that they were in line. Then the next mark could be chipped out. This is a common and usually effective method of maintaining a straight direction. Mind you, confident though I might be about going around in circles in this maze, if that shint Ahrinye decided to stick his oar in, why then, I might end up anywhere.

There were cleared areas within the clumped columns and here the accuracy of direction became a trifle more tricky. Only when I was satisfied—or as satisfied as possible—would I go on. Some time elapsed and once again I became aware of the hollowness of my inward parts.

The next section contained mirrored pillars set at wider spaces. My image danced crazily from surface to surface.

The faintest of hissing sounds echoed around me, bouncing in the maze. A fleeting glimpse past my own reflection in a mirror ahead showed a humped shape. The image was there and then was not.

Not for a single moment could I disbelieve my eyes.

Instantly, I swiveled about.

"By the foully diseased liver and lights of Makki Grodno!" I said to myself. The Scompeto crawled towards me with his scaly legs jerking up and down, his crop of tendrils writhing and the cross of his four jaws opening and closing, dripping slime.

The damn thing looked bigger than I recalled from that first brief meeting before the flood came. Now I abhor with a great abhorrence wanton killing. If something is going to kill you, then in all conscience you have to defend yourself. Unless, that is, your conscience precludes that course of action. In that case, you more often than not end up dead.

So, I decided I would use my brain and be very clever.

Moving swiftly but positively not running, I crossed the open space and passed between two columns. Although I cannot swear to it, my reflection revealed a self-satisfied, not to say smug, expression.

So, clever clever Dray Prescot turned to watch the discomfiture of the Scompeto.

Ha!

Before my very eyes, as they say in Clishdrin, the squat monster began to shrink. He dwindled. In no time at all he had reached a size that could pass easily between the pillars of the maze. "By all the Furnace Fires of Inshurfraz!" I burst out, as hot as any of those fabled furnaces. "The devil take the thing!"

Those tendrils, those jaws, although much smaller than they were, remained of a size to do nasty things to my hide. If I could pass between the columns, then the confounded Scompeto wouldn't be smaller than me, would he?

Oh, well. Reluctantly I drew my sword. I didn't intend to give Ahrinye and his crony Razinye the lip-licking satisfaction of seeing me run off. Oh, no, by Vox!

Pride, stupid, selfish pride! Many a high-flown fellow has been brought low by his infantile ideas of honor.

The scaly monster scrabbled across the floor. The slime dropping from those ugly fanged jaws increased to a gush as his appetite and bodily juices anticipated a tasty little tidbit.

He reached me and his tendrils writhed out to seize me up.

They'd pop me between that tooth-cluttered cross and—crunch!—I'd be chopped into four digestible portions.

With all the glittering reflections blinding in this eerie place, the blade of my drexer caught the light and flamed.

The tendrils struck. The blade swept around, lethally.

Even in that moment of smiting the thought occurred to me that this unholy thing could be a phantom. My sword would pass clean through the apparition. The notion struck me that Ahrinye, having proved to Razinye that, indeed, I did possess a brain, was now out to show my mettle in physical prowess.

All that metaphysical nonsense swept away as the avalanches of the Mountains of the North in Vallia sweep everything in their path to oblivion.

The steel struck. I felt the shock. Clumps of tendrils fell off, chopped away as one chops the icicles away from the roof guttering. Without a pause and ignoring the hissing whine of the thing, I whirled the blade back. More bits of the Scompeto tumbled to the floor.

These first two blows whistled in quickly, exceedingly quickly, by Krun. The poor damn monster had suffered, as his high-pitched shrilling indicated. I just hoped he could grow his face-fungus back. Without striking him further, I span about and hared off between the coruscating mirrored-facets of the columns.

Should he wish to follow, or if Ahrinye made him go after me, then I'd have to take this confrontation further, Opaz forgive me!

Running now, and with no shame in it, I cocked an eye back over my shoulder.

The Scompeto appeared reflected in the columns, half-a-dozen of him. The fang-jawed head swung from side to side. The scaly legs beat up and down, up and down. But—he did not move.

"Thank Zair for that!" I said, and stopped.

Staring back, the unwelcome realization hit me that I could see only the last sign I'd chipped into the crystal. "The Black Bat Caves of Gratz take it!" I exclaimed, annoyed.

Still, a more considered review of the situation convinced me that I must have run off at a more or less straight prolongation of my course. Anyway, at the worst I would probably only have veered a degree or two off the straight and narrow.

So, hoping that my reading of the situation was reasonably correct, I set about carving the next marker into the crystal column.

The squamous Scompeto with his blasphemous yellow-fanged four-jawed head just humped up and down as though he was lost and what had transpired was completely beyond his grasp. Poor innocent victim of his own nature! I just hoped his tendrils would grow back and Ahrinye would not punish him for his failure.

As for the other cramph, Razinye, would this demonstration have convinced him? Or would he demand further proof?

That, I may say, made me move very smartly along among the crystal pillars. That, as they say in Clishdrin, made me jump to it.

By this time as I forged along with my many dazzling reflections keeping me company I was thoroughly out of countenance with the whole situation. The reasons for all this, of course, were absolutely clear. The quicker Razinye was convinced, the quicker I'd be out of it.

The way now trended upwards. The air remained sweet. The floor changed to sharded crystal gravel, very crunchy and very blinding underfoot, so that I blinked. Only the steady crunch of my footfalls disturbed the silence.

By Makki Grodno's internal disasters! How much longer would this nonsense have to go on?

Now, for the sweet sake of Opaz, I cannot exactly say that the eerie silence of this weird place began to get me down; but, then, why did I deliberately stamp my feet as I went along? I crashed my feet into the crystal gravel so that the echoes rang in some kind of pathetic defiance. Defiance of the Star Lords? Ha! Still, that was me, the plain sailorman Dray Prescot, who would venture on beyond the bounds of commonsense.

Whether or not Ahrinye at last tired of toying with me, I couldn't say. He had to prove his plans to his new accomplice Razinye, and he was scarcely any longer doing that.

The forest of crystal columns abruptly ended and before me stood an open archway. As I say, I might have come to the end of the place because this was the end, or because the Star Lord had shuffled his artifact around to set me on the next step.

Inside the archway a stair rose up out of sight, luridly lit by a mixture of lights springing from the walls. The treads were formed from solid blocks of crystal. Ashlar masonry never fitted as well. The edges were sharp and clean cut.

Again, by Krun, the stairs could be natural, hewed out by consummate masons, or erected by sorcery.

What they were, I didn't care. I started up.

Now, on Kregen in perilous situations when you have to use a staircase it behooves you to proceed with the utmost caution.

I had no ten foot pole, so I used the sword to test each step. The crystal rang solid each time and up and up I climbed.

The head of the stairs arrived at last. The treads debouched onto a platform under a crystal dome not quite large enough to house a fair-sized city villa. The space under the dome lay bare, completely devoid of carpets, furniture, windows or people. The silence that I'd vowed would not bother me persisted so that I began to believe I could hear a ghostly echoing ringing in my ears. What appeared to be blue sky lay over the dome; it might have been sky, it could just as easily have been an Illusionist's trick and I was still deep underground.

The place was empty. So I sheathed my sword.

On Kregen, of course, one should never take anything for granted.

My irritable impatience with the brooding silence and the empty state of my insides, together with a general feeling of resentment and anger directed at Ahrinye and his crony combined to make me careless. Perhaps that was what the Everoinye were after. The instant my hand left the hilt of the drexer four men all dressed in green appeared directly to my front. They charged headlong for me, swords high.

Well, that was a comfort, by the Blade of Kurin!

Proper professional assassins do not as a rule run about waving their swords in the air like farm boys hoicked into the army.

Out whipped the drexer in ample time to meet the first blade. The two steels scraped together. So these lads were real and not apparitions. Very good. As I swung the sword to check the next attack I decided these would-be assassins must take their chances.

The fight did not last long. Everything that had happened lately must have got under my skin, infuriating me, to my shame. The clash of steel echoed under the crystal dome. They skipped about and cut and thrust so that I was able to take them in proper Krozair style.

They bled. Their wounds spouted red blood as I withdrew. When the last one fell I shook my head. That great blintz Ahrinye cared nothing for his tools. Mind you, I, Dray Prescot, was just one more poor devil he wished to employ to death.

A soft scraping above me made me whirl about, sword snouting. I looked up. A segment of the dome slid sideways revealing blue sky and white clouds, both apparently real.

When the opening grew wide enough to let me walk through I marched across the floor and looked out. A small railed platform glittered under the lights of the twin Suns of Scorpio. Stepping out I sniffed the breeze. Ah, wonderful, the bracing fresh air of Kregen!

A quick look back showed the four pathetic would-be assassins lying on the floor in their own blood. As I watched they thinned with the faintest suggestion of green light, and disappeared.

That blasted Ahrinye!

An enormous crash of thunder smote down so that I jumped.

The blue sky and white clouds seemed to revolve. The Suns vanished under the lip of the platform. Light smashed all across the void about me. A green spear-shaped wedge darted across to collide with a bar of red radiance. A spinning circle of blue flame coruscated between the two. Was there a hint of yellow, creeping up over the unseen horizon?

The upside-down sky crackled with noise and fire as the colors clashed. Everoinye, Ahrinye, Zena Iztar, oh, yes, they battled it out.

There was no Giant Blue Scorpion of the Star Lords. There was no pitching headlong into an icy nothingness. I felt myself dragged up. I could breathe—just. My eyes snapped shut as intolerable white light burned the universe about me.

The crash as I landed almost broke my back. I let out a huge gasp. I opened my eyes. Stark naked, weaponless, I was lying on a sandy beach where the sea lapped, and a hungry crab the size of a dog scuttled towards me with pincers raised.

Six

I, Dray Prescot, Lord of Strombor and Krozair of Zy, scrambled to my feet, favored this scuttling crab with a baleful look, and ran off.

Oh, yes, by Zair!

He was merely following his nature, like the scorpion in the fable with the frog. Had he been a scorpion, I might probably have hung around to find out what the Star Lords had to say to me. This crab would do his best to grab me with one pincer and do extremely nasty things to me with the other.

That, of course, could not be permitted. So I'd have no option but to turn him over on his back. He might writhe himself the right way up in time. That would be up to him and Whoever designed his body.

This reasoning was not purely metaphysical. Given that I detest having to kill anything, then the only honorable course of action for me, a Krozair of Zy and a Krovere of Iztar, was to run off.

So—Dray Prescot ran off sharpish.

When I say the pestiferous crab was the size of a dog I'm well aware that dogs come in various sizes. This darling fellow of a crab was the size of a well grown Saint Bernard. His pincers ready to cut in sideways in a gulping slash were as big as a mechanical digger's scoop of Earth. All the same, by Krun, tip him over on his back, and—!

This muddy green crustacean had been spared that fate. I felt glad for him. So, as naked as a new born babe, I toddled off along the beach.

The lack of clothes means relatively nothing on Kregen, depending, naturally, just where you are on that wonderful and terrible world. The lack of weapons is a mighty serious matter, mighty serious, by Zair!

Quite automatically, the moment I'd regained some sense after my arrival here, I'd checked the state of the heavens. Were there two Suns shining refulgently red and green up there? Or, was there only one small yellow sun? The last was a fate too hideous to contemplate, far too horrible to endure. By the Black Chunkrah, yes!

Of course, the size of the crab told me the truth, quite apart from the marvelous ruby and jade tinged shadows stretching across the sand. So, as my flight slowed I glanced back. The crab was just scuttling back to sea. I didn't smile; the situation, though, warranted a little facial grimace, by Krun!

The noise of the surf rolled in, and the susurrating slide as the waves receded filled the air with a familiar and reassuring ordinariness. Mopheaded palms leaned over the water on long slender trunks. A rocky headland enclosed a charming little bay where the waves broke in a white smother against the tumble of fallen boulders. Crank-winged gulls circled and glided overhead, screeching happily. Within the fringes of the vegetation higher up the shining beach brilliant splashes of color betrayed the existence of many luxurious flowers of all descriptions and fragrances.

This might well be a deserted island; it most certainly was not a desert isle.

Going steadily on I circumnavigated the head of the bay. A litter of timbers washing up and down against the boulders took my eye. Investigating, I soon determined that these were the pathetic remnants of a shipwreck.

Splashing down into the water and careful not to become trapped by the wash against a stone I secured a handy length of lumber. I swished the wood about experimentally. Well, by Krun, I'd used, aye, and fought with, a length of wood in lieu of a sword before.

Thus formidably armed, I strode on exploring my new home.

For, make no mistake about it, I was stuck here until such time as whoever had brought me here wished me to go somewhere else.

A tangle of impressions remained in my mind. There had been the omnipresent blue, which was probably a veiled representation of the Giant Blue Scorpion. There had been green, no doubt of that! That would have been Ahrinye. There'd been red, the red of the other Star Lords. Had there been yellow, a thin sliver, shining gloriously?

I couldn't be sure. If I'd not been mistaken then Zena Iztar had placed her presence on the scene there by the crystal dome.

If she had— Then I stopped that line of conjecture.

The sea glittered away to my right, palm trees bowed low to the left, and the ground trended upwards ahead. As I reached the apex of the little ascent and looked over and down, my thoughts about Zena Iztar washed away instantly.

Below lay a valley, not too wide, where one would expect a river to run down from the interior. The valley bottom bloomed green with vegetation and the vibrant hues of flowers. There was no sign of a river, or even of a stream.

Clear of the vision-obstructing trees I could see far up to the left where three distinctly-shaped mountains rose against the high sky. Each was a near-perfect cone, positively deluged in the greenery of close growing trees. Was that the center of the island?

Exploration there would have to wait. My disappointment that the river was dry came as a most unpleasant surprise. Phlegmatically I picked up four stones and trudged across to the nearest clump of palms.

The second throw brought down a coconut. The dratted thing broke on impact and coconut milk sprayed everywhere. I mentioned a few uncomplimentary facts regarding the Divine Madam of Belschutz, and hurled again.

This time I made a neat outfield catch, taking the coconut in both hands and rolling over on my shoulder, springing up ready to hurl the ball at the stumps. Well, that was the sensation.

The last stone produced the same result. The fallen stones served to bash open my prizes and I walked on, wooden longsword under one arm, thankfully drinking refreshing coconut milk.

The beverage was sweet and delightful, as was the flesh when I sank my molars into it.

The twin Suns of Scorpio, Zim and Genodras, were declining. A campsite must be found. A bow could be fashioned readily enough. A sharpened arrow, provided it is flighted reasonably, will fly straight enough to do the business. Anyone who has been coached by Seg Segutorio, the finest bowman of two worlds, ought to fill the pot.

Mind you, that would depend on the presence of game.

Perhaps I should stroll back and discover my crab friend. I am not particularly fond of fish, or frutti de mare, or shellfish; still, a hungry belly must be filled somehow or other, by Krun!

As I thus ruminated on my plight I realized my feelings were not an inner turmoil of seething frustration. That, by Zair, was strange! If you have dealings with the Star Lords then you learn patience. I'd taken a long time to understand that. Still, in life you have to play with the hand you are dealt. There seemed very little I could do to influence what happened.

Yes, I'd have to try to circumnavigate the island and see if there were other lands offshore. A boat or raft of sorts could be constructed. With these thoughts I still fully understood that the most logical way I'd ever get off this place was by the intervention of the Everoinye.

One puzzle, one obvious false note, was simply that there did not appear to be anyone here for me to rescue.

That is what I did for the Star Lords, getting myself hurled willy-nilly into dire peril to snatch some poor wight from a certain death.

Oh, well, I'd let the crab alone. Perhaps that counted?

One overriding fact remained paramount.

I'd not been flung headlong here for no purpose. Something was going on, something the Everoinye wanted done. Ergo, I'd keep my wits about me, make myself as comfortable as possible, feed myself properly, and generally be on the top line for the emergency when it eventually arrived. Oh, yes, by Djan Kadjiryon, I most certainly would!

Of course, boastful Dray Prescot babbling on like a loon with his black-fanged winespout wide open, had no conception of just what that dire emergency might be.

The Suns were now well down and their streaming mingled light lay across the land in swathes of shadowed crimson and verdigris.

About to head for the line of trees I cast a last look back at the beach. A jumble surrounded by splashes as the tide came in attracted my attention.

I perked up. This was more raffle from the wrecked vessel and I hoped there might be useful salvage. A big breaker filled with ale, now—that would not come amiss, by Beng Dikkane!

The beach was crossed in no time at all. Ropes, spars, planks, a whole raffle of detritus sloshed up and down with each incoming wave. Moving closer with a sailorman's hopes high I checked and stopped stock still.

A man's form swung up and down in the wreckage. He wore only a long white gown, now much discolored and soaked through. He lay on his side, one arm limply outflung.

I bent and turned him over.

The shock, the horrific shock, tore clean through me.

This poor damned shipwrecked survivor was a Shank.

His fishy face, small of jaw and round of contour, made me take a step back. The water lapped up over his body as the tide gained. His legs did not move as much as his upper body and peering closer I saw that his feet were trapped in lapping coils of rope.

Good cess, then! The tide would come in and drown him so that I wouldn't have to bother about bashing him over his head.

Unlike true fishes, he did have eyelids. These were closed. From where the robe clung to him I could see he possessed a fine physique. His other hand was tucked down around a rope. So he'd been trying to free himself, then. He'd tried, and he'd failed, and dropped unconscious and now he was going to drown.

Excellent!

So I, Dray Prescot, Emperor of All Paz, turned away and began to slog up the beach.

I halted. For the sweet name of Opaz! I should have known better. The flashing memory of my Delia commanding me to climb back down a damned great hole to rescue a young Wizard of Loh coruscated all across my mind. But this fellow was a Fish-head!

Standing isolated, as though in some limbo of decision, I tried to get my muddled thoughts around the situation.

Was this the—person—I was sent here by the Star Lords to rescue?

That was beyond belief.

Yet—yet I'd been flung here with purpose. I'd wandered around like a shiftless layabout, concerned about food and drink, weapons. I'd been heedless of greater things, higher demands.

Was this damned fishfaced Shank the real reason I was here?

In the end I believe it was not the Star Lords who made up my mind. Delia, Delia of the Blue Mountains, Delia of Delphond—ah, yes, the fairest lady of two worlds—she it was who convinced me.

Grumping away to myself I reached down and ripped the soggy ropes away from this fine fellow's feet. Taking him under the shoulders I hauled him out of the sea and dragged him all the way up the beach and dumped him down under the trees. He did not stir or moan. About to move on I arranged his slack body comfortably. "Now lie there and rot, you fish-faced horror!"

The declining suns threw deep red and green shadows into the furrowed tracks I'd made dragging the Fish-head up the beach. All these shenanigans in pursuance of my desire to refrain from wanton slaughter had delayed me. I was much later than I cared for in the important matter of finding shelter for the coming night.

And, notice, as I thus contumed these absurdly chivalric notions, never for a single instant could I accept any possibility of blame being attached to the divine Delia. Delia was, is, and always will be, above reproach.

The spot I thought looked convenient lay further along the beach, so I walked along smartly kicking sand. The breeze died away at this hour and the shushing of the palms fell silent. In floods of emerald and ruby I hurried along, cursing the damned Shank.

One thing was for sure, by Krun! I didn't want him too close to me during the night. After a brisk march I swung away into the tree line. The flowers were mostly shutting up shop for the hours of darkness, although later on the Moonblooms would open and perfume the night air.

So, like any green young coy instead of the seasoned campaigner I'm supposed to be, I hurried along. A kind of track or avenue lay between the trunks. This did not alert my senses. I can give no excuse. I acted like an onker, a veritable onker, a get onker.

The ground collapsed beneath me.

Engulfed in a smother of branches, leaves and palm fronds I fell head-long, head over heels, into the pit.

The smashing jolt of landing dazed me only a trifle and I glared up savagely, seeing at once that the sheer sides of the trap would prevent the climb out being easy. Still, I kept a grip on my length of timber. With that I'd damned well dig away until I did climb out.

Thus thinking, with all the intemperate nature that is in me, I felt a thwunking great crack on the head.

A last heavy branch across the opening of the trap had fallen. It hit me end on. That I reasoned out in the last few heartbeats before the black cloak of Notor Zan enfolded me in emptiness.

Seven

My kregoinya comrade Mevancy, face as flushed as the red sun Zim, said: "Oh, you!" My kregoinye comrade Fweygo used his tail hand to rub his chin in a most judicial way. Delia smiled and in her superb way smoothed the incident over. We were sitting in a little straw basket floating among the clouds. A shoal of fishes swam past, glinting as they vanished beyond a tropical forest.

A butterfly flew in and landed on my cheek. I didn't brush him off. He turned into a wasp and stung me.

The sharp prick made me open my eyes. I didn't exactly groan; but I made a glubby squashy sort of sound. Mud and dead leaves pressed against my face in a dim pinkish radiance.

Those famous old Bells of Beng Kishi were dinging in my skull. They clanged painfully between my ears, dulled as though ringing through yards of sailcloth. My hand brushed my cheek and a little scuttler tumbled off. Making an enormous effort, I rolled over.

Well, thank Opaz, I hadn't broken my back. My limbs also appeared in order and still attached to my aching body. The sharp sides of the pit reared over me, the opening clearly delineated. The mingled pinkish radiance of Kregen's two second moons, The Twins, flooded down. Odd noises echoed, the sounds of whatever they were out there in the center of the island.

Standing up, I did let out a little groan. Because of my baptism in the Sacred Pool of far Aphrasöe, injuries I suffered mended with magical speed. The clamor from the Bells of Beng Kishi hammering away in my head would stop soon enough. I picked up the length of wood I chose to call my jury-rigged longsword.

A long streak of shadow lay against the side of the pit.

I stared. I bent forward and looked carefully.

A rope dangled down from the lip of the hole.

Taking the rope into my hands I discovered it had been plaited from vines and fronds of the forest. The plaiting was extremely neat. I hauled a couple of times. It appeared to be securely fixed.

Beng Kishi's cacophony made rational thought difficult. I'd climb up and out on this remarkably-appearing lifeline and rest up a bit and then sort out some explanation. Whoever dug this trap would be back with the suns to find out what was for dinner this day.

So I'd better be about this business sharpish.

Anyway, whoever the trappers might be, they'd go hungry.

Despite the idea of trappers watching me from the cover of the palms, the necessity of morning ablutions remained. By Krun, I did not intend to allow a pack of mangy what-have-you stop me taking a morning swim. Apart from that, the salt water should soothe the bump on my head.

The splash around in the sea certainly did refresh. The Twins, eternally orbiting each other, cast what can only be described as a romantic flush over the waves. The next items on the agenda would have to be eats and drinks.

Thus life on Kregen is, romantic and practical, all bound up together on that gorgeous and barbaric world. Shaking water off and brushing my hair back, I waded in and so climbed up the beach. Only then was the stupid enormity of my conduct brought home to me.

Thinking of the beauty and terror of Kregen—my Val! To go off swimming about in the sea at night without a care in Kregen was the lunatic act of a stark staring madman! Monsters lurked in the water. Just why I hadn't been snatched up in mighty jaws as a tidbit eluded me. By the putrescent eyeballs and dripping fangs of Makki Grodno! I had to rid my old vosk skull of a head of this daze. When reality struck—as strike it would, by Krun!—I wouldn't last ten murs at this rate.

More coconuts would solve the immediate problem of sustenance although better arrangements must be made. Going past the place where the pit had nearly had me I noticed in the early palest rose and apple green light a second set of footprints alongside those I'd made earlier. Investigation revealed the interesting and sobering fact that small webs stretched between the toes. The prints were perfectly plain.

The rope I salvaged and coiled around my shoulder must have been plaited up by the self-same Shank I'd hauled up from the wreckage. If there were other castaway Fish-heads I doubted they'd care to give me the chance to climb out of a trap, no, by Vox!

The line of tracks followed the edge of the palms for a space and then turned—abruptly—and disappeared into the interior. Now just what had my new acquaintance seen?

The Suns of Scorpio rose splendidly, the new day was starting, and I had puzzles under my hand. I stretched. Splendid! But for the constant concerns of Paz and the overriding question of why I was here at all, I could throw myself into the promise of this kind of day.

No other tracks showed on this section of beach, apart from two parallel sets which were probably made by giant crabs. Unwilling though I was to kill the animals, maybe necessity would supervene.

The task facing me was to march inland towards the mountains and find water. Coconut milk was fine; all the same, by Krun... That confounded dry river bed worried me. That looked ominous. Still, you wouldn't have all this luxuriant vegetation growing without water. Thus ruminating, I strode on briskly, watching for traps.

The pit into which I'd fallen had been only muddy; there had been no discernable water. That meant I'd have to dig down a long way if I couldn't find any free water on the surface. Knowledge of forest craft would furnish tubers and roots from which to extract water. Oh, no, I wasn't going to die of thirst. From other forces, well, naturally, quite possibly, I'd receive my quietus.

From time to time I fancied I could make out footprints along the way; but they were far too indistinct for identification.

The smells wafting about on the bright air contained an interesting mixture of scents. Flowers in profusion, decaying vegetation, a suggestion of an elusive animal smell, all these fragrances combined with dust to form an interesting olfactory palette.

One fascinating fact about my fishy acquaintance was that he didn't stink of fish. Also, his blood was red. If there is any truth in the saying: 'Think of the devil' I wouldn't care to say. Still, I found it highly interesting that rounding the trunk of the largest tree so far encountered, I saw what lay at the side of the track.

Whoever had done this had done a good job.

I stopped absolutely still and silent. Four stout pegs driven into the ground with thongs attached stretched the Shank out by wrists and ankles. He lay spread-eagled, his chest hardly rising and falling. They'd stripped his white gown away. His eyes were closed. He had not heard me approach and I'd have been mightily put out had he done so.

Without moving I stood there and let my gaze rove around everything there was to see. Chummies might be hanging around. I had absolutely no wish to end up stapled to the ground—particularly as a glistening line ran from the Shank into the underbrush. The shiny sweet sticky stuff had been trailed over his body. They'd made patterns with it. If they were religious then they were a blasphemous lot, that was for sure.

Just how long fishface had been staked out I didn't know. The time must be short, because the ants hadn't yet put in an appearance.

Eventually they showed up, busily working their agitated way along the sweet trail. The ants had six legs, were red and were of a proper ant size. Very little would be left of fishface when they finished up with him.

A fleeting reference to both Makki Grodno and the Divine Madam of Belschutz crossed my mind. Was I to be stuck with this fellow for as long as I remained on this damned supposed-to-be deserted island? Rousing myself I went across to him, laid hold of a thong holding an ankle, and snapped it across with a jerk of annoyed resignation. His eyelids flew up.

He said something, all a gargle of spitting and hawking. I said nothing but broke the rest of his bonds. Reaching down I gave him a heave and set him on his feet. He let out a yelp; but he remained standing up, swaying. Well, I've always said the Shanks possess remarkable courage.

He waved his arms about and stamped up and down to get the circulation going. I thought I knew why I was thus acting in so odd a fashion when any good Pazzian should kill a Shank as soon as possible. My actions were all tied up with that very repugnance of killing, and of the way Delia looked at me. Well, by Djan, whatever was to happen now, I was stuck with it.

Now, the universal language of Paz is Kregish. Over on the other side of the world they speak their own different tongue, and this, logically, is called Schannish. The Savanti of Aphrasöe, who had first of all brought me to Kregen, had given me a language pill so we could converse. This also conferred on me the ability to handle Schannish, a strange tongue not properly understood in Paz.

So, now, this Shank said: "You may be a naked-skinned and uncouth barbarian who ought to be put down, and you don't understand a word I'm saying. These things may be true. But as Schandler oversees All, I must thank you for my life—for what that is worth."

Almost—almost!—I opened my black-fanged winespout and spoke to him in his own language. But Dray Prescot is a canny old leem-hunter in certain situations, even if he is the biggest onker in others. So, speaking Kregish, I said: "I dunno what you're babbling on about." I waved an arm along the trail. "We'd better get out of here."

He understood my meaning. I felt confident he didn't speak Kregish, although he might. Some Shanks learned enough to be able to tell the Katakis what they required and to give orders.

This fellow looked likely. He was limber and well-muscled. He stood lightly, well poised, ready for anything. The red blood testified he'd put up a good struggle before they'd roped him.

There remained in my aching head the wonder of why on Kregen I was carrying on like this. I should just break this fellow's neck like any damned Fish-head and get on with my own affairs. His look, although naturally difficult to read on that fish face, gave me the impression his thoughts paralleled mine.

This Schandler of his—god, spirit, demon, wife, whatever—could well be acting on him in the same way as the forces pressuring me.

I touched the plaited rope over my shoulder, and nodded. "Thanks, fishface."

He understood that, all right. His mouth, on the small side for a confounded fishy-jawed fellow, widened by a thumbnail. "Why I did that," he said with his hisses and clicks, "puzzles me still. To save a mere basich—" He shook that fishy head. "Astounding."

Basich, I said to myself. No, I don't remember that word. This fellow, though, used it in a certain high and mighty way I recognized. Now he was revealed for the first time not tangled in ropes, not unconscious, not staked out, he stood forth as your true blue damn-your-eyes aristo. Perhaps, by Vox, I had not wrought well here!

He put a stiff forefinger to his chest.

"Schanake." He spoke with so much conscious pride I felt like bursting out into a rude guffaw. He followed that with a rigmarole of titles and ranks, all high-flown, which boiled down to a captain and noble of the second degree. He stared at me expectantly.

This seemed to me no time to be hanging about exchanging courtesies, with a politeness excruciatingly impossible between Shank and Pazzian. He was making the pappattu solemnly. I wanted to get well on my way from here.

Anyway, what name should I give?

He showed he was a noble all right in a fierce flicker of that fishy face which I took to be impatience.

"Darjad." I pressed my finger against my chest.

"Darjad." I swear he managed to make the name sound splashy. He nodded that fishy face. "And is that all?"

I stared at him blankly, then allowed an expression of sudden comprehension to spread over my face. Now I nodded. "Kov of Ronaline Hill."

He reacted to that, saying sharply: "Kov!"

Well, it seemed reasonable to suppose that the Shanks had heard of the rank of nobility, equating to a Duke, in Paz. As to Ronaline Hill, if I say, first, that I'd never heard of it, and, second, that a ronaline is a strawberry, you will see in how trifling a way I tried to amuse myself at chummy's expense.

All the same, by Vox, if he was a noble of the second degree, then he might behave a little more sensibly in dealing with a Kov. How petty all these ranks and titles are, for the sweet sake of Opaz!

He stared around at the encompassing trees, that fishy face of his very suspicious. His nod was that of decision. He swung about, gestured to me, and set off.

Now I most certainly did not want to be tied to him. I sincerely wanted to be rid of the fellow. There was no way I was easily going to rid myself of the conviction that my duty was to strike him down dead. As far as anyone in all of Paz knew, there was no such thing as a nice Shank. So, instead of following him, I turned about and went in the opposite direction.

Some stern degree of self-control had to be maintained to stop myself glancing back over my shoulder. I did not hear him padding along after and I just hoped he'd understood. My fists tightened on the ersatz wooden longsword.

Schanake, this famous noble of the second degree, had gone on following the direction we'd been trending. Now I did not wish to retrace my steps back the way we'd come so after a space I turned and swung diagonally towards the beach. If he was intent on exploring the interior then I'd go on my circumnavigation of the island. By this time my insides felt as hollow as the big bass drum of the Fourth Churgurs, reputed the largest drum in the Vallian Freedom Army. A few coconuts assuaged my thirst for a trifling mur or two. I'd have to stop and make a determined effort to find drinkable water in the very near future.

Before venturing from the line of trees onto the beach I put a cautious eyeball around the trunk of a palm tree and gauged the situation.

Apart from a waddling giant crab, nothing moved on the yellow sand. The sea washed in and recoiled, endlessly shushing.

Although I kept referring to this place as an island it need not, of course, be. It could be a part of some mainland. I didn't think that was the case, not if I knew my Ahrinye.

Also, my unwanted Shank friend had not told me who had staked him out. Whoever they were, they were probably the same folk who'd dug the trap which had so nicely taken me in like a simple coy.

After that experience you may be sure I kept a sharp lookout. All the same, as I went along I indulged myself in the pleasant pastime of calculating the possible size of the island from the angle of beach curve and rate of progress—assuming the place was circular, of course. Naturally, it was unlikely to be round; the mental exercise did me good.

The beach narrowed to a rocky ledge much overhung with green creepers. Fortunately none tried to strangle me and then suck my juices. Opening out once more the beach turned into a nice little cove. Just as I spotted the body of a man drawn up above the tidemark I heard—or thought I heard—a rustling sound from the rear. If that dratted Schanake had taken it into his fishy head to follow me—well, then, what? The noise was not that of leaves in the breeze.

Going swiftly on I checked the body. The fellow was dead and he was a Shank. What had been done to him was ugly and cruel, so after one look I avoided that example of man's inhumanity to man and concentrated on the bottle and scrip still fastened to his belt.

The waxed stopper came out smoothly. I sniffed. A pale yellow, probably a Wantry from those spice islands of Donengil, the wine gave off a splendid scent to a thirsty fellow. Mind you, really it was too early for wine.

The shirring of shifting sand brought me around swiftly.

Schanake's fishy face bore a look that must be absolute fury. He came barging down waving his piece of lumber like a madman.

"Keep away!" he raved in his hissing tongue. "Stand back you naked illiterate basich!"

Spraying sand he slid bodily down on me, tumbling me over. He tried to snatch the bottle and scrip. Twisting, I kept them out of his grasp. "This is my friend Storori of Lights! Or was! You defile him by your touch—" He was shaking with anger—and another emotion, too, when he saw what had been done to his friend Storori of Lights.

43

Whether or not he was truly berserk was difficult to judge. He came at me like a maniac. The piece of wood whirled down at my head. Parrying, I twisted him away and started a hefty slash in return. Then I checked. In that fraction of time as I held my blow he recovered. Again he swung viciously. Again I slid the blow and this time I let my chunk of wood tap him lightly on the shoulder.

Why, in the blasphemous name of Makki Grodno, I did this I could not explain to myself.

The wine bottle and the scrip lay on the sand. He tried to force me away from them. The pieces of wood clashed. I took my length of timber into both fists. Now the Krozair Longsword disciplines would enable me to bash him on the head and knock him out. Then I'd take the wine and check the scrip for anything interesting. After that I'd walk off and leave him. I recalled the rope hanging down the hole. I'd leave him with his life.

We circled so that now he was facing up the beach.

Quite clearly he gathered himself. He was going to make a final charge and deal with me for once and for all.

His wooden sword lifted. The rudis hovered above his head. He stood, without moving, staring past me. His mouth opened.

"A Clikroit!"

Already guessing what I would see, I looked back.

The thing waddled out of the treeline, all orange and scaled, with a wide flat body which bent upwards, six legs on the ground, two clawed arms waving. The head was triangular, with a mouth that went back almost to the level of the crown. That mouth was choked with yellow chompers, glistening in the lights of the Suns.

The Shank stepped up to stand at my shoulder, staring.

Scuttling with their six legs going up and down alternately, squamous, vengeful, a whole pack of the things rampaged out onto the beach and started headlong for us. They wielded metal weapons.

"Now, Darjad," said Schanake, "we will see how a naked barbarian basich fights."

Eight

The things—Clikroits, as Schanake had named them—scuttled over the sand towards us. They clicked. Their six legs clickety-clacked against their armored shells, banded in orange and brown. Their wedge-shaped heads bobbed up and down. They brandished weapons and as they neared it was possible to make out they were blessed with an opposing claw to form a grip with the other six. Each stood in that right-angled bent up posture about the Shank's height, and he was by a couple of finger-breadths shorter than me.

It looked as though it was going to prove an interesting afternoon.

Schanake gave me a look, and I found I could read his expressions with growing surety. That lowering glare meant that he intended to fight to the death and that he intended I should do the same.

Well, now. Hold on! I wasn't at all sure that this situation demanded a great fight to the death. Not at all, by Djan! We ought to run off. That was the most sensible course of action here.

Harshly, knowing he could not understand the words, I said: "This is a waste of time. Come on, Schanake, let's get out of it!"

With that, to make sure he grasped what I was saying, I pointed away along the beach and started to move off. I made running motions with my legs, although I stayed on the same spot. "Come on," I shouted. "Wenda!"

His reaction should not have surprised me. I suppose an animal that grows into a human being over the aeons of evolution must develop responses very similar whether the animal be fish or fowl, as they say. He drew himself up, squaring his shoulders, head erect.

I sighed. This confounded situation wasn't even worth a ripe Makki Grodno salutation. He intended to fight. Obviously, some kind of obscure honor code had him in its grip. I knew all about that.

Oh, yes, I, Dray Prescot, had stood there like an onker ready to throw his life away for notions of honor. In their place, such notions were what made civilization run, sometimes. We'd gone down against the Fish-heads when they were taking our people of Paz.

"You miserable specimen of a scaleless larver!" He could hiss and click away as much as he liked, and all the time the damned Clikroits were scuttling nearer and nearer, and I stood there like a loon. I stopped my silly running motions. I glared at him. I hefted the stupid lump of wood. I kicked some sand about. I wanted him to know I wasn't a brainless great hero like him.

All the same, his mindless heroics made me stand with him, shoulder to shoulder, to face the scuttling onrush.

That first charge surged in over the beach and was seen off.

Now that sounds remarkably like boasting. The fact of the matter was, these carapaced Clikroits would have done better to have stuck with their formidable armory of claws instead of trying to use weapons not fashioned for them. They employed swords and spears, tridents and axes. Clearly, these were weapons salvaged from folk who'd been shipwrecked here in the past.

My unwelcome Shank companion fought well—that is, of course, an unnecessary observation. He clouted the wedge-shaped heads with an abandon that must be called wild. I really believed he thought this was his last great fight on Kregen.

Pretty soon I knocked a scuttler over and took his trident away. In a brief moment when our antagonists sagged back I shouted: "Schanake!"

He turned to look and I tossed him the trident. He caught it with the practiced ease of a trident fighter.

The sloshing word for thanks in Schannish was followed instantly by a yell of complete abandon. He just went straight into the things.

What could I do? With Makki Grodno and the Divine Madam of Bels-chutz boiling away in my head I helter-skeltered after him and charged slap-bang into the mass of orange and brown carapaces.

He was fighting for his honor. I was fighting for my life.

Much as I value honor in the right place, I knew which of the two reasons for fighting was more important right now. Anyway, my honor demands that I stay alive for Delia. Now that is real honor!

Pretty soon in the whirling fracas I grabbed an axe and this gave me a much better implement to crack shells and chop torsos.

All the same, well as we were doing, when a fresh bunch of the Clikroits appeared and started to scuttle down to join the combat the end looked to be inevitable.

Two lethal sweeps of the axe parted a torso from a body before me. Another of the things tried to slice my head off, so I ducked and let the axe swing around to chunk solidly into his side. He let out a screech and scuttled away as another brought a damn great two-handed sword down on me. He struck from the side at an angle and I had to hurl myself into a ball and roll over and over along the sand.

This was becoming far too close for comfort. We must disentangle ourselves from the remnants of this lot before the new mob joined in.

Springing up, I managed to swivel the axe to block the next blow. The two-handed sword sliced clean through the axe's wooden haft.

Only by an amazing contortion borne out of desperation was I able to minimize the effect of that massive strike. The blade glanced across my cranium. For an instant stars and comets enveloped me. I sagged to my knees.

With a frantic roll I avoided the next blow. The sword chunked into the sand. In the instant the Clikroit struggled to drag it free, I had him.

His claws felt cold and hard. The two-hander came free from his grip. One-handed I slewed it around as though chopping down a tree. The long blade parted his torso from his body, so mindlessly powerful the blow. I hauled in a huge lungful of air and glared about.

The reinforcements had not yet arrived. Schanake was down. His trident lay broken at his side and he was trying to defend himself with the stump.

Two Clikroits clearly considered he was ripe for the chop. They were so far gone back into their instinctive behavior they had discarded their weapons and were about to rip the Shank to pieces with their claws.

"Hai!" I bellowed, to attract their attention, and went hell for leather for them. They swung about. Schanake's fish face looked an unnatural green. Using the two-handed sword in both fists as was proper I swung up, reversed, sliced down and across and then back.

Where there had been two Clikroits ready to rip Schanake into bite-sized chunks, there were now four pieces of the things.

The Shank scrambled up as I glared around.

He started on some rigmarole about giving thanks in the name of Sereblind. I chopped him off with a snarl, pointed at the Clikroits, grabbed his arm and fairly ran him up the beach.

At first he made no resistance, completely bewildered. By the time we'd reached the tree line he was starting to struggle.

His whole demeanor was one of outraged dignity. I could read his expressions now and judge them from the context in which he employed them. I, he was furiously expressing himself, had besmirched his honor.

As we thus stood struggling half in and half out of the trees the carapaced horrors scuttled on, waving their purloined weapons.

Eventually, and quicker than sooner, I shook him into a state of sense. I waved my arms about. He made no attempt to hit me. The sword's blade was slimed with a brownish ichor, so I used a leaf to wipe the steel clean. He was panting, and, being a Shank, the gasping for air was more of a hissing.

"We must resist." His splashy voice sounded flat and curt. "I cannot flee. You do not understand this, not being a Shank."

He looked back at the oncoming scuttlers. He shook his scaly shoulders. "You are a mere basich, naked, scaleless. Yet you fight well, and have had the honor to save my life."

At this I had to look sharply away so as to conceal my reaction. The pomposity of the fellow! The absolute unconscious assumption of superiority! By Krun, it was nothing less than comical!

Swinging to face him, I said: "Schanake—" Then I stopped. What could I say? The situation was hopeless. So, there was one solution left. I'd hit him over the head, sling him over a shoulder, and take off running.

By Krun, that should sort out his ideas of honor!

All this time I'd been patiently cleaning the sword. More than one handful of leaves were required, I can assure you. He watched with an alert air, as though expecting trouble. He now recognized, I judged, that his noble airs and graces meant nothing to me.

So, I'd just have to be quick and smart in knocking him cold.

The scheme was to get him off balance, to make him totally unaware of what I intended. Just a few paces in from the tree line a useful looking branch of the right thickness jutted from a trunk. A couple of quick blows severed the branch. With the two-handed sword in one fist and the thick branch in the other, I faced him.

"Here, fishface," I held out the sword, hilt first. "If you insist on fighting—"

He stared at me in what was undoubtedly a dumbfounded manner.

Deliberately ignoring him I stripped the branch a little to make a club. It would serve until I could relieve the scuttlers of a weapon—Hell's Bells, it would have to serve!

My Fish-head accomplice swung the two-handed sword around. I judged he had some skill, and as an officer he'd use a sword as much if not more than the Shank's racial weapon, the trident. He favored the oncoming Clikroits with what can only be described as a baleful glare.

Two conjoined shadows fleeted down from the tree line where we stood and halted above the beach. The twin suns stood at our backs, so that we were in shadows. Only one object cast those shadows tinged with ruby and verdigris. I looked up. Already the flier was letting down. A very sharp pair of eyes indeed had spotted us. The Clikroits halted, waving their weapons frantically, making a hellish shrilling racket. The voller landed and men poured out to front the scuttlers.

That voller had a black shaped hull and brightly-painted squared-off upperworks. A group of crewmen started to run up the beach towards us.

Nine

Schanake swung about. He faced me with his body shielding mine from the gaze of his compatriots running up the beach.

Gripping my branch I prepared to defend myself from the two-handed sword.

His small mouth opened widely. Knowing, as he thought, that I could not understand his words, he used his free hand to push me in the shoulder. He thrust me back.

In Schannish, he spat out: "Go on, you must escape." Then, surprising me, he spoke the Kregish word for 'get out!'

"Schtump! Schtump!"

He made of the word a veritable splashing avalanche.

I lowered the branch. I gave him a look which he might interpret as surprise, thanks, relief. I said: "I'll see you again, fishface, never fear!" Then I ran off into the trees.

As I sprinted off I shook my head in disbelief. What in Kregen was the world coming to? Here was I not slaughtering a Shank, and here was a Fish-head saving me from his pals who were ready to butcher me.

Someone must have planned this. Whoever had brought me here, Ahrinye, the other Star Lords, Zena Iztar, surely knew what they were doing? Well, perhaps in the case of the Everoinye, possibly not. Were they senile? They made mistakes. Yet why would Ahrinye bring me here to tangle with a Shank? To prove something to his crony Razinye? I doubted that.

As I fleeted between the trees the sounds of Shanks' shouting died away to the rear. So that must leave Zena Iztar. She was by far the most mysterious of these superbeings who kept interfering with my life. I clung onto the thought. It reassured me, and there was no doubt about that, by Vox!

All the same, the Star Lords had told me they required the Shanks conquered. I, as this confounded idiotic Emperor of All Paz, with the wonderful charismatic power of the yrium, was supposed to accomplish that. If I failed, then my fate was already written. Back to Earth they'd fling me, four hundred light years through empty space. That, I could not tolerate. Once more the glorious vision of Delia flooded into my mind. Oh, no, Kregen and Delia were my fate.

That realistic approach to life was, obviously, the reason why there had been so many runnings off in my hectic career of late.

On that, I slowed down as if in instinctive rebellion. The trees clustered, wound about with vines, and the many startling flowers deluging the scene with color would have brought apoplectic pleasure to any plant-hunter of Earth. Minute attention to the ground at each step saved me from the Clikroits traps. Three of the pesky things in the length of fifty paces really was gilding the lily. The fourth in that set of traps contained the unconscious body of a fat, pig-like animal with six legs and a curly tail.

There was no joy in it for me, no sense of revenge or of vindictiveness. Anyway, I carried the poor thing up out of the pit with the aid of Schanake's rope and dumped him down some way off. I just hoped he'd recover before something else ate him, as is the pleasant way of nature upon Earth and Kregen.

The way trended between the trees and began to form a recognizable trail. Although I was checking assiduously for traps, it did not seem prudent to trot along a plain trail. Accordingly, I branched off into the tangle of trees. There seemed to me little chance that the Shanks would follow me from the coast, so I could go along taking my time and being ultra-cautious.

Presently the trees, as it were, lined up and I was walking along another trail. No signs of disturbance or suspicious leaves or other unpleasant artifacts to trap a fellow appeared. All the same, I cut off at a diagonal, always maintaining my heading.

In the wildwood trees grew as they do in a wood. All too soon I found myself going along an open trail and this time the trees arched together overhead making a green gloom.

Abandoning myself with the resignation of experience I just accepted all this and walked steadily on.

The quite obvious thought in my old vosk skull of a head was: "Who?"

The leafy green gloom lightened. Pale green light sifted down. Still I went on. The light brightened. Green damned light.

Search as I might, I could find no hint of red, blue or yellow.

The fellow was confounded persistent, that was for sure. He regarded the other Everoinye as senile. I tried to think of nothing as I walked resolutely on. Although, to be sure, I did imagine that I might well be senile, and past senile, by the time he'd finished with me.

The end of that particular jaunt came as I stepped out from under the last of the trees to find myself on a small grassy eminence. At the highest point in the center stood a small pavilion, all slender columns and little domes and tiled surfaces and parchment windows.

"Enter and take your meal and rest."

The thin scratchy voice, acrid as ever, floated in from nowhere.

Not deigning an answer I strolled over to the pavilion and went inside. Very comfortable, by Krun! A couch with patterned silk upholstery invited on one side. But the most important items rested on a round single-legged table. Solid food of the tropics on wide plates alongside white and brown bread without a single scrap of fish reminded me that Ahrinye knew me. At least, he believed he understood me. The flagons were chased silver—perhaps he'd learned something from putting in soft metal jugs!

I poured ale, ignoring the wine—for the moment only.

I sat down and tucked in. Of course, this was the last meal of the condemned man.

Ahrinye's sharp voice coiled in the warm air.

"You see how careful I am of your welfare. Serve well. The Everoinye have never known how to use you properly."

Munching away I marveled. I didn't think I'd always misjudged Ahrinye. Oh, no, by Vox! This was the fattening up process.

The disembodied voice went on to tell me what he wanted. Now this surprised me even more than the care for my welfare. My Val!

Here was a Star Lord actually spelling out in detail what he wanted me to do. I ate and drank and listened.

"Nath Arovan, the King of Muldaur, married a barren wife. One of his slave girls, Ismelda, now carries his twins. The queen, called Tovah the Tempestuous, incensed, secretly had the girl sold away to slave traders. The king believes she has run away and abandoned him. The slave traders sold the girl on to Katakis. The king is inconsolable and has sunk into a decline."

He paused here. I did not interrupt. He'd get to the point of all this rigmarole in his own good time, although what I was supposed to do looked pretty obvious. So I continued to stuff my face with all the food I could manage. By Djan! I didn't know when I'd get the chance to eat again, did I?

"You will fetch the shishi Ismelda back to the king."

I felt absolutely no surprise at this. After all, this was the reason the Star Lords brought me to Kregen after the Savanti had thrown me out. I went at their bidding to rescue people. That was my job. I can't say it was my living, for they didn't pay me—except for the odd glass of wine now and again. As now.

"Well, Dray Prescot? Have you nothing to say?"

"Why?"

"I presumed you would have something to say, you usually do."

"No. I meant, why is this little king so important?"

He made a cackling sound that might have been a laugh. "The king is of no importance."

So this was another job designed to fit in with the schemes of the Star Lords that stretched over centuries. The twins this girl was carrying were the important people here. No doubt when grown-up they'd say or do things that would alter the destiny of Kregen.

The acrid voice continued: "Remember, Dray Prescot. What you think you see may be Illusion."

"I'm aware."

The idle thought occurred—were the giant crabs illusions? They roamed the beach. Yet Schanake's body had not been eaten away, as might have been expected. Where I'd dumped him would be reasonably safe. Tangled up with that raffle of rope as he was, he'd have had not a chance in Kregen of avoiding the crabs' dinnertime.

A silence ensued so typical of conversations with the Star Lords. At length, a second whispering voice from nowhere said: "Is that all? It seems no great task." That was the voice of Razinye.

About to make some kind of answer, I was halted by Ahrinye's words and realized Razinye had spoken to him and not to me. Did I detect the faintest bluster in what Ahrinye said? The two Everoinye, whilst not actually arguing, certainly were slightly at odds one with the other. I gathered the presence of the Shank Schanake had not been a part of their planning. They were—and I felt rightly so—more concerned about what Zena Iztar might do if she chose to put in an appearance. They referred to that puissant and mysterious lady as the Shere'affo Iztar. All the same, by Vox, no glorious yellow light appeared in the tall blue sky to herald her approach.

Finishing the last of the repast I felt pleasantly full and so sat listening and sipping the wine.

Eventually they came to the decision that old fishface had really been shipwrecked here. The two Everoinye further decided that this odd co-incidence would not affect their planning.

All this smacked so much of the overweening self-importance of Ahrinye and, now, of his crony, that I actually felt my lips trying to form a smile. So I sipped wine instead.

When you deal with the Star Lords it's no laughing matter, no, by the dangling left eyeball and putrescent right nostril of Makki Grodno!

The couch on which I lounged comfortably, sipping wine, rose into the air. My feet dangled and with a quick convulsive movement I hauled them in onto the couch. We sailed out of the pavilion and slanted up as a voller climbs. The ground fell away below. Green with trees, ringed by a golden beach where the waves broke whitely, the place was an island after all. We sailed above the circling gulls.

Dwindling, the island became a mere dot in a wide ocean.

A last acidic command reached me: "Do not fail, Dray Prescot!"

As to that, the vaol-paol, the great circle of existence, would have the final say.

Mind you, for all his wine and rest and information, Ahrinye hadn't supplied me with any clothes or weapons.

The couch was very comfortable. The fact that the pretty silk upholstery was a pale green didn't bother me. The gold fringes added a nice touch. Green and Ahrinye went together, and although I still felt twinges over the color green in connection with the Grodnims of Magdag in the Eye of the World, they paled to insignificance when compared to the Star Lord.

High up as the couch flew I did not feel cold. I closed my eyes.

A jolt shook me awake. I must have slept for the Suns were gone. The Maiden with the Many Smiles shed her fuzzy pink light upon the ground. So we'd landed, then.

Stretching, I looked around.

Old sailormen instinctively look up at the stars. I did not recognize any of the star formations or constellations. Over to the right an orange light shone up from the ground. The continuous beat of noise sounded like a maniac beating Hell's Drums. Over to the left vague mountains rose against the pink-tinged darkness. The ground all about my couch and me looked to be parched desert.

I stood up. Well, Dray Prescot, I said to myself, you're here so you'd best get on with it.

Clearly the orange light and the noise were the items to investigate. Before that I caught a fold of the nice green silk and hauled, freeing by vandalism enough to wrap about my nakedness. Thus dressed, I set off.

The ground was warm.

That represented a puzzle. By this time the desert should be cold. The closer I drew to the light, the louder the noise. There was no sign of habitation or of humanity. Closer in I could see the orange radiance fanning up, clearly originating from a wide hole in the ground. The noise sounded like the rumble of thunder, a continuous rolling beat, yet I could just distinguish it was composed of many hammerings joined in succession.

Cautiously now I dropped to all fours and crawled to the lip of the hole. I peered over. I saw.

A number of triphammers were going full blast, worked by men and women on treadmills. All these people were naked as were those digging ore from the ground and those wheeling it to the hammers.

I saw the men with whips. In that eerie orange light from the furnaces, I saw them clearly.

Every damn slavemaster was a damned Fish-head.

Ten

I, Dray Prescot, Vovedeer, Lord of Strombor and Krozair of Zy, knew exactly where I was. By Krun, did I not! That conniving shint Ahrinye had callously dumped me down in Schan, homeland of the Shanks.

He'd threatened to do this before. On that occasion Zena Iztar had prevented it. As far as I knew no one who'd ventured to Schan on the other side of the world from Paz had ever returned.

So I lay face down staring appalled on that appalling scene in the quarry below. For all I knew the story of the declining king and the little slave shi-shi, Ismelda, was a complete fabrication designed to make me think there was a purpose to sending me to Schan.

If Ismelda was indeed down there eternally climbing the treadmill, or wheeling the ore to the crushing hammers or feeding the furnaces, the task of freeing her was a worthy one.

Her, and all the other Pazzians into the bargain, by Vox!

The Maiden with the Many Smiles shone down refulgently; but massy clouds drifted slowly across the heavens. Her light would be obscured from time to time. Hundreds of oil lamps hanging from poles helped the slaves to see what they were doing. Altogether there was far too much illumination to please a desperate fellow intent on sneaking down there on a rescue mission. Still, it was night time; during the day when Zim and Genodras rode in ruby and jade brilliance over all, the chances would be far less.

As an old hare I spent a little more time carefully studying the layout of the quarry and associated works. The crater extended for a considerable way and, all in all, was mightily impressive. The smells rising contained that fuggy, throat-tickling aroma of coal, fire, dust and the definite impression of human sweat.

What the Fish-heads had going for them down there was an entire production line. The slaves dug the ore, dug the coal, fed the furnaces. Every now and then a coruscating line of fire would branch into a tree shape where they were running off the pig iron. Down there it would be undeniably hot, by Krun!

Shadowed in fuzzy pink what appeared to be lines of shacks lined the side of the crater off to my right. They'd be the slave bagnios. The Shank guards obviously occupied the more splendid buildings on the other side. And, by Djan, there were a lot of 'em!

Now, as you will readily perceive, this confounded mission on which I'd been sent by Ahrinye differed considerably from those other tasks I'd undertaken for the Star Lords in the past. Then the main problem was deciding just who was to be rescued. Here I faced the old needle in a haystack conundrum.

One thing was as certain as the Suns of Scorpio rising every morning over Kregen: I'd have to discard my newly-acquired silk clothing. Throwing the strip of upholstery down I reflected that, anyway, it was green. Skirting out of sight around the lip of the massive hole I reached the edge to the rear of the slave quarters. The descent proved more of a slide and was not too difficult. I took great pains not to raise a cloud of dust and the moment I was below the level of the shacks' roofs felt secure from Shank observation.

Just as I reached the ground the shifting patterns of clouds parted to let The Maiden with the Many Smiles shine down. I froze.

The shacks were mere hovels constructed—if that is the proper word for their crazy ramshackle appearance—from bits of wood, drapes of canvas, abandoned barrels. Nothing in my vicinity moved. Taking a breath I moved steadily, not running, into the shadows of the huts.

The night was warm and the canvas flap over the nearest doorway had been flung back. Inside, light seeped in through chinks and gaps where the building's odd bits and pieces did not fit together. Silent forms lay sleeping down each side, twelve to each row.

In my hectic career upon Kregen I have been slave, more than once, by Krun! Sleep is precious. I did not have the heart to wake any of these poor devils up. So I just hunkered down inside and waited. No doubt the Shanks operated a system in which the slaves were allowed just enough sleep to keep them active at work.

This short time of waiting was not wasted—well, not entirely. I reviewed what I knew of this dratted job. Because I'd bathed in the sacred pool of baptism in far Aphrasöe, one benefit was an extraordinarily powerful memory. There was, though, no difficulty in recalling what the Star Lord had told me of young Ismelda.

She was not overly tall, of a pleasing shape, and her hair held that early-morning sheen, blonde and shining. Her eyes were blue. Ahrinye had implied she was not your witless, screaming kind of girl. As she was pregnant I foresaw a knotty problem there, by Mother Phrutil.

Once again I dozed off. This was a clear dereliction of duty. Yet sleep and I had not been much in each other's company of late.

Dawn lights creeping in through the chinks in the crazy walls woke me. The noise of the triphammers continued. I stretched and a damned great clangor started up just outside the door.

All the sleeping people started up at this racket. By the way they moved it was crystal clear that they knew what would happen if they were late for work. Cracking an eye around the door I was just in time to see four Shanks striding along. One banged a gong with a kind of demented vigor. The others beat on the ramshackle shack with sticks. They made a hell of a row. They wore armor and were girded with weapons.

They simply marched straight on, making no attempt to see if the slaves tumbled out for work.

A croaky voice said in my ear: "Dunno who you are, dom. The Opaz-forsaken Fish-heads might not be able to tell one apim from another. But I can. You're not in my gang."

I looked at him. He was not an apim like me, being a Fristle. His cat-man's face looked drawn, haggard. His fur was dull and bedraggled. He carried a balass stick. So the Shanks were able to employ slaves to order other slaves about.

"Llahal," I said. "I'm looking for a girl—"

"Ain't we all!"

"No, no." I described Ismelda. "Have you seen her, dom?"

He whacked the balass stick on the rump of a Honim going out the door, growling. The Honim yelped, but ran on.

"Couldn't say. You'll have to try the women's huts. Opaz help you if you're caught."

"Yeh," I said. "I can guess."

The Fristle waving his balass stick shepherded his gang out. No doubt they'd stop at the cookhouse first for nauseating slop. Still, that was more food than I was going to stuff down my gullet. Also, I saw again the deadening effect of abject slavery. As I was not in his gang he had no interest in me. His sole concern was to make sure he brought no punishment down on his Fristle head.

Skulking in the shadows I waited until the arrival of the shift coming off work. The wielder of the balass rod of this gang was a Rapa. His feathers were as dull and bedraggled as the fur of the catman, and his vulturine face looked just as haggard. His beak was bent to starboard. He stared at me, as he saw his gang in, without the slightest interest. Complete fatigue held all these poor wights in a stasis of indifference. They just threw themselves down on the floor and went to sleep.

Peering out I saw where the lines of women trailed dejectedly towards their huts further along the line. Knowing it was foolish to expect a miracle, I still stared at each woman hoping to pick out Ismelda.

By this time I was beginning to appreciate what a trap I'd put myself in. These poor souls would just go to sleep. I couldn't possibly wake any one of them up to ask the vital question I must ask.

Another item as certain sure as Zim and Genodras was that I wasn't going to steal a uniform and disguise myself as a slave guard. Then I thought a little more on that concept. With a suitable mask, might I manage to look passably like a Fish-head? H'm. Doubtful, highly dubious, by Krun.

By the pendulous organs and suppurating belly of Makki Grodno! What the blue blazes was I thinking! There was work to my hands, set by a Star Lord. How could what I had to accomplish stand against the few moments of lost sleep of a poor damned slave?

On that dire and demeaning thought I dodged out of the shadows and ran swiftly over to the line of dejected women. I seized the first by a naked shoulder and spoke with full authority into her ear. I asked her about Ismelda, describing her. I was urgent, domineering, hateful.

The woman, a Gon with wonderful silver hair to her waist, cast a frightened glance at me, and tried to walk on. "Tell me!" I brayed.

"Master!" she stammered. She was almost falling from tiredness. "I do not know this girl."

"Very well. Ask. Ask everyone. I shall enquire of you."

"Yes, master." She tottered and I hoisted her up and let her go trailing on with the rest of the women. Oh, yes, by Opaz! I had to steel my heart. I had to act like this puissant lord because a Star Lord commanded me. Do not think I enjoyed any single part of it!

Half a dozen other women later, asked the same question, all rewarded me with the same fatigue drugged answer. None knew of Ismelda.

By this time I knew my chances were running out. A damned Shank slavemaster was bound to turn up at any minute, checking all was well with the human workforce they drove so cruelly. I knew enough about slaves and their despicable slavemasters to understand that if I hit a Shank and gave him his quietus, the repercussions would be so horrific as to make me the monster of the scenario.

Frustration and resentment building in me burst out in a scorching thought that screamed in my head. This shint Ahrinye could hoist me up from one spot on Kregen and dump me down in another miles away. Well, then, why in a Herrelldrin Hell didn't he just lift up young Ismelda and transfer her to safety? Only a few moments reflection were enough to find a number of obvious answers to that. I suspected one cogent reason was the quarrel between the Everoinye. Thus stewing my brains I saw a Shank slavemaster walk around the corner of the hut.

Instantly my head went down and I slumped into that bent-backed slouching which is the trademark of slaves improperly treated.

All the same, the blintz flicked his whip at me. The metal-studded tip scored along my ribs. I jumped and let out a cry.

Fishface in his hissing, clacking voice snarled: "Get back to the men's huts, you flistis." I understood him all right. Yet here was an example of another epithet with which I was unacquainted.

Unsure of the proper slavish reaction I let out another yelp and shuffled off towards the men's huts. I moved faster than the Fish-head expected, for I heard his whip go crack! in the air at my back.

Acting with all the consummate skills I'd picked up with Ricky Tardish and his troupe I collapsed in the entrance to the shack. Very rapidly hauling myself inside, I trusted I'd avoid another blow from ol' snake.

Rolling over I looked out. The Shank marched past, coiling the black ugliness of the whip over his shoulder. Bad cess to him!

The fellows stretched out along the floor were all asleep.

Taking stock of my unenviable position—a position into which I'd hurled myself—I came to the sobering conclusion that I must follow a simple plan to stay alive. This wonderful Plan—called The Plan—would entail my joining the slave queues for food. There was no way I'd bring my mission to success if I was starving to death.

Thus it was that I hungered all that day and ventured out with the night shift. The night and day cycle being split in half by the majority of the slaves I realized was bad news. The rigidness of the system would hamper my efforts.

Very quickly as I joined the queues for slops and green bread I discovered that there were slaves on special duty. These people tended individual Shanks, cleaned their harness, saw to their domestic chores, even did a bit of gardening to grow green vegetables which the Shanks devoured along with their eternal diet of stock fish.

Everywhere I went I enquired for a blonde-haired blue-eyed girl.

Now being a slave for the Shanks is a bad business. The horrors do not bear recounting. Discipline is strict to the point of death. That fate I escaped, often only by the skin of my teeth, as they say in Clishdrin.

Very naturally there were a considerable number of blonde-haired blue-eyed girls slaving in the crater.

As the days went by with me dodging and diving and working now and then, not a one of these unfortunate ladies was Ismelda.

Every day the water boat flew in. She was clearly a very old flier with peeling paint along her upperworks and dints in her hull. She'd been fitted with a series of large tanks in her ripped-out interior and these were emptied by the force of gravity into heavily-guarded tanks set apart in their own select area. The desert outside, although not a true barren desert, was enough of a dry wilderness to deter any thought in a slave of escaping across the waste. Water was precious.

With the natural eye of a Kapt for any weakness in his enemy I realized that the water supply was the Achilles Heel of this set-up.

Twice in that first week supply boats flew in and returned carrying the ore that was the result of our labors. That, I reasoned, might very well be the way of escape from this almighty dump.

Growing tired of dodging about and still finding no trace of Ismelda, I decided I'd have to flex my muscles. The furnaces looked promising, so thither I went to suss out the situation.

The timber supports appeared most likely. In the dust and confusion, the baleful glow of the fires which sent waves of searing heat out into the compound made people look like devils from hell. Stripped stark naked but wearing clumsy wooden and rope sandals men and women toiled with the sweat pouring from them. The taskmasters wielded their black whips with a viciousness that brooked no argument.

That very self-same night, having boldly joined no less than three food lines, I started off.

Finding enough wood proved something of a problem. Reluctant to tear down any of the slave shacks for the consequences, I turned to the kindling piles stacked by the cookhouses. It is a truism to say that in any large organization if a person walked purposefully about carrying a piece of paper, a file, a bucket or spade, they would not be challenged.

Thus carrying a bale of wood over my shoulders, bent over, I trudged from kitchens to furnaces. I had the sense to keep in the shadows as much as possible. Three trips saw a tidy pile building up at the base of a timber support.

We in Paz were aware that the Shanks could not tell one apim from another, or any two diffs of the same race apart. They could, naturally, tell different diffs one from the other.

Standing in the shadows of the furnace, checking to see if the coast was clear, I heard a thumping great crash further along the line.

At once bedlam broke out.

Slaves began running madly away, their scrawny bodies shining with sweat in the fuzzy pink moonlight. Shanks were not whipping them back to work. I stared. Then I understood why there were so many Fish-heads here.

More crashes broke the night apart. A furnace two along from me abruptly toppled over, spilling a roaring mass of flame.

There were two sorts of Shanks in the crater. One type carried the whips and were the slavemasters. The others now came running out from their barracks, armed and armored, dressing in lines, forming fronts, soldiers every one of 'em.

Something out of the desert was attacking the mine. Whoever it was had catapults. More rocks battered down on the smelting works.

Apart from the formed lines of Shank soldiery utter chaos enveloped everything. Movement at the lip of the crater took my instant attention. Men were swarming down on rope ladders. Weapons gleamed. Arrows flew. Soon there was going to be an almighty great fight. And I, weapon-less, was stuck right slap bang in the middle of it.

Eleven

Hate, detest and fear the Shanks as we in Paz so fervently did, there was no denying either their courage or their discipline.

The creatures attacking into the crater looked to be well disciplined also. In the erratic light with smoke beginning to blow over the frantic scene, it was difficult to distinguish what they were. The hideous noises of combat spurted up into the night air. Clouds rolled past above so that only now and again could the fuzzy pink moonlight of The Maiden with the Many Smiles shine down.

Rocks continued to rain down, smashing up the smelting works. Now they were hurling firepots. One landed on my pile of kindling and the lot went up with a whoosh.

Time, by Krun, to depart!

Oh, yes. But—where to?

Where in this inferno of noise and fire and screeching maniacs would there be a safe haven?

All the slaves were racing in a panic-stricken mob away from the fight. That, of course, was sensible. Perhaps they knew where to go. Probably the fishfaces had given instructions in case of an attack of this nature.

Accordingly, off after them I ran.

Here, again, was another example of Dray Prescot running away.

Too true!

A stinking waft of smoke billowed across in front of me. Plunging on into the gloom I followed on in the direction the slaves had fled, hoping I was going the right way. Dark, animated figures appeared vaguely off to the right. About to chase after them, I checked.

A coil of smoke twined away, leaving a rift into which pink moonlight drifted. Clearly, unambiguously, the form of a man wearing scale armor jumped into focus. His sword, I noticed as one notices these things in the height of the moment, was slightly curved. He glared at me—and charged.

His face! Squat, compressed, wedge-shaped, with eyes set wide-apart, this visage from hell possessed slits for nostrils and a thin vicious gash for a mouth. The nearest I could come to a description in that fraught moment was that he had a snake's face.

In the next instant he was on me, hissing venomously.

Only the Disciplines of the Krozairs of Zy saved me. His sword blade was slipped, his neck was seized, his head was wrenched around. He struggled with the frenzy of one possessed of demons.

Well, I have battled demons before, and, in Zair's good time no doubt will do so again. Remorselessly the pressure bore down on his neck. The crunching crack of his vertebrae parting was followed instantly by a savage jerk in the other direction. His snake head lolled. His legs folded. I let him go and he collapsed.

Long before his limp body hit the ground his sword was in my grasp. The thing felt heavy for its size.

Glaring around for any of his fellows I must have presented a picture of barbarity. I could feel the blood thumping around my body. I was wrought up, I own it. I didn't give this snake-faced fellow's corpse a kick; had I done so it would have perfectly fitted my mood. Seeing no others as the smoke closed in, I carried on.

In our half of the world of Kregen we had many names for the Fish-heads, of which Shank was merely the most-used. There were Schnooprins, Schturgins, Shants. We called snake-faced Shanks Schtarkins, although that was not a strictly accurate name. The snake faces of Schtarkins were far removed from the sheer compressed ferocity of this fellow. He'd send a shudder along the spine, and no mistake about that, by Krun!

Pressing on as the smoke thinned I was aware of the change in the noises erupting within the crater. Gone were the heavy beating thumps of the triphammers. In their place the ghastly sounds of combat and the screams of terrified humanity spurted up like a devil's concerto. Irritably brushing the last tendrils of smoke away from my eyes I caught up with the panic-stricken slaves.

They were headed in a bunch towards the far side of the compound. There was not much in the way of habitations or of workings here and I'd not gone exploring here. A hole loomed up in the crater wall, and I couldn't swear I'd ever noticed it before.

Fighting one with another the slaves pushed and shoved their way through the hole, which was the size of a small temple doorway.

At the side a round stone, like a millwheel of the gods, waited ready to be rolled across the opening. No doubt there'd be an efficient wedge system to chock it shut. Once in there, the slaves were thinking, once in there and, by All the Names, we're safe!

Cynic in these matters as I am, I wasn't at all sure of that, by Vox! These unpleasant snake-faced newcomers, judging from their actions and the specimen I'd met, might not be baulked of their prey by a clever piece of masonry engineering.

About a dozen or so slaves remained outside and a huge hairy fellow was hurrying them through as fast as possible. The round stone began to revolve. Like some pagan juggernaut it rolled across the opening, remorselessly closing the gap. Shrieks and entreaties burst up from the poor wights left stranded outside. The massively-built man covered in hair picked up a hairy-pated Gon and hurled him through. He turned, seized a slip of a Fristle fifi and pitched her through neck and crop. The opening narrowed. The hairy fellow would never squeeze through into sanctuary now. The stone rolled shut.

The slaves left outside set up a caterwauling that tore at the nerves. Their experiences had drained them of all semblance of humanity. I came up to the hairy fellow and peered at him. At once my mind flew back to that ill-favored inn called The Ruby Winespout in Ruathytu.

"By Beng Brorgal!" I said, totally astonished. Beng Brorgal is by way of being the patron saint of tavern brawlers. "Dahram the Bold!"

The hairy hunk of humanity favored me with a glare from bloodshot eyes. "I was, dom. Now I am called Darham. I don't know you, do I?"

The shrieking slaves ran into the smoke. Dahram—who was now Darham—and I were for the moment alone. "We met briefly in The Ruby Winespout in Ruathytu. There was a quantity of blattering."

"I know it! A fine establishment where a fellow can take a skinful at his leisure. Aye, and find a bonny fight. "But you?" He shook his head. There was no wonder in this, for at that time I'd been wearing one of my disguise faces.

I said: "You mistook me for an unfortunate called Planath the Sly."

Now my dip in the Sacred Pool of Baptism in Aphrasöc has conferred upon me this memory that can reproduce verbatim conversations of many seasons ago. Yet most of the folk of Kregen over their long lifespans are able to remember much of what happened in their pasts. Darham looked not a day older from that time when Seg and I had supped in The Ruby Winespout, watching for spies, and Darham had made our acquaintance. We'd heavily blattered some assassins. This fact I mentioned. Darham screwed up his furrowed face. He rubbed that monstrosity he called a nose. He pursed his lips.

Then, with the effect of a geyser exploding, he burst out:

"Nath the Hammer! And your comrade, Naghan the Fletcher! By Uldor the Mighty, he was a powerful kampeon!"

"True," I said, soberly. "Too true."

"He is here?"

"No." Even as I spoke I felt two contrasting emotions. I could never wish dear old Seg to experience the horror of this place among the Shanks. But, by Vox, if he was here—we'd show 'em!

Darham's massive torso swelled, with muscles cording under his skin, yet his belly was flat as a discus. He blew out his whiskers. "We can't hang about here, dom. Them Neeshargs are worse than the Shanks."

"That's hard to believe. But I believe you."

"Keep to the sides. Keep in the shadows. Let the yetches of fishfaces and Neeshargs fight it out between 'em, by Krun!"

"Aye."

Following this man mountain of hair I padded swiftly along the side of the crater away from the action. Darham eyed the sword.

"Very smart, dom. I hope you did for the cramph."

"Yeh. Have you seen a blonde-haired, blue-eyed girl called Ismelda? It's absolutely—"

"Ismelda? Oh, aye. I fear for her, for once the Shanks discover she is pregnant the stinking cramphs will kill her out of hand. Far too much trouble."

Twelve

Darham the Bold might be big and hairy; he was no awkward lumberer. He moved with a sudden smartness belying his bulk. We crouched in the pink-tinged shadows under a store platform raised on its stilts. Across the crater sheer insanity roared and thundered away as the main body of the Shanks met and fronted the assembled ranks of the Neeshargs. They fought one another with a frenzy that spoke eloquently of an ages-old racial hatred.

"She cleans out some fishface woman's night utensils. They had me cleaning armor." His voice was a mere low growl. "Hanitcha the Harrower take 'em!"

Quite obviously the Fish-heads would fight maniacally to protect the quarters where their women lived. We needed to cross the intervening space from the stilted store platform. We were as far away from the fight as we could be without tunneling through the desert wall surrounding the compound. Everything took place in a jumbled, nonsensical fashion, so that it seemed to me I was carried along on a surge of action. If Ismelda still remained in the slave huts of the Shank women's quarters, if she did, why then, this was our best time of rescuing her.

Darham mentioned with disfavor the reason he was here. "Taken up like a coy in nets!" He'd grown tired of the strict Laws of Hamal and turned to the sea to follow his mercenary trade. He was a zhanpaktun who could wear the golden glitter of the pakzhan at his throat. The vessel sailing out of Ruathytu, caught in a hurricane and swept miles off course, had fallen in with three Shank vessels. They'd sealed the Hamalese ship's fate without trouble.

Eventually Darham wound up here, in this hell. He'd not been here very long so that his natural strength and optimism, together with his fortune in landing a cushy job, had not reduced him as so many of the other slaves were sorely brought down.

He looked exceedingly fierce and shaggy as he gazed out over the space we must cross to the slave huts where we hoped to find Ismelda. She had not run into the cave where Darham helped at the opening until he was too late to squeeze through.

Some folk of Vallia regard the people of Hamal as stolid and stuffy and altogether no fun. Probably they haven't rioted in the Sacred Quarter of Ruathytu. Every instinct told me Darham was a splendid fellow, a zhanpaktun, a swordsman, and, clearly, a man of honor.

Those thoughts and the fact that I was a Krozair of Zy explain my next action.

"Here, Darham." I handed him the sword. "As a mark of friendship."

Of course he was astonished. Without boasting I tried to convince him that he would make better use of the weapon if we were to form a team.

"Well, as Havil the Green is my witness—" He stopped abruptly. "By Krun! I haven't used Havil the Green in an oath since I first went for a paktun! You've rattled me, Nath the Hammer, made me look more than a little differently at—well, you know."

He took the sword, hefted it, said: "A trifle heavy." He cut and retrieved expertly. "Still, it will give a good blow!"

With that, and a very careful scrutiny of the ground, we broke cover and ran like March hares across to the shadows of the slave huts.

Darham's massive hairy chest expanded. "Clears the lungs, that."

When we ventured further on, where the huts clustered more thickly, I received the distinct impression my new comrade had been this way before. He knew where he was going. We both padded along lightly, although our footfalls were more than concealed by the racket going on as Shank fought Neesharg. The battle was now out of our sight. It sounded as though all the tinkers from hell were bashing their pots and pans with the frenzied intensity of maniacs. The screams spurted up.

From what had taken place it was patently obvious that the Shanks' plan for defense concentrated their forces to protect their barracks. The general slaves out in the compound had been provided with the bolt hole of the cave beyond the opening where the stone had rolled across. I fancied that if those slaves were all killed despite the sanctuary afforded them, the Fish-heads would shed no tears but simply go out and sweep up another bunch of human misery.

Oh, no, by Vox, these fishfaces were strictly out to protect their own. In doing that, they protected the privileged slaves.

Instead, as I'd expected, to be surrounded by the moaning wails of frightened slave girls, the shabby huts stood in total silence.

Did this mean they were deserted? I had to hope with fierce resolve that the women were keeping as quiet as trembling mice to save themselves.

Softly, Darham growled: "Up here."

The hut looked no different from any of the others. We padded silently up the mud brick stairs and Darham scratched on the canvas covering the doorway. "Ismelda?" His voice, normally a thundering bellow, penetrated with the force of his whisper.

The canvas whisked aside. A light, shaky voice, said: "Darham?"

"Aye, lass. Do not fear."

She stepped out of the hut onto the top step, limned in pink moonlight. Ahrinye had spoken sooth. She was pleasingly shaped. Perhaps some old crone of many seasons of experience might have guessed she was pregnant. As yet she showed no obvious signs. "Will they kill us all?" Her voice might be shaky; she stood firmly upright.

"No, no! We can escape in the confusion. Come—"

She saw me. No doubt I presented a pretty wild sight.

"Who—" Now one hand went to her breast. "Who is that?"

"A friend." Darham held out his empty hand. "Come."

She didn't dally. She was not as thin and hungry and exhausted as the slaves working the mines and the smelters. All the same, her ribs showed through her smooth skin. In that light her hair took on an odd color, and her eyes were mere pits of darkness.

Darham held her as she descended. She gave me a quick look, almost a furtive glance. "Llahal."

"Llahal and Lahal, Ismelda," I said. "Now we must hurry."

"Who—?"

The rumble from Darham must be amusement. "He calls hisself Nath the Hammer. I don't believe that to be his real name."

Darham clearly knew what he was doing. Assisting Ismelda he led us swiftly back into the shadows.

The first time we paused I touched Darham on the shoulder to make sure I had his attention. "I've seen small vollers flying in and out. I take it they're personal transport for the chiefs."

"Oh, aye. You've as much chance—those vollers are guarded like an emperor's virgin daughters."

"I don't doubt it. But—now?"

Ismelda, her voice far less shaky, spoke up. "Nath is quite right. The fish-face guards ran off to help fight those—those—"

"Imps from a Herrelldrin Hell." Darham looked at me. He was sizing me up again, no doubt remembering our first encounter in The Ruby Winespout. "Right, dom. But keep Ismelda safe."

"Oh, yes," I said under my breath. "Oh, yes, very yes!"

This little blue-eyed, blonde-haired young lady knew her own mind. She'd been lucky to have been picked to join the privileged slaves; all the same, I reasoned even dragged down by hard labor and poor food she would not have reached as destitute a state as most of the slaves. Now she led on in the moonlit dimness with a certain very definite swing to her hips, a most determined young lady.

We had to scale a brick wall to enter the voller compound. Darham fussed in a most officious way in seeing Ismelda over. I let him get on with it. To be frank, I was only too glad to have a useful ally in my task for Ahrinye.

Not a soul stirred. Of course, there were people of Paz who would say that even had the flier compound been crammed full with Shanks, there still would not have been any souls there.

Taking exquisite care we sussed the place thoroughly. At last, satisfied, we selected an airboat. There were four of them, and they appeared exactly the same, what must be a popular model. Ostensibly four-seaters, their two wooden bench seats could hold six. They were built of light wooden frames over which canvas stretched tautly. An arrangement of hoops in the stern could be lifted to form a canvas tilt.

The craft smelled of fish. I mention this only because it must have smelled extremely strongly for me to notice it in that place. I untethered the restraining ropes and threw them inboard. Fully living up to his name, Darham the Bold jumped in boldly and sat at the controls. Ismelda sat in the back. About to join her I was arrested by a shriek of alarm at my back.

Whirling about I made out agitated figures prancing about on a balcony at the rear of the women's quarters. They wore long skirts whose heavy writhing patterns were clearly visible in the moonlight. Their chests were covered by plastrons smothered thickly with gems. Their fishy heads were crowned with tall gem-encrusted constructs—I hesitate to call them hats, for they were far too stupendous for that. These Fish-head females kicked up such a din at the sight of us they must bring a score of Shanks running—if the fight went well.

"Take no notice!" snapped Ismelda. "Come on, Nath!"

The voller shot skywards, I swear, the instant my hand fastened on the gunwale as I vaulted in. Collapsing on the bench seat I slid helplessly along as the airboat swung in midair. For an instant I was entangled with rosy limbs and bare skin, much to my alarm.

"You are all right—?" I began.

"Fambly!" she said, tartly. Then: "Yes. No harm done."

"Thank Opaz!" I got out on a breath, most fervently.

"We can make the coast and escape." Darham sounded confident.

"Oh, no!" cried Ismelda. She sounded alarmed. "We cannot leave without dear San Mrindaban! We must find him and take him with us! We must!"

Thirteen

I, Dray Prescot, for the moment passing as Nath the Hammer, said nothing.

What could I say? Nothing!

Rather, by all the crawling bugs on the slimy hide of Makki Grodno, there was so much I could say that I was like to burst from not saying it.

Ahrinye had set the mission. We were well on the way to accomplishing the most tricky part. Darham was perfectly correct. In this Shank airboat we could fly to the coast, ascertain in which direction lay our proper course, gather supplies, and fly home.

And now some confounded san or other, so dear to the heart of this little spirited lady, required to be saved first. Jeehum!

But, and mark my words O ye of little faith in the workings of the worlds, there was more, much more.

She sat there along the bench, her mouth, dark in the moonlight, trembling so very slightly. She held herself erect, staring at me defiantly. The Twins, the two second moons of Kregen, were rising, and their combined light added to the pink radiance of the Maiden with the Many Smiles was enough to set a bright glitter in Ismelda's eyes. I was, Opaz succor me, going to have a lot of trouble with this determined little madam.

"But—" said Darham, as though coming out of a trance. "But, Ismelda—!"

"I can't leave the dear san. Oh, no."

Darham heaved up a sigh, keeping the airboat on a steady course although he twisted his head around to talk to us. "We will try. Where is he, this San Mrindaban?"

She made a movement of her bare shoulders like a shrug.

"Well, I don't know!"

"What—?"

"The dreadful Shanks took him off after we landed in Terzul."

"So," said Darham, breathing hard, "he is not in the compound."

"Well, of course not!"

As I said, there was more desperate news, much more, by Zair! I sincerely hoped that was the last of the bad tidings.

The way I saw the relationship between Darham and Ismelda was that he regarded her as the daughter he'd never had, or at least never knew about. She obviously regarded him as a pillar of strength on which to lean and, as far as I could judge for the moment, had a genuine affection for him, as daughter to father.

Now he shook his massive head, beard and curled moustaches quivering. Like me, he knew our chances were slim, although with a spot of luck and utter determination, we could escape. To have to go gallivanting off after some holy man or sage was going to load the dice against us with enough lead to sink a galleon of Vallia.

This bold hairy gallant fellow made up his mind.

"Right, fanshos," he growled out. "As Malahak is my witness, I, for one, will go and find this famous san."

As you will readily see, that left me with no alternative course of action. At least, as far as these two were concerned.

How contemptible I felt myself to be. Here was I, agreeing to go along with a sweet young lady's desires, with the support of a hairy great zhanpaktun, when the overbearing demands of the Everoinye dictated the opposite. I'd have to ignore Ismelda's pleas, somehow or other render Darham impotent to interfere, and then, obeying the commands of Ahrinye, drag Ismelda off to safety.

When I recalled the malevolent face of that hideous Neesharg, all bloodthirsty desire to rend everyone not of his race into tiny fragments, I had to remind myself that I was not here by choice. I had a task to perform. I was under duress. All the same, by Vox, I knew with a deep cold shudder right into my vitals, the last thing I wanted to do was tangle with any of those spawn of hell.

By the pendulous belly and gargantuan thighs of the Divine Madam of Belschutz! All I wanted to do was snatch Ismelda out of all this and then, when she was safe, high tail it as fast as possible back to my home in Esser Rarioch in Valka—and Delia!

As we soared on under the lights of the Moons, going I knew not whither, I grumped to myself that, anyway, Delia might well be off on some secret mission for the Sisters of the Rose, or some harebrained frightening task for the Star Lords.

"Thank you, Darham. Mrindaban will show you his gratitude in remarkable ways." When Ismelda spoke the name Mrindaban it dropped lightly from her lips. She made a tiny hum of the letter M before finishing with rindaban. She clearly thought a lot of the old buffer.

"Terzul." Darham swung the voller off on a diagonal. We'd been flying due west, now we slanted down south a trifle, WSW by West. "Terzul. We'll start from there."

We bore on through the night air and although I felt no cold, I began to feel concern over Ismelda's lack of clothes. We'd shot off so fast that by now we were well away from the orange glow of the crater and there was no chance of descending by Ahrinye's couch for more upholstery. Anyway, by Krun, the shint had probably taken it back.

I spoke up.

How, I wanted to know, how in a Herrelldrin Hell did Darham expect to carry on an investigation when he didn't speak Schannish? The wind blew his hair all over the place as he said that there were many slaves in Terzul and that some of them would surely know. San Mrindaban presented a portrait no one was going to forget.

Hmph, I said to myself, and lapsed into silence. On we flew.

Obviously we could not just fly unconcernedly into Terzul, which was a fair sized city on the coast where fresh slaves were brought. The Bold's plan was to hide the airboat some distance off. There were vegetation, agriculture and husbandry all along this coast, separated by substantial forests. We'd have no difficulty in hiding the voller so that no one would discover her, Darham assured us. He let out a grunt which in other circumstances would have been a laugh. We might, he told us, have a job finding her again for ourselves.

Sitting in the back seat of the airboat I asked Ismelda about this wonderful San Mrindaban of hers. She became animated. Her lips glistened in the moons light, her bare body vibrant with youth and health and the currently beneficial aspects of pregnancy. The san, she said, was truly a marvelous person. He had tried to help her, but the queen by treachery had discovered that. Mrindaban had been drugged. Shipped off with Ismelda, he'd taken a serious knock on the head which, she said sadly, had deprived him of his powers.

"What does he look like?"

"Magnificent!"

Then she shook that pretty head of hers. "Well—no. Not now." San means dominie, sage, teacher and is also the title given to priests and wizards. She hadn't said what her favorite san was. Now the effects of slavery had brought him down. His hair, jet black, sprouted atrociously. He had lost weight and his powerful face was shrunken. But his eyes! Ismelda said his eyes still retained their inner force. He was tall, and stooped, and his nose was, Ismelda said with a little choke in her voice, almost as big and beaked as mine, Nath the Hammer's.

Well, I warmed to the fellow more on that piece of news.

Darham leaned back. "We'll know him all right, by Krun!"

The voller was not one of your speedster types, but she was fast enough. Darham said she didn't handle the way Hamalese vollers did. There was a certain sluggishness in her climb. I nodded. We'd examined captured Shank airboats and found the two silver boxes that sustained flight and direction were not always silver. Some were bronze, others various alloys. There remained a great deal to learn.

So it was that just before Zim and Genodras arose in splendor to shed their glorious apple green and rosy radiance upon Kregen, we touched down in a forested glade. The voller was pushed under the trees where they grew thickly. Branches were bent over her. We did not cut anything down to conceal her. When those leaves died there'd be a glaring brown patch in the greenwood. Darham said he was satisfied.

This new companion of mine proved himself a man of parts. He brought in three furry creatures that might have been rabbits had they possessed twelve legs between them instead of eighteen. The firesmoke drifted up and dissipated among the trees. There were forest fruits to hand. I played my part by stripping a spout of bark from a tree I recognized, the shrimpa, and collected a liquid that passed as water. It had a quite pleasant taste, and was often used to sweeten Sazz.

The day wore on. We slept covered by leaves. Ismelda made no attempt to cover her nakedness with leaves and vines. It meant nothing to her in the company of comrades.

With remarkable suddenness the day was dying.

Rousing ourselves, we prepared to push on in our quest. With what, in another girl, would have been distressing frequency, Ismelda persisted in reminding us that we had—we just had!—to find San Mrindaban. What he must be going through! It doesn't bear thinking of! You must keep your promises!

And so on, and so on.

A raucous caw drifted down from the sky. Before I looked up I glanced swiftly at Ismelda and Darham. Both were busy with the little fire we had carefully built. They were moving, so I knew they were not held in a thaumaturgical stasis. Then, knowing they could not see or hear the Gdoinye, but wondering what they'd think of my talking to myself, I looked up.

Yes, there he flew, grand and contemptuous, all a glitter of gold and scarlet feathers. The Gdoinye, the spy and messenger of the Star Lords, a giant raptor with whom I'd had words. Now, though, I wondered if he'd come from Ahrinye or the other Everoinye.

He soared in wide planing circles about me. About to shout some jocular insult, I checked. With a movement swift and precipitous, he flicked over on a wing and went hell for leather down and through the trees where I lost sight of him. Now what was he playing at?

"This is supper, Nath. But we'll call it the first breakfast."

"Yeh, Darham. We've a lot to do."

We ate and drank from the forest's provisions and started to think about hauling the voller out from her concealment.

What made me look up? Had the fleeting visit of the Gdoinye alerted my senses? Whatever, up I looked.

A black bird, a giant raptor similar to the Gdoinye, floated over the trees. He was zigzagging and clearly was looking out for something. That something, I considered, must be the spy from the Star Lords. Instantly I hauled on Ismelda's arm, holding her still.

"Do not move, Darham! Silence!"

He gave me a stare, saw the determination on my face, said nothing. Ismelda started to say: "Nath! What on—?"

In a manner totally opposed to gentlemanly behavior, I clapped a hand across that pert and pretty mouth. So we stood, frozen.

Presently, through the leaves above us, I could just make out this unwelcome bird turning and flying off. He went in a different direction from the one the Gdoinye had taken.

What he was, was obvious. Who sent him—well, now that was a quite different question, by Vox!

Of a size with the Gdoinye, this black bird with his metallic golden beak and claws, conveyed altogether more menace. Oh, sure, the Gdoinye and I traded insults almost as a matter of ritual; but after those first fraught seasons upon Kregen the ripeness of the repartee lost much of true venom. Over the years the odd idea had occurred to me that the Gdoinye, no less than I, had a job to do.

Ismelda started questions about the black bird. Darham cut in with a sharp: "Watch out! There's a voller approaching."

Remaining in the leafy cover we waited quietly. The voller came on at a steady rate of knots and in a direct straight line.

That line would terminate at the exact spot where we stood.

"Mother Tulippa save us now!" Ismelda put a hand to her breast. "The Shanks have found us!"

Darham put one massive arm around her still narrow waist. I said: "Take a look at the flier. That's not a Shank craft."

The voller's lines resembled the fliers of Balintol called lifters. She was a swift, two-place job as far as I could judge. On she came directly following that ominous line. Darham hefted the sword in his free fist. The voller landed gently and then skimmed lightly over the grass until she came to rest just under the trees. The figure of a man stepped out. He waved an arm. "Llahal all!"

He walked firmly towards us with a litheness and grace in his step. He was apim, like me, and he wore an odd costume consisting of a very wide-brimmed hat festooned with faerling feathers. His coat was almost a doublet, and his breeches might have come from Vallia—except I had the suspicion they'd come from somewhere far further away. An enormously wide baldric supported a rapier of considerable length and the main gauche on his right hip swung from a narrower crossbelt. Much lace cascaded down around his neck. His moustaches, wide and curled, and his pointed beard a marvel of exactness, gave him a most dashing air. Finally, his black boots were turned over at the top to flop about just under his knees. The boots were polished to excruciating brilliance. Apart from that, his entire costume was silver.

"Llahal," growled Darham, very fierce.

"Llahal and Lahal," quoth this fine dandy, very bright. "May I be allowed to present myself? I am Larghos de la France."

The silver colored silk doublet creased as he bowed most gallantly.

Now in my description of him, you may wonder why I did not mention a short cape hanging from his shoulders. For one thing, the cape was blue and for another it lay folded over his left arm. Now he held it out to Ismelda. There was no need of words. She put the cape around her shoulders, and then gave that typical wriggle, snuggling into it.

"Thank you." She said it very prettily.

I wondered why she bothered to cover up her nakedness for this dashing fellow, when she'd not cared a fig with Darham and me. Perhaps because his lean face, bronzed and yet smooth, with the crystal blue eyes and the firm mouth and chin appealed to her.

So, acting in a very mean and petty way, I said: "You'll have to be mighty careful, dom. Some damn great black bird's been—"

"Really?" He interrupted with such grace I couldn't possibly feel insulted. "Parbleu! That Maksting is becoming troublesome."

"Maksting?" said Darham.

"Just a name we have for it. What the Cymbaro-forsaken thing's Schannish name is I've no idea."

"Yours is a two-place lifter." I spoke heavily.

"Precisely. Our friends did not expect a third member of your party. The wide-brimmed hat, which he'd doffed when bowing to Ismelda, went back with a slap. He turned to face Darham. "My regrets, dom. I cannot take you."

Ismelda, who was not just a pretty face, burst out: "I'm not leaving! Mother Tulippa strike me barren first! We must find San Mrindaban! We must!"

Darham gave me one of his hard stares.

Larghos de la France showed surprise at the young lady's words.

"But, I have strict instructions—"

She was having none of his instructions and she didn't even bother to ask whose they were. Darham still held her and, again, he glared at me. So, I nodded. The Bold growled out: "Do not fret about your dear san, Ismelda.

We will find him, Nath and me. And we'll bring him back as Malahak is my witness."

"Nath?" That jolted Larghos de la France. "I thought you—"

Rather loudly and trumpeting over his words, I told him my name was Nath the Hammer. I leaped forward and shook his hand warmly. I introduced Darham the Bold. Undoubtedly I made a clown of myself; but if I was to be Nath the Hammer for Darham, then I didn't want my general use name of Drajak the Sudden banded about. Perhaps later.

To relate how we cajoled Ismelda would be tedious. In the end we persuaded her and she climbed into the lifter observing the fantamyrrh. That gesture pleased me. As I say, a most resolute young madam, with a pleasing shape. The flier lifted out from under the trees. She rose swiftly and now Larghos de la France put on the power and she fairly fleeted away, devouring the dwaburs, as they say. In no time at all she was gone.

"Hum," observed Darham the Bold, and so fell silent.

To make him think of something else I asked him why he'd changed his name from the time we'd met in The Ruby Winespout. Oh, he informed me with comic gravity, he felt Darham was more sophisticated. I hid my smile. By Vox! I'd nothing to laugh about, had I? Here the Star Lords had sent their fresh young fellow all kitted out and in a voller to take Ismelda back. Deliberately—deliberately, mind!—they'd given him a two-seater. Two! Oh, no, those puissant Everoinye wanted poor put-upon Dray Prescot to stay here in hellish Schan. Why?

To rescue this confounded San Mrindaban, I supposed.

As to why that should be, well, I mustn't ask, mustn't meddle in affairs that don't concern me, mustn't I! There was a damn great lot of skullduggery going on behind the scenes, that was for sure. Yes, and when all these grandiose power games involved the Star Lords quarrelling, then I, Dray Prescot, intended to keep my head well down.

Fourteen

"San Mrindaban?" said Lokushi. He rubbed up his left tusk. Like the right it had a groove all the way around. That was where the pestiferous Shanks had removed Lokushi's golden tusk bands. For a Chulik, who are bred from birth as warriors and earn their living going out into the world as mercenaries, he was remarkably friendly. This, I assumed, must be one result of his capture and subsequent slavery. "No. But I know a polsim who might."

The cell-like room in which we talked had been dug under the foundations of a slave hut. We were not in the bagnios, for which I gave great thanks to Zair and Opaz. Lokushi said we were perfectly safe from detection. The Shanks may be slavemasters, he told us. They do not have the skills in man-management of your normal despicable Kataki. Thus it was that escaped slaves ran off into the interior, others formed what can only be described as a secret underground.

From the moment we'd entered Terzul we'd been spotted and picked up by members of one cell, that run by our Chulik friend Lokushi. Terzul was, as we'd been promised, a large city with many thousands of Shank inhabitants. The place gave me a creepy feeling, by Krun! Pazzian slaves labored everywhere, performing many different tasks, and divided up into a sickening kind of hierarchy. Some folk we saw strutted about wearing halfway decent ragged clothing and wielding balass sticks. Not a pretty sight, perhaps; but when you recall normal human nature you cannot be surprised.

One of Lokushi's men, a Fristle with mangy fur called Franco, went out at once. Lokushi, I saw, ran a tight ship.

Food was not in plentiful supply. I knew of the ways slaves supplemented their meager rations and this band of cut throats would let very little stop them from storing their larders. So I had no guilty qualms about eating and drinking. Well, not many.

The polsim, Lamki the Quick, came in with his rat-faced whiskers twitching.

"Yes," he said in that artful whining way of your polsim. "I saw the san. They took him off." He waited, his little eyes bright.

Lokushi put one broad hand onto the hilt of the dirk on the table. He did not lift it. Lamki the Quick swallowed and went on rapidly. He told us the Shanks had taken San Mrindaban off to work as a stylor on a place some way away. The nearest he could get to the Schannish was 'Stinshish' although, as he admitted, that was not quite the right pronunciation.

"Never heard of it, by Likshu the Treacherous!" quoth Lokushi.

I glared at Lamki the Quick. "What in a Herrelldrin Hell is this Stinshish?"

He jumped. His thin polsim face betrayed utter shock. I suppose I had spoken rather intemperately.

"I—I don't know—"

The yrium, that super charisma in me that was the reason the Star Lords had chosen me to be this stupid Emperor of All Paz, flared out. "Well, you'd better find out, hadn't you!"

Again the polsim jumped. "Yes—yes, master."

How petty all this was! Both Darham and I were still smarting from the last-minute failure of the Shank flier we'd liberated. She'd touched down in the last seconds of the life of her flier boxes. Now she was useless. I still smarted from the appearance of Larghos de la France. The Everoinye had prevented me from taking my new comrades by sending the fellow, and that, in view of the stricken voller, was something to be thankful for, I supposed. All the same, this got up my hooter.

May the Divine Madam of Belschutz take the lot and sink them in their own artifices! I was stuck with this task, therefore I had to go through with it, come what may. Dokerty take it!

Lamki the Quick proved his soubriquet correct. He took off running. Lokushi said: "By Kolsh of the Tusks! You have a rough edge to your tongue, dom!"

Darham gave me a funny look. "By Kuerden the Merciless! You scared the ib out of his mangy hide, Nath!"

"Your pardon, horters," I said, much mollified in tone. Lokushi had not removed his hand from the dirk. The Shank sword I'd given to Darham we'd had to hide outside Terzul. Although we could fight if we had to, I had absolutely no desire to get into a scrap right now, no, by Zair! "The matter of finding this confounded san is of the highest importance."

If that sounded pompous, well, then, so be it. These folk did not have superhuman immortal beings breathing down their necks.

A cheap mineral oil lamp, a mere floating wick in a dish, scattered our shadows across the walls and ceiling in a macabre fashion. Faces were harshly illuminated among the shadows. Oh, yes, we looked a right rascally bunch of throat slitters.

Which, as we were in Shank territory, was absolutely correct.

"How," growled Darham, "I could ever have mistaken you for Planath the Sly is beyond me. By Hanitcha the Harrower! You're enough to scare a whole army of the iron legions of Hamal!"

Ignoring that, for a thought had occurred to me, I snapped out: "How can San Mrindaban work as a stylor if he doesn't speak Schannish?"

"Oh," said Lokushi in an airy way, "the damned Shanks have us slaving away keeping their records with tally sticks. Don't need to understand their barbaric lingo for that."

"All right. What do you know about the Neeshargs?"

"Them, the spawn of hell!" He wiped his lips and ran a finger around the groove in his right tusk. "We call 'em N'shargs, or just plain hellish Shargs. The Shanks hate 'em, that's true, by Hlo-Hli. But they fear 'em. Oh, yes, they fear 'em all right!"

The day was well on the wane and despite the good offices of Lokushi and his henchmen and women there remained a very great deal of information I required, which, it appeared, they could not give me. Accordingly, when the twin suns set in their glory, as beautiful here as ever they were in Paz, I started out. The thought about the Suns of Scorpio shining over each half of Kregen in turn made me realize afresh how little Mother Nature cared for humankind's petty differences. The memory of Schanake rose in my mind, to be banished instantly.

Waiting until the radiance of the Maiden with the Many Smiles was hidden in clouds drifting sluggishly over Terzul, I reached the end of the row of shacks to look out into a wide cross street. Needless to say, Terzul with its creepy feeling looked quite different from an honest city of Paz.

Lamps shone indifferently down on the passers-by. Slaves were still hurrying about their fishfaced masters' bidding. The Shanks, too, or Schtarkins or whatever they were, strutted along in that casual air of authority. We'd have to figure out just what racial stock fitted to its proper name. That was another task I must set my hand to as soon as possible.

Pink-tinged shadows drifted across the street. Ensconcing myself in a convenient niche just inside the mouth of an alleyway, I set about selecting my target—not quite an assassin's kitchew—but near enough if it came to push of pike, by Krun!

The fellow was not too slow about showing up for his appointment. His clothes were of that silken, rich Shank variety with which they impressed others. His face resembled that of a barracuda. He marched along very importantly. Before he knew what was happening he found himself yanked bodily into the alleyway.

Speaking in the harsh, hissing, clicking Schannish I told him to keep still and silent. I held him facing away from me. I held his head pressed forward and down. Enough pressure applied and his neck would snap; but I just used enough to make him realize his predicament. He spluttered and hissed; but did not call for help.

The question was put to him.

"You flistis! I am a noble of the third degree. I'll have your head for this." He found it difficult to speak by reason of the grip on him. He was trembling and this I put down to his rage and affronted dignity; not to fear.

"Tell me!"

"Stinshish? I know it."

When he pronounced the name it had altogether more splash and hiss than Lamki the Quick's version.

"Tell me where it is."

An abrupt application of a fraction more pressure, quickly followed by release so that he could breathe again, brought the answer. This grand noble of the third degree was happy to tell me. I did not miss the irony in the terrestrial translation either. The place lay some goodly distance away from the coast. Shanks do not relish travelling far from the oceans. He gave me directions.

"Right. Clear off now, and be thankful you're still alive, you stinking basich."

He let out a sharp exclamation at this. Already my grip was loosening so that, moving with startling suddenness, he was able to twist around. In the vagrant shafts of pink radiance from the Maiden with the Many Smiles, he looked full into my face.

His reaction was one of complete and utter anger. In a spitting, venomous verbal onslaught he started: "Ishtish! A larver! To me! To—!"

I gave him such a belting crack on the side of that fishy face he went straight over and down. His head hit the cobbles with an almighty bang. Like a pumpkin dropped on rocks, his head broke.

So, like the onker I was, I stood there, stupidly looking down on disaster.

All too clearly the result of this night's handiwork stared me in the face. When the Shanks understood that one of their citizens had been killed by a Pazzian—a larver, a basich—despite that it was an accident, well, there'd be hecatombs and rivers of blood.

Of course, by Zair, it was all my fault, really. I, Dray Prescot, trying to be clever and act out the part of a Fish-head, had chosen the wrong expletive. Flistis, that was the name I should have used. Basichs and larvers were Pazzians.

Standing there like a loon and trying to work out a solution to this nightmarish impasse, I heard the racket of running feet and impassioned shouts battering along the street towards the alleyway.

Fifteen

The Shank's green ichor spread across the cobbles. I stared on him, appalled. What had I done? As the sounds of the hue and cry bellowed closer I knew exactly what I had wrought here. Although not of my willing, I'd brought horrific retribution upon the heads of the Pazzian slaves pent within Terzul.

Only seconds were left. I had to act. The attack of near panic had to be fought off. Do something, Dray Prescot! Now!

Moving very rapidly and as silently as possible I upended one of the rotund barrels stacked by the entrance to the alleyway and placed it carefully between the fishface's legs. No time for anything more fancy now; I just had to hope his fellow citizens would believe he'd stumbled over the barrel and cracked his head.

With that, off I loped, going very, very quietly.

In the next few heartbeats the shrill shouts spurted up. They'd found him, then, and now it was up to All the Names to convince the Fish-heads that what their eyes saw was the truth of what had happened.

Taking a short circuitous route, and most circumspectly keeping in the shadows, I arrived back at Lokushi's hideout. Now there are many people who tell confidants just about everything, on Earth as on Kregen. It seems they can't prevent themselves from blurting out all their boring details to their friends. Scorpions are not like that, in general. Many items in my life are still shrouded in vagueness. So, I did not tell Darham what had just occurred. I did say that we'd found where Mrindaban might be.

"Good. Let's get started, then."

The Chulik, Lokushi, who answered to the soubriquet of the Cranstemer, offered quite willingly to help us—if we helped him.

Darham huffed and puffed. In the end we both agreed. Lokushi rubbed his naked tusk and beamed one of those grotesque Yellow Tusker smiles, and told us what he wanted.

After my brush with the noble of the third degree, I was not altogether happy about venturing too often into the Shank-crawling streets of Terzul. Still, a bargain was a bargain. The third degree noble's tacit bargain with me had not been kept. Once again I felt the remorseless and intolerable weight of guilt descend on my shoulders. Detesting killing wholeheartedly, I suffered under this damned doom that was my fate.

So it was, the next night we ventured forth, a right pack of unhanged rascals about our nefarious business. All we had to do was rob a warehouse containing food of a far superior quality to that supplied grudgingly to the slaves.

Lokushi's gang knew their business. I'd been on enough food stealing expeditions as a slave and a soldier to play a full part. Darham, too, was no slouch in the illegal replenishment of supplies.

Everything went off smoothly, which, by Vox, came as a vast surprise to me!

With the confiscated food stored away we could eat and rest. Lokushi and all the other gangs of runaway slaves referred to their activities as the Holy War, and raiding the enemy was not stealing. Some slaves had made their headquarters outside the city. Their activities were far more dangerous because of reprisals from the military; the convoy raids and confiscations couldn't be blamed on Shanks. Still, these bandits for the Holy War referred to their drikinger activity as confiscations.

Our new Yellow Tusker acquaintance was as good as his word. We'd be escorted out of town by secret ways. We could each wear a breechclout and drab tunic once we were well away. Provisions went into two sacks fitted with straps. Lokushi pressed four large water bottles on us. "You may need them, doms." His words sounded ominous.

Understandably, he was most reluctant to part with any weapons from his meager armory. Darham surprised me. A trifle airily, he came out with: "Oh, we'll pick some up on the way."

So much for giving him a sword in a crisis!

A sack of provisions and two water bottles slung over my shoulders and the determination to secure weapons as soon as possible as my preparations, I was ready to set off.

The water bottles were fashioned from nawish hide, a kind of goatskin, and I just hoped they'd behave themselves and not leak. Also, I trusted we had enough water to last us to the first well.

The next night off we went through murky ways between the backs of buildings. We crawled through a disgusting sewer. We'd have to smell until the stink wore off by itself; our water was far too precious to squander on washing.

Lamki the Quick headed up the other three polsims in the team escorting us out. He'd whined that he'd failed to discover the whereabouts of Stinshish, as it was supposed to be secret. "The Fish-heads are concentrating an army there for some important war. That's all I know, save the blintzes need slaves there."

Lokushi had burst out with: "By Likshu the Treacherous! That is bad news for us all—aye, doms, and worse for your san."

We parted from the polsims, thanking them, and set off into the night. Neither Darham nor myself had even bothered to ask for riding animals. Anyway, the sewer would have baffled them, for sure.

As I trudged along in the darkness, fitfully lightened by brief appearances of the Maiden with the Many Smiles, I thought of Larghos de la France, as he called himself. That was cheeky, in itself, by Zair! My resentment had not lessened. Here I was, lumbered with some crazy mission, reduced in circumstances and walking on my own two feet. And that jackanapes Larghos, a kregoinye sent by the Star Lords, all dressed up like some comic opera tenor and in a voller, too! It didn't bear thinking of. So, I stopped that line of thought and tried to concentrate instead on what lay ahead.

A secret location, given to me by that unfortunate noble of the third degree, an army gathering, slaves taken up for the menial tasks—it all added up to skullduggery of a very high order.

By morning we'd reached the end of the coastal belt. Ahead stretched an uninviting territory. The Shanks did go in for agriculture in a small way, mainly for the production of green vegetables. Of husbandry there was a sad lack, a variety of vosk being the main animal. You could readily see why the Shanks went raiding all the time. Oh, yes, you could see it. You didn't like it, by Krun!

Resting until dark under the trees gave me time to draw more syrupy liquid from the shrimpas, thus saving our water. Twice during the day patrols of Shank vollers passed high overhead. I was confidently persuaded they were not searching for us.

Darham had already proved himself a good comrade and even in this somewhat miserable situation he could still crack a joke—aye, and laugh at it, too. I felt that he should never have been born a Hamalese. This rather demeaning thought I could think, despite that my very fine blade comrade, Prince Tyfar, was not only a Hamalese, but the heir to the throne, and, perhaps by this time, my son-in-law—that was, if my lass Princess Lela had made up her mind. One day she would, if Tyfar, too, faced up to it. Then Lela, known as Jaezila, would in due time become the Empress of Hamal.

As for the other girls, Dayra, known as Ros the Claw, would be off somewhere fiercely fighting for the Sisters of the Rose. And young Didi, daughter to Velia and Gafard, would also be embroiled with the Sisters of the Rose. Her aunt, Velia, of an age, would no doubt be getting into scrapes at her side. What a family!

About to ponder on the lives of the lads, I was snapped out of my reverie by Darham's brisk: "Time to march, Nath. Wenda!"

"Aye, Bold," I said. Then, mocking him, I added: "Quidang!"

This night the marching was altogether more arduous. The land we crossed was not exactly desert, being your flat dusty plain dotted with stunted bushes and unhappy grass. We kept a wary lookout for wild animals. On Kregen you never know when you'll bump into a raging monster, all fangs and claws, ravening for your blood.

We did sing a few songs, very quietly, and not many as our throats were not lubricated for the task. We had "She Lived by the Lily Canal" and "Lola's Sweet Armpits." Then we packed up and saved our spit.

The branches we'd pulled off in the woods remained untrimmed to a nicety. The leaves and twigs stripped off left two knobby lengths that were really more like cudgels than wooden swords; but we could not be choosy, obviously. We tried stones to sharpen them up; but each so-called rudis remained more like a bludgeon.

So the days passed. The provisions shrank and the water became barely drinkable.

A dark and horrific thought began to worry me. Suppose that shint of a noble of the third degree had lied? That was an idea I should have taken into account. Were we two walking to our doom?

Lokushi had been completely unable to supply us with a map. Clearly, any half-competent slavemasters bossing their victims about would never let them get their hands on maps. We marched in a land of which we had not the slightest idea of the location, save it lay in Schan. Oh, no, the Shanks saw to it that their captive basichs had no idea where to run away to.

More and more bothered by that dreadful thought that the noble of the third degree had hoodwinked me, I pushed on until morning with Darham striding at my side.

We scraped out a bit of a hole using our pathetic wooden swords. This was as much for protection from the suns as from the Fish-heads' aerial patrols. These increased as we proceeded and soon a pattern to their flying emerged. Strings of them, in straight and rigid lines, flew above—at night their lights moving constellations among the stars, during the day maintaining their impeccable formations.

Darham said: "We may soon be there, Nath." He cocked his head up.

"Aye—the vollers go and return along the direction we follow."

That day I felt like a naked new born halmfrey before its camouflage coat grew. Out of every ten cub halmfreys born, on average over the seasons only a pitiful four survived to adulthood. The thought did nothing to ease my concerns, even though appearances in the air tended to confirm we were going the right way.

Then, like a gift from Opaz in the wilderness, we came across cacti. The lack of knives or of any cutting edge tool could not deter us. Like madmen we dug our wooden weapons into the fat bole, and tore strips away until the water oozed. We lapped like hounds exhausted and thirsty from the hunt.

Mind you, although I was a trifle surprised to find cacti growing in this type of terrain, the discovery was bliss. I'd already determined that we must dig holes down near plants. Eventually the narrow deep holes would fill with what passed as water, earthy, yes, but drinkable to thirsty men. The obvious problem of our lack of digging equipment would be overcome by sheer doggedness and near-insane clawing at the ground. The water table here could not be so far down as to make hole digging for water an impossibility. The Names would not have willed that, for the sweet sake of Opaz!

Mind you, by Vox, I was really whistling in the dark, as they say in Clishdrin, if I banked our lives on finding water by that simple method in this country. It works splendidly in nice friendly forest or lush meadows. But here?

When Lokushi had mentioned the runaway slaves who set up bandit gangs for the Holy War in the interior, he clearly did not mean this land. By Krun, no! My thoughts, I sluggishly acknowledged, were becoming rambling. The effects of the journey worked surreptitiously on us, so that our steps did not carry us forward in the warrior's march.

If we poor benighted pair didn't die of thirst out here and were found and taken captive by the Shanks, they'd staple one of those damned great metal collars around each of our necks. Every collar bore an inscription in Schannish, easily readable. That way the fishfaces kept track of their slaves. Also, to the utter condemnation of all the gods or spirits or ghosts respected by the Shanks, the collars bit deeply into the Pazzian's necks. Blood ran down chests and backs, leaking freshly from under crusted dried blood scabs.

Opaz rot all Shanks! Yet—Schanake?

Muzzily I couldn't find a way around that conundrum. The twin Suns beat down splendidly—and remorselessly.

My idiot brain must be frying in my old vosk skull of a head. While there grew cacti, we'd quench our thirsts. Until one or other of us spotted a cactus safe to eat, we were in peril of dying of hunger rather than thirst.

A tiny yellowish-white triangle appeared over the horizon ahead. Instantly, I knew what that was. She bore on splendidly, all plain sail set, heeling to the breeze. All her larboard guns were run out. Flags floated about her like a halo, proud, imperious, golden and red, the flags of Spain.

About to yell: "Beat to Quarters! Clear for Action!" I checked myself. The black-devil cactus! Hallucinogenic!

My comrade abruptly leaped forward, snarling in a dry thirsty fashion that was in no wise ludicrous. Rather, Darham'd put the fear of demons up his foes. He leaped, and struck savagely about with his cudgel. With blazing ferocity Darham fought his enemies—the phantoms within his own drugged brain.

The hundred-gunner sailed past across the scrub and vanished beyond my left shoulder. Had she fired her batteries in a smother of smoke and pitiless tongues of flame I'd have said, aloud: "For what we are about to receive, may the Lord make us truly thankful."

Darham abruptly leaped straight up in the air. His bludgeon raked across in two slashing blows, left and right. Then he fell flat on his face.

He lay there, sprawled, breathing stertorously, a great hairy mass of a comrade.

How many times have I talked about the marvelous twin Suns of Scorpio? Of the glorious red of Zim and the sinister green of Genodras? Many and many a time, I know. Now those self-same suns poured down their carmine and jade brilliance relentlessly. My old vosk skull of a head felt as though at one moment it was going to explode, and the next as though it was clamped in a vice under intolerable pressure.

The wonderful and terrible world of Kregen revolved about me. I was lying down. The harsh sandy dirt felt like a feather bed. My eyes closed. After that it was not so much the Black Cloak of Notor Zan that enfolded me as the sensation of slipping away down into the shadows...

Sixteen

When I regained my tattered senses I slowly became aware of three things.

One, I was still alive. Two, I wore a damned great iron collar around my neck. Three, I was surrounded by a most dismal low-key moaning like a mournful wind soughing through dead branches.

So, I knew where I was.

Well, what more could a fellow from Paz expect if he got himself drugged and fell asleep in Shank territory under the surveillance of their air patrols?

The effort of opening my eyes proved not as painful or as difficult as expected. The bagnio was poorly lit by what looked to be the Maiden with the Many Smiles shining through cracks and chinks in the mudbrick walls. Rolling my head to the side I discovered the hairy form of Darham still well away into the land of Nod.

All about slaves lay on the bare earth, collared, miserable, moaning. The sound sawed at my nerves. Come on, Dray Prescot. You've been slave before and no doubt will be slave again. So start to plan how to escape this mess and get on the job for the Star Lords.

Of one fact in the case I was sure—wishing that I wasn't—and that, of course, confound it! was that the Everoinye wouldn't send a dapper little fellow and a smart voller to get me out of it. That still rankled. Yet I knew from hard personal experience the Star Lords did not send their Giant Blue Scorpion to rescue me. They'd whipped me off from the Heavenly Mines only because they wanted me to work for them at once. The task set to my hands existed right here, wherever here was, for I felt confident that San Mrindaban must be in this pesky Stinshish where the Fish-head patrol had dumped me.

So there was no reason for the Star Lords to lift me out of here, was there, by Krun!

Darham began to stir and groaned a bit.

"Kaerlan the Merciful save me now," he mumbled out as though his tongue filled his mouth.

"Amen to that," I said, and my voice, too, sounded cracked and old.

Well, perhaps the Lord Kaerlan did intervene in the succeeding days. Certainly, Kuerden the Merciless proved to be in evidence everywhere in the stinking camp of Stinshish. But we survived. We worked hard, digging, humping loads, carrying out all the menial tasks required to service the camp of an army.

The whipping and kicking were moderated, there was food, coarse but enough, and the laboring hours were reasonable.

"Fattening us up for what lies in store," a mangy-furred Fristle told us, glumly. "Eat while you can, doms."

During the days of toil that followed we picked up a good picture of the camp. If you have a wide plain with a river flowing from the hills, blue on the horizon, and many tents and picket lines, I suppose it is only fair to assume one camp will look much like another.

That theory appears sound. In parts, of course, it was. But—but this Shank army camp! Oh no, by Zair, this was a fishface excursion of a quite different stripe.

The creepy feeling I'd experienced in Terzul seemed to me to be concentrated here. Oddness, what could rightly be called squiffiness, a sense-disorienting placement of things, everything that was not Pazzian kept an unsettling grip on our minds.

In these days, naturally, we made enquiries as to the whereabouts of San Mrindaban. One of the great attributes of my new hairy comrade was his absolute lack of rancor against fate—or of Ismelda—in landing him in this horrific situation. He'd given his word. He was a zhanpaktun with the gold pakzhan at his throat, and that recognition of prowess from his peers was not lightly won, not lightly at all, by the Blade of Kurin! He'd committed himself and he'd go on to success or death.

Eventually we discovered the san worked in a large marquee heavily guarded by Fish-head soldiery. The structure consisted of a number of large tents joined to form the outside ring to the marquee. Unless a slave had a right to labor in there, then no slave would be admitted. Queyd-arn-tung!

Darham said, back to his growly way: "Easy. We change collars with a couple of fanshos who work in there."

"Right."

As I said, he earned his nickname of The Bold.

We found that the slaves of the marquee, a simple name to distinguish them from the common run of slaves who worked around the camp, did not leave their quarters. San Mrindaban did not venture outside.

"Best time, Nath?" demanded The Bold.

"It may not matter if they work in shifts in there. Still—night time, I suppose."

"Aye, by Krun!"

Accordingly, that night after a supper of stock fish and cabbage, or what purported to be cabbage, we set off.

Darham's excellent plan to change collars with a couple of marquee slaves now out of the question—and you may imagine the air turning blue with the epithets of disgust about that!—we had to act with the utmost caution. And that is a mighty understatement, by Vox!

Lines of slaves bent under their burdens took supplies to the marquee. They made piles of sacks and jars under an open-sided awning. There must be a horrendous amount of good grub in there, by San Belshui of the Steaming Pot! The fishfaces strengthened the guard when supplies were brought up for the internal slaves to take away inside. So, logically, Darham and I went around the back.

Either we were very lucky or the weakened guard couldn't do a proper patrol. In the event, we cut a slit with the edge of a broken pot and slipped inside.

I sniffed. Darham sniffed. "What's the smell?"

The canvas walls enclosed a small space filled with jars. We trod carefully. We sniffed again. Eventually we understood the smell was that of scents from the perfume jars. So accustomed had we become to the eternal fish stink of the camp little else penetrated our nostrils.

The place lay very quiet between its canvas walls. We came across no one. My back began to itch. This was past creepy to eerie.

Darham, in the lead, abruptly jerked back so that I had to haul up sharpish. We stood stock still like a couple of statues.

A succession of soggy thumps sounded through the canvas just ahead on our right. They were intermingled with other squashy sounds. Darham dropped to all fours, stuck his head around the edge of the canvas, pulled back very swiftly. He motioned to me and we changed places. I looked.

By the light of two lamps four Shanks were torturing a Shank woman. She was naked, with a lump of wood jammed into her mouth and held by cords cruelly bound about her head. What Shank ideas of beauty were I wasn't sure. I'd heard that fishface women were regarded as servile creatures by their men folk, lacking respect. They were totally unlike the ladies of most of the lands of Paz—not all—where women were their own women, open and free partners of their menfolk. This poor creature had tiny, pretty scales, and I guessed she must be a prize beauty who had misbehaved.

Without thought I tensed, ready to spring in. A massive hand fastened on my shoulder and held me fast. Darham's growly whisper breathed in my ear. "Hold still, onker! They're only Shanks."

I felt—what did I feel? The injustice and inhumanity in the world? The hatred and cruelty? Oh, yes, those. I felt shame. Darham was right in a horrible way, and San Mrindaban waited.

That was the moment, when I raged against the inhumanity of humanity, that the sounds spurted up ahead.

There were hissingly shrill Shank voices raised in anger. There were the unmistakable sounds of steel on steel, followed by chopped off screams. Darham flung me a look and we dived into the nearest cover, which happened to be a remarkably ugly statue of a Schtarkin in heroic pose. We huddled in the shadows.

The swift helter-skelter of running feet heralded the appearance and immediate disappearance of a running girl. She was a Sylvie, one of that race of diffs whose women are voluptuous almost to the point of parody of the female body beautiful. Her eyes glared in absolute terror. Her scarlet mouth was wide open; yet she couldn't scream for the utter horror that gripped her. She was entirely naked, which made the scene even more painful. Darham said nothing.

Now heavier footfalls approached. We crouched lower. Four Shanks came into view carrying bloodied swords. They were talking amongst themselves; but for the moment I scarcely listened. In the lead strode my old fishface mate Schanake.

All that they were saying added up to the fact that they were going to kill the bastards and take the lady Stasia away to safety.

Darham remained so still you'd have thought he was dead. The fact was that if he'd moved too much, he would be dead instanter.

The four Fish-heads led by Schanake passed by and we didn't hang around to hear them sort out those bastard torturers. We scurried on in the search for San Mrindaban.

The corner around which the panic-stricken Sylvie and Schanake and his gang had appeared revealed further bloodshed when we turned it.

Three Fish-head guards lay in their own green blood, their weapons fallen, their wounds grievous to death. To myself I said that my fishface dom really did mean business, by Krun!

With a low, snarly growl of triumph, Darham leaped for the swords. There were two of them, a straight cut and thruster and an ankster. The other weapon was a typical Shank trident.

"Which one d'you fancy, Nath?"

"You choose, Darham."

"Thank you, dom. I'll have this one." He picked up the straight cut and thruster. It was not a Havilfarese thraxter but not too dissimilar. I hefted the ankster. The double curved blade sheened blue. The weapon felt good in my fist.

We left the trident as being too conspicuous. My Val! As though a couple of slaves parading about with swords belted to their waists were not conspicuous! Still, they could be hidden when we'd finished this night's nefarious doings.

The Bold gave his opinion that whilst he was grateful for the weapon, all the hullabaloo could have happened on another night.

"It may work to our advantage, dom. There are few folk about."

"True, by Krun!"

I found it strangely comforting to have a fellow at my side who apostrophized dear old Krun—by Krun!

In addition, and thanks to Opaz and Zair!—that poor creature being so dreadfully tormented was about to be released. I hoped Schanake would not be too lenient on the torturers.

Eventually we struck lucky and ran across a couple of slaves who knew the whereabouts of the stylors in the tents surrounding the marquee. Thither, cautiously, we went. We did, unfortunately, meet two fishface guards. The savagery with which The Bold flung himself into action gave the Shanks no chance. They went down without even the chance to screech.

Put that down to Schanake's account, I said to myself with what philosophy I could muster. We prowled on and left the tridents.

These two poor dead Fish-heads had green ichor for blood. Schanake's was red. Here was the conundrum of races reinforced.

Two little Ochs leaped up from their stools where they'd been transferring the notches from tally sticks onto paper. That paper was not the superb quality bond from Aphrasöe, and, too, it had probably been taken from a stricken Pazzian trading vessel.

"The san?" They each waved their four upper limbs about in bewildered apprehension. "Yes, yes—he works just here."

A deep basso voice spoke over their chatter. "Let a man get some sleep, Onko. And you, Nath the Quill, you sound—"

The man who stepped in must be Mrindaban. His hair was still black and it sprouted heavily all over the place almost rivaling Darham's mop. The voice might be deep, it held a note of tiredness. He stopped speaking the moment he saw us.

"Please do not be alarmed, San Mrindaban," I said.

"I am not alarmed."

His nose was indeed a fine beaked specimen. But his eyes were as Ismelda had said. Their color was almost nonexistent, a pale transparent glisten. But they commanded and demanded so that you could imagine you looked clear through them to the man's soul. You wouldn't forget those eyes in a hurry, by Vox!

"I see you carry swords and are not of the marquee slaves."

"Aye, san," growled Darham. There was satisfaction in his tones. He looked about after the fashion of a chavonth locked in a cage. Already he was planning the best way out.

Calmly, I said: "We have come on the request of the lady Ismelda to take you out of this place."

He took that in, digested it without surprise. He shook his head. "Oh, no, my friends. I cannot allow that—"

"What!" Darham swung about, massive and hairy, and filled with the adrenalin rush. "We've come to rescue you!"

I held up a hand. "Tsleetha-tsleethi. Softly-softly."

"I cannot possibly leave now." Mrindaban waved a hand vaguely in the air. "My studies are nowhere near complete. Why, I've barely mastered the parsing of the most simple Schannish."

Darham just gaped.

I said: "You speak Schannish?"

"Yes. Well, to be truthful, no. But I progress, I progress."

That confounded itch up my spine became as pronounced as the carbuncle on the backside of Beng Thrax. My Val! Here we were, out to rescue this sainted san, and he was just like a stuffy professor wrapped in his arcane studies and perfectly oblivious of the outside world. It was enough to make that saint hurl his halo on the ground and jump on it, by Vox!

The Bold growled out: "We do not have much time, san. We must leave right now."

"Leave? Ah, no, my impetuous friend. You must understand, it is vitally important for all Paz that we learn the Shank's language." He waved that hand in the air again. "This new Emperor of All Paz we have to unite us, this shaggy clansman of genius, Dray Prescot, will value such knowledge above gold and jewels."

Amen to that, I said to myself.

"But, san—you can't—I mean—you are a slave—"

Evidently, Darham had no conception of the ferocity of the pursuit of learning. That is the hardest taskmaster.

Well, by Makki Grodno's pendulous unspeakables and putrescent nostrils, apart, that is, from the Star Lords.

"That is enough, horters!" The latent power in Mrindaban showed itself now. "Please thank my dear Ismelda for me. Now, I must take my sleep. Vardgan the True Clepsydra knows, the Shanks allow me little enough rest as it is, without unwanted intrusions."

Well, by All the Names, what could you do with the man?

Abruptly he opened those compelling eyes wide and all his force flared forth. "Ismelda. She is well?"

"Yes, san," replied Darham, much taken aback. "She is safely on her way back to Paz. Must be there already."

"I am relieved. She is a very precious lady. Now, thank you for your intentions and remberee."

With that he turned about and walked not quite steadily back past the canvas. So, Ismelda was right. Her dear san was much sunken in body—but in spirit! Oh, no, by Djan! That flared as brightly here in these dreadful surroundings as ever it must have done back home. And I still didn't know what Mrindaban's discipline was.

"Remberee," I said. Darham mumbled out a: "'beree, san."

My fist went around my back and rubbed across my spine.

"Let us—" I started. The Bold got out: "Aye."

He was really choked up about the ironic situation, although he wouldn't call it ironic, by Krun.

The two little Och stylors concentrated so closely on their work I swear their noses almost touched the paper. Leaving them and the scene of our discomfiture we started back the way we'd come. Before we reached the canvas enclosure where Shanks had died we branched off through a gap into the adjoining tent. Distant shouts increased in volume. Guards would be running from all directions.

I found myself hoping Schanake would escape safely. If he kept the damned Shank soldiery off our backs I'd be grateful.

By the smells the next enclosure must be the kitchens.

There were bound to be slave cooks there, for any headquarters of an army has grub on the go around the clock. So we ducked across the next gap and saw a flapped opening in the canvas wall.

My bump of direction fancied that led outside.

Like any sensible person, seasoned kampeon or green coy, we peered outside before venturing on. A damned great rout of Fish-heads galloped past from left to right, waving their weapons and shrilling menacing threats in Schannish, calling on all kinds of arcane spirits and devils to catch the perpetrators.

They were after Schanake all right. Darham grunted, as though lifting a boulder, and stilled. He'd break out the right way when the appropriate time arrived.

Why the devil I should worry myself over the welfare of a stinking fish-face escaped me. But that Shank woman, the Lady Stasia, clearly meant a very great deal to Schanake. I understood that.

The somewhat arcane words of San Blarnoi occurred to me as apposite. 'If you cannot understand the pain, it is torture. If you understand the pain, it is not torture.'

Many pundits over the seasons had made much of that, arguments and counter arguments. Make of it what you will.

Darham sucked a breath. "We've been lucky so far, by Krun!" His massive hairy body crouched by the opening was a mighty comfort, I assure you, to a compatriot in nefarious goings on. "We'll have to lose these swords, Kuerden take it. Otherwise, we are dead men."

"Hide 'em where we can find 'em again in a hurry."

In a quiet interlude in all the excitement rousing the camp, after a fresh mob of Shanks raced past and went hullabalooing across to the cavalry lines, and so leaving us in, as it were, a vacuum of action, we sneaked out and burrowed into the shadows.

Following the Maiden with the Many Smiles, the Twins were up. The Twins, sometimes called The Dahemin, eternally orbiting each other as they orbited Kregen, shed their particular pinkish radiance upon the world. In the shadows we could skulk. In the open we were like clay pipes set up in a rifle range on Earth.

In the blended shadows Darham shook his sword, and scowled.

"By Krun! A sword in my fist—maybe I spoke over hastily,

Nath—maybe—maybe we could steal something that floats and go down the river—I hate to discard a weapon—"

"Maybe, Bold." I spoke as equably as I could. "Mebbe. Still, the Shanks will have thought of that. Slaves sailing off down the river. Bound to."

"Aye." His scowl became deeper.

Casually, I said: "You're taking the san at face value?"

What, he wanted to know, did I mean by that.

So we discussed our dilemma, there in the streaming pink moons light as the camp shook with the clamor of Shanks chasing Schanake and his pals. Ismelda had taken our promises. The object of our rescue bid did not wish to be rescued—well not right now. By Darham's talk of slipping away by river, I assumed he considered our obligations discharged.

For my part, I'd gone along because of my word to Ismelda. The Star Lords had not interfered. That did not, of course, mean they wished me to hoick San Mrindaban out of here. After the job finding Ismelda was over I could go my own way until they required my services once more. All right, then, Dray Prescot. Will you, too, skulk off and leave the san happily learning Schannish?

Of course, naturally, inevitably, the glorious face of Delia glowed radiantly into the forefront of my confused mind. Smiling, she put a finger to her lips. I could feel the dizzying sensations sweeping me away. So that was that. I told Darham I'd be hanging on here in the camp ready to rescue Mrindaban when the time came.

We looked into each other's eyes. The Bold's scowl now drew his shaggy features into one enormous grimace.

"We-ell—" He growled out. "We-ell—"

Seventeen

The fleet sailed majestically about us. This gathering of fliers, an Armada of the Clouds, drove on in the rigid sailing lines so typical of Shank aerial doctrine. Darham and I and many other slaves were packed into a weyver, a barge-like voller, with tremendous carrying capacity. Pazzians called them Quoffas of the Skies. The fishfaces regarded these highly useful barges with a degree of contempt. They called them Bishters. A great concentration of flying vessels about us, we flew on under the streaming mingled lights of the Suns of Scorpio.

Where we were going, and why, naturally, we had not the foggiest idea in all of Kregen.

Out to raid our own Paz; that was the general consensus among the slaves huddled in the weyvers.

The fleet was heavily stocked with provisions. No one knew that better than us. We'd carried the lot aboard, hadn't we?

Many of the slaves became extraordinarily apprehensive over the treatment handed out by the Fish-heads. We were given more palatable parts of fish, rather than heads and tails. A kind of gruel, served in baked clay bowls, didn't taste of fish—well, that is a stupid remark. Everything about the fish-face menu held the tang of the sea. Still, this gruel did taste more like a porridge than anything else available. There was bread, stale, of course, and mostly crusts. The cabbage that was not cabbage was served up more frequently and on two occasions we received cheese in the form of rinds.

All this pampering of the slaves frightened some of them so that they became ill. They didn't talk. They sat crouched over, their hands clasped around their heads. Some couldn't stop shaking.

Whatever was in store for us at journey's end, clearly, was highly unpleasant.

The view from the bulwarks of the weyver was restricted to what flew higher than us. A few white clouds, cirrus, drifted into sight. Darham perked up. "Getting somewhere, Nath."

"Aye."

In confirmation, that evening the tame cook slaves handed out yalloms. These look and taste just like bananas. Mind you, their yellow skins were soft and heavily marked with constellations of brown spots. The fruit was soft almost to the point of mushiness. Of course, they carried the taint of fish. We ate them ravenously.

"Quick energy, Bold." His cheeks were widely distended so that his hair stuck out like a sweep's brush. He swallowed mightily. Then he reached across for another handful and started stuffing that into his black-fanged winespout. I could not criticize. I was doing exactly the same, as fast as I could, by Krun!

What it is to be a slave! You know nothing. You go where you are told. You get whipped and beaten. You slave. Yet when these puissant slave-masters give you better food, take care of your welfare, you are even more frightened out of your wits.

Despite all this, Darham the Bold with his: "We-ell—" had decided to remain. He'd voluntarily accepted this ghastly existence instead of regarding his promise to Ismelda as cancelled when her precious san announced he didn't want to be rescued.

This meant, of course, that we'd had to discard the two swords. You may imagine with what reluctance The Bold had parted from his blade. Still, amusing me, he'd perked up. "When the time comes, Hammer, we'll snatch fresh weapons. Hanitcha the Harrower take it else!"

A mere audo of Shank soldiery, consisting of eight swods and a deldar—to give our Pazzian names for the section and its commander—guarded us in the weyver. Darham's black glances at the fishfaces concerned me so that I said, a trifle sharply, I confess, that he should confine his loathing to that proper to a slave—that is, to non-existence. He stuffed in the last yallom, and agreed by a nod of the head. Slightly surprised by his ready acceptance of criticism when I'd expected an outburst, I did feel the relief.

The guards produced sharpening stones and started to put keen edges on their weapons. A little two-place voller dropped down and out stepped a Fish-head very well dressed and armored, with a tall headgear of colored scales. He gave orders, smartened up the audo and with some pompous language for remberees, flew off.

"Tonight." Darham spoke with authority.

"Aye."

We'd counted only four crewmen to run the weyver and they kept close in their cabin at the center of the craft. They were armed, naturally. Heaping piles of empty sacks suggested hard work ahead.

Among the fleet flew deeper-hold cargo vessels which we called binhoys. Whatever plunder the Shanks were after, they made provision for a hell of a lot of it, by Krun!

The guards, whips at the ready, moved closer to we slaves and made unmistakable movements to indicate we must keep silent. We would, of course. No one in his right mind wants ol' snake licking the blood from the stripes down his back.

Some familiar Pazzian words were known to some of the Shanks. Schanake had known some, for example. Now one of the guards with a face like a dogfish managed to splutter out: "Shastum!" Silence!

The most hated word slave drivers shout at their prey is the infamous command: "Grak!" This means work until you drop, and then if you don't work on after that, you're dead. The Shanks had difficulty in hissing that foul word, although they managed to click it out roundly enough. We understood. Oh, yes, by All the Names, we subdued and beaten slaves understood!

With the setting of the suns on that evening She of the Veils put in the first appearance of the moons, having overtaken the Maiden with the Many Smiles in their orbits. Some unfathomable attraction had always drawn me to She of the Veils, making her my favorite of all the moons. A golden light permeated her rosy radiance, and the shadows grew richer for that nightly brilliance. Clouds drifted across her glowing face and Kregen darkened into shadows.

This powerful armada of Shank fliers would cast a heavy shadow upon whatever and whoever proved to be the targets and the victims. There would be much wailing and gnashing of teeth at the end of this nights work, to the chagrin of Opaz.

In that grim thought I was only half-right.

There would be much agony, blood and death. But I was wrong to ascribe that horror to any lands of Paz over which Opaz held sway.

Above us the clouds parted to allow the radiance of my favorite moon to shine down upon the world. Ahead, clearly visible, the warships of the Shank fleet moved forward, away from the freighters. The night rested still as a corpse upon Kregen.

The moment I saw the shadowed mass floating in thin air before us, on the very instant that I spotted the floating island of the air, the volgendrin, I knew what went forward here. I knew at once what the Shanks sought in this secret night raid.

Pashams!

These honey-melon sized fruits tasting like old sweaty socks and smelling like the sweepings of a totrix stable were prizes valuable above gold and gems. They were practically inedible. Slaves who in their desperate hunger tried to eat them vomited all night long and through the next day, too, by Vox. Oh, no, these fruits were not food. Dried, crushed and ground up, they formed one of the ingredients of the silver boxes that powered fliers.

So, if that was the way of it, as, indeed, it was, we were in for a big night. A mighty big night, by Djan Kadjiryon.

Mind you, the Shanks built their fliers differently from us. They used power boxes that were not silver but bronze or brass or some other metal. The question here was, why did they have to sneak up surreptitiously like this in the night with an army to raid a vo'drin for their pashams? This was a conundrum to set alongside so many other puzzles that beset me in the terrible and beautiful world of Kregen.

Our Shank guards were now very much on the qui vive. With action imminent the Fish-head soldiery were taking no chances with the slaves in their charge. Still the night lay silently all about.

In his breathy whisper Darham said: "A vo'drin. Aye, I served a stint on one of them out by the Mountains of the West in Hamal."

The irony of this revelation did not escape me. At the moment I did not wish to dwell on my long and practically fruitless quests for the secrets of the vollers' silver boxes. I'd had successes, of course, as the great flying ships of the air of Vallia proved. Their silver boxes lacked some of the required ingredients and thus could only lift a vessel in the air, they could not propel the craft. For that we relied on the ethero-magnetic keel, as the sages called it, to provide the proper functions of a ship's keel as the wind bellied her sails and drove her along among the clouds.

Darham clearly was ruminating on his time out there by the Mountains of the West. "I wasn't particularly voinsh there." Voinsh is one way of say-ing happy. "Still, we had one or two ding-dongs with the wild men from over the mountains. That livened us up." His hand went automatically to his throat as he went on: "'Course, I was only a mortpaktun then." His hand clasped emptiness at his throat. The jerk with which he ripped his hand away and the growl that rose to be immediately suppressed, told elo-quently of his feelings now.

Our weyver slowed right down. Two others drifted above us off the lar-board beam, and three more off the larboard quarter. We were waiting. You didn't need to be a genius to guess why we tarried like this.

The volgendrin was big, all right. Even the Volgendrin of the Bridge, out there in West Hamal, which was really two of the flying islands joined together, came nowhere near in size to this beauty.

Lights dotted the black mass, here and there, not many. The clouds were indeed thickening, and on a guess I'd hazard they were alto-cumulus, which meant we might be in for rain later. The Shank fighting craft in their rigid formations showed no lights and they vanished in the shadows as the glorious face of She of the Veils dimmed and disappeared.

In that close-pressing darkness the nauseating sounds of combat seared into the silence like a hot iron on flesh.

At once the frightened slaves set up a jabbering.

"Shastum!" hissed and clicked the fishfaces. Whips flicked out in the darkness to crack heavily where chance took them.

A young Hytak lad, Clandi, of the tailed Hytak race of diffs, let out a yelp at my side. A vagrant shaft of pinkish golden radiance reached down to reveal Clandi gripping his arm. He saw Darham and I watching him.

"My apologies, doms. By Vox, it caught me by surprise."

The racket quietened down. The slaves moved restlessly, huddled, appalled at what lay in store for them. The noise of the battle on the vo'drin flowered into the night air. Now Darham showed me another facet of his fascinating character.

"Listen, fanshos," he said in his heavy penetrating whisper. The Shanks did not splutter at him to keep silent. "Clandi, you can fly an airboat?" At Clandi's nod, Darham went on: "There was a fellow I knew, a pilot in the Emperor Nedfar's air service, who was the most marvelous flyer in the air, a real flutkamp." By this he meant an Ace. Now other slaves were craning forward to hear. In his bold, straightforward way, Darham calmed them down as they listened.

"Well," he went on, "this fellow, Nath the Clepper, he was, might be the most wonderful flyer in the service. He could judge the height and speed and distance of another voller absolutely." Here Darham paused. He sucked in a breath. "But he had no idea how to land a voller."

Of course, his auditors wanted to know the rest. The Shanks, who couldn't understand a word, recognized the change in attitude of their slaves and allowed The Bold to continue.

"What did he do? I'll tell you, fanshos. He stopped over the spot where he wanted to set down. Then he'd gently pull the silver boxes apart, slowly, slowly. The craft would go down more slowly than a drunk getting up the next morning. Inching down, a bit at a time, he'd yank the boxes apart the instant he touched the ground." Darham looked around. "'Course, he bent a few airboats in his time. But he was such a flutkamp the flutkapts kept him on."

The air marshals of Hamal are a canny lot, that I do know. Anyway, you couldn't land like that in a conventional terrestrial fixed-wing aircraft. Ships like the marvelous Harrier can, of course. And helicopters do, too. But your normal Kregen voller pilot just swoops down to touch the ground and skid to a peremptory halt.

The little anecdote had calmed the slaves. As I say, this was another and refreshing side to my new comrade.

All the same, as I was Dray Prescot, the supposed Emperor of Emperors, the Emperor of All Paz, with plans in my old vosk skull of a head for the future, I was more than a little dismayed at the lack of fighting spirit of these slaves. If they thought of themselves as slaves I had a hard task ahead. Whatever my new dom Darham might think, I had plans.

Many times in my hectic rackety life on Kregen I'd pontificated against the despicable institution of slavery. Delia and I had eradicated the disgusting custom in the lands over which we held sway. I'd raised slave armies to fight their slave masters. But this poor lot? I fancied I might count on Clandi. By his way of speaking he hailed from Vallia. Who else? Darham, Clandi and I could hardly hope to fight the opposition that would be pitted against us.

By the disgusting diseased liver and lights of Makki Grodno! There had to be a way! And so long as I was Dray Prescot, Krozair of Zy, I'd find it, by Zair!

That was all fine fustian stuff. The clangorous noise of the fight on the volgendrin continued to sully the night air. Yes, of course I had a plan. A simple plan, to get the slaves to rise and chuck the damned slavers over the side and take the weyver and high-tail it out of here. But, again, with this spineless lot?

I've quoted many and many a fine epithet and round oath used by the good folk of Kregen. Perhaps you have heard, what, a tenth of the wondrous ways of cussing people upon Kregen? I could call this poor collection of scared people famblys, hulus, jinkas, zigging great onkers. None of that would matter. The desperate need was to motivate them into doing what I required, what was necessary.

Darham spoke, bringing me back from unprofitable theory. "If this is supposed to be a raid—they aren't doing too well—shoulda quietened the opposition down by now—"

"Yeah," I said. "Agreed."

On that, the little two-place voller swooped over our craft, the officer aboard her yelled down, and our Shank guards and crew jumped to obey. The weyver rose and turned toward the vo'drin.

In the erratic pinkish golden moonlight details of the vo'drin stood out clearly one moment, to be veiled in shadows the next. Stars scintillated above as we moved purposefully in for a landing.

Darham's assessment seemed to me to be accurate. Dark masses of troops fought bloodily hand to hand. The uproar, screams, shrieks, moans, blended into a nightmare symphony. The Shank army who'd brought us here for this supposed lightning raid were making heavy weather of subduing the soldiery standing guard over the pashams. We slanted down with other freighters aiming for a cleared space beyond the conflict.

Fringing the area, the long dark bulks of warehouses rose to the height of a three-storey house. They looked heavy among the slender trees with willow-like drooping foliage. Those warehouses must be crammed with the fruits we'd come to steal. As I'd said, a big night ahead, and now that was complicated by the fight roaring away only a few hundred paces from us.

The cargo craft touched down and at once the Fish-heads flailed their whips, driving us out and towards the warehouses.

A quick glance at the fight, clearly revealed in moonlight, showed that disaster could be imminent. A wing of our Shanks—if I may distinguish the rasts thus—swayed back under pressure. Darham grunted unpleasantly. "They'll give way any second."

"The prospect, Bold, is unappealing."

Blueness stole in like a devotee of Diproo the Nimble-fingered. The blue radiance hovered more strongly above me. I knew no one else could see that ghostly radiance.

At this moment of crisis the Star Lords sent their Phantom Blue Scorpion to seize me up and hurl me somewhere else about Kregen.

Events followed so fast I'd no time for anything else. The shape of the Scorpion wavered, trembled. It surged about and then swung away from me. The blueness quivered a hundred or so paces off, between me and the fight. A shape appeared below the Scorpion.

The blue radiance vibrated and thinned. From that eerie light a figure walked out towards me. I stared and my old heart gave such an almighty thump I thought it would jump clean out of my mouth.

The most glorious lady in two worlds swung lithely on towards me. She wore her russet hunting leathers, with a mail shirt underneath. Her rapier glittered unsheathed in her right fist, and her left hand was covered by the cruelly sharp steel Claw.

At that precise moment the Shank battle line gave way. Fish-head soldiers broke and ran. Swiftly chasing them vicious Neeshargs hacked them down mercilessly. The rout roared on towards our Shanks and the slaves clustered by the warehouse.

And—between us and the swiftly approaching carnage walked Delia, Delia of Delphond, Delia of the Blue Mountains. In only moments she would be overwhelmed and all the lights of Kregen would go out.

Eighteen

I, Dray Prescot, Vovedeer, Lord of Strombor and Krozair of Zy, went berserk. Everything became highly charged. My vision was surrounded by blood. The noise of the combat thinned. My actions became vague to me. A Shank guard lay bloodily on the ground at my feet. His sword was in my fist. I ran. I raced forward like a maniac.

Delia had seen the danger. Her Claw lifted. She could rip the face off a Shank with that lethal weapon. My head felt as though it was bursting. I could feel nothing of physical pain. Mentally, my agony scythed into my brain like a chainsaw.

Imperiously, Delia pointed her rapier off to the side. I looked. Yes, she could be right! There was a chance, a slim chance. It was all we had.

Between two of the warehouses the shadows beckoned invitingly. If we could reach there in time! Once in there the shadows would hide us. We'd scuttle off like woflos pursued by nikchavonths.

Do not be amazed, my friends, that Dray Prescot could think like that. Oh, no! Where Delia is concerned honor is everything: my only honor is for the safety of Delia. So we ran.

Delia ran superbly. Well, what is there that she does not do superbly? Perhaps her aversion to sickness may be called otherwise; but as she has proved, when disease strikes and people depend on her, then, once more, she is superb.

The slap of feet cracked out abaft and I turned with a quick savage readiness to rend and destroy. Darham and Clandi panted along at our backs. In that swift backward glance the scene out there was etched on my mind.

The slaves, shrieking in abject terror, fled. Their Shank guards ran in front of them. They were racing for the weyver. The rout of fishface soldiery thundered on following them. The Shargs just kept on straight ahead, slaying, slaying.

We four flung ourselves into the shadows and crouched down. We must have presented a sight as we stared out from between the warehouses. I thought we'd succeeded, then Delia snapped: "There are a couple of those pesky Neeshargs who've seen us."

"Aye, my lady," rumbled Darham. "And here they come!"

I said: "You know their name? Who they are?"

"People we know told me."

So there was a story there, then. Clandi piped up: "My lady, how did—" He stopped, wet his lips, went on: "I am surprised—"

I gave him a real good old Dray Prescot glare, not the Devil Look, and in my gravel-shifting voice, said: "The pappattu is, Clandi, this is the Lady Alyss. You would do well to remember that."

"I will, I will—"

"This hairy morsel is Darham the Bold."

So the pappattu was made and Lahals exchanged, and then the Neeshargs ran across to our shadows.

There was just time for Delia to say, with a very wicked tone to her voice: "And you are?"

Of course! These fraught moments were really addling my brains. "Nath the Hammer, if it please you, my lady."

Then I stood up, swung the Shank sword, and fronted the Shargs.

They were what they were. Deadly killing machines without mercy or compunction, they shrieked some gibberish and charged.

Their compressed, flat faces, with those staring eyes and wide lipless mouths, showed no other emotion than a joy at killing. The blades crossed, swiftly, swiftly! They were good—I would not say they were especially good, for they were foot soldiers without the special skills that were no doubt possessed by their commanders. Keeping both their blades in play to the front I made no attempt to force them back. The less attention we attracted the better.

The one to my left tried to spit me. A quick beat and riposte and my borrowed sword slid into his throat. I swiveled at once, half-ducking, ready for the next. I needn't have bothered.

A loud thwunk! crunched out. Darham stepped back, looking pleased, holding a chunk of timber he'd ripped from the warehouse wall. The Sharg just crumpled up and fell without a sound.

"Very nice, Bold." I said.

"Ha! It was a good blow—I'll admit that!"

So now we had more weapons to add to our arsenal.

Clandi kept glancing at Delia, and away. The way I figured it, he wasn't sure she was Delia, Empress of All Paz. After all, how could she be here? Why, in the name of Opaz, should she be? Yet he must have seen her at some time, probably in Vondium. Kings and queens where immediate media coverage is absent are not often seen by the ordinary folk. Whilst I might regret that, it is decidedly convenient when these high and mighty folk go adventuring around Kregen.

Confident that he had not recognized me, or had never seen me before, I could concentrate on our immediate next steps. I burned with the desire to take Delia into my arms and hear her story—that must wait.

Darham said: "Best get away—I mean—this vo'drin is big enough to hide on—till we can steal a voller."

The weyver that had brought us here rose into the air. Only some of the slaves were aboard, the majority left stranded simply ran blindly every which way pursued by the Shargs gripped by blood lust. Some headed for our shadows.

"Time to move!" Delia spoke sharply. Clandi jumped.

What story she and I could think of to explain her presence here, a female basich, clothed and armed, escaped me. Delia would dream up a story, there was no doubt of that, by Vox!

We cleared off back from the warehouses. The main combat flowered its nauseous noises into the night. Rows of pasham bushes led onto woods. Thither we went, very sharply yet most circumspectly.

"Handy, is he, Darham, with a chunk of wood?"

"Oh, aye, my lady. As old Hack 'n' Slay would say, indubitably. And there's a thought to make you blanch—those two together!"

And Delia laughed.

Leaving the rim of the floating island to our rear we progressed on. The sounds of combat dwindled. There were hills ahead, sharply pointed with narrow valleys between. Everything was smothered in vegetation. Deep within the volgendrin would be the enormous reservoirs kept filled by rain which gave rise to the springs and streams. We'd not thirst for water. Food, though, might be a trifle more tricky.

Darham took the lead, moving like a hairy strigicaw through the surrounding shadows. Clandi, the only one of us able to wear some of the fallen Shargs' armor, took the rear. Darham and I just didn't fit into any of the armor, which happened to be scale shirts. We'd tugged on some clothes, though, breechclouts that appeared to be made from fish skins. Delia's delightful nose wrinkled up at the smell; but I assured her she'd soon grow accustomed to the eternal stink.

Our marching arrangement gave Delia the chance to talk quietly to me. She asked if I remembered one of her handmaids, Rosala. I nodded. "Clandi is her grandson. He was very very young when he first saw me. I don't think he really remembers."

"If he does, he'll stay mum. He's a Vallian." By that I meant that all Vallians were devoted to Delia of Delphond.

When she went on to tell me how and why she'd arrived here I felt so many varied emotions chasing around in my old vosk skull of a head. I shuddered at the terror for her, yes; but I really believe my chief feeling was one of amusement. True! As Opaz is my witness!

She'd been on a harebrained mission for the Star Lords and successfully completed that. Then they'd wanted her to go off to Zumbaya. She heard the Everoinye discussing some late developments and my name was mentioned. Now, Delia is Delia. She'd asked the Star Lords what went forward with her husband. Ahrinye and his sidekick, Razinye, had at last shown their hands. The Everoinye might be old beyond belief; perhaps they weren't quite as senile as I'd often cussed them out for.

The upshot was, the Star Lords went along with my staying in Schan. San Mrindaban would prove useful to their plans. When Delia discovered where I was, she'd gone spare, as they say in Clishdrin.

"I told them a few home truths, by Roz the Flame! Yes, I let 'em have it!"

At this I didn't know whether to break out in a cold sweat at the risks Delia took, or to burst out into a coarse guffaw at the delight in the situation. My Delia! My Val! What a wonderful girl she is! And here we marched along side by side and I could not take her into my arms as every last blasted bit of me wanted to do.

"So I told 'em I wanted to go, too."

"That stupid Giant Blue Scorpion," I said. "He fumbled again. He dropped you right in it."

"He did his best, Dray."

"Humph!" I said in the best quarterdeck tradition.

Delia went on to say she'd contacted our comrade Wizards of Loh. Apparently they had enormous difficulties in trying to get through to Schan. Still, they were going to do what they could. Selah!

To think of Delia in her imperial fashion telling the Star Lords a few home truths. To imagine the scene! Superhuman immortal beings they might very well be, I'd bet a zorca against a calsany they'd been shaken up a trifle—more than a trifle, by Vox, when my Delia gets going!

The point here was, folk in Paz regarded Shanks as devils from every single one of the various hells available. The idea of actually going to Schan was akin to going to certain death. Even the Star Lords had prevented Ahrinye from sending me earlier. This time he'd sneaked his schemes past them until they caught up with him and Razinye.

There was probably in Pazzians' imaginations no fate worse than being miraculously dumped down in Shank infested Schan. Yet Delia had trounced a group of superhuman beings so that they'd send her there!

Well, there is only one Delia, Delia of Delphond, Delia of the Blue Mountains!

One startlingly obvious fact in our present imbroglio was the sheer awe in which both Clandi and Darham held Delia. This had nothing to do with the way in which she had so mysteriously appeared. Their feelings of awe and admiration and sheer reverence stemmed from the fact that Delia was Delia.

If I grow maudlin, the reason is obvious.

I told Delia I'd have to go up and take point to relieve Darham. Before that I said: "Have you seen an ugly raptor, like the Gdoinye, called the Maksting? Only he's not gold and scarlet. He's black."

"Not seen, no. But heard about, yes. Larghos de la France told me—" My mouth opened. Then I clamped it shut with a snap. Delia's quizzical little look was enough to spell it all out. She went on: "The Maksting can track Kregoinyes if they move about Kregen physically. Well, at least, that's the theory up there—wherever up there is. Larghos had to be very slippy to avoid the thing."

So Delia had sussed out the dapper kregoinye, too. I asked about Ismelda. She was doing fine. The besotted king had set up a nice little villa for her. The queen, presumably, fumed in fury in private. In a weird way justifying our actions for the Everoinye, Delia gave it as her opinion that the twins would probably create a cause célèbre when they were come to maturity. "Or start or stop a war."

At that, with the utmost reluctance, I went up for'ard and took over point from Darham.

Later on we rested up beside a shallow brook that tinkled over a gravel bed. We took turns to stand watch until the Suns of Scorpio rose, palest green and flushing rose. To our joy we found paline bushes. We did not have hangovers; but the juicy yellow berries served to dull our hunger.

Delia pointed imperiously at an odd little bush with tall narrow leaves, and Clandi jumped to dig it up with his sword. The fat white tubers were not only edible, as Delia told us, but were delicious. "Lompas," she said. "Unmistakable." But then, you see, Delia's fieldcraft is superb.

The sharp peaks ahead, green and shining in the lights, arrayed in random ranks, promised better cover. That morning we penetrated the narrow valleys, finding welcome food, and by evening set up our makeshift camp at the entrance to a cave, which was dry.

Clandi was asleep in the cave, and Darham just ducking his head to enter. Delia and I stood outside the entrance, silently.

The blueness which stole down to envelop us crept stealthily. Delia and I clasped each other. We looked up. Yes, there he was, the Phantom Giant Blue Scorpion of the Star Lords, hovering over us.

"What now, my heart?" whispered Delia. "We aren't finished here."

"We are together—" I said and up we went, hurtling head over heels, cavorting helplessly through the blustering cold. Through the weird other dimension used so effortlessly by the Everoinye we sailed away, bound for what new fraught adventure—who could say?

Before we landed the blueness thinned beneath us. We were the right way up. Below, many campfires burned. The Shank vollers were neatly lined up, squadron by squadron. Slaves toiled, loading the freighters with sacks that undoubtedly contained pashams. So although the fishfaces had been unsuccessful where we'd attacked, they'd won here. There was not a sign of a Neesharg to be seen.

That brief glimpse was all that was vouchsafed us. Locked in each other's arms, we went hurtling headlong down into the Shank camp.

This time the Scorpion dropped us down in the right place. At least, I judged so, for we found ourselves in a clump of trees, under good cover. The leaves and ground in the open were wet, so the expected rain had, indeed, fallen.

The dappled lights from the Suns were just beginning to fade as the evening wore on. The sweet after-scents of rain on grass and leaves filled the air. These pleasant reflections were broken in a harsh and ugly way as the Fish-heads, hissing and clacking, rapped out "Grak! Grak!"

"Look." Delia pointed. "That fellow fits perfectly the description of San Mrindaban given to me by the Everoinye."

"Aye." There he sat with papers spread before him on a wooden crate. He worked away taking up the records given him by the tallymen. You could see his importance to the Shanks all right. "How—"

"Oh, the Star Lords want him rescued."

I said nothing for a bit, then: "Well, he refused!"

"So now, if he won't come of his own accord, we take him." So, of course, this explained all the machinations going on behind the scenes. The Star Lords were not so far gone in senility as to be unable to turn Ahrinye's schemes to their own advantage.

Of course, how I, Dray Prescot, suffered in the middle really didn't bother those high and mighty immortals one whit.

Looking around carefully, I located where the smaller vollers were parked. We'd have to liberate one of those if we were to succeed. I anticipated with dark forebodings the reactions of the san. Well, by Krun, he'd be lifted up and carried off. That was what was!

The slaves appeared a docile lot, worn down more by fear than bad treatment. Just like the bunch of poor devils who'd flown in with Darham and me, they were highly unlikely to put up a fight.

"We'll have to be slippy."

Delia gazed purposefully around the camp, sizing everything up. I knew that shrewd brain in that beautiful head was working away on overtime. She nodded. "Yes."

So that was that. We would follow Delia's Plan.

One thing was obvious to me; it was likely to be a far better Plan called The Plan than anything I'd concoct in the time available.

With the going down of the Suns and the lowering of the shadows we moved. In her pouches Delia had a firelighter, so we were able to make quickly twisted stems to form torches and light them. We hurled them right merrily, too, by Vox! At once the camp became engulfed in commotion. Shanks ran every which way. Slaves just cowered down with hands over heads, desperate to keep out of whatever was going on. A whole pile of sacks went up in flames. A voller began to burn. We could not keep this up for long. Our positions would quickly be revealed by the direction of the flung torches. So we sprinted most rapidly about our two tasks after setting the fires.

Delia shot off to the small voller park with a: "Don't be late!"

I headed straight for Mrindaban. Running fast I reached almost to him seated at his crate before any of the fishfaces reacted.

Two came for me. There was no time for niceties. One, left, reverse, two, right. They hissed as they fell and I raced on.

The san looked up quite calmly. "I thought it might be you."

"Come on, san. Time to be gone."

"I told you, Nath the Hammer. I do not wish—" He couldn't say much more as I seized him up, slung him over my shoulder and scampered off.

The blade in my fist ran with green ichor by the time I gained the voller. I did notice in all that inferno that not a single Shank had red blood. The confusion racketed up like a carousing night in Sanurkazz before the jolly mobiles trundled up.

Into the voller with him, over the coaming after, Delia thrusting the levers over, and away we went, soaring up into the night sky of Kregen.

Circling high, climbing, we passed across the rim of the volgendrin. The strangeness of all this action taking place on an island that floated about in the sky was enormously strengthened by the abrupt appreciation of the drop beneath us. The ground lay wreathed in shadow.

"That's that, then," I said. I gave the san a look. "This is for your own good. So there's no use in arguing."

That impressive face of his with those strange eyes clouded. Then, sharply, he nodded. He'd reached a decision.

"Very well. I surrender to superior forces. Let us go."

He'd not given any flicker of emotion at seeing an incredibly beautiful woman, clad for war, flying the airboat. He went along to the bench seat at the rear and lay down.

"We'd best head west."

"Aye," I said. "I believe that to be the nearest coast."

"What, Nath the Hammer, do you think you are playing at?"

"What?" I said, stupidly.

"There is something we must do first."

About to burst out with some rigmarole about doing things for the Star Lords, I checked. Of course! I'd been so wrought up, I'd missed the obvious.

"Absolutely, Alyss. We must go and find Darham and Clandi."

"Exactly!"

Nineteen

Now that I'd calmed down from the fraught emotions urging me on, a puzzling fact that had been bothering me surfaced.

"Y'know, it had been raining and things were damp. Yet the torches burned splendidly. And the Shank stuff went up—"

"It wasn't all that wet!" Delia spoke with a bite.

"Well, I fancy that—"

Delia gave me such a look that I clamped my black-fanged winespout shut instanter. "Oh, there was nothing magical about it." She swerved the flier sweetly in the air. "You're imagining things."

So, naturally, I realized that in chattering on about perhaps the Star Lords really and truly helping us, my words would inevitably attract the intent interest of San Mrindaban. All the same, by Krun, perhaps the Everoinye had dried things, given us an assist.

If they had, I did not think it was because they wanted the san so urgently. It most certainly was not because I was involved. Oh, no. Oh, sweet no! It would be because Delia was here.

True or false, that thought gave me enormous comfort.

"Have a look aft, Nath. Can you see anyone following?"

"No. Not with the antics you've been flying. Still," I added more somberly than I relished, "as soon as the clouds clear and the moons shine through, they'll see us."

"Which means we must get down sharpish." We flew on heading for the steep little hills where'd we left our new comrades. Presently, Delia, in a musing way, said: "Y'know, I find these volgendrins very weird. Highly eerie. Massive islands flying through thin air."

"Not at all!" broke in San Mrindaban. "It's just the Chakarj Effect. A perfectly natural phenomenon." We swiveled to stare at him. His dark outline leaned forward and he went on to say that the Chakarj Effect, being part of the natural order of things, did not rely on thaumaturgy or prayer. "I have rejected sorcerous magics and religious miracles. What power I have is different, and, if I may say, in my view far superior."

These words made me leap back in memory to the continent of Loh and to a remarkable man, San Ornol Wanlicheng, and his pretty, devoted student, Xinthe. My guess need not be true. By Djan, there are so many diverse religions and disciplines of sorcery on Kregen that even with the long lifespan of Kregans, one man might never encompass them all.

Trying to make my voice as calm as possible, I said: "You are, perhaps, one of the Pilgrims. A Wayfarer, a Pathfinder."

Although the darkness of encircling shadows concealed his features, the utter shock in his voice could not be disguised. He burst out with: "And what do you know of the Pilgrims?"

Still speaking evenly, I told him I'd met a man in Loh who had opened up his vision of Alternative Magic. He disliked the title of san. By following various Pathways in the human brain, it was possible to perform what mages called sorcery, and religious folk miracles.

"This man—his name?"

"Ornol Wanlicheng."

Mrindaban sucked a breath. "You have been privileged."

"I think so, too. He told me of Lisa the Forthright—"

At this Mrindaban let out a croaking cry, almost a squeak, as though someone had struck him in the midriff. "If only!" he cried it out. "If only!"

After that he rambled on a bit in what can only be described as maudlin self-pity. He had never had the opportunity of meeting San Ornol. As for Lisa the Forthright—well, if he didn't believe in gods he certainly referred to Lisa in terms fit for a goddess.

Alternative Magic functioned in the human brain so that men and women could perform what would otherwise be called magical and miraculous acts without sorcery or religion. It worked. I knew it worked. It had saved me from a bloodthirsty pack of werstings.

Then She of the Veils smiled down, all golden and rosy, and flooded the face of Kregen with nighted beauty.

The Pilgrims, folk who followed the Pathways, were few in number, and scattered about. Mrindaban had first been instructed by a wandering scholar who had himself been instructed by San Ornol. Ornol, once a religious devotee entitled to be called san, in rejecting thaumaturgy and gods, denied himself the title. Mrindaban, by contrast, as an academic, once he'd mastered enough of the Pathways, joyed that he might now be addressed as San Mrindaban.

Delia said firmly: "There's the cave."

That old savage clansman's twitch in the back of the neck made me turn about quickly. "Aye. And there's a damned Shank voller on our tail."

No other airboats could be seen flying after us and I rather fancied this fellow had not followed us from the camp. He was more likely to be one of the standing patrols the Fish-heads ran over the volgendrin. With the raid only as successful as the curate's egg, the fishfaces wouldn't care to hang around too long. Delia swung the voller away immediately on my caution.

Two tiny figures popped out of the cave, and even more abruptly dodged back.

"They'll be all right." Delia stated a fact in her inimitable way. She sent the voller up in a soaring arc, seeking shadows.

After that there was nothing I could do to influence the situation. Delia is such a superb pilot with skills even old Darham's flutkamp Nath the Clepper never dreamed existed, she simply took control of what happened. The little voller gyrated, swerved, soared and dived, so that the Shank patrol flier acted like a bemused coy at the flying academy.

This action gave me time to reflect more cogently on the fresh information from Mrindaban. Alternative Magic, although a product of the human mind, could not be compared to hypnotism. Apparently, hypnotists tell their patients that what they are required to do is 'effortless effort.' This is far from the strict requirements of following the Pathways. To reach along these mysterious trailways of the mind demands immense effort. Absolute dedication and concentration will carry the Pilgrim from one corner to another, until the goal is reached. That goal varies with the individual. I wondered just how far Mrindaban had toiled within the Pathways in his own brain.

Abruptly, Mrindaban sat up. "I feel sick."

"Well, san, hold on. We don't want you following your meal overside." Thus spake Delia, tartly.

The thing was, Delia was really chucking the voller about the sky.

Y'know, Delia of Delphond is the most wonderful and kind-hearted lady in two worlds. Yet, where professional competence is in question, or where urgent matters must be settled, she can be—well—strict. I hardly dare to presume to say callous, for that would be blasphemy. No, Delia knows what is right and proper in any given situation. If the san wanted to bring his guts up, all well and good. But that little weakness could not be allowed to stand in the way of what had to be done. And in this the Star Lords had no authority over her decisions.

I stared hard at this famous san of Ismelda's. He clutched on with a grip of death. His powerful face assumed the color of old cabbage cooked too long in the pot. He was a Pilgrim. He knew the arcane arts of following the Pathways. He'd spoken almost contemptuously of the Chakarj Effect, as though the whole phenomenon of volgendrins was familiar to him—and scarcely worth mentioning.

Well? And wasn't my automatic thought perfectly natural?

Do not forget, I, Dray Prescot, quite apart from being a supposed Emperor of Emperors, Emperor of All Paz, am a wily old leem hunter, a savage clansman of Segesthes, as well as being your plain sailorman.

Yes, by Djan Kadjiryon! If it could be done, then I'd make damn sure San Mrindaban did it, may the Divine Madam of Belschutz and all her bodily imperfections drop sploshingly upon us!

All the time, as I thus pondered on what might be accomplished, Delia wove her magic aerobatic skills through the moons-light drenched night sky of Kregen.

By this time Delia had the Shank flier thoroughly confused. Poor old Mrindaban, still clutching on for dear life, leaned over the side. His shoulders heaved. What a shame!

In the erratic shafts of light streaming through gaps in the clouds the volgendrin appeared to dance and prance about beneath us. The Shank had no hope of catching Delia, yet the fellow clung on stubbornly. Just like a fishface! I leaned forward and spoke softly to Delia. Her responding laugh came as a spring of clear water in the desert.

"But if you fall—" The laughter in her voice stopped almost, I fancied, on a quick choke of emotion.

Without further ado, my Delia swung the flier into a new series of maneuvers. In no time at all we came swooping up on the tail of the Fish-head voller. With precise timing Delia slanted in from his starboard quarter and I stood up and leaped.

Mind you, by Krun, I hit the rear bench seat an almighty bang!

The two Shanks in the front twisted around. They'd been taken completely by surprise. Anyway, they wouldn't think anyone could be so crazy as to risk a wild leap in the half-light from flier to flier.

I cannot be boasting when I say that Dray Prescot is crazy enough to perform so maniacal an act, rather it is an admission of foolhardiness. Yet my Delia had sanctioned the leap!

One Shank received a finicky little thump under the ear which stunned him sufficiently for me to take the other fishface into my grip. He started to struggle and in the ensuing fracas I had to upend him. He went over the coaming yowling. The other Fish-head came back to life and whipped a short fat dagger at my throat. The dratted thing almost had me. With a savage jerk of my head I avoided the blade. This fishy specimen followed his crewmate over the side.

The voller sprang about the sky like a mayfly with one day of life to enjoy. Taking the controls into my fists I gentled the craft down and then brought her to an even keel and so rode neatly alongside Delia. She smiled brilliantly at me. I waved back.

The other major moons were up now. In their mingled lights a face appeared over the coaming. The color of that drawn visage was an amazing amalgam of green pallor overlaid with the sheen of gold and rose. San Mrindaban's mouth opened. "Wha—?" He stared at me in our new flier. "Where'd you go, Nath the Hammer? How—?"

"Oh," said Delia, offhandedly, "he's fond of tricks like that."

In the carrying bin fixed along the forepart of the voller rested a bag made from woven fiber, something like the Shanks' attempt at raffia. Next to it stood four wicker shapes that could, thanks to Beng Dikkane! only contain ale flagons. They must be the loot from a raid on an unfortunate Pazzian vessel. Elation filled me.

The bar that retained these valuables when the flier swirled about in the air snapped open faster than a leem strikes. I snatched up the bag and a flagon and held them high over my head.

"Treasure!" I yelled across the wind swirling gap.

At least, we had a trifle to sup.

Delia pointed up. "Shanks!"

Yes, there they were, four of them, flying a rigid line ahead formation. On that, both our vollers helter-skeltered towards the ground and cover.

I followed Delia in under overhanging trees and pulled the controls to off. Silently, we stared up, and the san's face remained that intriguing greenish color.

Abruptly the vollers peeled off and went swooping down.

A rapid search of the trees over the little valley above which we hid revealed a small airboat flying fast. It headed our way, clearly attempting, as we had, to find shelter. The voller had no chance.

Half a dozen darts and a few hurled rocks from the catapults drove the flier over on her side. Bits of her hull flew off. She crashed into the trees and was lost to sight.

"Well." Delia gave her opinion that although she felt sorry for the crashed passengers, as they were Shanks there was no real harm done. "Still, they could have survived if the trees broke their fall."

"Aye. Just."

The night wore on swiftly as the Moons crossed among the stars. We waited a long time before moving off. The Shanks we had spotted might well be gone; there would be others out on patrol. No doubt some of the detested Neeshargs were still hanging around.

When at last we took off and rapidly and silently flew over to the cave, I, for one, looked every which way. We saw no fishface ships and so swooped down and drove gently into the cave entrance.

Darham rose from the shelter of a boulder, sword in fist.

"You coulda got yourselves killed like that."

"Where—" started Clandi, and then, in his fashion, stopped.

"You wouldn't believe it if I told you." Delia was decidedly brisk. "Nath the Hammer has found provisions. Let us eat and drink."

There was Shank bread and cheese, and, of course, fish. Also, there were onions. The ale, Darham hazarded a guess, was from Dorinth. "A trifle hoppy, but welcome, fanshos. Very welcome."

The fact that there were hops meant the drink was beer and not ale; but a trifle like that didn't matter to Darham was concerned. Oh, no! Glug, glug, glug!

Young Clandi had the utmost difficulty in refraining from staring at

Delia all the time. Of course, the youngster was hopelessly in love with her—along with uncounted millions of others. Still, I found myself wondering if he did remember meeting the great Empress of Vallia with Rosala his grandmother all those seasons ago.

If he did eventually decide that Delia was really Delia, I had no doubt, as I'd mentioned, that he would keep his mouth shut and carry on as normally as possible.

A heavier darkness outside the cave heralded the approach of dawn. The general consensus among my comrades here was that we should fly to the west coast and thence back to Paz—wherever among the continents and islands we might end up. That should be done during the night, and there was not enough of this night left.

This general consensus of opinion did not suit my plans.

I said to Delia: "Let's take a turn outside." She knew at once I needed to tell her something and, knowing me, that I wanted to ask for her views. We stood together, quietly talking in the darkness with the breathing night all about, hushed at the approach of dawn. When I'd finished she said in her calm, practical voice: "If it can be done, it should be done. The importance to Vallia is difficult to exaggerate."

The first rosy flushings of light spread across the sky. The dark shadows retreated. Somehow or other, with Delia at my side, with the rising of the Suns of Scorpio, I felt a great uplifting of spirit and a tide of confidence that it could be done and we would do it.

During that day we rested up, ate and drank sparingly, and I told San Mrindaban what I wanted. Rather, what Delia and I would like him to do.

Studying the san, you could see his importance swelling up. His gaunt appearance, the wildness of his hair, together with those startling eyes, all added together to give him back a great deal of his shrunken impressiveness. He sat with his back against the cave wall and closed his eyes. "I shall review the situation," was all he said.

The rest of us went off to the other side of the cave to leave the san in peace. He had told us his studies in Schannish progressed well. He explained the raid after pashams. Until recently the volgendrin had floated over territory belonging to the Shanks of these parts. Then the dreaded Neeshargs had arrived and driven the fishfaces out. Without the volgendrin there were no pashams, therefore no source of one of the ingredients needed to power fliers. If the Shanks couldn't retake their territory within a reasonable time scale their vital flying forces would run down. So a raid in force became the only logical answer to the problem.

"The Fish-heads hate them Snake-heads," said Clandi. "Even though they get along with the Schtarkins, who have—"

"Aye," rumbled Darham, not expecting Clandi to finish his sentence.

"But Hanitcha the Harrower knows, them Shargs have faces an honest snake'd be afeared of."

In my new optimistic mood I did not wish to allow the usual black tide of despair at mankind's follies to overwhelm me. Fishface and snakeface detested each other. There were racial rivalries in Paz. One nation did not trust another, and, it would seem, especially if they shared a border. Yet the Star Lords commanded me to be the Emperor of All Paz and weld all those disparate forces into one to face the Shanks.

How long, I wondered, fighting despair, how long before the ghastly Shargs invaded the fair lands of Paz?

A soft rustle and a cough, a clearing of the throat, brought me back to the here and now. San Mrindaban stood up. He passed a hand over that wild hair, which immediately sprang out again in a tangle.

"It can be done. And I can do it."

I, Dray Prescot, smiled.

"Excellent, san! Excellent!"

With the demands of a Pilgrim on him, renewed vigor brought a faint flush to his gaunt cheeks. Those amazing eyes caught the lights of the Suns and sparkled. He stretched.

"Yes. I can do it. It will not, of course, be easy."

"You did not expect it to be easy, did you, san?" Thus Delia, soothing, understanding, the metaphorical hand at his brow. What a lady she is—and manipulative, too!

Mrindaban went on to say we had to find as central a location on the volgendrin as possible. Not the exact center; but near. He added, with more than a little smug superiority, that his duties for the fishfaces and his studies of Schannish gave him advantages in many directions. So, he knew which way to go.

The mingled streaming radiance of Zim and Genodras slanted in at the cave entrance. The sterns of the two vollers were partially illuminated as the red and green shafts of light crept across the floor.

"Better shift the vollers into the shadows." I started for the two fliers. The others followed.

The operation was not tricky, just a matter of moving a few paces; all the same I was glad Delia offered to control the craft.

She observed the fantamyrrh and leaped gracefully into the nearest flier. By just inching the flying boxes closer she caused the voller to rise. Then we laid hold of the ropes and hauled her round. That one done we turned our attention to the second.

Again observing the fantamyrrh, Delia boarded.

The unmistakable sound of crossbows being cocked reached into the cave and echoed around the rocky walls like a doom tocsin.

Just outside the entrance six Shanks stood in a rank. Four leveled their crossbows at us. The other two lifted their swords. In mere heartbeats those cruel steel bolts would skewer into us.

Darham turned to face the Shanks. His ribcage swelled. His face turned purple. He ripped out his sword.

"Hanitch!" He screamed the battle cry out. "Hanitch!"

Sword snouting he started to hurl himself at the row of Fish-heads and the deadly darts aimed at his heart.

My old foretop hailing voice beat out in a bellow so loud it drowned Darham's yell of 'Hanitch!'

"Stop!" I fairly smashed the words at the Bold. "Darham! *Llanitch!* Halt!"

The ferocious shriek in my voice and that word of command to halt used by sentries hauled him up. Before he had time to say any more or to react, before the deadly crossbows loosed, I shouted again.

"Schanake! Stasia! Schanake!"

I jumped forward and held up my hands, high, palms out.

Then I waited for the crossbows to loose.

Twenty

Darham said: "I'd never have guessed you was a kov, Nath—I mean, Kov Darjad."

"Nath the Hammer'll do fine, Bold."

Schanake said something to which Mrindaban contrived a reply.

The desperate shout had worked—thanks to Opaz. The crossbows had lowered on Schanake's command. He did not, of course, recognize me. But a basich who knew his name could only be the one he'd encountered on that deserted isle.

While he talked to me and quelled his wonder that his new comrade was a kov, Darham kept shooting dark glances from under his eyebrows at the four Shank crossbowmen. They sat in a line on the other side of the cave, crossbows resting on their knees.

"Look at 'em," said Darham. "That one on the end keeps gripping and ungripping his bow. They don't trust us."

Shocking all we Pazzians, the Lady Stasia spoke in broken and halting Pazzish. "Not be alarmed. The noble lord Schanake orders. Rest. See you our—state—"

In her calm voice Delia said: "That was nobly spoken, Lady Stasia. Bravely done."

Well, yes, we could see the state they were in. Two of the soldiers wore reddened bandages. Schanake himself had a cut over one eye. Stasia's clothes, like the others, were in a sorry condition. They'd survived the crash of their voller, shot down by the Shargs, but, by Krun, only just.

All the same, despite their obvious distress, the atmosphere in the cave remained tense. Well, of course it would. Here were disgusting Shanks in converse with what were, without doubt, equally disgusting Pazzians in the eyes of the fishfaces.

The Lady Stasia looked as though she would pass out any minute. We'd brought up water in an empty ale flagon, and now Delia, all concern, dampened a rag and offered to bathe the Fish-head lady's scaly forehead. Stasia allowed her to do that beneficial act.

Mrindaban, in his execrable Schannish, asked why the Shanks were chasing the noble Schanake.

Weakly, Stasia got out: "Me. Zoronsh, the noble of the second degree—he—wanted—"

Rapidly, Schanake said that she should not try to speak but rest. Mrindaban understood the gist of that. Officiously he told us that the Lady Stasia should rest.

In a roundabout way I felt certain Stasia would not comprehend I asked Mrindaban if one voller would suffice for what we had to do.

He nodded. "Yes. Better with two; but one will—"

"Good. Then tell the Lord Schanake that we can spare him a voller."

"What!" burst out Darham. "Stinking fishfaces! By Kuerden the Merciless, I'd—"

"Hold your water, Darham, my friend. This is bread cast upon the waters." I didn't say that but used a Kregish expression. "Seed thrown to the gods."

"Hanitcha the Harrower take it, Nath, or Kov Darjad! Shanks! Dealing with 'em as though they were honest human beings!"

"Some must be, Bold. And there's the color of their blood."

"Yes, well," he grumped, and so fell silent.

Clandi piped up: "Yes. The Lady Stasia is a fine looking lady—for a Fish-head."

I gave him a glare. "Don't you start."

Delia favored me with one of her intense stares. "In the Lady Stasia's condition she ought to receive the attentions of a Puncture Lady as soon as possible."

Something in Delia's words brought me up. "Condition?"

"Of course. She does not show much. But—"

"By the colossal thighs and pendulous bosom of the Divine Madam of Belschutz!" I fairly groaned. "You're doing another Ismelda on me! Very well, that settles the matter. A flier they shall have."

Somewhat drily, Delia said: "With those crossbows they rather settle the question for us don't they?"

Darham caught the drift of all that. "Another Krun-forsaken fishface to pollute Kregen."

"Oh, come on, Bold! Surely you must acknowledge the awe and mystery of birth!"

The tension eased after the Fish-heads understood they could take a voller. Oddly, the power of the crossbows seemed out of it. A tentative, a very fragile and untrusting friendship, might grow. Between the Lady Stasia's labored Pazzish and Mrindaban's equally halting Schannish, we had the story of the lovers.

As the story unfolded, Delia smiled at me. "A Fish-head romance," she said, softly. "A fishface love story. Who'd have believed it?"

Among the Shanks, as, unfortunately, among us, rivalries and festering hatreds disfigured their civilization. Schanake came from another island, to which he'd been sailing when shipwrecked. The Lady Stasia, in that time, had been taken by this noble of the second degree, Zoronsh. That he had green blood and she red meant only that they couldn't produce offspring, otherwise they were compatible. These two were very clearly passionately in love. I began to regret that I'd heeded Darham's advice, and done the sensible thing in not rushing in to rescue Stasia when she was being tortured. At least, that would have saved her some moments of agony.

They'd brought provisions from the wrecked voller and these they shared with us. Green-blooded Shanks and inimical Shargs waited somewhere outside, we did not doubt. And here we sat, all nice and cozy, breaking bread with fishfaces. Incredible!

A blue pillar of radiance, wavering, unsteady, began to form opposite Delia and myself. I knew no one else could see this eerie manifestation. The blue thickened sufficiently to reveal a cheerful face crowned by an enormous turban in peril of toppling over one ear.

"Lahal, my dear Lady Delia and lahal Jak. This is very difficult and I cannot stay long."

Delia spoke very quickly, chopping me off. "It will, I expect, be a fine night. We will depart then." What she said made perfect sense to the rest of the company. Also, it told our comrade Wizard of Loh, Deb-Lu-Quienyin, appearing here in ghostly form from halfway around the world, what he wanted to know—apart from the fact we were still alive. The cheerful image swathed in pallid blue light nodded and the turban toppled dangerously. Delia added: "At the center." The Lady Stasia looked up at this cryptic announcement.

The blue radiance vibrated, thinned, wisped to nothingness.

Back home in Vallia Deb-Lu would be coming out of lupu now, returning to the normal world from that strange other dimension frequented by mages. That would not be the same place used by the Star Lords, for sure! Deb-Lu would be telling our friends that we still lived. Delia gave me a little smile, and I knew she was thinking with me that the thought brought a warm feeling to us.

Mind you, a wily old hare always keeps his eyes and ears open, so all during that pleasant scene I'd been listening to the soldiers talking idly. Successful so far at concealing my knowledge of Schannish I'd no wish to spoil that little ace up the sleeve now.

The weird item about the fishface soldiers' conversation was that whilst alien to my ears, it still retained the flavor of fighting men's talk Kregen over. For one thing, they complained about their immediate superior officer, even though he wasn't here.

The day waned and the Suns sank and some of the Moons came out.

Stasia said with a hiss and a click: "Remberee time." The hiss came when she added: "Please."

"Thank you," said Delia, gravely.

So we saw them off and Darham did not cease from being highly suspicious until the voller vanished into the shadows. Then he said: "By Hanitcha the Harrower! I don't really believe it. This is one scrape I shan't tell the paktuns in The Ruby Winespout. No, by Krun!"

Then it was our turn to leave. With Delia piloting we scudded across the landscape of the vo'drin until we flew through a valley that was more like a sheer-walled cleft in the hills.

"This will do." Mrindaban was back to being important again.

We landed and the learned san instructed us to find a cave or fissure in the rocky walls. Clandi found what was required, a cave with a narrow entrance stretching away into pitch darkness. Delia's igniter tube produced flame to set the twisted fiber torches afire.

As in any properly provided airboat, the bag of tools lay in its recess under a seat. Hefting it out, I said: "I'll be as quick as I can." Then I started to remove the bronze and balass orbits containing the power boxes from the flier. These were of bronze.

Darham gave me a hand to lift the whole power complex and by the time a bur and a half had passed we had the lot deep in the cave.

"I am truly glad to be in here," said Delia. "I kept hoping the torches would not attract either Shank or Sharg."

We all, with the exception of Mrindaban, helped to install the power complex in a rift in the strata of the cave wall where we jammed the lot in with rock above and below.

"That'll have to do," I said. "San?"

"Yes, yes. Now I must concentrate."

He took his time. He sat with eyes closed, breathing evenly, wandering about in the Pathways in his mind. Alternative Magic in dealing with natural phenomena required dedication and energy. Mrindaban's forehead began to shine, and sweat drops ran down.

Rose and golden moonlight abruptly flooded the narrow entrance. She of the Veils drowned the world of Kregen in her radiance. I walked up and looked out. This seemed to me a perfectly natural act because of this particular fascination I have of my favorite moon.

On this occasion She of the Veils served me well—very well, by Vox! They were plainly visible creeping along the cleft-like valley. They knew we were in the cave. They sought to trap us there and butcher the lot of us out of hand.

If my lady who drifted so regally among the stars had not drawn me out—we'd have been done for instanter. As it was, there did appear to be a hell of a lot of them. Their snake-like faces with those staring eyes convulsed with hatred as they spotted me. Surprised or not surprised, we were in for it now.

"Bold," I said, speaking softly. "Quietly. We have company."

On the instant he was at my side, breathing hard. His hair in the light of the Moon was marvelous to behold.

To my enormous terror, I knew Delia would be taking her Claw out of its bag and strapping it up over her left hand. There was absolutely no way I could keep her out of this fight.

The narrowness of the cave entrance meant that we could stand only two abreast. That meant, hopefully, that the Shargs would come at us two at a time. If they shafted us—well, by the Blade of Kurin, they shafted us.

By using the Disciplines of the Krozairs of Zy I could flick incoming arrows away. But that wouldn't last all night.

At my back Delia in her light voice said: "Two at a time. We take turns. And no argument, Kov Darjad, known as Nath the Hammer!"

"Yes, my lady."

And, by All the Names, was there another lady like her on two worlds?

When they put in their first charge they did not hurl themselves at us like wild leems. Oh, no. They were far more savage than leems. A peculiarity of their race appeared to be a love of the arme blanche. They did not shaft us. They simply came on in a headlong rush with naked steel glittering before them.

So—we fought.

For all their ghastly ways, the Shargs were bonny fighters. Darham fought magnificently. I found perfect confidence with his massive hairy bulk at my side. So we cut them down, and took our wounds, and fought doggedly on. We had the advantage of the cave. Without that the fight would have been over far quicker than, inevitably, it was going to be.

Darham did not scream war cries. He fought hard and economically. The Shargs set up a screeching, all a rigmarole of pagan names that meant nothing. Soon that din was swept out of my hearing as I allowed myself to flow into the Disciplines of the Sword.

Through that hollowness ringing emptily in my ears Delia's commanding voice cut with the precision of a scalpel.

"Time to change!"

"Not yet!" I managed to get out, and sliced a snakeface's guts open. Another reared up to take his place. "No time!"

Darham took a wound on his left upper arm. He staggered back without a sound, and then recovered and so surged forward again, savagely.

This, then, was the last great fight.

Everything became a blur and only the Shargs to the front were real in this phantasmagorical world.

They pressed on, shrilling, and my sword dripped green.

A Snake-head to my immediate front swung his two-handed sword at my head, and I ducked. Like some magician's stage trick, a long Lohvian arrow, fletched with the rosy feathers of the zim-korf, pierced through his neck, standing out halfway each side.

A voice called over the shrieks.

"Well, my old dom, I see you're up to your neck as usual."

Twenty-one

There is little more to relate about this adventure.

To my surprise and a mixture of admiration and terror, I found Delia had been fighting alongside me for some time. Darham's wounds would trouble him until the needleman attended him.

Seg strode up to the cave, brave and gallant in the rosy gold moonlight. With him were—well, *everybody* seemed to be there.

Delia's Claw dripped green. Our friends crowded up, stalking over the sprawled corpses of the Shargs. You know the names of these folk, the sea of faces stretched and every one was a comrade. I tell you, for the Love of Opaz and Zair, that moment felt good, very very good!

Deb-Lu-Quienyin was there in person. His ghostly apparition had found us and he had guided the fleet. And the ships! Mighty Skyships, with rows of frowning varters and representatives of all the various regiments of the Guard Corps crowding their decks, mingled with the smaller vollers, and all equally ferociously armed.

Inch said: "Kytun is taking your Djangs cleaning up the vo'drin. And Hap Loder is doing the same with your clansmen. There are Vallians and friends of Vallia all over the place."

Kov Turko chimed in: "Now if you'd taken us with you, Dray, in the first place—"

Other people were talking and laughing—I ask you, laughing amid the slaughtered snakefaces—but they were all good-hearted folk. Delia was greeted by her kapts of the Jikai Vuvushis. All in all, this was going to turn into a splendid celebration.

A voice at my back spoke with considerable acerbity. That voice was owned by someone who was extremely annoyed.

"Is anybody listening? I have finished. Are you going to fly—or what?"

San Mrindaban walked out. He stared about on the scene. His mouth hung open. "What—what—?"

The famous and learned san had been following his Pathways and remained completely oblivious of what had happened.

Clandi said: "I'll tell you all about it, san."

I brisked up. "San! It is done?"

"Haven't I just said so?"

"Ah, yes, of course." I started to re-enter the cave. "Then I give you my thanks, San Mrindaban. Now you must meet my friends."

Seg and Inch and others came along with me. I showed them the flier controls wedged into the crevice in the strata.

"The good san, through his knowledge of natural phenomena, using Alternative Magic, has released the vo'drin from its anchor. The Chakarj Effect persists freely."

"By the Veiled Froyvil! You mean we're drifting about?"

"Precisely."

"And, by Ngrangi, the voller's power boxes will—"

"Precisely."

After that we all stood about, silently, contemplating the marvels and mysteries of the Chakarj Effect and Alternative Magic.

Then I told the assembled company that there could be only one pilot for the vo'drin.

"The majestrix is off with her Battle Maidens," said Korero.

"I'll take upon myself the honor of fetching her!" boomed Nath Javed, old Hack 'n' Slay.

He returned, side by side with his empress and not a pace in the rear as would be considered proper in many parts of Kregen.

"It works, then?" She smiled. "I knew we could rely on San Mrindaban." That self-important worthy swelled with pride. How changed he was from the poor reduced slave Ismelda had told us of!

Somebody brought a seat and willing hands positioned it before the makeshift controls. We had to shoo people out of the cave for the crush. Delia looked up. "Now I shall begin."

"May Zair and Opaz smile upon this work."

With that Delia pushed the control levers over with her sure, firm touch. We all felt the difference under our feet. Now the island of the sky was not drifting idly about—unfettered to the ground beneath, it was being driven purposefully along. San Quienyin told Delia the course, she moved the controls delicately, and then locked them. "I think it would be nice to go outside and look."

So we stared up waiting for the new day to dawn when Zim and Genodras would rise in splendor. I knew in my bones that the bards of Vallia would make a great song of this adventure. Also, I knew exactly where near the Heart Heights of my island stromnate of Valka we would position the vo'drin. Mrindaban would bring the Chakarj Effect back, and, lo! Valka and Vallia would have their very own vo'drin.

This was, as they say, a very fine consummation of what had been a pretty hectic affair.

We saw no Shank or Sharg vollers when the Suns of Scorpio rose. I trusted Schanake and his Lady Stasia would reach their island safely.

All in all, a very satisfactory night's work. As I said, there is little left to say.

Now I needed to go along with Delia, Delia of Delphond, Delia of the Blue Mountains, for a very serious heart to heart talk.

We turned to go and the gathered Pazzians drew their swords. Then, as the High Poets sing, they waved their swords aloft in a forest of flashing blades. They roared the accolade.

"Hai Jikai! Hai Jikai!"

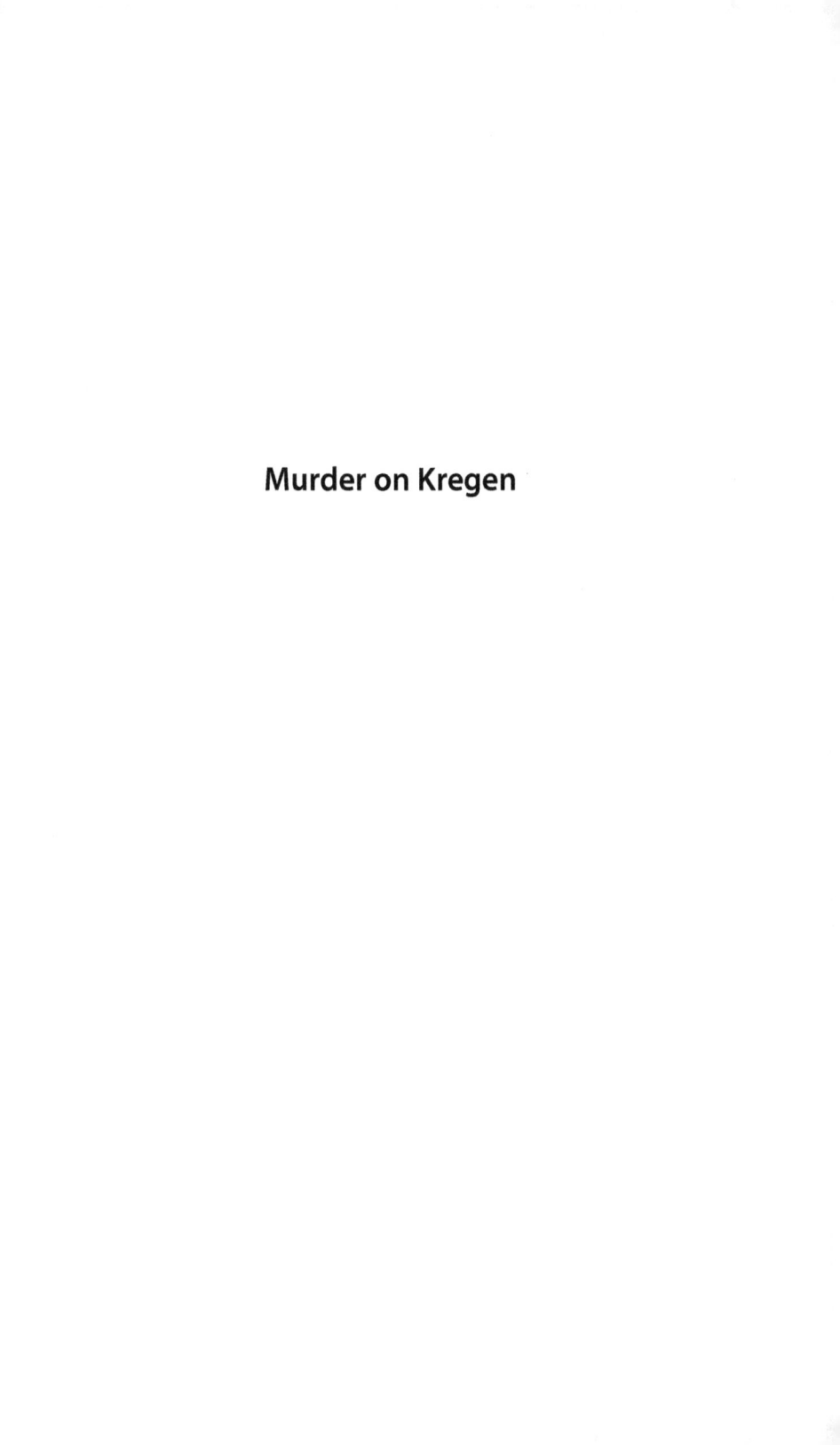

Murder on Kregen

A note on the Spectre Cycle

A new page turns in the unruly life of Dray Prescot and all his strengths and inner resources will be required to confront fresh problems and perils. For those readers who have not hitherto encountered the story of Dray Prescot, this volume, *Murder on Kregen*, the first book of the Spectre Cycle, is an admirable place to begin making Prescot's acquaintance.

He has been described as a man above middle height with immensely broad shoulders who moves like a hunting cat, silent and lethal. There is about him an abrasive honesty and indomitable courage. At the same time he presents an enigmatic figure for there is much about him we do not yet know. Educated in the harsh conditions of Nelson's Navy he managed to gain the quarterdeck but after that his career waned. Only when he transited to Kregen under the twin suns of Antares were his true qualities given expression. The Star Lords, furthering their mysterious ends, demand that he unite all the continents and islands of Paz as an emperor. This task is beset with innumerable difficulties. He and the divine Delia have abdicated as Emperor and Empress of Vallia—and we believe one of the chief reasons was simply so they could go adventuring abroad on the cruel yet beautiful world of Kregen under the Suns of Scorpio.

The early parts of this book contain events that Prescot could not have known about at the time but learned later. They have been placed here for the sake of clarity.

So, join Dray Prescot as he rides south from the port city of Zandikar on the inner sea of the continent of Turismond, the Eye of the World, with his blade comrade Seg Segutorio and the Princesses Velia and Didi of Vallia. Of course, as is the nature of Kregen, they face unexpected peril.

But first...

Alan Burt Akers

One

A wild dark streak haunted the reputation of the Vorner family down through the generations and many times in their turbulent history dishonor stained their family name. Young Tralgan, son of Lord Nalgre Vorner, radiated a sunny disposition that charmed all who came into contact with him, so that folk said perhaps the black blood had at last all been drained away.

Here, under the battlements of the gate leading up to the castle, Tralgan stared sickly upon the dozen crossbows aimed for his heart.

"Do not move, Tralgan! The Judge will have no compunction in ordering the crossbowmen to loose."

The saturnine features of the Judge confirmed with chilling authority what Ornol Lodermair said was true. He and the Judge stood side by side under the shadows of the arched gateway. The glee and raw triumph in Lodermair's voice struck through Tralgan like a hurled javelin.

His full lips trembled with a despair he tried to mask with rage. This fellow, this Ornol Lodermair, a cousin detested all Tralgan's life, now arrogantly laid claim to the castle and lands of Culvensax. Lord Nalgre Vorner, Elten of Culvensax, had died as all men die in Opaz's good time. His son, grieving at the news, hurried home to be met by this debacle.

"I am the true Lord of Culvensax!" Tralgan spoke stoutly; but he could hear the quaver in his voice. "You usurp my rights at your peril, Ornol!"

Lodermair sneered at this, dismissing Tralgan's words out of hand. The Judge said sharply: "The papers are all in order. The late Elten Nalgre's will is testified and witnessed. Kyr Ornol Lodermair is now legally the Elten of Culvensax."

The twin Suns of Scorpio struck ruby and emerald fires from the steel heads of the crossbow bolts. The suns shine glinted off the silver pakmort at Tralgan's throat. Until the death of his father had brought him home to claim his inheritance his sole ambition in life was to take the next step up the mercenary hierarchy and to wear the golden pakzhan at his throat, to be a zhanpaktun.

The tableau at the gate appeared to him to be divorced from reality. Many of the citizens of the town gazed with wide eyes upon the scene, held back by the spears of the town's militia. A dry smell of dust hung on the air; the crowd made little noise. The dark color mounted in Tralgan's cheeks. His heavy face with the full lips and curled nostrils of the Vorner family gave a sudden shocking reminder that Elten Nalgre was indeed Tralgan's father, the stain of the black blood unmistakable.

His right hand curled into a fist around the hilt of the sword hanging on his right side. Those who understood these things noticed this, and that Tralgan did not grasp the rapier scabbarded to his left. He wore light armor, suitable for travel. His groom with the animals, detained by spearmen a little way off, looked on with an expression compounded of horror, alarm and pity.

Tralgan stared up past the arched gate, up and up to where the castle of Vornerhold soared against the sky. He knew every one of those pinnacles and towers, every embrasure, every room, every hiding place. Here he had spent his childhood. His arguments with his father usually ended in raucous laughter as they embraced and made up—what son had not quarreled with his father? His mother he did not remember. Now this blood-sucking leech Ornol Lodermair intended to steal all away from him. His fist tightened.

"Draw your sword, Tralgan, and you are a dead man." The thick passion in Lodermair's words disgusted Tralgan. But he relaxed his grip. He was bold and reckless, yes; he was not stupid.

When he spoke he surprised himself at the steadiness and calmness in his words. "That will is forged. My father left—"

"Your father left all to me, his favorite nephew!"

Tralgan turned to stare at the Judge. That subservient person blinked, although he did not flinch back. "I claim my right to be heard by the nazabni. She rules Urn Vennar for Princess Didi under the hand of the Emperor. I am a loyal subject and will be heard. You cannot stop—"

"I can do what—" began Lodermair with ferocious passion.

The Judge halted him, hand on arm. "What Kyr Tralgan says is sooth. The case can be taken to the nazabni."

Watching them with hatred suffusing every particle of his body, Tralgan saw the Judge whisper swiftly. Lodermair nodded.

"Very well." Lodermair raised his voice. "All can see I am a just lord. All must be done legally. The case will be taken to Nazabni Ulana Farlan at the capital."

Yes, there he stood, this Ornol Lodermair, plump, full-fleshed, hands on hips, jaw jutting, triumphant. He wore the buff clothes of Vallia as though, Tralgan considered through the rage and contempt, as though he were a respectable Vallian. His curly-brimmed hat sported a bunch of feathers in ochre and silver, the old colors of Vennar before the province was split. He lifted his left hand and gestured impatiently to the guard captain. Three rings glinted on the fingers of that fat hand. As the guard captain gave orders to the Deldar, Tralgan wondered with a sudden and devastating switch of mood to gloom and despair, how many of those rings belonged to his father.

The Deldar, like most Deldars, creaked in his armor as he bellowed, as all Deldars bellow, commands that brought a detail of spearmen up to surround Tralgan. He saw the chain. They actually had a chain with which to imprison him. That dark blood rose again, chokingly, and once more his mood switched.

Sparks of red and green fire bounced from the chain as the twin suns, Zim and Genodras, streamed down their mingled radiance.

The chain with dangling manacles lifted in the Deldar's fists.

Tralgan struck the fellow once, a clean blow to the jaw.

The unfortunate officer staggered back, collided with a couple of his spearmen and they all fell down in a tangle. Tralgan bellowed louder than the Deldar: "No man chains me! That affront to my dignity will not be tolerated. By Vox, Ornol, you're a cramph among cramphs!"

Turmoil ensued. Lodermair yelled something about rasts and cramphs, tapos and squirms, waving his arms. The Judge stepped back smartly. The spearmen waited for orders. The cadade, as a competent captain of the guard, crisply told the fallen Deldar to stand up. He eyed Tralgan. "Very well, Kyr Tralgan. No chains. Just walk with us to the castle—if you please."

Now Tralgan didn't recognize any of these jurukkers of the guard. They were all new employees, for he'd been away adventuring for longer than, perhaps, he should. He did recognize the quality of this cadade, though, this Jiktar Claydoin Ma-Le, who was a Pachak with two left arms and a very brisk manner with him, after the way of Pachak diffs. So he merely nodded and started off through the gateway on the ascent to the castle—to his castle, as soon as Princess Didi's nazabni, ruling in her name, saw the truth of the matter.

There was no doubt the Vorner family had committed many dark and bloody deeds over the seasons. His father, Nalgre, had—well, decided Tralgan, better to push all that aside. He intended to bring lightness and joy to Culvensax. Some of the mercenary guards his father employed proved unworthy of trust. Perhaps this new lot were cast in a different and better mold. The Jiktar, Claydoin Ma-Le, had given his Pachak nikobi and would serve faithfully. Tralgan was fully aware of the quality of Pachaks; his father had never employed them. As a youngster, why that was so had never occurred to Tralgan. He hoped his father had changed in his later years.

The castle fortress of Vornerhold contained extensive dungeons, a testament to the bad old days. They didn't put Tralgan in a cell; he was ushered into a small suite of rooms in the Thoth Tower. The cadade, a hint stiffly, said: "I am instructed to allow you to keep your rapier and main gauche. The rest of your weapons must be surrendered." He gestured with his upper left. "A matter of form."

There did not seem much else for it; so Tralgan stripped off the fighting sword, the short-hafted axe, the terchicks strapped over his right shoulder. The long Vallian dagger was taken. The Pachak told him that he had not served two months of the Maiden with the Many Smiles. He hesitated, and Tralgan obtained the clear impression that Jiktar Ma-Le was not altogether happy serving in his new post.

"Elten Ornol Lodermair—" he started.

He was chopped off abruptly. "I am the Elten!"

"That is not my province, Kyr. I serve my nikobi."

After that a meal was served up and Tralgan ate as any paktun will eat when the opportunity affords. He prowled around the chamber restlessly. How long would the nazabni take to rectify this treachery?

A shaven-headed Gon arrived to say he was required in the Elten's chambers. Controlling himself, Tralgan followed the Gon upstairs where he'd played as a child into the suite of rooms once occupied by his father. Sneeringly, with heavily-armed guards to hand, Lodermair informed him that word had been sent to the nazabni. "As you and all the world can see, I am a just lord."

The Judge was not present and Tralgan hoped he'd fly as fast as he could. He was confident that Princess Didi would never allow injustice in her province of Urn Vennar. The nazabni was the daughter of old Nazab Erinor Farlan, who'd been appointed to run Princess Didi's province by the emperor. There was a new Emperor of Vallia now, Drak, and his wife Silda was the new empress. Tralgan reposed every confidence in the swift course of justice in Vallia.

The Gon, very obsequious in his servitor's uniform, took him back down the stairs. He did not speak. He pushed the door open and Tralgan walked into the chamber.

He stopped stock still. At once, he saw it all. He'd been duped like any green coy. The Judge and the cadade lay sprawled in the center of the room. A great deal of their blood had been spilt to sink into the carpet of Walfarg weave. The coarse smell of blood stank in the room. Tralgan's fighting sword stuck up from the chest of the Judge. His axe was embedded in the cadade's skull. The murder scene could not have been more explicit.

Making a stupendous effort to keep control of himself, Tralgan swung around. The Gon and his bald buttered head were gone. The heavy beat of metal-studded boots thudded along the corridor and a group of soldiers marched into view.

At their head a ferociously-feathered Rapa urged them on.

"Stand still!" The Rapa's voice held a crisp note of authority. He wore the rank badges of a Hikdar, so he was probably the second in command, the shal-cadade, to the poor devil of a Pachak with his head cleft in by Tralgan's axe. "What is the cause of the commotion?"

"You should know!" spat out Tralgan. He felt physically sick. He'd been gulled, trapped, and he was only too well aware that nothing he could say or do would get him out of this mess.

Events brisked along after that. The charade was played out to the last full stop. Lodermair arraigned him, judged him, condemned him. He would be sent to wait in prison until the nazabni pronounced on his fate.

Even then, even at this low stage in his fortunes, Tralgan still had the greatest hope of Vallian justice. He would explain everything. The will could be proved a forgery. There was not a drop of blood on his clothes. How explain that when those two poor devils had spouted blood everywhere? Tralgan began to breathe more easily. He'd get out of this imbroglio and take up his inheritance. By Vox, he would! There was justice in Vallia.

After all, a nazab, the governor of an imperial province, was equal to a Kov, the highest rank of the nobility. A nazabni was equal to a Kovneva. These folk held dread powers in their hands.

Thus confident of his own future, Tralgan was not so far gone in blind hatred as not to feel compassion for the cadade, Jiktar Claydoin Ma-Le. Everyone knew Pachaks served with loyalty. He most certainly had not deserved this hideous fate. As for the Judge—his name, Tralgan gathered, had been Nath the Righteous—well, perhaps he did deserve his fate. Righteous he certainly was not.

They took him off in a well-guarded narrow boat along the canals to the new capital. Since the Times of Troubles a new sense of freedom and enterprise flourished in Vallia. Gafarden bustled with business and commerce. The city, named by Princess Didi in remembrance, might be new, expanding around a small town situated on a promising site, it was prosperous and the Gafarden folk fully intended to be more prosperous still in the future. Tralgan was flung into the dungeons below the ancient fortress that dominated the old town. In the rooms above lay the quarters of the town dignitaries. Here Nazabni Ulana Farlan lived and ruled the province of Urn Vennar.

A small-boned woman, who habitually wore her hair tied into a bun, she had only recently taken over the reins of government when her father, the nazab, died. She was still in mourning. There was no automatic transfer of power for the nazabs and justicars who administered the imperial provinces. Ulana Farlan must be confirmed in her post by Princess Didi and receive the blessing of Didi's uncle, the Emperor Drak of Vallia.

She relied completely on her chief pallan, Nath Swantram. He, as the chief minister of the province, knew everything there was to know worth knowing. A one-time soldier who now had many irons in a multitude of businesses and was, thereby, wealthy, he harbored the desires obvious to a person of his rank, wealth and ruthlessness.

His nose and left side of his mouth were disfigured by a sword slash in a long-ago battle. The scar remained, both physical and mental. Sometimes he was called Nath the Clis. He did not care for this, and, anyway, there were many men called Nath the Clis on Kregen. His robes were sumptuous, much bedecked with gold, although he had toned down the gorgeousness of his attire during this time of mourning.

Coming into the nazab's office on the bright, breezy morning following Kyr Tralgan's incarceration in the dungeons below, he felt in a particularly good mood. The drinking session last night in his private quarters had left him with a purse heavy with gold. His thoughts centered on the prim little woman seated at the desk, her dark hair tied just so. No, this was no longer the nazab's office. This was now the nazabni's office. Well, if his plans bore fruit, as, by Klass the Reiver, they would! he'd be the nazab and this would be his own office.

The two discussed the business of the day in matter of fact tones until Nath the Clis said: "There is a matter of a murder—two murders—at Culvensax." He related the grim details of the story and added: "There is no doubt of Kyr Tralgan's guilt. The decision of his execution is a mere matter of form. It would not be wise to trouble Princess Didi. Anyway," he waved a beringed hand: "She is away visiting King Zeg in the Eye of the World."

"Ah, yes." Ulana Farlan relied on this man, yet she was well aware she must rule herself, and be seen to rule. She must make decisions. All the same, Nath Swantram understood affairs of state. His advice was sound. If she went running to the princess at every little problem her credibility would soon be in doubt.

"There is no doubt of Kyr Tralgan's guilt?"

"None whatsoever."

Nath the Clis placed the death warrant on the desk.

"This is a part of my work I can never grow accustomed to. I remember how my father hated signing death warrants."

Very smoothly, the chief pallan said: "Yes, justice and duty are hard taskmasters."

Nazabni Ulana Farlan, governor of Princess Didi's imperial province of Urn Vennar, signed Kyr Tralgan Vorner's death warrant with a firm hand.

Two

For the period of a few grains of sand dropping down either side of the hour of mid a faint wash of red and green light drifted across the topmost iron bar. For the rest of the time the barred window remained shrouded in shadow. They allowed him a lamp in the cell and had even enquired if he was one of those folk who could not bear to live under a single light but must have two sources of illumination mimicking Zim and Genodras.

The bed was hard, the floor carpetless and the ablutions primitive. Stone walls and iron bars were no novelty to Tralgan. This cell was by many moons vastly superior to the disgusting pit those Opaz-forsaken driking-ers had stuffed him in when he was employed as a paktun by Kov Panral over there in Pandahem.

After the first few days the smell ceased to trouble him. This was only because he grew used to it, not because it improved. The food, coarse and not plentiful, kept him alive.

Kyr Tralgan Vorner, rightful Elten of Culvensax, needed to live, to stay alive, hungrily waiting for news from Princess Didi.

Sure she would not fail him, Tralgan was yet fully prepared for hesitation, and determined to carry his complaint to the emperor himself in Vondium.

The jailer, a stunted Fristle whose hair had been burned almost all off his left side, brought the food. He was taciturn. On the next day in his slurred sing-song voice he informed Tralgan that Pallan Nath Swantram would visit him tomorrow. Between that announcement and the Pallan's appearance, blazing hope and black despair alternated, shaking Tralgan in their grip as a leem shakes a ponsho.

Swantram entered with a perfumed kerchief to his nose. He spread his hands. He was polite. He sympathized deeply with Tralgan's plight. The spreading of his hands convinced Tralgan the man was attempting to be sincere, in that he had to take the perfumed kerchief away from his nose. "The news is not good, Kyr Tralgan."

"Tell me."

"Princess Didi declines to intervene in the case on your behalf."

The shattering tide of despair overwhelmed Tralgan. He sagged back on the bed. He put his hands to his face and rocked backwards and forwards. Hope—all dashed!

"No!" He started up. Despair had to be overcome. "The Emperor!"

"I have, of course, my dear Kyr, immediately applied to his gracious eminence the Emperor Drak."

Fresh hope burst up in Tralgan. "Then the emperor must see the justice of my case! He must!"

"Yes. I have the utmost sympathy for you. I have—" here Nath the Clis's voice took on a confidential tone—" I have personally expended a considerable sum in furtherance of your cause. Gaining access to the emperor in these matters is seldom simple."

Tralgan's experiences abroad had given him an insight into the ways of corruption. He understood the high ones of Kregen demanded tribute to assist unfortunates. Mind you, he'd been given to understand that since the emperor's father's time bribery was no longer rife in Vallia. Still, this pallan understood politics.

"Thank you, pallan."

Nath Swantram stared about the cell, kerchief well up to his scarred nose. "I had not realized, my dear Kyr, that they had placed you in such a dolorous situation. I shall have this rectified immediately. A person of your quality should not be confined here."

"You are very kind." Tralgan coughed. "In the matter of—ah—expenses in connection with the emperor—"

Swantram held up his hand. "When you have your estates we can talk about expenses." After a few more pleasantries the pallan took himself off. The next day Tralgan was moved to an upper room where the twin Suns of Scorpio shone radiantly through the barred window most of the afternoon. The food improved remarkably. The bed was soft and the ablutions most satisfactory.

The effect of having someone of the pallan's position and power on his side lifted Tralgan's spirits. Swantram believed him! All would yet be well.

A sennight passed in which time the pallan visited every other day. He was solicitous to the extreme. His servants installed a splendid paline bush in a ceramic pot. The lush yellow berries themselves did much to cheer the prisoner up. There was no news from the emperor. Swantram counseled patience and radiated hope.

He informed Tralgan that Nalgre Lodermair strutted importantly in Culvensax, as the Elten. "I can prove the will is forged, my dear Kyr. You shall, in any event, come into your inheritance."

"I want to see that cramph punished for his treachery."

"You shall, my dear Kyr, you shall."

"The thought of him, there, where my father—" Tralgan's heavy face flushed with all the dark blood of the Vorners. "I'll have him punished if it's the last thing I do."

The pallan coughed a trifle uncomfortably. "Ah—h'm—if the murders are proved, they are of necessity outside the scope of your inheritance."

Tralgan wanted to know—by Vox!—what the pallan meant.

"Only, my dear Kyr, that whatever happens—whatever happens—your resolve should be to deny Lodermair the fruits of his treachery."

Tralgan Vorner swore by the Sword of Kurin that if he was damned to hell he'd stop Lodermair and see him beggared and ruined.

"If I'm stalking through the mists of the Ice Floes of Sicce I'll have Lodermair out of Culvensax! By Opaz, I'll have him!"

On that the pallan, professing great respect for Tralgan's resolution, took his leave. His scarred face held an expression of satisfaction. Only later, when Tralgan had calmed down a trifle, was the import of the pallan's words borne in on him. He mulled them over. Well, then! By Vox! He would. Confident of the emperor making a decision in his favor, Tralgan yet formed an icy resolve that whatever happened he'd dislodge the usurping bastard Elten Ornol Lodermair from Culvensax.

Vorner believed that the officials would not be negligent. The Emperor Drak and his father had instilled an understanding into the various officials of the new Vallia that justice, truth and mercy must govern the land. Corruption would not be tolerated. If any of the High Ones ruling Vallia contravened those precepts, then Tralgan would have no mercy on them either. His revenge would encompass all.

The visits the pallan made to the comfortable cell increased. He would sit in one of the two chairs as Tralgan strode about the floor ranting and raving, calling upon All the Names, foaming at the injustice he had suffered. A polite, almost distant look, made the scarred face a mask through which Tralgan, far too obsessed with his own passions, had no thought to penetrate.

The mental pressure, cunningly worked on and enhanced by Pallan Nath the Clis, wrought mischief within Tralgan. He felt himself being brought low. Surely, he would abruptly burst out, time after time, surely the emperor must have sent word by now!

When that day came, when the pallan entered the cell, flanked by three pairs of Fristle guards, Tralgan Vorner's world came to an end.

"He refuses!" Tralgan screamed. He could feel his lips writhing, his body burned, sweat varnished his face. He shook. He collapsed on the bed. This, then, was the end.

Nath the Clis said: "I have spent considerable treasure to help you. I grieve at your misfortune. But you are a man, a noble, of courage. You will see what needs to be done."

"You're going to kill me." Tralgan's words sounded like dry gravel crunched underfoot. "How?" This was, suddenly, the most important information he must learn.

"Swiftly and easily, I assure you, my dear Kyr."

"There will be no torture?"

"Those days in Vallia are long gone. Now I want you to concentrate your mind on what to do about your great enemy Lodermair."

"You know what I have said."

"Yes. But he remains in possession of your estates—"

"Then he must be dispossessed. You have a plan?"

Nath Swantram explained in a smooth, even, most reasonable tone of voice. The plan was, in essence, simple. Nath the Clis would benefit from Tralgan's will, the spurious will would be proved forged, Nalgre Lodermair would be expelled from Culvensax. Arrangements could be made for his early demise. Tralgan would have his revenge.

Such was the hatred suffusing all Tralgan's thoughts, the rage burning in his body, he agreed. The papers were brought, the bokkertu completed, Tralgan signed. The Fristle guards witnessed.

The guards wore the insignia of Urn Vennar, their banded sleeves bright with Didi's new colors. Their furred bewhiskered cat faces remained blank. They were paid handsomely.

The death warrant having been signed by the nazabni some time ago, explained Nath Swantram, the execution must be secret, else the strict little lady would want to know the cause of the delay. The disposal of his body concerned Tralgan. Now he was en route to the circumambient Mists where he would fight his way through the Ice Floes of Sicce to the sunny uplands beyond, he became calm. He became resolute. "You will give me proper burial?"

"Assuredly." What the pallan did not say was that he could not possibly take the slightest risk in disposing of Tralgan. The usual means of getting rid of executed criminals was no longer open to him. The nazabni would ask damned awkward questions, for sure.

"There is a secret passage." The pallan touched his lips with his kerchief. "You will see. Let us go."

They went out, the guards surrounding them, and they went down.

They went down a long, long way.

"This castle is old, yet it was built upon a site even more ancient. There are no records. The builders must have been a nation old before the time of Delia, the Mother Goddess."

That, reflected Tralgan, was a damn long time ago.

They reached eventually a corridor of rough-hewn masonry. An alcove to one side, eerily shadowed by the torches and the lamp carried by the Fristles, revealed a trapdoor, also of stone. The guards hauled on the bronze ring and with a screech that, uncomfortably, sounded far too eldritch for Tralgan's liking, the slab lifted.

The lamp was lowered on a rope. The rope paid out a considerable length before the lamp reached the floor below. They looked down. The place was an oubliette, a gourd shaped hole in the ground, walled in by masonry. The brief circle of illumination down there revealed scattered bones and an indistinct floor. A rope ladder was thrown down. "Through there." Nath the Clis pointed. "You, Fenrio, go down. Take the provisions and release the rope."

"Quidang, lord," snapped out one of the guards with a rush basket over his shoulder. He descended smartly enough and presently the empty rope's end came up. The Fristle reappeared at the lip of the trapdoor and the pallan motioned to Tralgan.

That young man took a deep breath. If this was the way out—this was the way out. So be it, by Vox! Knowledge that Lodermair would be destroyed nerved him. He went down the ladder.

Two rungs down, he stopped, stared up, and said: "You know, pallan, I did not murder the Judge and the cadade."

Nath the Clis made a vague gesture. Tralgan went on down.

He reached the bottom, stepped off the ladder which, instantly, whisked away aloft. "I am to go forward alone?" shouted up Tralgan.

"Of course. I know you did not kill those two. But it is too late now." The pallan's words bounced eerily about the oubliette. "You have your burial, as I promised you." With a crash like the last trump, the trapdoor smashed down.

Only then Tralgan Vorner realized how he had been gulled.

The gray blank walls of the oubliette appeared to crush in on him. The stones sparkled with nitre in the light, dark streaks of moisture ran down, and he stepped upon brittle bones that snapped with the finality of death.

No clean swift execution awaited him. He would finish the provisions so mockingly provided, the lamp would gutter and be extinguished, and Tralgan Vorner, rightful Elten of Culvensax, would die the hideous death of thirst and starvation.

All that dominated his mind in that moment of awful realization was hatred. Absolute and remorseless hatred for all those who had tricked and betrayed him and brought him to this fate convulsed him with the single purpose of revenge.

Three

The arrow did not miss. Well, by Krun, that is a supremely superfluous remark! Of course the arrow did not miss. The shaft had been loosed by Seg Segutorio, the finest bowman of two worlds. With perfect calmness and precision he selected another arrow, nocked it, drew and loosed all in that marvelous flowing rhythm that is the hallmark of the warriors of Erthyrdrin, the finest of all the many Bowmen of Loh.

Rollo the Runner, his red Lohvian hair afire under the twin suns, loosed and struck his mark. "That's three more of the shints gone." Although no longer the hot-tempered young fellow-me-lad he'd been, wearing now the sterner face of maturity, he was clearly as pleased with his shooting as any youngster at the butts might be.

"Aye." Seg checked his next shot and stared calculatingly across the grassy valley. Clumps of bushes concealed some of the attackers. A shrill and most unpleasant howling caterwauled on the air. "That leaves around thirty of 'em, Rollo."

"And those dreadful sand-leems!" Didi spoke without a tremble as befitted a Princess of Vallia and a Sister of the Rose. "I declare, their racket is worse than the drums and bagpipes of the Yinfitter people." She glanced across at Velia. "Would you say?"

Princess Velia lifted her bow, shot, hit her man, and said: "Oh, aye. Infinitely."

Seg laughed, his fey blue eyes bright, his shock of black hair sheening in the suns light. He delighted in these two Sisters of the Rose, and if they sometimes called him 'Uncle Seg' he joyed in their mutual love for one another. "You ladies have seen the world."

What was abundantly and horrifically clear was that if these desert tribesmen, the Ancidoins, with their half-tamed sand-leems, succeeded in the attack, nobody in the little hunting party would see much more of the world. They'd be groping their way through the Mists of Sicce. The thought was not refreshing.

To the rear stretched the last of the forest. Ahead the grassy valley and plain led to the dry dunes of the desert. This area was the last outpost of the Kingdom of Zandikar to the south. The hunting party had left their camp among the trees and ridden south to find suitable game for the evening's supper. They were not the contemptible kind of hunting party that rode out to kill anything they ran across. King Zeg and Queen Miam, in the port city of Zandikar on the shores of the inner sea, the Eye of the World, up north, recognized that their sway to the south ended where the desert began.

The lean, lethal shapes of the sand-leems appeared to slither across the ground. Leems are dangerous wild animals. They come in various types including volleem, snow-leem, and here, the sand-leems who acted as surrogate hunting dogs for the Ancidoins only because in their feral minds they understood this would bring them food more easily than fending for themselves in a poor land.

So far the desert-leems had not been released from their leashes. The tribesmen wanted to shoot us up first. They saw how few we were, even including the handful of guards Zeg had insisted we take with us. If they could shoot most of us, then the leems would not suffer too much from our shafts as they charged in. If this puts a gloss on the character of the desert tribesmen, so be it. They were only doing what they always did when times were hard down south. News was that the oases were not as fruitful this season. The River Zinkara, running into the Eye of the World from the Mountains of Ilkenesk, over to the west, would support some of the wandering desert folk. Some ventured north into civilized lands to see what they could lay their reiving hands on.

The position of the party, half-concealed in a little gulley, was not too promising. A few straggly bushes afforded cover. Arrows fletched in a variety of birds' feathers fleeted in, to thunk into the ground or tangle up in a bush.

Already two of these confounded arrows had found targets, and two of Zeg's guardsmen were wounded.

The Suns of Scorpio slanted past the hour of mid. Once night fell the tribesmen would sneak up, their curvy daggers hungry.

A wide-winged shadow fleeted undulatingly across the valley, a twin shadow, red and green. A raucous squawk screeched down. No one in the hunting party looked up.

"You great nurdling onker!" The itchy voice from above irritated like fingernails scratched across glass. "Onker of onkers!"

Nobody in the party spoke; but several of them loosed at quickly-glimpsed shapes hiding behind bushes and rising to shoot.

"Well, Emperor of Onkers! Speak up! The Star Lords are mightily displeased with you."

At this I did look up. I shouted: "What's new, you bird of ill omen?"

"You need not take that tone with me, Dray Prescot! You are not on a specific task for the Everoinye. Yet you wantonly place your life in danger."

The damn bird up there, circling, peering down with a beady eye, clad magnificently in golden and scarlet feathers, had bandied words with me before, aye, by Zair, many times! I'd thought we were getting on a trifle better in these latter days. Now it appeared just because I was in danger from these pestiferous desert folk the Star Lords had become cross with me.

I yelled up: "You mean if I'm in danger because the Everoinye put me in peril, that's all right. Is that it, you scrawny bird?"

"You obey their orders, Dray Prescot! Never forget that!"

The spy and messenger of the Star Lords curved splendidly up aloft, riding the air. No, he couldn't be called scrawny. All the same, by Vox, he'd get the rough edge of my tongue.

Then, in that instant, blinding terror engulfed me.

If I disobeyed the Star Lords they could banish me four hundred light years back to Earth, the planet where I'd been born. They'd once kept me there for twenty-one miserable, horrendous years. Should they do that now, then my people here would be left alone to face what would come. Seg would struggle to the last, the truest blade comrade a man could ever have. My daughter Velia and her niece Didi might suffer beyond comprehension. Rollo—well, Rollo was a Wizard of Loh. He, at least, might fashion something from this imbroglio.

So, cringing in my ib, I called up: "The position here is as you see it. Chance ordained it." I drew a breath. "What is your suggestion, Gdoinye, to extricate us safely?"

Now I had far too much experience of the Star Lords to expect them to whisk us all up and out of it. They didn't work like that. Their delicate hands—for they had once been as human as me—attempted to guide the destiny of Kregen in subtle ways beyond the full cognizance of a mere mortal human being. Sometimes they made mistakes. Well, now, if they wanted me alive—as I understood was their desire—then perhaps they might reveal a little more of their hand. I doubted it. But, by Krun, it was worth a try!

The Ancidoins used short bows. Their range, naturally, fell far short of the Great Lohvian Longbows in our fists. The word Great is here used correctly in context. The tribesmen were, however, within the range of their smaller bows. In not only range does the Lohvian Longbow excel; in the hands of a master archer like Seg it is deadly accurate.

We had two casualties. The tribesmen had at least a dozen by this time, and more damage continued to be inflicted on them as the Lohvian Longbows sang.

Naturally, as the Gdoinye wished, none of the other members of the hunting party could see or hear him. In addition, on this occasion at least, he arranged things so they didn't hear me, either.

After my question the Gdoinye continued to circle. He did not squawk down an insult. He remained as silent as one of those poor devils of self-mutilated monks of Caneldrin. So, thus, as I waited for the flying oracle to solve the riddle, the tribesmen, no longer relishing our shooting, released their pet sand-leems.

Didi said: "If I am to die, I do not regret the pilgrimage to my parents' tomb. But I am deeply sorry that we must all suffer death because of my wishes—"

Seg said: "This Gafard was a man, as I hear. And Velia—"

"Seg." I spoke quietly. Seg shut up at once.

The Velia of whom my blade comrade spoke, twin to Zeg who now ruled in Zandikar, mother of Didi, wife of Gafard, had died in my arms across the sea in the land of the Green Grodnim. As we waited, bracing ourselves to shoot fast and accurately, my thoughts went to Velia. Oh, yes, we had found her and Gafard a fine plot in which to lie. Their memorial was not elaborate, being dignified with many flowers. Inscriptions detailed all Gafard's titles, Sea Zhantil and all the rest. Yes, and the name 'My Lady of the Stars' was inscribed there, also.

The time was short. Leems run fast. In a matter of moments the ochre hides would be upon us.

A dull overcast spread across the land. Along the valley from the flank a wide low cloud billowed, dun colored, the color of the leems, the color of the desert.

Rollo exclaimed: "A sand storm!"

The swirling particles of dust and grit hurled low over the ground. Ruby and emerald shadows entwined in the folds of sand, rolling over, tumbling, throwing a ghastly hue across the ground.

So swiftly the sand storm arose it reached along the valley and struck the howling, racing leems in full cry. Between that confrontation and our party, ready in the gulley, lay an open stretch perhaps twenty paces wide.

Half a dozen lean lethal shapes broke free of the cloud and, screeching, charged full at us.

There was no need for orders. Seg took out two of the horrors, the princesses and I took one each. My bow went into the dirt, the Krozair longsword came out of the scabbard with oiled sweetness, and swept around in a cunning stroke that cleft the last leem in two.

"H'm," remarked Seg. "Is that it, then, my old dom?"

"It would appear so."

"Well, by the Veiled Froyvil!" Seg spoke in huge disgust. "And we did not have a wager on it!"

The two princesses laughed at this, for the wagers on shooting in dire situations between Seg and me were famous in Vallia—aye, and through the books and plays, notorious throughout Paz.

Reasonably enough, given the circumstances, it was Rollo, very seriously, who had to say: "A sand storm? Over this grassy valley? I did nothing. But I fancy there was thaumaturgy at work."

I kept my old black-fanged winespout fast shut.

Could it be? By the diseased left eyeball and rotting teeth of Makki Grodno! Could it be? Could the Star Lords have intervened and sent this unnatural sand storm to save my hide?

Four

The insidious effects of blind hatred corroded Tralgan Vorner's vitals. His skin burned. His eyes felt as though they protruded on stalks. He shook. He sweated in the dank chill of the oubliette.

Brown decaying bones crunched underfoot. He glared about as a hunted escaping prisoner glares upon the werstings who are about to leap on him and tear him to bloody fragments.

The light of the lamp, so mellow and normal, revolted him at its incongruousness in this place of horror. The oubliette engulfed him. The incurving walls in the gourd shape prevented any attempt at climbing out.

"By Chunformo the Shatterer of Chains!" He choked on bile. "This is not the finish of me!" The corroding hatred bit away at him.

Glaring about, he saw a place in the masonry where someone had been picking the stones away, leaving a dark opening. That someone must once have owned some of the skeletal bones strewing this place. Whoever it might have been, the tools used still lay there; tools fashioned from the bones of a poor wight thrown down here, what—centuries ago? Such was his rage and hunger for revenge, Tralgan seized up a bone and threw himself furiously at the walling stones.

He worked frenziedly, stupidly, gasping for breath in the dank stagnant air, clawing at the recalcitrant stones. Some long dead prisoner had begun this painful escape—and had failed, had died before the escape route had been completed. Tralgan Vorner, sweating, obsessed, burning with malignant passion, determined that he would not fail. He would not, by the corrupt entrails of Benga Shuna!

Whoever the poor benighted soul might have been who'd hacked away here before, he—or, by Vox! she—had progressed well. The dislodged stones lay piled neatly to the side. Tralgan was able to insert his full length into the opening. Grunting with effort, he pulled himself out, brought the lamp across and took up the bone tool with fresh resolve. "Sweet Opaz!" he gasped. "Aid me now!"

Hauling out the next block, and dreading that the whole tunnel would collapse upon him to finish him for good, he struck earth. Dirt tumbled down at his frenzied blows. The bone broke.

Cursing as only a seasoned paktun can curse, he wriggled his way back. The lamp's yellow radiance revealed the bones scattered across the floor. Tralgan selected a stout-looking femur and went maniacally back, hacking at the face of the tunnel he was creating.

Yet through all this, like a tremulous candle flame set in a window, he remained aware that he was sane enough to know he was not insane. Perhaps he ought to have been driven makib by these experiences. He ought to be, as they say, barking mad. But he felt himself to be sane, driven by hatred and the thirst for vengeance.

A shoulder blade makes a handy digging tool. He was alert to the danger of driving into the earth; collapse of the tunnel would be inevitable. He must shore up. What to use? Tralgan Vorner, smothered with dirt and dust sticking to his sweat, his eyes red-rimmed, laughed there in that place of horror. What to use indeed!

Bones.

Crawling back he blinked. That felt as though red hot sand paper had been rubbed across his eyes. His mouth was clogged with the ashes from the Furnace Fires of Inshurfraz, or, the way he choked, with detritus from far worse places in hell.

The rush basket contained standard oar-slave rations. A heel of dry bread, an onion—not too far gone—and a rind of cheese not too green. An orange colored gourd held brackish water. At the shape of the gourd Tralgan grimaced. The shape was the shape that imprisoned him down here. He felt no surprise at the food; it was absolutely normal for those in slavery or those condemned to death.

The water helped with the clinkers in his mouth.

Taking up a bone and the lantern he crawled back past the end of the masonry and attacked the tight-packed dirt.

At the third blow the earth puffed and moved of its own volition. For a moment of blind terror he imagined the whole roof collapsing upon him, to bury him for all eternity. The earth wall slid away from him. The noise reverberated like the sliding hiss of a tide receding across pebbles. Willy-nilly, unable to halt himself, he skidded forward with the falling earth. The lantern went over and went out. In blackness so intense he felt the darkness invading his soul, Tralgan pitched head first down the tumbling slope.

He hit bottom. Winded, flat on his back, he lay there trying to breathe evenly, trying to master himself. Dirt spattered down over him and he scrunched up and crawled away before he was buried. One hand held before him feeling for what might obstruct him, he went on.

Opaz, he said to himself. The Hand of Opaz pushed the earthen wall away. Opaz held suffocation and burial apart from me. Now he felt a renewed faith, a firmer resolution. Now he knew his vengeance must be consummated.

Further proof that The Hand of Opaz was with him came with the faint glow ahead. Fire crystals embedded in the earth illuminated his surroundings in light, pallid and gruesome. To Vorner, the light shone with sweet promise.

As he went on, buoyed by new hope, masonry clothed the walls. No bricks had been used in this building. The walls exuded a palpable sense of ancientness. These were the foundations, far below the castle above, the very roots of the olden-time fortress long abandoned and forgotten. What stories these stones could tell!

"I'll see that black-hearted villain Lodermair into the jaws of hell yet!" he said to himself, pressing on. "And the rest of the traitorous crew with him!"

The thought of revenge on all those who had wronged him kept Tralgan Vorner sane, determined, and moving as fast as he could. He was tired, no doubt of it; but his hatred would not let him rest.

Abruptly, with the suddenness of a cataclysm, all his hopes were blown away as a hurricane whirls away the flimsy reed huts of the Shalaam river folk in their mud delta. He stopped, his mouth hanging open, panting. He felt a physical pain knife through him.

Before him rose an ebony-black door, blocking the way, shutting off the corridor. The blackness writhed with carvings. In the eerie light, for the fire crystals were not the normal pure white, but of a cloudy grayish sheen, the fantastical images of beasts and monsters undulated as though mocking him.

The slab existed in front of him. There was no lintel, no architrave. Wall to wall and ceiling to floor, the balass-black impediment frustrated all further progress.

To Tralgan the words carved around the circumference of a circle upon the door, glimmering weirdly in the uncanny light, struck with a prosaic contempt. The words spelled out a curse.

Among the portrayed monsters and demons the words spelled out a curse of ultimate evil upon all those who attempted to venture beyond the forbidding portal.

"To a Herrelldrin Hell with your curse!" He flung himself at the black obstruction. He scrabbled with stiff fingers at the edges, trying to find a gap, a slit, anything. He felt all across the obscene carvings, feeling for a protruding knob, a lever, some hidden device by which the door could be opened.

He found none.

For some time after that his will failed and he beat at the barrier with clenched fists, screaming, kicking, as perilously close to insanity as could be and yet retain a vestige of his own self.

Finally he collapsed in a huddle still feebly trying to beat on the door.

How long his exhausted stupor lasted he could not tell. The black and often brutal blood of the Vorner family began subtly to penetrate through his veins and arteries with a pulse that would not be denied. He lifted his head. He was Tralgan Vorner. He would not be beat. No, by Vox! There must be another way.

He pulled himself together, ignoring the aches and pains, the thirst, the rumblings in his guts. He stood up. He went back along the corridor away from that thrice-damned door. Once more, as he now fervently believed, The Hand of Opaz lifted him up. He found the narrow crack slanting between the stones of the wall. Breathing as evenly as he could, trying to keep the dust from clogging his mouth and nostrils, he wormed his way through.

The Hand of Opaz might lift him up in a metaphorical sense; a pace into the crack he stepped upon nothing and fell straight down.

They had reclined in their sumptuous tombs whilst empires rose and fell, whilst religions waxed and waned. Nine of them there were, nine, the magical and mystical number of Kregen. The Nine Thaumaturges of Sodan, the nine wizards who in the long ago had tried to usurp all power and rule Vallia.

Their sarcophagi, arranged in a wide circle, feet pointing outwards, encrusted with inscriptions, gleamed. Not a spot of dust fouled their shining richness. King Rikto the All-Glorious, who by trickery had entombed the nine wizards here, at least allowed a little magic in their last resting place. A scrap of glamour kept all dust and decay away.

Deep beneath the earth the nine thaumaturges lay, yet their tomb's roof stretched above, clear, transparent, glassy. Fire crystals shed a mellow radiance into the elaborately furnished chamber. Deep purple drapes clothed the walls. Gold glittered everywhere. King Rikto, triumphant in his struggle, yet harbored a deep and uneasy sense of doom at what he had accomplished. These lavish surroundings, where treasure and labor had been poured out without stint, should placate the restless wizardly spirits.

At the center, at the focal point where the nine heads pointed, rose a marble altar. This, again, had been placed there at King Rikto's bidding. Once it had adorned the Temple of Sodan where so many evil rites had been performed that folk said you could smell the devil stink fouling the air all about. That blasphemous object was safely buried with the Nine Thaumaturges of Sodan.

The ages had passed. King Rikto's name was now unknown, not a single reference in any of the hyr lifs so preciously guarded in libraries mentioned him. He, like his times, was forgotten.

The silence here had brooded for centuries. Nothing stirred. Kregen could roll around the twin Suns of Scorpio until at last the planet fell into the crimson fires of Zim; nothing changed here.

As though Doomsday had at last arrived, the roof split open. Shards of glass flew to ring against the sarcophagi. The noise shocked into the aeons-old silence. A hurtling human figure smashed through the glass roof, twisting and turning, arms and legs flailing.

No doubt somewhere in the sunny uplands beyond the Ice Floes of Sicce, King Rikto the All-Glorious felt an abrupt pang of alarm.

Tralgan Vorner felt as though his body had been dismembered and scattered to the four corners of Kregen. A sliver of glass stuck into his thigh and he dragged it out with a sudden and savagely petty wrench. Dark blood welled from the cut. He cursed and for the moment ignoring the blood—for as a paktun he'd taken worse wounds—he stared about.

Where in a Herrelldrin Hell was he? A glass roof, here, deep within the earth? Gold, lavish furnishings, nine sarcophagi, tombs of eye-blinking sumptuousness, a sacrificial altar? He ripped a shred of cloth from his already tattered clothing and wrapped it around his wounded leg. He stood up and tested his strength. Well, by Vox, he could still stand and walk—aye! and run too, if he had to.

The most important item in this weird chamber lay at the far end. Forcing his aches into the background of his mind, still wincing from the fall, he started off, limping slightly, towards the arched opening where the foot of a staircase showed the way up.

He thought, and then pushed the thought away, that perhaps this staircase led up to the other side of that thrice-damned black door. Well, if that was so, then he must use all the hatred and lust for revenge still burning brightly within him to go on.

He climbed the stairs one at a time. He reached the top. He went along the gold-encrusted passageway. He came to a golden door. He knew without a flicker of disbelief that this was the other side of the black door. He licked his lips. He gave the golden door a kick, which hurt him, turned around and went back down the stairs.

The thing was obvious. Whoever was buried down here had not been intended to be seen again. They'd been walled off. The door shut them in. Fini.

By the time he reached the burial chamber the frustration in him hurt worse than his wounds and his toe where he'd kicked the door. He could not allow himself to be buried here along with these people. He had a task to do. His hatred must nerve him and his vengeance must be slaked.

He was hungry and thirsty; but above all he was tired. A paktun can sleep on an empty stomach and has to do so at distressingly frequent intervals. Tralgan found an upholstered couch among the plethora of furniture, flopped down, and was instantly asleep.

He awoke, still stiff and sore, a little refreshed and with his insides complaining. There was no food here, that was obvious. Had any nourishment been left for the ibs of these people on their journey through the Grey Mists, then it would surely have rotted away centuries ago. There was a great deal of gold and many many jewels. Tralgan Vorner was a mercenary, a mortpaktun. He would not leave without as many gems as he could carry, no, by Bonny Nath Makchun, the King of Reivers!

With a professional plunderer's meticulousness, Vorner inspected the chamber. The place was eerie. He would not allow the silence and the pressing purple drapes, the omnipresent tombs, to dampen his spirit. Take the gems and then escape! The central altar presented a splendid sight to a looter. The marble was encrusted with gems. A single superb emerald, situated at the top, where no doubt nubile virgins' throats had been slit, attracted him.

He touched it. The odd fact was, it was loose.

Now all during this fresh upsurge of his mercenary training he was aware that the treasure at his fingertips would immeasurably aid his vengeance. He could buy men and women. He could wreck his hatred upon those who had betrayed him. Greed mingled with hatred and, within the confines of the chamber, appeared almost to smoke upon the air.

Perhaps King Rikto's little magic to purify this place assisted. Perhaps it was only the outpouring of hatred from Vorner. There was, undeniably, magic in it. Tralgan took up the emerald.

He heard the creaking first. He was aware of a sharp tingling throughout his body, obliterating his pains. Streaks of green fire surrounded him, hissing, building a web that sparked and spat tongues of emerald flame.

He yelled and leaped upright, glaring about, staring with sick horror upon the ring of nine sarcophagi.

Brazen gongs beat stunningly within the chamber. The tombs moved. The tombs moved! Smoothly they revolved so that very quickly the heads were outwards, the feet pointing towards Tralgan.

The lids of the sarcophagi began to lift. They swung aside. A second lid appeared within each golden glowing sarcophagus, lifting up, revealing—Tralgan Vorner screamed.

Things rose into view from the tomb. Rotting corpses, men and women, trailing rotting vestments upon their rotting skin, the nine dead and decaying bodies of the Thaumaturges of Sodan rose up to confront Tralgan Vorner.

He dropped the emerald. He swung about, this way and that, shaking, seeing those ghastly eyeless skeletal faces that yet bore down on him with a gaze he knew picked out his every detail.

"No!" He choked it out, hands held before him. "No!"

The nine corpses grinned.

Five

"If," said Rollo with a fine judicial air, "we'd brought the voller with us we would not have got into that unpleasant fight."

Rollo the Runner hailed from Loh, where airboats were more uncommon than seeing the seven moons of Kregen turning blue. He had learned to pilot an airboat skillfully, yet it was interesting to note how he still pronounced the word voller with such meticulous care.

"Oh, aye," said Seg in his fine free way, riding his zorca with the easy nonchalance of perfect knowledge and skill in zorca handling. "Oh, surely. But, Rollo, you'd have us miss that little scrap? And you so keen about your archery."

Rollo, as a Wizard of Loh, had come on a great deal in the magical arts since he'd been tutored by our comrade Wizards of Loh.

Still, he hankered to be a great bowman, emulating Seg, practicing shooting when he should have been studying the arcane tomes and learning spells and going through the prescribed exercises that mages require to be able to practice their craft.

Our little hunting party cantered quietly through the forest heading north to Zandikar. The pack animals held our camping equipment, for we had decided to move on, and now we were looking forward to finding a good site where we might settle down for the night.

The two princesses were chattering away as they always were, always with something to talk about between them. Aunt and niece, they were heartbreakingly alike, for they bore the same blood. Yet Velia had the soft brown hair of Vallia, while Didi's hair bore a darker tone, the heritage of the black curly mop of Gafard her father. Ah, yes! Gafard! Rog of Guamelga, The King's Striker, Prince of the Central Sea, Sea Zhantil—and all the rest of his glorious titles that were now as ashes thrown upon a slagheap. He had been a man.

Now both these splendid young ladies were Sisters of the Rose, capable with rapier and main gauche, with whip and Claw. Oh, yes, time marches implacably on and children grow up and the world turns and they take their places, and neither the Savanti nor the Star Lords can halt a single second.

Well, to be truthful, the Everoinye can meddle with time, although I knew they made a mess of it from time to time. Ha! Dray Prescot, making a pun! Deplorable, by Krun!

Didi had made her pilgrimage to the memorial to her parents. We'd taken this short holiday break before flying back to Vallia. The excitement was now over, we'd say the remberees to Zeg and Miam, and then we'd be off.

Mind you, that oh so convenient sand storm posed me puzzles. Had the Star Lords intervened to assist us? I shook my head and geed up my zorca to keep up with the tail of our little group. If the Everoinye had taken a hand, then perhaps—as before—I'd reached a further plateau of understanding with them. The Gdoinye had vanished on the instant, flirting his wings and volplaning up into the blue vastness of the sky. I had carried out many of the tasks set to my hands by the Star Lords. Whilst their purposes remained unclear, individual missions had to be accomplished. Otherwise...! So, now, riding along comfortably with this holiday group, I understood that another and fresh task was to befall me.

Jade and rose shafts of light fell dappled through the leaves above. The sweet air of Kregen breathed all about us. The way trended down to a clearing and a burbling brook. The wonderful world of Kregen can be a most marvelous place for any soul alive to take delight in and relish every tingling second.

Hikdar Frazan ti Relzana spoke to his Deldar, Landi the Harness—there was a scurrilous anecdote about Landi's nickname—telling him to send a couple of outriders down to scout the stream. The two jurukkers speeded up their zorcas and cantered down towards the grassy slope. King Zeg in providing this little guard—an audo of eight men commanded by Landi the Harness—had given overall command to Hikdar Frazan who was by way of being your dashing and handsome cavalry officer. His ferociously brushed-up moustaches were the envy of his comrades and the despair of swooning young ladies.

Now he turned his zorca and waited for me to catch up. His bright, open face with the wonderful blue eyes and those moustaches expressed a genial good humor, finding joy in life.

"Majister. Would you wish to camp here?"

"Looks a good spot, Frazan."

He nodded respectfully, chivvied up his mount and rode off to organize our resting place for the night. A fine, upstanding lad, whose grandfather was a roz, the term in the inner sea for kov, duke; one day he'd come into his inheritance and take over the roznate.

He passed the two princesses, giving them a courteous wave from the saddle, and with Deldar Landi rode down towards the stream. Princess Velia trotted her zorca over to ride alongside Seg.

Princess Didi trotted over to ride alongside me.

Her face, gloriously beautiful at any time, now shone with the high color of the setting sun Zim.

We talked amiably and easily as we rode along. There existed between us thankfully little of any embarrassing generation gap. Remember, these two serene yet fiery princesses were no empty-headed girls. They'd been thoroughly educated at Lancival, the secret headquarters of the SoR. They were well able to run their own provinces of Urn and Thoth Vennar. Of course, they far preferred to be off around the world adventuring. So our conversation was no idle babble, far from it.

One point Didi raised, that was to have far reaching consequences, by Vox!—concerned her unease about her new nazabni, Ulana Farlan. "She tries to be like her father was. I am not sure."

"Her father I knew well, a fine man. The daughter—I've little information. Anyway, it is a matter for you and Drak."

"Yes. If it comes to it, I shall act for the good of Urn Vennar. Ulana will have a generous pension."

Seg swung about in his saddle, lifting a hand. "A gold on it, my old dom. First to the water! Hai!"

"Hai!" I hallooed back to him and instantly set my zorca to pelting along with the breeze flowing past and the rattle and creak of harness and the soft pounding of hooves.

Inevitably, the two princesses joined in the race. Well, they would, wouldn't they, seeing they were Ladies of Vallia.

Very difficult to judge out of the two ladies who reached the water first, very difficult, by Krun! Seg and I reined up. The four zorcas had earned their drink. We all dismounted. Velia went across to Seg, holding her hand out. Didi stood by me.

"Well, Uncle Seg? And where is my gold piece?"

My blade comrade laughed his great laugh and hauled out a coin that winked in the declining suns' rays. It was a gold Zo piece, named after the king who'd reined in Sanurkazz all those long seasons ago. "Here, you saucy imp." The coin flipped up, spinning, and Velia's pink palm closed over it unerringly.

Didi said absolutely nothing.

Very quickly the preparations for camp were well underway. The two princesses, as seasoned campaigners, took their share. They appeared to find tasks well separated one from the other. Hikdar Frazan ti Relzana superintended, lending a hand here and there. He, too, seemed to find work away from the ladies.

Seg strolled over, already polishing up the new bowstave he was building. Well, when wasn't Seg Segutorio building a new bow?

"We were well beaten in the race, my old dom."

"Aye."

"You've noticed the girls?"

"Aye."

We sat comfortably under the branches of a tree for a while, not speaking. Seg polished his bowstave. I got on with thoroughly cleaning my Krozair longsword.

"Romance," said Seg, at last. He shook his head. "It's a real devil at times."

"Aye."

He gave me a quick glance from under the eyebrows, his blue eyes fey and knowing. "You can't blame young Frazan."

"No."

Again, we sat in silence.

The cleaning rag in my fist, working smoothly over that remarkable blade, I looked at Seg. "It's going to be a right moil if the girls won't speak to each other. It's all come on rather fast." I own, by Krun, my voice carried an edge of testiness.

"I'm prepared to wager," said Seg, casually and yet with meaning, "that neither of 'em'll make a go of it with Frazan." He turned the bowstave over, looking at it critically. "Anyway, I would wager young Frazan has a girl in Zandikar."

"Probably."

Deldar Landi the Harness walked across. "Jernus—dinner is ready, if it please you."

Seg leaped up, gripping the bowstave. "It pleases me, Del Landi. I could eat three wild leems and look for three sweets."

So that was how the matter of the two princesses and the Hikdar of the moustaches was left for the moment.

The meal was good. We all tucked in. Velia sat at one end of the table; Didi at the other. Frazan sat in the middle. Rollo, next to me, sensibly said nothing. Seg, affably, said: "If Inch was with us now that long streak would be happier than where he is at the moment."

"Aye." We missed Inch—and, for that matter, we missed all our comrades. Delia was off somewhere, either on behalf of the Sisters of the Rose or the Star Lords. What that divine lady got up to when not with me gave me nightmares. Still, she was capable of anything. That was the only comfort I could glean from her absence.

Rollo, lifting his goblet of wine, abruptly gasped. He sat upright, stiff, eyes staring. The wine spilled red upon the cloth.

"Khe-Hi!"

Instantly, Seg and I turned to stare narrowly upon the young Wizard of Loh.

Rollo nodded. He was now under perfect control. "Yes, Khe-Hi. I understand." He nodded again. "I will, san, at once."

We knew what had just taken place. Through that uncanny other plane where wizards spent a deal of their time, our comrade Wizard of Loh, Khe-Hi-Bjanching, had just gone into lupu and communicated with Rollo. The last whereabouts of Khe-Hi which I knew, he'd been visiting Deb-Lu-Quienyin in Vondium, capital of Vallia.

Rollo took a sip of the wine. "Deb-Lu sends his regards. He and Khe-Hi have become aware of—" He paused, sorting out the right words to try to explain arcane lore to folk who were not mages. "There have been unexplained sorcerous—ripples, waves, in Vallia. They are investigating. The power of the thaumaturgy is very great."

Now it was frighteningly clear to me that two Wizards of Loh so far advanced in the arcane arts as our two comrades would not trifle to warn us in far away Zandikar unless they suspected grave danger. After all, Drak was Emperor of Vallia now. Still, he would have been warned first. Ling-Li-Lwingling, Khe-Hi's wife, would most certainly be aware of this new situation. I shivered with a sudden and totally unwelcome premonition of evil days to come.

As though Lexarm the Black Bastard, the spirit of evil who enjoys piling misery upon misery, chose us for his disgusting sport, a wild whooping started up all about us. Under the last rays of Zim and Genodras lithe forms burst from the shadows, racing towards us. Schnarlers, squamous, toad-like creatures, they threw themselves at our peaceful dinner party. Steel glittered. In the next second they were upon us, screeching, fanatically determined to slay us all.

Six

The corpses of the nine Thaumaturges of Sodan sat up and leered upon Tralgan Vorner.

One hand gripping the carved edge of the altar, Vorner swung about, this way and that, bent over. His head jutted as he twisted and turned looking for a way out. There was no way out. He knew that. He knew it with the same deadly assurance he knew he was condemned to the lowest pits of an unimaginable hell.

A nauseous waft of disgusting decay flowed over him. These dead things stank! His feet appeared rooted into the marble floor. He could not stir from this spot, the focus of the eyeless gaze of the undead.

He tried to swallow and failed. A miasmic mist fell over his distended eyes. The kaotim, the undead, remained perfectly still. The only sound in the chamber came from Tralgan's hoarse, unsteady breathing, his mouth wide open and gasping for air.

He managed to swallow down. His eyes flicked from side to side. His gaze searched desperately and uselessly for a way out. He was doomed. So much, then, for his fierce longing for revenge, so much for his vaunted hatred.

Try as he might, Tralgan could not move. He stared appalled upon the kaotim. Even if he could have moved, there was no escape.

Tiny lambent flames rose from the coffins. Multicolored, sparking, they gyrated from coffins to floor. The flames began a macabre dance across the marble, springing about, swaying, a blasphemous dance of doom.

The prancing slivers of flame reached Vorner. They climbed his legs, encircled his waist, crept up over his chest. They formed a halo about his head. He felt no heat. Instead he experienced a vibration that drove down into his psyche. His ib recoiled from this sorcerous invasion of his own personal privacy. All that he had ever been, all that he was, his everything, lay flayed bare under the dance of the flames.

Noise beat about him. Hammer blows of sound crashed into his ears from all around this dread chamber. The uproar coalesced into words, recognizable sentences. Tralgan realized he was listening to a single voice, magnified a hundredfold, bouncing in reverberating echoes through his skull.

"I am Rafan-Ymet!" The multitude of echoes thinned to a single penetrating whisper, hoarse, menacing, sending the stark shivers up Tralgan's backbone. "Remember! I am Rafan-Ymet, known as the Ineluctor. I speak for all—for now." Tralgan hunkered down, covering his ears with his hands, shaking. The occult voice seared into his brain as a red-hot brand sears into a slave's skin.

A vast sigh filled the chamber with echoes, as the other eight corpses confirmed what their spokesman said.

The eyeless face of the cadaver altered. Sparks flew. In the blank orbits light grew. Eyeballs, red and white, appeared as though floating unsupported in the boney eyesockets.

"You think of hatred. What do you know of hatred? Have you spent centuries locked into a tomb of darkness? Your petty betrayal is as the mewling of a woflo beside the roar of a leem!"

Vorner tried to speak, and could not. He wanted to scream out that he understood hatred. He knew the corroding turmoil in his guts, the agony in his mind. "I know about hatred!" He shouted it out, shocking himself, passionate with the emotions torturing him. "I know!" He panted with the sheer exertion of speaking; but he had broken the fell hand of fear upon him. "If you want hatred and revenge, then I know, I know!"

"Oh, yes, Tralgan Vorner, rightful Elten of Culvensax. We understand. Your hatred has given us life."

With a sudden pitch into a different tone of voice, Rafan-Ymet went on speaking in a smooth, highly-cultured way, like any high-flown noble addressing an assembly of his peers.

"We have been wrongly imprisoned here for so many centuries the rocks have worn away in that gulf of time. Yet you have given us the impetus to resurrection." The voice now almost caressed Vorner. "Perhaps we owe you a meed of thanks."

"No, no!" babbled Tralgan. "I—"

"You will be of use to us. Your revenge shall be ours."

"Yes—yes—"

"I, the Ineluctor, will guide you. You shall have your revenge." The sheer volume of spite and deep-seated anger vibrating in that smooth voice overpowered Tralgan Vorner. "Oh, yes, mere mortal man, you will gain your vengeance. But our vengeance upon our enemies will be so far greater than your pettiness can conceive as the irresistible force of the Tides of Kregen is to a child splashing in a paddling pool."

"Yes, yes," hawked out Tralgan, beside himself with terror. "Oh, yes, I agree. Absolutely! Oh, yes, whatever you say!"

"Good. You will do our bidding without question. I shall be with you, night and day."

Tralgan looked up with reddened eyes as the ghastly thing floated up free of the sarcophagus. Trailing tattered vestments and rotting skin, it hovered above him. Malevolent eyes gazed down, isolated and glaring within the hollow eyesockets.

The dancing scintillant flames died and vanished. Tralgan knew where they had gone. They had penetrated his very being.

His fear dwindled. He saw the doom laid upon him. He licked his lips.

Well, by All the Names! He welcomed his fate; he clutched it to him with all the ardor of a lover clasping his mistress in stolen moments of secret passion. He would have his revenge! These apparitions of dead wizards would aid him. So be it! He was the rightful Elten of Culvensax, and he would have his inheritance, come what may!

The black blood of the Vorner family rose up in him, demanding, compelling, overriding every other feeling. Vengeance!

But—there was more!

Oh, yes, Vorner's revenge was to be bought at a price. That this price was the usual one did not deter him.

Rafan-Ymet widened that lipless mouth where the rotting teeth stood as timber breakwaters stand eaten away by the sea. "You understand? You are prepared—aye, willing—to devote your ib, your spirit, to your revenge?"

Vorner nodded savagely.

"You wish to sell your ib?"

"Aye."

"So be it. Then I shall be at your shoulder from now on."

Those multicolored flames, dancing, caressing, which had entered Tralgan's body and being, carried with them the dire presence of the thaumaturge, Rafan-Ymet the Ineluctor. Now he was a part of Tralgan Vorner. Yet—"I shall appear when necessary. You will obey my commands. We will, together, have every vengeance owed to us, yes, by the Nine Arcades of Sodan!"

Tralgan had heard wizards swear by the Seven Arcades. These ghastly remnants of an older age, perhaps, knew more.

Rafan-Ymet floated back to his sarcophagus, trailing rotting vestments. "You may take what you will of treasure. You will leave the emerald in place." The corpse sank down into its coffin. "Your escape is plain. Remember, I am always with you!"

The coffin lid closed soundlessly. The other eight lids shut.

Then, one after another, with the booming sound of drumbeats of doom, the nine sarcophagi lids slammed down. The echoes smashed against Tralgan's ears.

He picked up the emerald and replaced it on the altar. He stared around upon the heaped treasures. He would be an immeasurably rich man. He licked his lips. This was the beginning of his vengeance!

Seven

No time for bowshots. Time only to leap forward into action.

On Kregen, even during a peaceful dinner party, fighting men and women habitually carried a sufficiency of weaponry. The Krozair brand leaped from the scabbard. The toad people, screeching and croaking out their guttural staccato, swarmed out of the red and green dappled shadows. We met them, fronted them. A frenzied fight began as the last rays of Zim and Genodras sank into darkness.

These damned Schnarlers, creeping out of their swamp homes, preyed upon innocent travelers. Their whole tribes were bandits, drikingers, taking what they could kill and rob from caravans whose protection was not sufficient. We had to defend ourselves, there was no other option.

Seg's superb physique corded with muscle as he swung his sword, hacking, lopping, thrusting. Hikdar Frazan's Krozair sword leaped about lethally, for he was a Krozair brother of Zamu. Rollo, not to be outdone, employed his drexer with cunning expertise taught him back home in Esser Rarioch. The guards fought doggedly, dour, professional fighting men, earning their hire.

But the girls!

The two princesses of Vallia, both Sisters of the Rose, both mistresses of their arts, cut swathes of destruction through the croaking toad people.

They were not using their whips. In each right hand the slender length of a rapier pierced and impaled. But their left hands!

Their Claws glittered in the yellow lights of our lanterns. All too awfully that bright razor sharp steel dulled in the dark sheen of blood. Schnarler blood, red as any apim's, ripped from heads that no longer contained faces, dripped.

The combat sprawled across the camp. The Schnarlers were fighting for loot which their rapacious life-styles demanded. We were fighting for our lives.

For the moment, their rivalries in the romance business forgotten, the two princesses fought side by side, splendid, lithe, mercilessly Clawing those foolhardy toad creatures who sought to drag them down. We all fought with the desperate dedication of those who struggle to save their lives.

But we took our lumps. A guardsman—I believe his name was Nalgre the Fornstetter—reeled back with a sword still jammed between the bones of his neck. He attempted to slash his blade across the abdomen of the toadman who had struck him, and who was trying to drag his sword free. He failed. He collapsed in a bloody huddle. I started across but Seg was there before me. His brand went *schissh* and the Schnarler stood bereft of a head.

For a tiny space there occurred one of those uncanny pauses that mark combats where extraordinary physical exertion drains the muscles of force. "D'you see the girls, my old dom?"

"Aye. Magnificent. Still—we'd best keep an eye on 'em."

We glared about in the lanterns' light, blood-spattered, drawing our breaths, seeing the next wave of the onslaught about to break upon us.

Nalgre the Fornstetter turned over on the ground, shaking his limbs in the last spasm. He could not speak. His eyes burned on us. Seg bent to him. "Rest easy, dom. You'll see the sunny uplands soon." With Seg's broad reassuring hand on his shoulder, Nalgre the Fornstetter died.

In the next instant we were at handstrokes. Swords bit and cleft. Blood flowed to stain the grass in greasy streaks. We held our own—just.

Now, if you think I, Dray Prescot, Vovedeer, Lord of Strombor and Krozair of Zy, enjoyed this disgusting combat, then you know little of me. By Zim-Zair! Yes, fighting has dogged my footsteps during my life on Kregen. The memories of many a battle, many an affray, haunt me to this day. The shedding of blood, even that of malignant folk determined to slay me and my friends, is repugnant to me. But vaol-paol, the great wheel of life and death, turns remorselessly. This fight was none of our seeking; yet fight we must.

Even as I smote and leaped and so smote again, I was fully aware that these Schnarlers from the swamps merely obeyed their own instincts, their own lifestyle. Like the scorpion, they did what they did because they were who they were.

All the same, by the disgusting liver and lights of Makki Grodno, since they tried to kill Didi and Velia, not to mention Seg and Rollo and the others in our peaceful party, they had to be stopped. Finally.

That damned scorpion of the fable had a lot to answer for, by Krun!

So ferocious our defense, so many the Schnarlers lost, their attack faltered. On my side of the fight they drew back a little. Their croaking screeching noises continued, a cacophony compounded of sheer hatred, bravado and the desire to intimidate. Abruptly, like a mountain splitting, Seg shrieked: "No! Didi!"

I whirled. Didi was down on one knee. Her blood-fouled Claw tangled with a toadman's spear. Her rapier was gone from her right fist. The Schnarler lifted his other hand. A sliver of steel glittered evilly in the lights from the swaying lanterns.

Without thought, instinct alone nerving me, I drew a throwing knife from the sheath over my right shoulder, and threw.

A damned confounded devil-doomed Schnarler rose up between Didi and myself. The white folds of flesh at his throat pulsated as he croaked out his toad screeches. The terchick struck straight through that fat vibrating flesh, struck on, struck him down. But Didi was left vainly trying to defend herself as the toadman drove the dagger down.

I saw Hikdar Frazan, poised and limber in that flashing instant, I saw him lift his Krozair brand, seize the forte, hurl.

The blade, sure, gleaming, deadly, scythed into the toadman in the same moment that he brought his dagger down.

The Schnarler went over backwards, spouting blood. Frazan, leaping like a leem, was on him. Frazan's dagger finished the work begun by his Krozair longsword. The toadman flopped, wriggling.

"Didi!"

The despairing cry shrieked up from Velia as she battled with three toadfolk to her front and flank. Even as I started across, my guts churning with the direst apprehension, Rollo sprang, as it were, from nowhere. His drexer wielded with painstaking skill sliced into the nearest Schnarler fronting Velia. Between them they had that flank covered, so I—and I admit with due humility and with a resounding Chusto oath—went bald-headed for the clump of toadmen who'd broken through to do so grievous damage to Didi.

What then ensued was not pretty. Well, by Zair, there is precious little about fighting and warfare that is pretty. The whole passage at arms hullabalooed silently, it seemed to me. I was conscious of smiting, thrusting, ducking, spinning about to slice toadmen from the side. Blood, of course, spurted everywhere. After a time I heard, as through a veil, Seg's voice: "They've all run off, my old dom." Then, with a sigh: "Didi is alive but hurt."

I was shaking. I shook in every limb, every particle, every single atom of my being. Didi!

A cursory wipe to my eyes, a stiffening up, and: "How—?"

Seg's strong, mellifluous voice calmed me: "She will live. The baptism in the Sacred Pool of Aphrasöe ensures she will recover. All the same, Dray, she needs a Puncture Lady or a needleman very soon. Quicker than maybe, may Erthyr the Bow favor us."

My vision cleared and the red mists rolled away. I stared about on the lantern-lit scene, appalled. Bits and pieces of toadpeople lay scattered about on the grass. Dark greasy streaks showed where the blood had flowed. I shook my head.

"Seg, Seg. This has been a bad business."

"Aye. And now—"

"Now—" I yelled. "Rollo! Go into lupu! Get a voller here! Tell King Zeg! Do it!"

Rollo did not answer. Immediately, he began his preparations. Now Rollo the Runner remained disenchanted with the idea of going into lupu and entering that weird other plane of existence to roam freely over Kregen. He'd jumped when Khe-Hi contacted him. He was a deal better now than when I'd met him over in Loh. He was, in truth, a proper Wizard of

Loh. Quickly, I added in a shout louder than I intended: "And tell him to put doctors and nurses aboard!"

Rotating with arms outstretched, slowly at first and then more and more rapidly until he was spinning dizzyingly, Rollo went through the arcane rituals. Our other older Wizards of Loh could enter lupu practically instantaneously. As I watched, feeling feverish with apprehension for Didi, I couldn't, even then, prevent a thought that Ra-Lu-Quonling—for that was Rollo the Runner's real name—would master the art sooner rather than later. Rollo was a good comrade.

Leaving him to get on with it, and looking sadly around the blood-soaked scene, I went off to find Hikdar Frazan. Frazan, as a Krozair of Zamu, had perfectly upheld the values of the Krozairs.

I greeted him as one Krozair Brother to another, using the prefix of honor accorded to us.

"Pur Frazan!"

He looked around, drew himself to attention. "Pur Dray!"

What I wanted to say was obvious enough, even redundant. All the same, I damned well meant to say it.

"You have my sincerest thanks, Pur Frazan. It was a magnificent throw. You saved Princess Didi." Then, because the friendly rivalry between the Orders of Krozairs upon the inner sea of Turismond affords lively debates, I added, cheerfully: "The cast might have been made by a Krozair of Zy."

"Ha!" His bright, amiable face with those startling blue eyes broadened into a smile. "Oh, Pur Dray, I daresay a Brother of Zy might well have missed the throw."

Oh, yes, a fine plucked 'un, this!

Then Frazan added in a serious voice: "I think Zamu may be closer than Zandikar."

I conjured up the map in my mind's eye. Zamu certainly was further south on the coast, with the promontory called the Nose of Zogo thrusting to the north east between Zamu to the east and Zandikar to the west. But Frazan was of the Eye of the World, not of the outer continents and oceans.

"Yes," I said, very judiciously, "but I believe you are thinking of riding our zorcas there. We have an airboat coming. The discrepancy in the distance is a nothing."

He screwed his face up. "We-ell—I suppose—"

"Again my sincerest thanks and deepest compliments on your throw."

So he just said: "It was Princess Didi."

Anyway, there'd be doctors and nurses arriving in the flier. Zandikar was more like home to Didi than Zamu. I did not question my decision.

Now Rollo was crouching down with head thrown back. His eyes were mere cusps of white. He was sweating. His ib was somewhere off through the ethereal planes, communicating the urgency of our need. I looked at the ground between us—looked and felt a great wave of grief. Deldar Landi the Harness lay there in a vile pool of his own blood. Good men had died here. We had defeated the toad people; the cost had been high.

Even as that gloomy thought filled me with remorse, shouts lifted from the camp. I stared up. That was quick! Far too quick for Rollo to have delivered his message, by Zair!

A voller drifted down, a dark shape between the stars. The Maiden with the Many Smiles shone fuzzy pink moonlight along her flank as she touched down. Men and women ran from her towards us.

The voller was not one of your gigantic skyships, all deck piled on deck, with a multitude of towers and fighting galleries, a massive armory of the clouds. She was a trim craft, a two-decker, with rows of ports through which the ballistae frowned menacingly in the moonlight. She had fighting galleries aloft and along each side of her keel. Many treshes fluttered from flagpoles, their proud devices difficult to read in the uncertain light. By her lines she'd been built in Hyrklana. Well, that made sense. The king of Hyrklana was that right rip of a tearaway, Jaidur, the younger brother of King Zeg of Zandikar.

Frazan stepped forward to greet the newcomers.

The yellow radiance of the camp's lanterns picked out the glittering and imposing figure who led the people from the voller. He looked what he was, a proud and imperious king, just but firm, a killer of the Green Grodnims, a true Krozair of Zy. He stalked on, followed by a crowd of guards, courtiers, functionaries. He looked absolutely splendid, there in the shifting lights of the lanterns and the streaming pink moonlight of the Maiden with the Many Smiles.

He spoke to Frazan briefly, and strode straight on. He stalked up to me with that unmistakable swagger of authority.

I just stood there, left hand on sword hilt, waiting.

King Zeg of Zandikar halted before me. His jaw went up.

"Lahal, father."

"Lahal, Zeg. You are well?"

"Aye, thanks to Zair and Opaz. Pur Frazan has told me of the hurt to Didi. Where is she?" Then, as an afterthought so common to powerful, obsessed sons: "And you, father. You are well?"

"Oh, aye, middling. Didi needs urgent attention. How came you to be here, right now, when we need you?"

"The Zair-forsaken Grodnims have hatched a plot against us. They have sent a clandestine force south to raise the folk here."

So that explained why we'd been attacked twice. The Green Grodnims of the northern shore of the inner sea continued to wage constant war against the Red Zairians of the southern shore. This contest I'd hoped—vainly—would cease. If the Grodnims had somehow managed to inflame the wild folk beyond the southern borders of the Zairians, then the situation was perilous in the extreme.

"Didi," snapped Zeg.

I gestured to the tent where the princess lay. Zeg, without another word, stomped off, his armor glittering. Well, of course, he was concerned for the life of his niece. Didi's mother, Velia, had been Zeg's twin sister. Like any twin, he was aware of the gaping loss in his life. Didi had in a way more profound than Velia his sister—the second Velia—helped to fill that gap.

Under Zeg's urgent and intolerant urgings, the medical staff of the voller hastened to work their healing magic upon Didi. The flier was called *Zairfaril*. She was a unit of the small air service Zeg was building up. I felt relief that Didi was in good hands.

Mind you, by Krun, the dip she'd taken in the Sacred Pool of far Aphrasöe meant that she would recover from wounds far more rapidly than any needleman or Puncture Lady could expect or comprehend.

A voice at my back, somewhat more peeved than plaintive, said: "I see that my efforts were not required."

I swung about instantly. "Not so, Rollo. Anyway, the task of going into lupu was good exercise for you." I gave him a hard look. "You did well. You'll just have to practice more."

"Oh, aye. Oh, aye. By the Seven Arcades! Don't I know it!"

The carcasses of the Schnarlers were dragged off a good way so that the wild animals might re-introduce their constituents back into the food chain. Our own dead we buried with all due ceremony, with appropriate prayers to Zair. The inner sea shared the concept of the Ice Floes of Sicce with some of the lands of the outer oceans. I trusted that Deldar Landi the Harness would find his way past the Grey Ones and through the Mists and so come safely to the sunny uplands. The loss of fine strapping fighters for Zair like him grieved me, as did all the stupid useless throwing away of young lives in this apparently incessant disease called warfare and battle.

Landi was dead. But there was every chance, in the way of your rough and ready soldiery, that his scurrilous story of the harness would continue to be told in barracks and over camp fires for seasons to come. Such, I suppose, is fame, by Krun!

Later, when it was reported to me that Didi was comfortable, Zeg strode over and said: "Those devil Grodnims must be stopped from building a powerful base down here. They are taking an enormous risk; but the prize is worth it to them."

I gave my lad King Zeg, who'd been called Segnik after Seg Segutorio, a stare. "So you're after them?"

He explained that the vollers of his air service were searching. The quickness of his arrival here was due to the supernatural speed of the Wizard of Loh's communications. Khe-Hi had told him of the occult manifestations in Vallia, and Zeg had assumed the responsibility of informing me. Now, he told me, he had to be about the business of chasing Green Grodnims. "They call themselves the Kaofaril, and they will not surrender."

Kaofaril—lovers of death—is a way of saying suicide squad. Plainly, Zeg had a very great deal of trouble on his hands. He went on to say that he was sending off one of his smaller airboats to take Didi back to Zandikar.

From there, I supposed, she would be flown back to Vallia.

"Not so!" He was haughty, brisk, the very picture of your kampeon, a Krozair of Zy and deadly adversary to the Grodnims. "Not so! She will stay in Zandikar and be looked after until she is well."

There was no point in arguing with this powerful and indomitable son of mine. Didi would get the best care available. I nodded.

"Very well. Our hunting party had best make all haste back to Zandikar."

"Aye. All haste. This area is no longer safe."

What had been puzzling me could now be asked. In a calm voice I said: "The Grodnims inhabit the northern coasts of The Eye of the World. Zairian patrols would have reported their swifters sailing to our southern coasts with a landing expedition." I took a breath, already guessing the answer, and dreading it. "So how have these Zair-forsaken Kaofarils managed to land their forces so far south in our hinterland?"

The frustrated bitterness in Zeg's reply wounded me.

"Airboats! The devotees of Makki-Grodno have bought vollers. They fly by night to stir insurrection among the folk of the southern marches." He shook his head. "They will do us a deep mischief if we cannot root them out before they are too firmly established."

This news—dire in the extreme—meant that the balance of power between red and green of the inner sea was tilting in the favor of the Green Grodnims.

"Where do they buy their vollers?"

"By Zim-Zair!" Zeg's words held all the boiling agony of a man barely able to control his frustrated emotions. "I wish I knew!"

Eight

Zeg organized a small flier from *Zairfaril*. The airboat was like a pinnace, trim and fast. They carried Didi out on her stretcher and I looked down on her. She was so pale she looked as though she would wisp away any second. Had she not taken that baptismal dip in the Sacred Pool of the River Zelph in far Aphrasöe, the wound would have killed her for sure.

Her hand stirred faintly, so I took it into my hand, holding it with trembling concern, feeling the desolate ache of wounds and pain and death.

"Paz," she said. Her voice barely reached my ears and I bent closer. She called me Paz, for was I not supposed to be this famous puissant Emperor of Emperors, the Emperor of All Paz? That notion was the idea of the Star Lords and one in which I had little faith. Still, young Didi called me Paz in all seriousness. "Paz. I am troubled—about Urn Vennar."

"Rest easy, my love. Velia in Thoth Vennar can—" And then I stopped my babbling foolish tongue.

Velia gave me a dark look.

"I stay with Didi."

"Of course. I wasn't thinking straight—"

Didi took a labored breath. She was stuck with acupuncture needles and the clean yellow bandages already showed the dark stain of blood. "Paz. Nazabni Ulana Farlan—you know my doubts—I am—I am not sure." She panted with the effort of speaking. Velia bent closer with a swift upward glance of annoyance.

"Hush, Didi, dear. Don't worry your head—"

"But I must. Urn Vennar is my province—I am responsible for my people. Paz!" She stared up, her brown eyes enormous in that pallid heartbreakingly beautiful face. "You will go there—see what—you will—"

"Rest easy. I shall go there and make sure all is well."

"Then—I am content." Her eyelids closed.

Velia, very much your Princess of Vallia and a Sister of the Rose, snapped curt orders. "Didi needs rest and proper attention. She will gain neither lollygagging about here or in the flier." Then, like the cutting flick of a SoR's whip: "Bratch!"

The trifling matter of a disagreement over a dashing cavalier was completely forgotten. The love between the two princesses had never been forgotten, had never died.

The little flier rose into the air and the remberees were called. A promise to Didi was cast iron. Whatever happened, I was bound to fly to Urn-Vennar and sort out whatever trouble was brewing there. As for the great and wonderful Emperor of All Paz bit: well, you who listen to these tapes will know full well my feelings there!

Zeg said: "She will live, praise be to Zair. Now, I am off to do the duty that brought me here. The damn Grodnims—"

"Aye," said Seg. "But we are for Zandikar."

Zeg looked at Seg, for whom he'd been named. "Sometimes—" he shook his head, that haughty Krozair son of mine. "Sometimes I wish—" Then: "I remember Esser Rarioch. The times we had there, Uncle Seg, shooting in our bows. Time is a damn hard taskmaster."

Seg let rip one of his stupendous laughs. "Well, King Zeg who was young Segnik all those seasons ago in Esser Rarioch, you've done well out of growing into a man!"

In my old gravel-shifting voice, I growled out: "You were scouting these Zair-forsaken Kaofarils, I believe, Zeg. You'd best get on with it, then."

He stiffened up at once. That proud and haughty face tautened. "I leave immediately. Remberee, Seg." He swung away, then half-turned. "Remberee—father."

I sighed. Even as Seg returned the remberees I regretted a millionfold the twenty-one awful years the Star Lords had condemned me to stay on Earth so that I'd not seen my children grow up.

Zairfaril lifted off, turned, rose and vanished among the stars.

The decision to strike camp and move off, tired as we were, was unanimous. Presently we were riding along under the radiance of the Maiden with the Many Smiles, dozing in our saddles. We had outriders out; we were not molested further.

Later on, jogging along, I heard Rollo the Runner talking to Seg. He was not aware that I overheard.

"You're becoming a fine bowman, Rollo." Seg sounded confident in his open-hearted way. "Your swording—"

"Oh, aye!" Rollo said with more than a touch of bitterness. "I am a Wizard of Loh, and people must think me a fool to want to be a warrior like you and the majister. His swordsmanship is—"

"Is remarkable, Rollo. Just so. But you will learn."

"I would say more than remarkable, by Ling-Loh!"

"Yes. Well, like me he is an old hare. We've taken our lumps."

Now, as you may imagine, this accidentally overheard conversation left me highly uncomfortable. Rollo was a Wizard of Loh, intrinsically a most powerful person. If he wanted to emulate Seg and me and turn himself into a bowman and a swordsman then were we not to blame for this ambition? Well, not Seg. From the first days I'd met Rollo he'd prated on about being a warrior. Deb-Lu had schooled him into wizardly ways far more subtly than the overbearing pundits back in Whonban, yet still Rollo harbored these romantic military desires.

Shortly after that as we rode along, She of the Veils rose into the night sky and shed her refulgent golden pinkish radiance across the land. I always feel comfortable when She of the Veils shines so magnificently among the stars.

Seg reined up beside me. In that streaming moons light he regarded me hardly, head tilted on one side. "H'm, my old dom." His voice was hard and practical and yet that fey quality rode through. "You're too hard on yourself. It was not your fault you were dragged away when your children were young. Zeg loves you, y'know."

I found I had nothing to say.

Seg went on: "And young Rollo. If he gets himself killed in a fight, well, that's his business."

About to reply, I clapped my black-fanged winespout shut. A spectral glimmer of blue light grew and broadened ahead. I reined in at once and Seg hauled up alongside. The night breathed softly about us. The others in the party carried on, their mounts taking them away from us. I stared narrowly on this oval of blue light, expecting to see one of our comrade Wizards of Loh manifest himself—or herself if it was Ling-Li—and solidify into a representation of the sorcerer who was probably halfway around the world of Kregen.

We had been through fraught times. By the foul intestines and maggoty heart of Makki Grodno, I said to myself, what now!

Rollo, up ahead, reined round and cantered back. Clearly, his sorcerer's training had taught him enough to recognize thaumaturgy at work. The blue dazzlement swelled and coalesced.

Why, I wondered fretfully, this time hadn't Khe-Hi chosen to communicate with us through Rollo the Runner himself?

As I thus waited so intemperately for the blue radiance to thicken into the likeness of a wizard, an odd tickle of thought fleeted through my mind. When the Star Lords sent that eerie sand storm—if, mind you, they had—why hadn't they instead simply snatched me up out of that unhealthy situation to hurl me down somewhere else? Maybe this was a strong clue to the fact that the saving sand storm was no work of the Everoinye. All the same, it had clearly been a supernatural phenomenon. Not, as you know, that they are all that rare upon the remarkable world of Kregen. Not by a long chalk, by Krun!

The blueness coalesced. A man stood before us clad in long vestments decorated with runes of an archaic nature, his face pale and with a mournful tinge. His turban was a miracle of tightly-wound silk. He gestured impatiently, as though admonishing students.

"San Nal-Hi-Munting!" said Seg, in a hard voice scarcely suitable for addressing a Wizard of Loh.

"Majister," said this Munting, inclining his head by the thickness of a butterfly's wing. "There is news."

Now I hadn't previously met this Wizard of Loh. He had been recommended by Khe-Hi as a master practitioner of the arcane arts when Seg was looking for a sorcerer to add to his entourage. Wizards of Loh take on the great ones of Kregen as clients. Wizards of Loh do not work for anyone; they have their clientele. For Seg Segutorio, as the Emperor of South Pandahem, it was proper he should have a powerful thaumaturge at his court.

Munting went on to say that the island of Pandahem had been ravaged by hurricanes of exceptional ferocity. Over in the west of the country the damage had been most severe. Enormous waves crashing ashore ripped away masonry defenses and demolished brick structures. Winds of incredible velocities simply blew away everything in their paths. Sadly, there had been great loss of life. Down in the south-west tip of Pandahem stood the powerful and wealthy city of Pundalad. Along with the other free cities of the southern shore Pundalad had joined the confederation of peoples put together by Seg for mutual self-defense.

"There were ugly scenes, majister. Riots, and waves of mass hysteria. Pandrite the All-Glorious has been forgotten. The city council question their allegiance to you."

Seg's handsome face twisted. Now he, like me, put little store in the panoply of empire. We both knew that folk had to stick together in the hostile world of Kregen. Here was a clear example of that principle in action.

"I suppose," said Seg, "the Empress Milsi has already gone?"

"Immediately the news reached Croxdrin. She has given orders that the whole empire must assist the people of Pundalad." Milsi was her real name, although she was Empress Mab and Seg was Emperor Mabo. The Wizard said she had been dealing with the situation splendidly and had calmed the populace of the city and brought in relief. Then a second series of hurricanes struck. The council felt it was time to call for the Emperor Mabo. Seg didn't swear. He just said: "I'm on my way."

"One of these airboat things is being sent," Munting told him. "It will rendezvous with you at the designated spot." The blueness faded, thinned, vanished. Nal-Hi-Munting in distant Croxdrin had come out of lupu and would report to Milsi.

Quite matter-of-factly, I said: "These are evil tidings, Seg. I shall fly with you. Maybe I can be of help."

"By the Veiled Froyvil, my old dom! Of course you would be of immense help in all kinds of ways. But—" Here he stopped, his head on one side, regarding me in a somewhat quizzical fashion.

"But what?" I said, a trifle truculently. "I'll have rescue people and builders and resources flown in and— What, in the sweet name of Zair?"

Seg's smile dazzled me. "You're the best comrade a fellow could ask for. But your memory here is addled. You have a prior commitment." He kept his zorca tranquil with one broad hand. "In fact, by Erthyr the Bow, I daresay you have two."

I said absolutely nothing.

Rollo started to say something and Seg hushed him.

I just sat there on my zorca like any lumpen loon. Of course I had a prior commitment. Two of 'em, by Krun! This devious infiltration by the Kaofarils of Grodnims could become so serious that the Krozairs would send out the great Call to Arms. The Azhurad would sound and every Krozair brother in the Eye of the World would answer. Aye, and so would the brothers adventuring on the Outer Oceans. To fail to answer—well, that had once happened to me and I'd been dubbed Apushniad, accursed, and had been cast forth from the brotherhood of the Krozairs of Zy. You may well believe I would never let that hideous fate befall me again.

Even before that, though, there was the matter of the promise to Didi. I was bound to go to Urn Vennar and sort out the problem of this troublesome nazabni Ulana Farlan. I would do that with joy for the sake of Didi, and that, by Vox, goes without saying, too!

All the same, mind you, conscious though I was of the importance of both missions so different in apparent magnitude, a rankling sense of injustice gnawed away at me. Always, it seemed superior forces imposed their wills upon what I wanted to do. I wanted to go and help Seg and Milsi. Promises and honor constrained me. Well, by Krun, I'd ask Drak to send ample help to the stricken island.

So I sat my zorca and sorted out what I was going to do.

Y'know, I, Dray Prescot, Vovedeer, Lord of Strombor and Krozair of Zy, have been called an onker, a consummate idiot, so many times the retelling is not worth the effort of spent breath.

Blueness fell about me as the shadows of evening drop from the eaves. Coldness struck in shrewdly. I looked up. I didn't bother to curse. Up there, vast and overspreading the sky, the blue shape of the Giant Phantom Scorpion hovered over all. Winds smote me. Supernal forces tossed me up and down, around and around, like that proverbial chip in a millrace. Up I went, head over heels.

The Star Lords called me to do their bidding.

Perforce—I went.

Nine

The circular room gleamed whitely all about me. Walls, floor, ceiling—all shone with polished whiteness. The shuttered door through which the hissing chair had brought me closed. A last wash of red light vanished. I had seen no sign of the green of Ahrinye, or of the glorious golden yellow of Zena Iztar. Now the whiteness of scraped bone enfolded me.

At the center of the room a single-legged round table rose into view. A flagon and goblet rested on that white surface.

Without waiting for an eerie unseen voice to bid me drink, I went across and poured. Red with that promising tint of blueness, the wine went down smoothly enough. I mentioned Mother Zinzu the Blessed.

When at last it sounded, the voice rustled like the sere leaves of autumn. "Dray Prescot!"

"I'm here."

"There is work to your hand."

"Surprise, surprise." Now I was not light-headed, nor did I wish to commit the equivalent of galactic suicide. These beings of such incredible age and powers were not to be trifled with. Although, mind you, even in these latter days when I felt I was getting along better with the Everoinye, a sarcastic twist or three did not come amiss.

"You are being favored highly. Extremely highly! You are to assist a kregoinye for whom we entertain the liveliest regard. He stands for all the qualities demanded of those who serve us. You will do his bidding faithfully."

About to say: "You're not talking of old Strom Irvil of Pine Mountain, by any chance?" I kept my black-fanged winespout shut.

"Look!" At that I swung about sharply. The flagon was gone from the table. Now that shining white surface held a harness of link mail of the finest mesh. "You will be properly attired."

I knew mail of that quality. As I divested myself of the coarser mail of the inner sea and donned the splendid armor, I said: "You are sending me to the Dawn Lands."

All the time I forced myself to keep an even tone. I had been outfitted by the Star Lords before; it was not their usual practice. Normally they hurled me down all naked and weaponless. I did not want them to see my surprise.

Even to me this smacked of pettiness; but I felt vaguely that this course of action kept me, as it were, on an even keel with the Star Lords. Not that a mere mortal man could ever hope to match them. Still, I tried to circumvent them when I could. Dangerous, of course; exhilarating, absolutely, and really and truly vitally necessary.

"The kregoinye is called Surrey. Serve him well."

That was all. The door opened, the chair hissed in and halted and I climbed aboard. Out we went along the rainbow corridors and into the blue radiance of the Scorpion.

I didn't want to go to the Dawn Lands. No, by Vox! I had work to do in Urn Vennar. And the Azhurad might sound at any time. Stuck down there in the Dawn Lands in Havilfar I'd hear the Great Call to Arms all right. The trouble would be in finding a way back to the Eye of the World in time. Confound the flaming Star Lords!

Where I was being sent, a weapon of the order of the Great Krozair longsword would be a novelty, not to say a laughing stock. The folk of the Dawn Lands, reputed to be the earliest inhabitants of Havilfar, when they fought each other used thraxters and a variety of other lethal ironmongery.

When they fought one another! Ha! The countries of the Dawn Lands were in constant turmoil, ever at war.

The blueness took me away into cold and blustery winds. I just composed myself and waited for the landing. The dratted Scorpion had fumbled before now, and had dropped me when the swirl of sky colors battled. My faith, therefore, in the Giant Phantom Blue Scorpion was much weakened.

As for the Krozair brand, well, this remarkable sword is not a long, long sword. Although ostensibly a straight two-edged blade, it has this subtle and beautiful curve from hilt to point within the confines of the two edges. This cunning curve enables the wielder to deliver the slicing blow which is so effective in battle, allowing the blade to carry on with the momentum of the swing. The Krozair brand would snug under my cape, as it had done so on many previous occasions.

My astonishment at the magnanimity of the Star Lords increased as I touched down. Well, knowing them, the apparent magnanimity.

As the blue mists cleared I found myself standing between two fluted columns at the top of and to one side of a magnificent flight of steps. I'd landed without a bump or crashing sprawl on my back. The twin suns were almost gone, so that the mobs caterwauling away at the foot of the steps were luridly illuminated by spitting torches clasped aloft in grimy laboring hands. There were men in armor among the mobs. Ranked along the top a thin line of guards in fancy uniforms looked to me far too fragile a force to halt that lot down there when they charged up, hollering and yelling blue murder.

What they were shouting, occasionally chanting in unison, was unpleasant hearing. "Death to the diffs! Death to the numims! Death to the lords!"

A closer look revealed the ominous fact that all the folk in that manic mob were apims, Homo Sapiens sapiens like me.

A swift glance back showed me the palace rising above the steps. By the deliquescing eyeballs and suppurating tonsils of Makki Grodno! Did the Star Lords expect me to take on this lot and stop them single-handed? The guards evidently shared my viewpoint, for they fidgeted and fingered their weapons nervously. I judged they'd break and run the moment the first of the bloodthirsty crowd started up.

The guards were the usual mix of jurukkers, Rapas, Fristles, numims, Khibils. There were no Pachaks. Also, there were no apims.

"Prescot!" The voice rapped hard and flat, like the crack of a twelve-pounder. "Get yourself over here and keep your head down!"

Because I'm an old hare, and not because of the fierceness of the command, I whirled around and jumped. Such was the velocity of that leap into the shadows I almost knocked down the fellow standing there beckoning to me with a brown-gloved hand. He staggered back. Then, proving his warrior quality, he gathered himself and thrust upright.

"You're damned sudden, Prescot!"

I didn't bother to answer, turning to see if our little collision had attracted attention. The guards were shifting from foot to foot. It would take only one bold fellow to leap up the first steps to make the whole little juruk flee. Beyond the mobs a kyro stretched, fitfully illuminated, with buildings lining the far side. The indistinct figures of people there, mostly women and children, told of the feelings of these folk. The situation was plain. This was a rebellion, and the apims were out to kill the diffs.

With absolute certainty I knew that within the grand palace the lion-people who lorded it over this city would be girding themselves to go out and show this damned rabble of apims just who was master.

Also, there would be their women and children shivering in anticipation of what was to befall them. Altogether, an ugly scene.

The reason why two kregoinyi had been dispatched here was obvious. The numim lords were to be saved. Well, I've rescued enough people in my time working for the Everoinye; this time the task looked formidable in the extreme.

Turning my attention to this fellow Surrey I realized he was sizing me up as best he could in the swaying illumination of the lamps strung along the architrave. He wore sensible black leathers over a mesh mail shirt that, I'd wager, came from the same place as mine. His rapier and main gauche looked reasonable enough; the fighting sword hitched above the hilt of the rapier seemed to me unusual and I fancied I'd take some interest in that blade in the future. The most remarkable thing about Surrey was his hat. A high-crowned, floppy-brimmed creation, it sported an aigrette of faerling feathers.

"You'll know me again," he said in that rasping voice.

"You're supposed to tell me what's happening here."

"I don't know you, Prescot. The Everoinye have told me very little about you, save you do not like authority." He looked away, out over the restless crowds surging back and forth, their torches flaring. "Dray Prescot—I suppose you come from Vallia and are named after the emperor." He sniffed, turning back to me. "What an onker he was! Abdicating! Can you imagine renouncing all that power?"

A beam of light from a swaying lamp fell across his face. He jerked back into the shadows. That face—apim—held a compressed look of hunger in its down-drawn lines. The dark moustache formed a straight bar above his mouth, which tightened with annoyance at the betraying beam of light. That is what I sensed, for I doubted if he would feel annoyance with himself for putting his face in the way of the light. He was, I judged, a man who liked exercising authority.

I said: "I'm waiting."

"Very good. Do as I say and you'll be all right." He went on to say we were in the city of Larnydlad in the independent kovnate of Larnydria. We had to save the kov and his family. There were strong reasons to believe the kov's retainers and fair-weather friends had already deserted him. The guards would run soon. It was all down to we two kregoinyi. I thought but didn't speak that this was all familiar stuff. If we moved fast we'd be fine.

Whilst he'd been speaking I'd kept my sailorman's eye on the rioting mobs below. Now a fellow who's been the first lieutenant of a seventy-four in Nelson's Navy knows how to spot the ringleader of a mob. There were two likely candidates below, gesticulating and haranguing.

The correct solution here would be to send in a snatch squad and arrest them. With their motivating power gone, the crowds could disperse. That, as I say, was the theory. Of course, by the gargantuan thighs and thomplod hips of the Divine Madam of Belschutz, the snatch squad would consist of me and this Surrey fellow, if he chose to join.

I fancied he had the mettle for the job, so I was surprised, after I'd told him, that he shook his head. "No! Don't try to rise above yourself. Remember, I command here."

That was true, being a command from the Star Lords. All the same, this attitude of arrogance was quite different from the attitude of running the show shown by my previous kregoinyi comrades, Pompino, Mevancy and Fweygo.

"Very well." Then, with an irony he probably would not appreciate, I added: "Lead on." Mind you, he could have been recruited from Earth.

He gave me a sharpish look, as though detecting something more in my tones than appeared, nodded his head so the aigrette fluttered, and started off into the shadows between the columns.

He clearly knew the way, for he led off without hesitation, taking me along ornate corridors where the plush drapes hung and the room-sized pictures adorned the walls. There was no one about. They'd all run off, that was for sure.

Pretty soon we were running. This suited me, for this thing had to be done nip and tuck. The throne room was empty as we sprinted past. Beyond that, luxurious chambers opened out into the private quarters. Here, in a small bedroom, we found what we sought.

The hollow ghostliness of the deserted palace could saw on a fellow's mind. The place breathed uneasiness. The man who reared up as we entered, oddly enough, restored normalcy. He flourished a sword and swore at us. He wore armor and his lion-man face twisted in anger and contempt.

"You murdering apims! I'll show you how a numim can die!"

Surrey spread his arms wide. He shouted. "Kov! We are here to save you, not kill you! Put up your sword. We must hurry."

The kov looked past us, whiskers flaring, eyes wide. "There are only two of you—but you are apims. How can I believe you?"

"By our actions. Now, kov, please—"

This numim lord was not old, although on Kregen people's ages are often difficult to assess by reason of their very long lifespans.

A weak cry from the bed made us all turn. A woman tried to sit up, and failed with a painful gasp, and so sank back. A single glance at her chalk-white hair, her gauntness, showed she suffered from the dread disease known as chivrel. Kregans are in mortal fear of chivrel. This, then, was the reason the Everoinye had sent two of us.

Two lion-men cubs crept out from under the bed. One was a stout lad, the other a remarkably pretty girl; they were heartbreakingly young. So Surrey and I had a job on our hands.

Speaking with intense precision, Surrey told the numims they must abandon any idea of taking very much with them—"Just a few gems to feed you"—and in no time we were organized for the flight.

"You will carry Kovneva Esme." Surrey gave his orders. "Kov Randalt will care for the children. I shall go first."

Now there were two lines of decision here. One was that Kov Randalt was in mortal fear for his little family. The other was that the kregoinye Surrey possessed the presence to order and be obeyed. Probably there was a little of both. In any event, we hurried from the bedchamber and started quickly for the rear of the palace. Kovneva Esme weighed as much as a little schoolgirl. Randalt did say to me: "You have no fear of catching chivrel?"

"It is not catching. Hurry on."

Some large ornate chambers later we paused for a moment where two passages crossed. Surrey took his bearings. I stood beside him whilst Randalt hushed the children. I said in a low, hard voice: "I would prefer you to call me Jak. I do not use—"

He looked at me and a brief smile touched his lips. "You, too? I just use the name Surrey. I'm Otto—but don't call me that. You have a cognomen? Sometimes I'm known as Otto the Lance."

Not prepared to reel out the string of names I've been called, I simply said: "You've already used it."

He cogitated a moment. Then: "Ah! When you leaped into the shadows. I'd barely told you to get your head down."

"You were rather—impatient."

"Yes, well, I was wrought up and I thought for sure you'd be seen." He gestured down the left hand passage. "Come on."

So, having sorted out the pappattu, we padded on.

He didn't seem such a bad guy, after all. Perhaps the arrogance I'd detected could be put down to the apprehensions of the situation. He was the leader, and, Opaz knows, leaders share the greater part of the burdens. Even so, he'd not considered that when talking of the abdication of the Emperor of Vallia.

Surrey, who was really Otto the Lance—was he then Surrey the Lance?—pushed through gilt double doors, saying they led onto the waiting chamber for those coming in by the main rear entrance. Looking past Surrey I saw the shambles strewn across the paving. Contorted bodies lay in pools of drying blood, slick and greasy. The throat-catching stink of spilled blood hung in the close air.

Kov Randalt choked out: "So that is what happened to them!"

Mingled with the bodies of apims the corpses of numim warriors pathetically attested to the fight they had put up. This explained the scene at the front of the palace. Kov Randalt did have, it would seem from this gory evidence, some jurukkers loyal to him.

Without thinking or hesitation and using the voice of an emperor giving commands that would be instantly obeyed, I rasped out: "Look to your children, kov!"

He jumped. Then, seeing the truth of it, he bent to the children, shielding their eyes. Mind you, by Krun, kids on Kregen are a hardy lot—however much one might wish otherwise in a more perfect world.

Kovneva Esme moaned, wrapped in bedclothes in my arms. The children started to ask questions in their high voices. They didn't like the nasty smell.

Thick columns supported the roof where shadows lurked. The lamps had not been tended lately, and smoked and threw fitful light about as though we stood in a Shadow Play.

A white shape flew from the high gloom. A pure white dove circled briefly in mid-air. With a graceful flick of a feathered wing the dove turned and rose and vanished.

Not sure if Surrey had seen this phenomenon, I was about to call to him when he moved off smartly, half-turning his head back over his shoulder to say: "Come on. Hurry."

That betraying turning back of his head undid him.

From the shelter of a thick pillar a man stepped out. His body was for a fractional moment limned in blue light from an unseen source. He was on Surrey before the kregoinye turned back to face front.

"Stand still, or you are a dead man!" The voice was mellifluous; the content savage with purpose. "You! Put down the kovneva. Gently!" A sword's point pressed against Surrey's throat. "Accept the needle. You have failed in your kidnap attempt. I do not wish to slay you both—but, as Jalam the Judicious is my witness, you deserve to be tossed contemptuously down to the Ice Floes of Sicce!"

A bright spot of blood appeared on Surrey's throat where the sword point pressed relentlessly in.

Ten

The moment hung, tense with the prospect of imminent and sudden death.

Now Otto the Lance, who liked to call himself Surrey, was a kregoinye chosen by the Star Lords. The Everoinye do not make their choices lightly—although they'd told me often enough how dubious they considered me to be—and the folk who serve them are masters and mistresses of their professions.

This sprightly newcomer in the shadows was a mere dark shape. His sword blade pressed in, digging deeper, demandingly.

Thinking to give Surrey the chance, I said: "Quidang, notor!" and bent to place Esme down, making sure she rested comfortably in the bedclothes.

Surrey reacted as a true kregoinye. He took the chance.

He moved with supple speed. That strange sword of his flicked, the stranger's brand swept sideways, and in the next instant the two faced each other, their weapons poised for hand-to-hand combat.

The newcomer stepped out into the light, nimble and confident. He wore fawn leathers with fringes, tall boots and black gloves. I saw his sword clearly, very clearly.

Seeing that weapon, the most deadly sword in all Kregen, I knew Surrey would have no chance in a fight, odd sword or not.

I said in my old gravel-shifting voice: "Hold!" I stepped forward, consciously using all the yrium with which I have been blessed and cursed, employing that super-charisma to enforce my will, that dark power for which the Star Lords suffer me and employ me.

"Put up your swords! We are friends!"

They both swung their heads to gape at me.

"You—!"

"What—!"

I ground it out. "We are here to rescue the kov and his family. You, stranger, are here for the same reason. For the sweet sake of Martine the Cheeks, let us get out of this pestiferous place!"

Well, now! They were both primed for a fight. They were trembling with passion, with their pride on the line, ready to go, come what may, death and destruction or arrogant victory.

How long that tableau held I do not know; I can say it seemed to go on for ever. Wondering if I should say: "Happy Swinging!" and thus betray secrets I wished concealed, I felt the wash of relief flood through me as they stepped back. Both flourished their brands in salute and then scabbarded them with two flat smacks.

This Surrey might be high in the confidence of the Star Lords; from his actions I judged he was not aware of the existence of the Savanti.

Now the two children were crying, Esme was making little gasping noises, Kov Randalt held his sword as though he couldn't understand how it had come into his fist. The stink of drying blood cloyed in our nostrils. The pressing gloom of this close-columned chamber lowered down over us. Time, by Krun, to go!

When I picked up the kovneva I hushed her, trying to reassure her that all was well. The kov scabbarded his thraxter. Surrey and the Savapim gave each other questioning looks, and then the Savapim gestured gracefully, and Otto the Lance took the lead. We went swiftly from that place of death.

By the time we reached the doors which would let us out, these two had talked and made the pappattu, for Surrey said: "This is Tyr Hangrol ti Ferstheim." That, I surmised, was not the name he'd been given at baptism. "He has everything arranged, apparently."

This Hangrol nodded. The doors were wide open, left like that when the apims had burst through. We fugitives hurried out and down the steps, looking about in the pink-tinged moonlight from the Maiden with the Many Smiles. We saw no one. Parked—neatly, by Vox!—just past the last flickering torch, a two mytzer carriage waited with drawn curtains.

Without hesitation this Hangrol opened the door and gestured to the kov to enter with his children. He jerked a hand at me and I put Kovneva Esme down gently on the upholstered seat.

Stepping back, I drew Surrey away. "Is this what the Everoinye require, d'you think?"

The pink moonlight washed his face with color, emphasizing the strength of his jawline. Shadow from his moustache blotted his mouth. "This Hangrol tells me he can escort the kov and family to safety. He is an apim. It appears that if these rioting apims killed the numim notors, then the whole weight of retribution from the diffs of the country would fall on them. There would be a general massacre of all apims." Surrey shook his head so the tall hat shook. "He does not want that."

So that explained it. I saw the reasons why the Savanti, whose apparent avowed intent is to make Kregen a place for apims alone, would want to save the lives of diffs. This apim revolt would be totally counter-productive to the plans of the Savanti of Aphrasöe, the Swinging City.

Hangrol climbed up to the box and took up the whip. "I thank you. I take it you won't be coming with me?"

Surrey shook his head and called: "Rembraee."

"Rembraee," said the Savapim, and whipped up.

I said: "That was all damned casual."

The mytzer carriage clattered off into the pink moonlight. "There are things to do with the Everoinye of which you are not aware, Jak. In this instance, his masters and ours desire the same outcome."

Soho! I said to myself. Perhaps this fine fellow does know of the Savanti.

In that case he was extremely brave or exceedingly foolish to take on a Savapim armed with a Savanti sword.

Now, I surmised, our task was done. Now we could go our separate ways. I had a great deal to do, and the quicker I shook the dust of Larnydria from my boots the better, as they say in Clishdrin. This was an isolated task accomplished for the Star Lords, with no significance for the future. Well, as you shall hear, in that I was woefully wrong, by Krun!

All this exercise had given me a thirst worthy of the father of Beng Dikkane himself. Thinking to essay a trial of this Surrey as to his knowledge of the Savanti, and to get my wet, I suggested we find a tavern open at this time, well away from the rioting mobs. He agreed at once, so I said: "That sword Hangrol had. Deuced odd."

"I agree." We started walking away from the palace. "It surprised me. The Everoinye gave me this sword. Hangrol's looked very much like mine, as though somehow he'd managed to copy it." He laughed. "Of course, that idea is nonsensical. What would he know of the immortal Everoinye?"

I didn't say a word. Not a single bloody one. I strode along in that refulgent roseate moonlight, seething with anger. Rage and resentment engulfed me. My Val!

Again Surrey knew the way. No doubt the Star Lords had briefed him thoroughly, just as they'd given him a sword newly copied from the Savanti sword. He gave me a quizzical glance.

"You all right, Jak?"

"Yeh." I managed to get out. "Never better."

"Good. The Everoinye will be giving me a new assignment very soon. I always enjoy the challenge."

What I thought I will not repeat. He went burbling on in a cheerful enough way as we walked round to where the lights showed the nightlife of Larnydlad was hotting up. By this time, by my reckoning, the guards should have fled and the mobs should be wrecking the palace and looting what they no doubt considered their dues. Good luck to 'em!

The thought occurred to me that perhaps the Star Lords felt my Krozair brand was sufficient. Maybe they thought that was enough, and the provision of a superior sword—copied from the Savanti!—totally unnecessary. Well, by the Blade of Kurin, as they usually dumped me down naked and weaponless, the question did not arise.

Next time they dragged me up to see them I'd damn well ask the question. Weapons on Kregen are life.

And, of course, death.

Very quickly we discovered that the lights of the city did not illuminate any night-time high-life. Torches hitched to corners revealed empty alleys. The taverns were all closed. The place had a dead smell to it.

"What we should have expected." Surrey spoke philosophically.

My annoyance over the Star Lords' shabby treatment of me in the matter of their new sword coupled with the undoubted dryness of my throat made my response somewhat harsh. "You know your way around this city, Surrey. The Everoinye told you. Where do we go to find a wet?"

He laughed lightly, quite amused at my tone. "Yes, Jak. A little action does dry the throat."

Well, I grumped to myself, by Krun, you couldn't fault him for that, could you? And, of course, here was another example of the helplessness of we great kregoinyi finding ourselves dumped down into strange surroundings with no friends or ports of call. "Cheer up, Jak. We're finished here. The Scorpion will arrive soon."

Grunting some unintelligible reply I looked about at a loss. A dog barked, lonely and remote; otherwise no sound disturbed the city. The mobs were inside the palace, then, having their fun. From the Savanti's point of view they'd spared a numim family in order to save the many apim inhabitants of Larnydlad from retribution.

Before the shuttered front of a tavern—The Disabled Duck—the blue radiance glowed into being. The shape of the Phantom Giant Blue Scorpion hovered over us. Surrey went flying up, arms outstretched. He dwindled into the ambient blueness. No one who was not a kregoinye in the normal way would ever see that astounding vision.

"About time, too!" I said. In the next second up I went. Headlong into the blue vortex of wind I hurtled. "And I'll have something to say to the Star Lords!" I sounded uglily malignant.

Coldness struck through to my marrow. Up and then down, around and around, and finally with a thumping great smash, I was catapulted out of Larnydlad—to where?

Yellow sunlight dropped about me. Absolute dismay gripped me and my vitals shrank. The thrice-damned Star Lords had flung me contemptuously back to Earth!

Was this a punishment for my recalcitrant attitude over their new sword? How long, this time, would I be banished from Kregen?

As you know, it is not my intention to spend long in this narrative over my sojourns on Earth. There was, indeed, work to my hand here and I spent a somewhat messy time in the Balkans. When that business was done and the ragged refugees found new homes, I was free to go about my own desires. Well, that is sarcasm supreme. My desires were to return to Kregen at once.

There had been work for me here; I felt strongly that the Everoinye also intended to remind me of their power—I'd mouthed off at them, and this was the dire result.

That trip back to Earth threw up one astonishing fact.

How many times have I said on Kregen that I was four hundred light years from the planet of my birth? Many and many a time. To my utter astonishment I found that new astronomical research put the distance of Antares, Alpha Scorpii, at five hundred and twenty-two light years distance.

Obviously, the distance in itself made little or no difference. But I had the footling feeling that had I provisioned myself for the journey then I'd have run out a hundred and twenty-two light years short. Despite the ridiculousness of the feeling, I shivered a trifle at the idea I'd been much further away from Earth than I'd imagined.

When, at last, at blessedly last, the Blue Scorpion swooped down on me, I was thankful past words to be returned to the horrific and marvelous world of Kregen—five hundred and twenty-two light years from the planet of my birth.

Eleven

When I awoke the freezing cold had gone and warmth once more clothed the land. For a few heartbeats I just lay on my back, relishing the gentle rocking of my body. I was in a boat; no doubt of that.

I was back on Kregen, there was no doubt about that, either.

A raucous squawk screeched down from above. "Wake up, Dray Prescot, Emperor of Onkers! There is no time for you to lie on your back like a sluggard!" My eyes flew open. Oh, yes, there he was, turning in tight circles directly above me, a dark shape against the light. Although I couldn't make him out properly, and my eyes blinked a few times accustoming themselves, I knew his black beady eye regarded me with his habitual disfavor, head cocked on one side.

Sitting up smartly, I realized I wore all my kit and weapons, and, amazingly, the superior mesh mail shirt from the Star Lords stretched over my shoulders. I swallowed down. "Well, you bird of ill omen! What do you want?"

"There is work for the Everoinye to be done!"

"When isn't there?" I snapped out churlishly.

The Gdoinye ignored that. "There is a great evil let loose upon the land. It is there, for the Star Lords sense it. But it comes and goes, and there is no sense to it."

"Where away, you foolish bird?"

"Urn Vennar."

Instantly I became deadly serious. Khe-Hi had warned of sorcery. Urn Vennar—although I'd been away from Kregen for only a short time, I trusted Didi was now fully recovered. She intended to sort out her problems in her province. Could this great evil be connected with the Nazabni Ulana Farlan?

"You will go—" started the screech from the air.

"Aye, aye, I know."

By this time I could make him out more clearly. Abruptly, he flipped over and went flying off under the rays of the twin suns, his wings pounding furiously at the air. I craned to watch him. He flew directly towards a white speck that must be the Savanti Dove. With that awe-inspiring stoop of a raptor, down he went helter-skelter.

The white Dove eluded him with a supple twist and swarmed away aloft. By the time the Gdoinye recovered from his dive, the Dove had flown.

In the next instant the Gdoinye vanished.

I let out my breath. Looking about I knew at once were I was.

Buildings of various heights and different styles lined both banks of the canal. Just opposite me a four-storey edifice constructed of pretty pink brick had one end rebuilt in a duller red brick. That end had been knocked into pieces during the Time of Troubles and despite our best efforts we'd been unable to find a pink brick to match. I was afloat on the Laringen Cut, which joined the Great Northern Canal where Nath the Hides' warehouse stood.

Sometimes when I return to Kregen from Earth it seems to me that many seasons have gone by, and at other times barely a sennight.

On this occasion the latter served.

Everything about the dangers promised in Urn Vennar rushed in upon me. There was no time to lose. All the same, I did hope that dear old Seg had sorted out the damage from that confounded hurricane—and that King Zeg had the Kaofarils under control.

A coarse voice hailed from the rear: "Hoi, fambly! Look where you're going!"

I swung around. I sat in a little dory and the craft was about to be struck by the blunt bows of a lighter impelled by four long sweeps. Seizing up the oars I rattled them into the rowlocks and gave way, hauling the dory out of danger. The lighter went past in a great wash of foam. "My apologies, dom!" I yelled. The sweeps went in and hauled and came out with that practiced twist, and the lighter surged past. A catastrophic ramming had only just been averted.

"Use the eyes the Good Opaz has given you!" With that last admonition, the lighter pulled away.

When Vondium burned during those dreadful times and the old emperor had been foully murdered some of the Proud City survived practically intact. Not a lot, true, but some. Now as I pulled along I felt satisfaction at the progress of the re-building program. Drak was doing a good job as Emperor of Vallia. I'd see him, of course, and get what information he had on the state of things in Urn Vennar. Then I'd have to hotfoot it there and Drak would have to spare me a voller.

What was more important than anything else, I'm sure you know. I hungered and thirsted for news of Delia. To see her—well!

Naturally, even on Kregen, dreams don't always come true. Mind you, by Djan, dreams on Kregen come true far more frequently than on Earth!

This time the dream was not fulfilled. Delia of Delphond was not in Vondium. She'd be off adventuring for the Everoinye or for the Sisters of the Rose. And, still, by Vox, I didn't know which of those two missions made me tremble for her safety more.

The Emperor Drak and the Empress Silda were away on an imperial progress through the south-west of the island. These journeys were necessary to keep the people of Vallia in touch with the center. So, perforce, I went to the serious men and women of the Presidio who ruled Vallia in the absence of the emperor. They now occupied a brand new building, the Presidium, which was not all gold and ostentation, but was a place for practical work. It was large, to house the many branches of the government. When I'd been emperor I'd found the Presidio most useful in freeing me from much of an onerous workload.

They jumped to assist at once and gave me all I asked for.

So, the following day, after some stupendous meals and meeting old friends and dealing with a mass of correspondence, I observed the fantamyrrh and stepped aboard my new voller. She was a swift seven-place craft called *Purple Violet*, and I loved her at first glance.

From the aerial platform atop the Presidium the elders called the remberees, and I hollered them back against the wind rush—and we were off, flying up through the marvelous air of Kregen, darting through the streaming mingled ruby and jade radiance of Zim and Genodras.

Some good news had been given me: Drak had immediately sent rescuers and resources to Seg to assist in the aftermath of the hurricane. The violent fury of wind and sea had abated, and down there in South Pandahem they were trying to rebuild and get back to normal.

It surely is a wonderful thing to be the master of a wealthy and powerful empire! And, by Krun, I'd been only too happy to shift that burden onto the broad shoulders of Drak. So I flew northwards.

The news about the hunting party in the Eye of the World cheered me. Didi stayed in Zandikar with Velia and mended apace. Rollo the Runner had taken himself off to Whonban, the mysterious place in Walfarg in the continent of Loh where Wizards of Loh were born and received their education. He'd fallen out with his tutors when young, I wondered what had taken the scamp back there. A girl, probably.

As for King Zeg—his news was that for the moment they were

containing the inroads of the Kaofarils. You may imagine my relief that the Great Call to Arms had not yet sounded. Had the Azhurad gone out when I was on Earth, and I had not answered, then I'd be Apushniad once again. That was a fate not to be borne.

The slipstream slammed against the low windscreen and I sat comfortably ensconced in flying furs and silks, munching on a handful of palines. The rich yellow berries invigorate the digestive system and are one of the great joys of life on Kregen. *Purple Violet* flew north towards Urn Vennar with the thrum of air past her hull like music in my ears.

To be thus flying above the land of Vallia on Kregen with the beaming rays of Zim and Genodras all red and green about me was undeniably an idyllic experience. All the same, I missed the simple fact that Delia of Delphond, Delia of the Blue Mountains, had not arranged the provisions and packed the hampers and seen to all the necessities of such a flight. Oh, yes, how in so many more profound ways I missed that superb lady!

So be it, then! A pallan of the Presidio had been appointed to look after my needs. He had performed his duties punctiliously. He was extremely zealous. Extremely! His name was Rango Nalgre na Voilarmin, and his nickname was Nalgre the Punctilious. That name was well-earned. He'd taken it upon himself to inform Nazabni Farlan that the Emperor of All Paz was about to visit her province. He chided her that all should be in order to receive so august a guest.

At a stroke, therefore, any ideas I harbored that I could arrive in Urn Vennar incognito were dashed. I could not be Jak, or Dak, or Chaadur, or Kadar, or even Drajak. Again outside pressures forced me into rigid pathways. I must be Dray Prescot, Emperor of Emperors, Emperor of All Paz, and ex-Emperor of Vallia.

What a lot of piffle! I shall spare you the unending rote of greetings that met me, the constant repetition of majister this and majister that. Just take it that they called me majister from crack of dawn to set of Suns—and through the night, too, by Krun!

Still, all was not gloom and doom. The good folk of the Presidio and Urn Vennar did not know of the technique taught me by the Wizard of Loh, Deb-Lu-Quienyin, who was a good comrade. He had shown me how I might change the appearance of my face so that close friends could not recognize me. Mind you, by Krun, the process still stung like a million bees cavorting over my craggy old physiognomy.

That was a small price to pay—and, anyway, the painful effects were lessening each time I used the technique.

So, I could be Drajak or any other of the names I used if I wished. As *Purple Violet* hurtled on through the streaming suns shine beaming from the Suns of Scorpio, I rather fancied that I'd be feeling a few bee stings in the near future.

Drak, Silda and Delia had visited Didi in Zandikar whilst I'd been away on Earth. The rest of the family had managed to tear themselves away from their compelling pursuits to visit. Zeg remained fiercely possessive of his niece and everyone agreed Didi would be best off if she stayed to mend in Zandikar. The mean little thought occurred to me that I was glad to have been out of that argument!

So, I shall spare you the tedious details of the reception and the displays to greet me in Urn Vennar. They put on a good show, though, give them credit for that.

During the shenanigans I had to wear fancy clothes with a mazilla so tall I fancied the jeweled high collar would jangle against the chandeliers. The food was good, and the wine reasonable. The dancing brought back happy memories and when, as is inevitable in Vallia in Paz, the singing began, I joined in lustily.

We had many of the old favorites. There was a new song in Vallia at this time, a chirrupy little tune that ran around like a puppy chasing its tail. The words were a rigmarole of nonsense that could be interpreted as one wished. It was called the Otlora song because the singers made their own sense out of the nonsense.

Here on this Earth a common custom is to name children after the reigning monarchs. This is not done in Vallia. Seg, in naming his first born Drayseg, flouted Vallian custom because he was not Vallian, hailing from Erthyrdrin in northern Loh. So, therefore, when we sang that diabolically clever song, 'Old Drak Himself', everyone knew exactly who was meant. Of course, the song had been written for a long dead Vallian Emperor; nevertheless, now it referred to my lad Drak. So, I sang the song right lustily, by Krun!

These frolics gave me time to take stock of the nazabni. She reminded me of a little gray rabbit, crouched down, ears flat. Trim, neat, the bun confining her dark hair wound excruciatingly tightly, she had a firm round chin which reminded me of her father. Appearances can only go so far to reading a person's character. She appeared to act with firmness and decision. As the jollifications trumpeted on with fetes and tournaments and song, I judged she relied far too much on her chief pallan.

As for her chief pallan, Nath Swantram, known as Nath the Clis, I knew his type passing well. A fellow who'd risen in the world through ability and ruthlessness, there was absolutely no difficulty in guessing the dark ambitions simmering in the breast beneath the magnificent robes. He would repay watching. He was all attention and flattery. Yet in him and the nazabni I detected a febrile undercurrent of unease.

With much circumlocution and painful delicacy they got around to asking me why I'd flown into Urn Vennar. The transparently honest answer served. Until the Princess Didi recovered she was concerned about her province and wished only to help through me. Any problems would be dealt with fairly.

"Problems!" said Ulana Farlan, with a tiny laugh more suitable to a schoolgirl than a nazabni. "Oh, no, majister. Apart from all the usual and tiresome chores, we have no problems."

"Quite," added Nath the Clis.

That night I altered my face only by a small amount so that the bee stings were hardly noticeable, and sallied out into the city of Gafarden in simple clothes. I carried weaponry—naturally, by Vox!

A drink in a tavern here, a wet in an inn further along, gossiping, listening, sizing up the mood of the people, I came to a conclusion. Given that Nath the Clis was efficient and that the nazabni listened to him, then the pair were lying in their teeth. I felt absolutely that they could not be in ignorance of what was going on.

There had been murders. Two Chuliks had been found up an alley dreadfully mutilated. Both were members of the city guard. Both their faces were contorted in a fixed rictus of insupportable terror.

A Fristle had been found in four different locations, neatly dismembered. He, also, had been a member of the city guard.

These three jurukkers had served in the personal guard of Nath the Clis. His captain of the guard, a powerful-looking Rapa hight Ringald the Iarvin, supervised security wearing a worried face.

So far in Gafarden these events had not caused a panic—after all, Kregans live more closely to murder and mayhem than even the inhabitants of the most unruly cities on Earth. What caused most alarms were the expressions of fearful terror—of horror—stamped on the faces of the victims.

Nath the Clis must have tight hold of his subordinates for not a single word was spoken in the palace about the murders. Maybe I was putting too much importance on the affair. "A few murders in the back alleys of the city, majister," he'd say. "One expects that." And, unfortunately, that was true. All the same, I sensed the general unease about the place, a lurking fear that would not exist if these murders were merely routine thud and blunder crimes.

The next morning Nazabni Ulana came down to the second breakfast dressed more splendidly than usual, and with a certain amount of makeup on her small face. Among those partaking of the meal a fine-looking man took my attention. Clad in the uniform of the Vallian Air Service, with many bobs across his chest, he radiated confidence and careless charm. His hair was by a tone or two lighter than the usual Vallian brown, giving him a leonine countenance.

At his side a slip of a girl simply soaked up the airman's charisma. She stood still, listening to him; but she gave the impression she was dancing on air. Her pert face glowed, looking up.

Nath the Clis introduced them. "The Lady Ahilya Vorona. Jiktar Yavnin Purvun."

I gave them the lahals and we talked for a few moments. I fancied they'd make a fine couple. I finished my cup and, politely, turned away as old limping Ornol the Books nodded to me. I saw Nazabni Ulana Farlan. She stood awkwardly, one hand flat on the table, the other to her breast. Her face seemed dipped in wax. She stared with her brown eyes wide upon this bright kampeon, Jiktar Yavnin Purvun.

He remained completely oblivious of her and of her look. He busied himself in finding replenishment for the Lady Ahilya's cup. Then Ornol the Books started to tell me of plans to build a new library, which he wanted me to ask Didi's permission to name after her. I assured him she would be delighted, and congratulated him on all his good work to bring enlightened culture to the new city of Gafarden.

Ulana turned away, abruptly. She walked from the breakfast room with short, choppy steps. Well, this moil was no business of mine. Still, I did feel a pang of sympathy for the nazabni. There was no doubt at all that the gallant airman, Jiktar Yavnin Purvun, was a splendid example of Vallian manhood. The Lady Ahilya must be well satisfied to land such a fine catch.

The breakfasters departed to see about the business of the day. A guard entered, looked about, saw Nath the Clis and went over. They talked quietly, heads together. Then, quickly, they left the room.

No decision was required for me to follow them. They hurried along the passage. After a few turns the guard pointed to a door and Nath Swantram knocked. He knocked officiously. Hanging back unnoticed, I watched. He knocked again. The door did not open.

The guard said: "I saw him go in, jen. He is due on parade."

"Well, by Vox, why doesn't he answer and open the door?"

After more fruitless banging, the chief pallan said: "Break the door down."

The door was stout lenken wood. The guard trotted off and returned with three of his comrades, all armed with axes. So, curiosity getting the better of me, I sauntered along and joined the group.

When he saw me, the Clis swallowed down. "Ah, majister."

I nodded and the guards went at the door. After some lusty swings and a splintering of wood chips, the door smashed back.

We all entered, to stand stock still at the scene that met us.

Crouched in the far corner, the Rapa cadade seemed to be merely a blot of blood. His hands were lifted above his head for protection, and they gleamed yellow-white as the bones showed through the tattered flesh. Blood splashed the furniture and curtains. As we stood, petrified, he slowly toppled sideways into the pool of blood. On his face such an expression of horror as no man should suffer told that he had died in mortal terror.

An examination of the room revealed that the windows were barred and the door bolted from the inside.

"How can this be!" Nath the Clis put a hand to his scar.

One of the guards said: "No one could have got in, jen."

Harshly, I ground out: "Yet he is dead."

To myself I added: "And dead in the classic locked-room mystery."

Twelve

Confusion reigned. In no time at all the news spread throughout the palace and went like a prairie fire into the city. The enigma of the locked room tantalized. People openly connected all the murders in conversation, and rumor piled upon rumor. Doors were locked tightly at night, few people ventured onto the streets.

Beside the tortured body of the cadade, Ringald the Iarvin, we found a shield-shaped piece of paper. Blood spattered its whiteness. The figure one, boldly inscribed, superposed pictures of a fighting sword and an axe.

This made me think on. There had been three previous murders, so how could this be number one? Unless, of course, they were not connected. My conviction was that they most certainly had something to do with one another. Maybe whoever was carrying out these crimes didn't rate three jurukkers as important. He'd—or, by Krun, she'd!—started with the captain of the guard. Who, then, was number two?

And—would there be more after number two?

There was history to all this. So I cornered the chief pallan in his office and put the question directly.

After a couple of burs of talk I stood up, abruptly, and bid him remberee, and stalked off. He gave absolutely nothing away, vowing that he understood nothing of the murders. His hands were clean, he said, and he wished only to get to the bottom of the affair as soon as possible. And, all the time we'd talked, I'd felt this powerful current of unease flowing from him like a psychic wind.

Now, all the ordinary folk of Kregen, the so-called 'little' people, wanted much the same things as their counterparts on Earth desire. They wanted a nice wife or husband, a nice house, nice children, nice friends, a nice job to last them all their life—although, by Krun, that changed with the passing of the years. They would like a nice preysany to ride, or a mytzer carriage for the family, just as an Earthly family would like a nice motor car. Also, they would like to be able to take nice holidays in a nice holiday location.

All these nice things the ordinary folk would like.

What they did not like and resented happening in their city, despite their knowledge of the unruliness of Kregen, was a string of horrific and unsolved murders taking place on their doorsteps.

Elders of the various guilds, the priests of the many temples, the grave merchants, made their representations to the chief pallan.

You had to admire the skill with which Nath Swantram fobbed them all off. The murders were isolated and unfortunate incidents. The guards were on full alert. Take proper precautions, and no harm could befall you or your families. The unrelated cases would soon be solved and the unhanged rogues of murderers brought to justice.

Oh, yes, he did a fine job and not once would he allow any further approach to the nazabni. The chief pallan would take care of everything, as he always did.

Now, having told you of the desires of the so-called ordinary folk of Kregen, it is essential that I add that the flame of ambition burns fiercely there, too. In one sense, this fine lordling Nath the Clis represented that wish-fulfillment to a nicety. Comparisons between Earth and Kregen are deceptive. Never forget that Kregen is not like Earth in so many ways. Oh, yes, Earth is, as I have said before, a most wonderful world. There is a great deal yet more to be learned about Solterra. But Earth is not Kregen.

One widespread custom on Kregen is that of the mercenary trade. Your ordinary girl or boy can become a paktun, and if she or he is lucky and brave and resolute, why—the whole world is open for the taking! These thoughts made me wonder if there was any significance in the fact that all the four murders had paktuns as the victims.

Just after the hour of mid that theory received further impetus. A Rapa—what was left of him—was discovered among the garbage in the yard at the back of The Skoll and Durkon, a rowdy tavern frequented by those without the wherewithal for more pretentious premises. Now, in the normal course of events this murder would be put down to a quarrel among the tavern's clients. In this case that dreadful look of total horror was stamped indelibly on the Rapa's face.

He, too, was a paktun and had been a member of the palace juruk.

There was no shield-shaped piece of paper with the number two.

These facts tended to confirm my tenuous theory. The best place to start the investigation was at the beginning. There was no apparent reason why Ringald the Iarvin should enter that particular room. It was merely an office devoted to the domestic staff's needs, where the captain of the guard would not normally be seen.

So I asked to see the guard who had raised the alarm.

The jurukker, Banko the Swarthy, was apim. He stood rigidly to attention in the small room placed at my disposal by Nath the Clis. "Sit yourself down, Banko." I pushed a flagon of ale and a jug across the table. "Take some refreshment."

He obeyed with all a swod's alacrity when a wet was in sight.

He had newly joined the palace guard and looked to be promising. He had his eye on the next step up the paktun's ladder, the bronze pakchav. Prompting him now and again, I got him to reprise what he had said about what he'd seen.

The cadade had been on his way from the breakfast chamber to take the mid-morning parade. Banko saw him abruptly halt, look about 'like a hunted rat' and then fairly hurl himself into the room and slam the door shut with a crash. Banko heard the bolts smash home.

That seemed to be that. "Were you alone, Banko?"

"Well—as a matter of fact, no. A man in the corridor saw exactly the same. He asked me what was that all about."

The next step was obvious and I asked that the second witness be brought in.

He was found and came into the interview room, and I offered him the same courtesy shown to Banko. His name was Nalgre Nevko, a gentleman of Vallia. He'd been a paktun, wearing the silver pakmort, and had recently returned to Vallia with a tidy sum in savings and the desire to establish himself. From him I received the distinct impression of a man of determination, despite the way he sat casually, who, as a koter of Vallia, would make his mark in society. He was politeness itself, and the 'majisters' spilled from his lips.

"Yes, majister, I saw that poor devil of a fellow run into the room. I couldn't understand it. I've been a cadade in my time."

We had a short pleasant conversation about the places he'd served and I warmed to him, one old paktun to another. In him I saw a deep-rooted strength of character, and felt a comrade could stand with him in the turmoil of battle and rest assured.

He was too young to have served in the Times of Troubles, and he said all his family were gone to the Grey Ones. Now he wanted to settle down and lead a useful life for Vallia to justify their belief in him. Also, he added, he would like to be prosperous, by Vox!

He wore decent Vallian buff. He carried rapier and main gauche. Like Jiktar Yavnin Purvun, his hair was lighter than the usual Vallian brown. He had a small scar along his left cheek. When we said the remberees he coughed and said: "I have enjoyed our talk, majister."

"So have I, Nalgre. If you think of anything else, contact me at once. This is a serious business."

His thin lips in that hard face, beginning to part in a smile, closed with a snap. He nodded. "Yes, majister, a nasty business."

When he'd gone I ran over in my mind what he'd said—or, rather, what he hadn't said. He was interested in antiquities. Well, there are very very many folk on Kregen interested in antiquities. They like to discover ancient tombs and sepulchers. They like to go delving after treasure. There is some, not much, genuine interest in the past from a historian's angle. The main thing Nalgre Nevko hadn't said from his point of view, was to ask outright for my help. He'd obtained an invitation to breakfast; the nazabni had disappeared so what of business he proposed had, perforce, been postponed.

By his mettle I judged he wouldn't have used the word 'abandoned'.

As you know, many and many a time I'd given a helping hand to deserving folk, remembering my own penniless days on Earth. There seemed every chance that the next helping hand would be received by Nalgre Nevko.

As for my interest in the murders, well, put that down to plain old curiosity, coupled with my promise to Didi. Problems are sent to us to be solved.

In pursuance of that I wrote a letter and had one of Nath the Clis's merkers travel down to Vondium to deliver my message. The recipient was Naghan Raerdu. Oh, yes, you will recognize the surname.

And the first name, too. But this was not Naghan the Barrel who had been my own personal secret chief spymaster for many seasons. This new Naghan Raerdu was the grandson. He was as thin as a leather thong where his grandfather had been as fat as a—well, as a barrel.

Naghan Raerdu well understood the tasks required of a spy. His father had decided to be a zorca breeder and had done well. So the grandfather told his tales to the youngster, and, fired up, the fresh Naghan Raerdu took over his grandfather's office. I welcomed him. Lean as a lath, he could pass unnoticed, just like his fat grandfather. The letter required him to use his skills in Gafarden.

He'd acquired a nickname, Naghan the Slippy. This referred to his physique. To the very few people who knew his qualities, the soubriquet perfectly described his character and aptitudes.

The next morning saw the beginning of the Day of Opaz Resplendent. There would be religious services, much dancing and singing, and processions along the boulevards. The citizens would gyrate along the flower decked avenues, chanting with incessant rhythm: "Oolie Opaz! Oolie Opaz!" This would last all day until the Suns of Scorpio declined and, exhausted, we could repair to taverns and inns for refreshments—and, as this was Vallia, more singing.

Because I was the Emperor of All Paz—ha!—I was press ganged into attendance, and would escort Nazabni Ulana Farlan. This I welcomed, as I needed further information on the lady before making a judgment. Well, the Day passed with all due ceremony. A small group boarded a narrowboat to return to the palace. I was not surprised to see Jiktar Yavnin

Purvun there, for he was your hero to the life. With him, of course, was the Lady Ahilya Vorona, clinging to his arm.

The Pallan of Canals, plump Lorgon ti Thrandor, with his even plumper wife, Thisi, swelled at the importance of the company they kept. Two or three other functionary couples made up our number, together with Koter Nalgre Nevko. No doubt he had passed gold to secure his invitation. I couldn't fault him too highly on that.

The chief pallan, Nath Swantram, boarded another narrowboat to lend his dignity to the important folk aboard. So, a happy throng, we sailed along the canals as the water gleamed emerald and ruby in the last of the suns. The Maiden with the Many Smiles rose into the star-studded sky and cast down her smiling pink radiance.

The Day had passed successfully and now, as we steered towards the branch cut that would take us to the palace, clouds gathered and overspread the stars and the Maiden with the Many Smiles.

Shadows dropped down about us making the pretty colored lanterns strung about the narrowboat bright spots of light. They gave little overall illumination. The boatman in his holiday uniform knew the way and headed unerringly into the mouth of the branch cut. For the moment no other boats accompanied us. We continued to turn, our wash sloshing away in a fan, ghostly gray against the dark water.

"What—?" shouted fat Lorgon ti Thrandor. As the pallan of canals he might be fat and fussy; he knew his job. The boat scraped alongside a wooden jetty, rocking the passengers. Everyone held on with grips of steel. The dark water overside—oh, no, dom, don't on any account fall into the canal waters of Vallia!

The pallan's angry shout was cut short by a meaty and ugly thunk.

The haft of a throwing knife protruded from his throat. As his wife started to shriek in terror, Jiktar Yavnin bellowed: "Jump ashore, now! Bratch!"

A quantity of confused yelling and struggling began as the boat's passengers struggled, jumped, fell, ashore. A flick of my eyes showed me the boatman leaping into the water and striking out boldly for the far bank. That rast was in the plot, then.

Because we koters of Vallia were out on a Day of Festival we wore only rapier and main gauche apiece. In the terrified company there were but two men capable of putting up resistance—Yavnin Purvun and Nalgre Nevko. Oh, and me.

As the stout gentlemen and their half-fainting ladies scattered away in search of hiding places in the bushes, a small hand touched my arm. Nazabni Ulana Farlan stood at my side. In her other hand she clasped a long Vallian dagger. It had, I noticed, a pretty ronil hilt.

She nodded tautly towards the black-clad assassins as they raced towards us. "They desire my life."

The leading stikitche hurled a knife. The thing glinted once and then chingled against the blade of my rapier, tweaked across Ulana's breast. Before any more terchicks could be hurled, the assassins crashed into us. There were six of them. There were three of us, and a small, frightened but brave woman with a dagger.

Now stikitches know how to use the assassin's tools of their distasteful trade. Curtly, I snapped at Ulana: "Stay at my back!"

She gasped, so I stepped before her. The warm night air shivered with the screech of steel on steel as blades crossed. Give my companions for the night, Nalgre and Yavnin, full marks. One was a mortpaktun, which speaks for itself, the other an officer in the Vallian Air Service. Their rapiers twinkled right merrily.

Not that, by the Blade of Kurin, there is anything merry about the kind of fighting one has to adopt in these circumstances in order to stay alive.

The first savage passage at arms left one assassin dead, one stupifiedly grasping a shoulder from which his arm dangled uselessly, and a third falling back onto the grass where Nevko promptly spitted him through. Also, it left Yavnin with a long cut across his cheek.

As the assassins gathered themselves to spring on us again, a shout lifted from the shadows of the bushes. "You shints! I'll have your liver and kidneys for breakfast!"

A figure bounded across as the clouds cleared. He wore holiday finery and he brandished a sword. In the next instant we were at it hammer and tongs. Now the odds were even as far as numbers were concerned, the fight went our way. The stikitche with only one arm battled gamely; but he went down as the newcomer cleft a slicing blow across his neck. Yavnin spitted his man. Nevko, adroitly avoiding a lunge, twisted and swirled his rapier flatly. He almost decapitated the assassin. Rapiers can slash with deadly effect as well as thrust.

In the pink radiance of the moon the grass stained darkly. The women hiding in the bushes were trying not to make a noise, and succeeded in stifling their cries to unsettling moans. We looked about. The four of us were wrought up. Stikitches are unpleasant at the best of times, and this attack smelled vilely of treachery.

The Lady Ahilya ran fleetly to Yavnin and clung onto his arm. "You're all right? You're all right?"

"Yes—better not to look at the corpses."

Nazabni Ulana sheathed her dagger. Her color was up. "Where are my guards?"

Whoever had organized this murderous attempt had also suborned her guards. That mystery would be probed. As the important functionaries emerged from the shelter of bushes, hushing their womenfolk, I turned my attention to this imperious newcomer. He'd shouted 'shint!' and the sword he employed so effectively was a lynxter. Yet he looked a Vallian, although with heavy dark features and lips thicker than thinner. He began to wipe his blade on the black clothes of a dead assassin. The others were all chattering away, and declaring how dreadful all this was. Ulana held herself bravely, although I saw the small tremble in her lips, clamped. "Let us get to the palace!" she said, savagely.

"I'll pull the oars," declared Yavnin. "All aboard."

In the aftermath of a potentially disastrous incident like this, folk often act in strange ways. The quicker they all reached the palace and had something to fortify themselves and started to regain normalcy, the better.

I went across to the newcomer, cleaning his sword. "Llahal and Lahal. We are much beholden to you."

"Llahal and Lahal. Never did like stikitches, dom."

"How came you here—it's well out of the way."

He looked up, the heavy features softening. "Went for a kiss and a cuddle. But the lady was reluctant—by Vox! What happened to her?"

At once he started to run back to the bushes. I shouted after him: "Your name, dom?"

"Tobi Vingal," he yelled back.

"Come up to the palace in the morning—see the guard commander."

He vanished into the shadows of the bushes. If the lady was reluctant she'd probably have sheered off by now. The racket of the fight was no inducement to stay waiting for Tobi Vingal.

The light had caught the bronze glint at his throat. He struck me as likely and reckless. So, I turned and walked back to the boat and Jiktar Yavnin Purvun pulled us back along the cut to Ulana's palace.

Thirteen

Amazingly, the flung knife had not killed Lorgon ti Thrandor, Pallan of Canals. He'd been wearing an ornate clasp at his throat to fasten his light boat cloak, and the knife lodged in the elaborate curves of gold. He went about with a yellow bandage around his throat, for the knife's tip had just nicked his skin. He told everyone who cared to listen that, indeed, verily, he was thrice-blessed by Opaz.

The post-mortem on the incident threw up the significant fact that the new cadade who had replaced the dead Rapa had not been told to supply a separate guard for the boat trip back to the palace.

He was a khibil, very red-whiskered and supercilious, demanding and receiving somewhat higher pay. Jiktar Pranton the Faranto wore the silver pakmort at his throat. I, for one, did not believe he would be derelict in his duty as the cadade.

So—what conclusion did that lead to? When a general, or a politician, plans a campaign one of their most pressing needs, if not the most important, is information. Correct information can save the lives of thousands of soldiers, can gain thousands of votes. I itched for Naghan Raerdu to arrive. Perforce, whilst waiting, I had to scratch around myself.

Nath Swantram was beside himself with fury over the attack on his naz-abni. He could offer no explanation why there had been so serious a lapse in security. I was not present when he interviewed the new captain of the guard; but Jiktar Pranton the Faranto emerged from the pallan's office with a khibil face as scarlet as the setting Zim.

The corpses of the assassins had been collected up and searched and, as anyone who knew the ways of stikitches upon Kregen could have said, nothing of significance was found.

Because of Ulana's insistence that the attack had been directed against her person, I gave little credence to the theory that the assassins had been hired to kill the Emperor of All Paz. As far as the great plan of the Star Lords to unify all the continents and islands went, we progressed, slowly, it is true. I did not think that any ruler of his own country who objected to joining in the scheme would employ stikitches to kill the Emperor of All Paz. Mind you, by Krun, that was always a deadly possibility. So far, I'd not had to force any ruler or any country to join up. That would be totally counterproductive, a point I had been at pains to spell out to the Everoinye.

The orders I gave the guard commander of the morning watch, a Hytak, Deldar Nath the Rumphious, were precise. He was to bring that rascal Tobi Vingal directly to my office. I really wanted to know how he'd fared with his lady love. I presaged a trifle of doom there!

Although this unfortunate business of the attack on Ulana was clearly of importance, I knew I must not lose sight of the greater problem. We had a serial killer in our midst. If he—or she—was not rapidly apprehended then more poor devils would be shuffled off to the Ice Floes of Sicce with awful grimaces of utter terror engraved on their features.

I still felt strongly that the two cases, Ulana and the attempt to murder her, and the serial killer who obviously intended to number his principal victims, were not connected.

All the same, by Krun, as an ancient san of myth once said: "A prudent man will put on two coats when venturing out into the snow." Under my normal Vallian buff I wore the superior mesh link given to me by the Star Lords. I wondered if that was their intention, and then pooh-poohed such a wishy-washy idea. The Everoinye had given me the mail shirt for my trip to the Dawn Lands. They'd simply forgotten to take it back.

Anyway, as San Blarnoi adds, "An even more prudent man does not even think of venturing out into the snow."

That was all very well and true; all the same, I had to venture out into the dangers of these cases to honor my pledge to Didi.

Lorgon ti Thrandor, ostentatiously fingering the bandage around his throat, had, in his capacity as Pallan of Canals, made enquiries about the treacherous boatman. The fellow was called Ven Norgad the Sweeps. He was not to be found. He'd absconded, leaving a wife and four children to fend for themselves in their narrow boat.

"The attempt failed," pontificated Lorgon, "and now Norgad is in fear for his life from the person who paid him." He snuffled up a good lungful of his office air, and added: "And from me!"

Commiserating with him on his lack of news, I hoped he would soon discover the whereabouts of Norgad the boatman, and left his office.

My quarters were on the other side of the palace and I had to pass by the front on my way back. The usual crush of people milled about in the anteroom past the main entrance with its guardroom. Walking on I was just about to enter the corridor leading to my office when a voice hailed jocularly: "Lahal, dom! I trust you're in fine fettle this morning after last night's little knock about."

Here he came, striding up with a big smile beaming on that heavy-featured face, hand outstretched. He wore proper Vallian buff and his wide-brimmed hat sported a jolly red and yellow feather.

"Lahal, dom," I replied, shaking his hand. "You look fit."

"Oh, aye. Can't let a bit of a fracas spoil breakfast, now."

"Quite so."

At that point a Hytak loomed up at Tobi Vingal's shoulder. The morning guard commander wore a look like the break of season's thunderstorms over the Pilotus Mountains—black with fury. He grasped Tobi's shoulder and span him around.

"I told you to wait for me! Why—"

"Oh, aye. But I spotted the fellow I've come to see. No harm done, is there, dom."

Deldar Nath the Rumphious drew in an enormous breath so that, like any Deldar, his armor creaked. He was about to let rip with a Deldar's tremendous bellow.

Quickly, I rapped out: "It's perfectly all right, Deldar Nath." I used this form of address as a formality to let him see I was serious.

His huge breath deflated as he said: "But—majister—!"

Tobi's whole attention had been abruptly taken by a beautifully-formed Fristle fifi swaying past with a shopping basket crammed with fruit. Her large, liquid eyes slid sideways to Tobi, and away, and her tail with its pink bow flicked upwards saucily. Tobi sighed. Then, swinging back to the guard commander: "Majister? You said—is he here? Where? I'd deem it an honor just to say Lahal."

Deldar Nath the Rumphious's ferocious features drew out into a smile—a most knowing and satisfied smile of triumph. He made the pappattu with all flourish and ceremony.

When the introductions were at last finished, Tobi Vingal rolled his eyes up. He stood to attention. He said: "You will have my head off, then, majister?"

"Oh, I think not just yet awhile." To the Deldar I said: "Thank you, Nath. I'll take charge of this ragamuffin now."

"Quidang!" bellowed Nath the Rumphious and turned about smartly and marched off with a crash. Folk tended to step out of his way.

"Come along, Tobi. Let's find some parclear or sazz."

"Sazz," he said at once. He perked up. Bright as a new-minted coin, he adapted himself to situations as they arose. He was very, as is said these days, streetwise. Confident, reckless, happy-go-lucky, he was all these. I wondered just how many seasons of life he had left before his rash ways shipped him off to the Ice Floes.

The sazz was poured from the jug, luminously pink and just sweet enough to allow it to slip down effortlessly. He sprawled back in the chair opposite my desk and was at once fully at ease. The heaviness of his features, his high color mantling the skin, stood in odd contrast to his manner and character.

Now my own Guard Corps had been much reduced of late and as I'd been out of the country so often Drak had taken them under his wing. Make no mistake, though, the kampeons of ESW and EYJ and the other regiments were vowed to Dray Prescot. Drak and Silda had taken my lads on their tour of southwest Vallia to keep them busy.

So, I intimated to Tobi Vingal that, had he a mind to it, I could offer him employment. He jumped at it. He'd had to leave Loh, where he'd been in the guard of some king or other, because the girl's father had sicced a whole posse of heavies on him.

I said: "Loh is a big continent. He couldn't have found you if you were cautious."

"That's right, majister. Still, I was homesick for Vallia."

"That I can understand. And call me jis. It's shorter."

"Quidang!"

One of the under chamberlains knocked and entered and said two koters wished to see me, Yavnin Purvun and Nalgre Nevko. At my instant acceptance of the visit, in a few murs the two were ushered in. The lahals were said, more sazz was poured and so there we were, the four fighting men who'd protected the life of the nazabni last night.

Well, by the Nymph's Button, we got on famously. Before we parted at the hour of mid we'd agreed to meet that evening to find what Gafarden could offer an airman and three paktuns in the way of entertainment. If you find it strange that a so-called emperor could thus sally forth as though he were a normal citizen—well, the many stories and plays of Dray Prescot circulating everywhere primed folk in that belief.

In the afternoon a blue radiance grew in my room and Khe-Hi appeared. He looked worried. The evil our Wizards of Loh sensed was growing. I confirmed the reports of the murders and Khe-Hi tended to agree that they must be a part of what he called 'This Great Evil'. "But there is a lot more to the deviltry than mere murder. By the Seven Arcades! We are groping in the dark here!"

All I could say was: "Keep in touch, Khe-Hi."

The blue glow dimmed and faded and Khe-Hi would be coming out of lupu in Vondium—if that was where he was currently living.

In this account I fear I have been remiss in omitting a somewhat lurid detail. When Tobi visited me and we had talked he'd been at pains to sit a trifle sideways. My curiosity about his lady love was well and truly answered. He sported a truly beautiful shiner, an eye blue, black and purple, a prodigious bruise across half his face. The lady had swung a half brick in a handbag, I shouldn't wonder. My delicacy in not alluding to this facial appendage resulted in my omitting to mention it to you who listen to these tapes.

Of course, by Krun, human nature being what it lamentably is, I felt a broad smile growing all over the inside of my face. Poor old Tobi! He chased 'em—and they clouted him in the eye!

Ever the optimist in affairs of the heart, Tobi would be confident that tonight when we hit the town he'd find the charming lady of his dreams. Cynical old reprobate that I am, I found I was looking forward to Tobi's next encounter with enormous gusto.

In due course, therefore, that evening I dressed in good Vallian evening clothes ready for the meeting. No thought was required to strap on the rapier and main gauche. I flung a deep cherry-red cape about my shoulders and drew up the silver clasps. Halfway down the second corridor I stopped. I fingered my chin. Hm'm—well—yes. So I turned about and marched back to my room. Far better, by the Blade of Kurin, to have your battle implements to hand just in case. So I hauled up the scabbarded Krozair brand beneath the cape. I admit I felt all the better for that comforting weight on my back.

I told my three carousing companions that they should call me Kadar. If they wanted a cognomen, then Kadar the Blade would suffice. Whilst the name of Dray Prescot is well known by reason of the plays and books, the face of that miscreant is not at all well known. And that, by Vox, is as it should be—totally unrecognized.

Beside his rapier Nalgre Nevko wore a fighting sword. The clanxer, the old straight cut and thruster of Vallia, had been largely superseded by adaptions of the Havilfarese thraxter and, more particularly, by the drexer. This, a very superior sword developed by Naghan the Gnat and myself, owed much to what I could remember and adapt of the Savanti sword. Yavnin wore a regulation drexer with his rapier.

It fell to Nevko to quiz Tobi. "Why d'you wear that foreign blade, Tobi? What's wrong with a vanxter?" This name, vanxter, was given impartially to any of the various patterns of fighting swords newly developed in Vallia.

We sat comfortably in The Roildon and Renang, an establishment of the better class where the wine was good, the floor covered in tile rather than rushes or straw, and the serving wenches undeniably pretty. Tobi laughed in his easy way, quite belying the heavy sullenness of his features. He drew the blade and twisted it in the air.

"My old lynxter? This sword has served me well. When I took employment in Loh, at the very first engagement my clanxer broke." He grimaced at the memory. "I liberated this from a Chulik who took a deuced long time to die, by Vox!"

Yavnin nodded. "And no rapier and dagger, Tobi?"

"Never learned to use 'em, Yavnin."

I thought I detected a tiny note of insincerity in Tobi's answer. Still, this was his business. So we drank and talked quietly, interesting professional and technical stuff. The evening wore on.

As a wary old leem-hunter, I noticed we all drank sparingly, nursing the glass. This confirmed my opinion of my new companions as men of quality. In the new Vallia after the Times of Troubles, with the lead given by the armies we'd created, drunkenness was very rare. Oh, sure, there were still plenty of drunks; they were frowned on. We knew how to have a good time without becoming stupidly soaked in drink. When I say drunkenness was rare and yet there were plenty of drunks still, I speak of the ratio, you understand.

We went on to The Frolicsome Nit and from thence to The Rokveil and Aeilssa. The floor was strewn with rushes, the wine was merely passable and the serving wenches were hearty knockabout girls.

I noticed that Tobi used 'By Vox!' almost as an afterthought. He more frequently came out with: 'By Lingloh!' or 'By Hlo-Hli!'

I wondered just how long he'd spent in Loh. When I managed to guide the conversation to a point where I could casually ask him, he proved evasive. "Oh, a good long time, Kadar, since I was a green coy when I went." Then, sipping his drink, he added a comment which puzzled me. "They don't much care for their own Wizards of Loh—well, really they're Wizards of Walfarg—over there. I got along with 'em."

One thing you could say for Koter Vingal, he was not at all overawed by the company he kept. All pomposity aside, an emperor is not always an easy sort of person to get along with. Oh, yes, well, I know I'm not your usual kind of emperor at all. But a Jiktar in the Vallian Air Service rates respect. And, too, Nevko was a mortpaktun, Tobi a chavpaktun, so there was respect there, too.

Yet this rapscallion laughed and drank in his free and easy way, perfectly politely, as though he caroused with these folk of quality every night in the year. Then he spotted a serving wench who was far and away more desirable than any of the others carrying their trays of jugs of ale and goblets of wine. He perked up. You could almost see the sparks flying off him.

Tobi quaffed off his wine and stood up. "If you will excuse me, koters, I have a little pressing business to hand."

"Pressing!" scoffed Yavnin. "I'll wager she has a man to care for her tall as a pine tree and wide as a barn door."

"Quite likely." Tobi twirled his hat between his fingers. "Still, doms, I'll wager he hasn't a tenth of my charm."

At that we all burst out laughing, even me. "Good luck, then, you rogue," said Nevko, still laughing. "I'll wager that—" He stopped speaking suddenly, and lifted his goblet jerkily.

"What? What, Nalgre?" demanded Yavnin.

"Oh—I wonder how you'll explain your black eye, Tobi."

Tobi laughed in his easy way. "That's my pallan jaunting to capture the queen." The Jikaida reference was perfectly clear. You could on Earth have said it was his ace in the hole. He winked his good eye at us. "Her sympathy for me will know no bounds."

At that moment, a furious row erupted over by the windows. Loud voices raised, fists crunched home, bottles flew. We all looked over. A knot of battling men reeled about crashing into tables and chairs, overturning flagons. Yavnin stood up sharply.

"Those are airmen! And the locals are blattering them cruelly. By Vox! I'm not having that!"

He started off across the floor. Men and women scattered away from the brawl. The object of Tobi's intended affections dropped her tray as a bottle whistled past her pretty head. Tobi yelped and ran towards her. Pandemonium broke loose.

Nevko shook his head. "I have to go outside, Kadar, if you will excuse me."

I waved a negligent hand. "By all means. I do not intend to get a black eye like Tobi's. I'll be here." Nevko nodded again and went towards the rear doors.

The whole milling mass of fighters surged this way and that. By the time Yavnin reached the brawl the inevitable happened and he was in time to follow as the struggling confusion smashed welteringly through the window. In a gargantuan smash of glass and splintering wood the lot toppled through the window still striking and kicking.

I just sat where I was and sipped my wine.

With the catastrophic disappearance of the brawl some semblance of peace and quiet returned. The landlord ran about wringing his hands. All three of my drinking companions had gone. The ripe aromas of spilled ales and wines rose to clog the air with fresh odors. The night's entertainment was perking up, then.

Finishing the glass I poured another. The place quietened down.

I wondered if our Tobi was having more success this time. There was no sign of Yavnin or Nevko. Naturally my mind started to fret over the various problems besetting the city of Gafarden. Only twice was it necessary to decline the offers of young ladies, and I placed a silver piece in their hands to maintain the peace and quiet.

That peace and quiet was shattered by a fresh outburst of yelling. This time the shrieks told me the situation was entirely different. People in mortal terror spilled into the room, running crazily every which way. I stood up. Crazed men and women ran screaming for the doors leading out to the street. I looked past them.

A terrified fellow barged straight into me, his head turned to stare back. I held my balance and grabbed him, twisting. His face looked like the wrung-out dishcloth flung down after washing up for the annual barracks dinner. He gobbled out words. Now slang along the streets changes over the years, and what is fashionable one year is derided as old-fashioned the next. I will not repeat his words for they were the typical gibberish used by denizens of street culture. Suffice it to say I understood. He was talking about a horror so great he could not describe it. I released my grip and threw him away.

The weltering rush of people all passed and I stood alone in the center of the floor.

The thought occurred to me that perhaps it would be highly prudent for me likewise to run off. I am a firm believer in running off so as to return—with reinforcements—later.

Nothing stood between me and the far doors from where the people had fled screaming in terror. Perhaps I *should* run off. But I wanted to know what was going on. What had caused this utter panic?

So, not fast, not slowly, I walked towards the rear doors.

The doors stood ajar. I peered down the short corridor leading from the adjoining chamber of The Rokveil and Aeilssa.

I saw—oh, yes, by Djan-kadjiryon—I saw!

In a single all-encompassing glance I absorbed that horrific picture. Immediately I leaped back and to the side beyond the doors. I dropped down to one knee. I swallowed down—hard! Then I put my head around the corner to look once more upon that demonic scene.

The monstrous thing should be dead; but it was alive. The stench churned my stomach. Rotting flesh dangled. Slime dripped. Brown bones protruded through tattered strips of skin. The blasphemous thing had once been human, apim, and now it shambled from one side of the corridor to the other. It clasped the head of a man in one skeletal hand. The rest of him lay scattered about the floor.

I saw the eyes! Two red orbs glowed within the hollow sockets. Twin glaring spots of crimson hung unsupported in darkness.

Before I could make up my mind what to do, the undead creature shrilled piercingly. Truth to tell, I just didn't know what to do for the best. My fist grasped the hilt of my Krozair brand and I half drew. The thought occurred that probably cold steel would not harm it.

It writhed in a flurry of rotting flesh, remnants of robes dangling. It twisted sinuously—and shrank! It thinned. It became a slender wisp. Straight for the door it undulated, under the door it slithered, squirming through the narrow gap between door and floor.

The blasphemous undead monstrosity vanished.

I let out a breath. All I could think of was—so that solves the mystery of the locked room murder!

Fourteen

I, Dray Prescot, Vovedeer, Lord of Strombor and Krozair of Zy, had to make a chilling decision. And that fateful decision must be made quickly.

Well, then, better to meet that dire fate with a sword in my fist. The Krozair brand felt good. As firmly as I could I marched up to the door in the side of the corridor. My left hand did not tremble as I grasped the handle, which surprised me.

I flung the door open.

The room was empty.

I sucked in a lungful of air which still carried the foul taint of the undead creature. Now what? I turned about and a voice hailed from the corridor. "Hai! Anyone here?"

"Just me, Yavnin," I shouted back and stepped to the door.

He was staring a trifle sickly at the remains of the poor devil ripped to pieces. "What deviltry's been going on here?"

The door at the far end of the corridor opened before I could answer and Nalgre Nevko and Tobi walked through. They stopped stock still. Without thought, swords appeared in the hands of my companions.

I shook my head and sheathed the Krozair blade. "This is no time for swords, koters. This is damned black sorcery."

Not one of them had seen this flesh-dripping, stinking, skeletal ambulatory corpse. They didn't know what to make of it. Well, by Krun, neither did I! This spectral apparition had a material body, otherwise it could not have done what it had. The thing must come from somewhere and, clearly, had a purpose to its actions.

A patrol of the city guard turned up to sort out the brawl between the locals and the airmen. They were quickly apprised of the new situation. The grisly remains scattered in the corridor were collected up and removed.

The landlord was called and, trembling, managed to identify the gruesome exhibits as once being his barrel master, Nath the Ale. Then the landlord was messily sick.

This death did not fit the pattern—at least, in my opinion. The unfortunate Nath the Ale happened to be in the wrong place when the undead monster struck. So—what had been the thing's real purpose?

When we looked in the next room along the corridor, we found out.

The Gon's bald buttered head shone in the rays of a cheap mineral oil lamp. A dagger protruded from his chest. He lay askew on a pile of old sacks. He'd died easily compared to the person who had killed him.

Once again the fellow was crouched in a corner, smothered in blood. His face bore that awful look of absolute horror. This, then, was the work upon which the monster had been engaged. His escape had been interrupted by the barrel master and the clients coming from the adjoining rooms. They'd been supremely fortunate to get away.

Bending, I picked up a scrap of paper carefully placed on the murdered man's chest. Shield shaped, it bore the figure two and a roughly drawn picture of an axe and a vanxter.

So—that settled the question of connected murders.

All this tale of blood and horror I have recounted in almost a quiet matter-of-fact manner. Believe me, I could feel the deep dread within me, the sense of ancient evil existing when it should be long buried and forgotten. Those patrons of the tavern would need great comfort to recover—some would never regain their proper senses.

Enquiries would have to be made. Quite clearly, our night out had finished, so I invited these three new companions up to the palace. In sober fashion we went up to the deren and to my room. Wine was poured; snacks provided. A little Och lady brought the food. The news had outrun rumor. There were, thankfully, no longer slaves in Vallia, and the Och serving lady, Flostan, knew all about it.

"To think I chided him for leaving his breakfast," she said, chattering on in her artless way. A long time servitor, she was by way of being a favorite of Princess Didi's. "When he said he was leaving the palace I couldn't believe it. He said he was coming into money." She shook her head and wiped her face with her middle left. "And now, it's too dreadful to think what happened to him."

"Who?" said Tobi in his affable way.

"Why, master Garan the Stick."

A few more words elicited the fact that master Garan the Stick was the Gon who'd died with a dagger through his heart. He'd been an under chamberlain in the palace. His throwing up his employment on the promise of coming into money perplexed his friends.

"He didn't come into money," said Nevko. "He came into a dagger."

Flostan wiped a plate fussily with her yellow cloth and went on to say perhaps he'd expected the money from Elten Ornol Lodermair.

"Oh?" said Tobi. "Who's he?"

"Why, he was the one so dreadfully killed by—by—"

"Quite, Flostan," I said. "Best try to put that out of your head. It's all over. We're well-served here. Get you to bed."

She shook that little oval Och head and muttered something about sleeping safely when ghastly monsters crept about Gafarden. When she'd gone I was only too well aware that many a person would lie uneasily in their bed this night.

Yavnin said: "So the Gon was blackmailing this Elten, and he killed him. Then—"

"And then this thing murdered him—" cut in Tobi.

"And then—" Nevko began. Someone else interrupted, and so we went on discussing and arguing and trying to make sense of it.

At last they went home and I had a few burs sleep and was up early. There were many questions to ask and much work to do.

Judge, then, of my pleasure when later that morning in my office the door opened soundlessly and a lean, lanky, gangling figure, as it were, sidled in. He wore clothes of so stunning effacement and moved so silently that, by Krun! you had to look twice to believe he was really there. I stood up and made a foolish remark.

"Naghan. Lahal. No under chamberlain to see you through—" I stopped myself, and clapped my old black-fanged winespout shut.

"Lahal, jis. Oh, I just sort of, like, wandered in. No one offered to stop me."

In Opaz's truth, my guess was that no one had tried to stop Naghan Raerdu, known as the Slippy, simply because they hadn't seen him.

I sat him down and poured parclear and laid out the whole situation here in Gafarden in Urn Vennar. He nodded once or twice and I knew he was making mental notes of salient points.

"These appear to be classical revenge murders."

"Someone with a twisted mind, obsessed with vengeance, yes."

I told him I'd been through the records from the time Khe-Hi first discovered 'the Great Evil.' I'd found nothing significant. The death of this Elten Ornol Lodermair gave us a fresh start. How was he connected with the Rapa blackmailing him? All the deaths were of people working in the palace—except Lodermair.

Naghan the Slippy stood up. One minute he was sitting down sipping his parclear, the next he was on the way to the door, saying: "I'll look into it at once. Remberee, jis."

By the time I answered with my remberee, the door was closing on him—soundlessly.

I fancied that even the ghastly undead creature might miss seeing Naghan Raerdu. By Vox! I just hoped that was true!

Shortly after that, Tobi came in and flopped into the chair. He looked thoroughly disgruntled. "You were right. She had a graint-sized fellow waiting for her. I had to be very polite." Then, because he was Tobi, he heaved up a laugh. "By Lingloh! I do pick 'em!"

Of my two other new companions, the four of us drawn together by companionability and the fact we'd stood shoulder to shoulder to fight off bloody-minded assassins, Yavnin was escorting the Lady Ahilya and Nevko had business with some important merchants of the city.

"It is surprising," said Tobi, "how the city keeps going. The news of this Opaz-forsaken thing is everywhere, yet people still go about their daily affairs."

"Ever been to Culvensax, Tobi?"

"No. Never, jis. Why?"

I told him I wanted him to go through the records for the past season to find any reference to Culvensax. "Anything at all, mind."

"Quidang!" He stood up at once, downed his parclear, and went.

The door opened with a squeal and closed with a crash. The difference in exits of Naghan and Tobi was most marked. Anyway, Tobi wasn't in good form. He'd accepted the parclear instead of his usual sazz without a murmur. And the door brought back memories.

I looked at my hands. They did not tremble, yet I felt they should be shaking at my thoughts. When I'd opened the door under which that Opaz-forsaken undead thing had squirmed, I'd felt myself to be the biggest fool in all of Kregen. Oh, I daresay if it got out the playwrights would mark this up as another wonderfully bold and brave deed on the part of the hero Dray Prescot. I knew damn well I'd been a reckless onker. Still, at the time, it seemed the thing to do.

A totally ridiculous and unexpectedly powerful craving swept over me. I felt an overpowering need for a good cigar. The feeling was quite irrational, of course. Smoking is a mug's game. How glad I am that the habit of smoking and fouling the air is unknown upon Kregen. All the same, a nice fat cigar, right now...

Thinking of Earth I realized that my old briar, perfectly packed with good rich dark tobacco, would be far preferable at this stage in my deliberations. Opening the desk drawer I took out two shield-shaped pieces of paper and laid them out. I pushed them about with a forefinger. Number One and Number Two. How many more were there to be before we solved this ghastly puzzle?

One interesting fact was that the paper was that superb Savanti bond, far superior to the ordinary Kregan paper. How significant was that? Did it have any significance at all in all this mess?

For the rest of that day and most of the next I was caught up in tiresome duties consequent upon the rank and position thrust upon me. Many dignitaries and notables had to be given the opportunity to bask in the reflection of the emperor. Ha! All a nonsense, of course, yet one had a lively sympathy for these good folks' ambitions. They were trying to make of the new city of Gafarden a worthy capital of Princess Didi's province of Urn Vennar. Perhaps the very word province stiffened their backs in pride.

At any rate, these meetings and functions gave me further insight into the state of mind of Nazabni Ulana Farlan. Her chief pallan I wouldn't trust with a bent copper ob piece. Ulana was so besotted with Jiktar Yavnin Purvun that she appeared a wraith of herself. She was absent from so many functions and duties that folk remarked on it. My impression of her, vastly improved since she'd tried to stand staunchly with her little dagger as the stikitches raced in, was now coupled with a lively feeling of sympathy. It is the very devil when the object of your affections yearns for another. Ask poor old Tobi!

In the event, I found myself coming to the firm conclusion that Didi must discuss with Drak and Silda the replacement of Ulana with a new Justicar for Urn Vennar. With Didi still recuperating and far away, the decision would be left with the emperor and empress.

I must confess that the decision, unpleasant though it was, relieved my mind of the burden. There would be fresh opportunities for Ulana. I'd see to that.

As to her relationship with my new comrade Yavnin—here I heaved up a sympathetic sigh—there seemed little hope of a happy outcome. The Lady Ahilya had her feet well under the table there, as they say in Clishdrin.

The letter I sent Drak and Silda was very carefully worded. Very carefully composed indeed, by Zair! Ulana would be discharged from her position under some pretext—and health seemed the most likely—and a new Justicar would arrive. I found a petty little laugh in the consideration of just what Nath Swantram, Nath the Clis, chief pallan, would make of that, and just how he would react.

On the very next day three more murders were reported.

Reluctant though I was, I felt it my duty to visit the frightful scene. The small gaming room at the back of The Potion and Quill was like a hecatomb. Bits and pieces of the three Fristles lay scattered about, their fur ripped and bloody. One of them, called Fenrio, less distributed than his two comrades, had received a mineral oil lamp in the face. He'd caught fire and burned. The smells were disgusting. I left as soon as I decently could.

No numbered shield of paper had been discovered.

That afternoon Tobi Vingal reported back. He remarked on the latest crop of murders, shaking his head. He'd sifted carefully through the records and had come up with some interesting facts.

Naghan Raerdu, earning once again his nickname of the Slippy, appeared in the room. I looked across and waved him to the other chair.

In making the pappattu between them I studied them closely. They might resent another person thus closely in the emperor's confidence. I'd have to watch that. Naghan's research dovetailed into Tobi's.

Essentially, they told me that some time ago, just before Khe-Hi sensed the new evil upon the land, the heir to the Eltenate of Culvensax had returned home to claim his rights. He'd murdered the cadade and the Judge when his cousin proved to be the legitimate heir. He'd been arrested and condemned to death before he could murder Ornol Lodermair.

"It all fits, jis," said Naghan, and Tobi nodded in confirmation.

"Aye. But where does this damned supernatural undead thing fit in?" I brisked up. "Right. We have a lead. We must discover a lot more yet."

We had a name to follow up. A name that might be the vital clue we needed.

That name was Tralgan Vorner.

Fifteen

Drak wrote that Silda and his imperial progress through south west Vallia went well. Rumors had reached my lads of the Guard Corps that their Kendur was back in Vallia. They grew fretful. Drak said that he'd have to release them very shortly so they could join me in Urn Vennar. He was disappointed at my report on Nazabni Ulana Farlan. He'd written to Didi telling her that he was relieving Ulana. She'd be asked to join the court for a short while. Silda wanted to talk to her. Drak was sending a justicar to take over the province. This was Nath Verunder who'd been a Kerchurivax of the Third Phalanx, and managed to carry on after his wound but who was now better employed as a justicar. He'd be flying in in two days' time.

Then Drak went on to write that he was mightily disturbed by the reports of a series of bloody murders in Urn Vennar. Was I doing anything about this?

At this I stopped reading and let out a remark about Makki Grodno. All the same, I knew a little about my eldest lad, and knew he was putting in the sly dig. Well, by Vox, he'd inherited that little foible as much from Delia as myself.

This kind of atrocity was exactly the sort of event that was supposed to have finished in Vallia after the Times of Troubles, Drak wrote. The marks of the pen fairly scored the paper. As Drak would have dictated the letter, it was abundantly clear the stylor had his nose well down to the paper and was jumpily responding to Drak's mood.

As soon, he said, as this imperial progress was over, he'd be up to Didi's province to sort things out.

Yes, that was my lad Drak, a real true blue emperor, and I wouldn't have him otherwise. Silda sent her love. The signature scrawled bold and powerful and more deeply indenting the paper than the nervous stylor's writing.

The Suns of Scorpio still shone in the sky over Urn Vennar and life went on. Whilst people kept to themselves and took care over their meetings and journeys, there was not as yet a general feeling that Gafarden faced a full scale crisis. People remarked that all the murders involved members of the palace guard, except for Elten Lodermair, and they conjectured in their down-to-earth way maybe he wasn't quite all that he should be as a noble of Vallia. So they took comfort from these facts and believed the murderer would not come near them.

Life, then, in Gafarden went on, if a trifle uneasily. Naghan Raerdu continued his slippery business in worming out more of the secrets of this affair. Tobi Vingal waltzed in on the morning full of the joys of spring. He didn't have to tell me, but he did. He had found a new lady love. Her name, he said, brushing his lips with his fingertips, was Tassie. She was absolutely gorgeous. Mayhap at last his luck had changed. "Excellent, Tobi," I said, briskly. "Now find Yavnin Purvun and Nalgre Nevko and ask them if they would care to join us in an aerial jaunt to greet the new justicar, Nazab Nath Verunder."

"Quidang!" He reached the door, opened it with a squeal, and then swiveled. "Jis—ah—" He coughed. "May I bring Tassie?"

Without change of expression, I said: "Yes. Oh, and I suppose you'd better see if Yavnin would like to bring the Lady Ahilya."

He nodded and set off, slamming the door at his back.

The next item on the agenda was to check with the chief pallan the full details of the trial and execution of Tralgan Vorner.

Nath Swantram spread his hands. It was a perfectly routine matter, he told me. Vorner killed the cadade and the Judge and would have murdered the Elten had he not been apprehended. It was, he said, an open and shut case. Then, fingering his scar, he added: "The odd thing was, majister, that at the end he repented of what he had done. Lodermair had forged the will, that was proven, and could never have profited by it."

"Explain."

"Lodermair was called to Gafarden to account for his actions. Of course, he died before the nazabni could pronounce her verdict."

"So how did Vorner repent?"

Here Nath the Clis stood up and paced across my office. "Why, majister, he desired that his cousin should not profit from his criminal action. Tralgan Vorner made over his will to me so that justice could prevail. This ghastly murder supervened."

I sat back in my chair. "So you're now the Elten of Culvensax."

"It would seem so, majister."

Oh, he was smooth enough all right. I called for the papers and everything was in apple pie order. I felt in my bones he was a rogue; but of proof there was nothing.

The chief pallan said that, naturally, he would be flying out to welcome the new nazab. His formal sympathy for Ulana Farlan rang hollow in my ears. He said the remberees most politely and went out quietly. Only when he'd gone, I realized I hadn't said that I and a party of friends would also be flying out to greet the new nazab.

As was proper for his rank, the chief pallan flew in an official voller provided by the province. She was a small craft carrying only the pilot and Swantram's party of three functionaries. I must admit to surprise that he hadn't chosen to use a more prestigious craft crewed by the Vallian Air Service.

The cloak he wore against the chill of heights made me think back a few seasons. My Val! So long ago, and yet like yesterday... The cloak gleamed pure white with ling furs. It made of the chief pallan a striking figure.

When my companions joined me on the landing platform Swantram's flier had already taken off. A huddle of clouds drifted in from the west and a few drops of rain fell. Sometimes a chilly wind swept off the Black Mountains and then the folk of Vennar donned thicker coats.

The Lady Ahilya wore a shimmery silvery number that reached down to mid thigh and was perilously suspended by two narrow strings. If she wore any underclothes at all I couldn't tell; but before I could make some comment about the cold, Yavnin heaved up with a massive cloak over his arm. This was white, too; although not ling. Ahilya turned her face up to him, laughing, flushed, and I suffered a sudden pang as the image of Ulana's face rose unbidden in my mind.

Nalgre Nevko joined us carrying a wicker container of wine bottles. If

I call Nalgre Nevko by his surname I merely followed a custom to distinguish between the many men with the same first name. When Tobi strode up a girl walked at his side, holding his arm for reassurance. She was of that oval-faced, full-lipped, heavy-lidded eyes beauty that some fellows find irresistibly attractive. Her trim figure was sensibly clad in flying leathers. Tobi swelled with pride.

When the pappattu was made she spoke up firmly enough; yet she was still uneasy about this company Tobi had brought her into. Here was another example of the dreadful effects of rank and perceptions of position upon perfectly ordinary nice folk. If the Lady Ahilya started to ride upon her high zorca, to coin a phrase, I might have to be a trifle tedious. Tassie worked in the records office, and that was where Tobi had met her and chanced his arm. So far, so good. Would Tassie be another to land him a black eye? Poor old Tobi!

Yavnin made professional remarks about my flier, *Purple Violet*. His leave was reaching its end and he would soon be off to Vondium to take command of an Air Service voller. From what he didn't say I gathered his new command was not all that he'd hoped for.

Somehow or other I had to get this little party into a holiday mood, although, Zair knew, with all the problems besetting me flying off for an aerial picnic could alleviate only a tithe of them. Nevko was determined to have a good time. The clouds parted, the magnificent ruby and emerald rays of the suns streamed mingled about us, a bottle or two was opened, and we were off. The Lady Ahilya laughed and draped the white cloak about her silvery self.

The six of us in the party meant there was a spare seat. When I'd suggested Ulana might accompany us if she was not flying with Swantram, she'd shaken her neat head. "Thank you, majister. No. I am to fly back in the airboat bringing the new nazab. I will wait here."

The real reason she hadn't accepted my invitation was laughing with Ahilya as we climbed into the sky. Poor Ulana couldn't face the torture that kind of proximity would bring.

Not one of us mentioned the murders, for which I was grateful.

Yavnin moved up to take over the controls whilst I went back to find a goblet. Ahilya at Yavnin's side made a very pretty picture.

In his raffish way, Tobi came out with: "Now we'll see some pretty sharp Air Service flying, eh, Yavnin?"

Tassie pulled his arm, her face turning pinkish.

"It's just straight forward now, Tobi," said Yavnin. He pointed ahead. "And there they are."

"Oh, Yavnin! I can't see them!" Ahilya's voice rose almost to a squeal. "Where are they?"

"That's Air Service eyes for you," quoth Tobi, laughing.

In that, of course, he was perfectly correct.

Up ahead a small airboat drove towards us. Beyond her the dot against the sky's brightness must be the voller bringing the nazab. Clearly, Swantram and his party had gone aboard her, and this explained his choice of so small a craft.

As we waited to close the gap I reflected that I knew little of young Lady Ahilya. Her parents came from Orvendel and she'd met the gallant Air Service Jiktar when visiting a school friend in Vondium.

She knew nothing of Ulana's hopeless passion for Yavnin and I fancied he had no idea, either. Had they known, I surmised their reactions would be to feel sorry for the prim little nazabni. Then they'd shrug and try not to feel guilty, and say this was the way of the world.

The oncoming airboat swirled up and past. Nevko was just opening another bottle. The pilot gave us a cheery wave and we waved back. No doubt he thought what a jolly picnic party we were.

We did not heave the empties over the side. That was not the done thing in Vallia, for who knew on what poor wight's head the bottle might fall?

The nazab's flier drew nearer and I recognized her as a packet airboat, a trim craft with sweet lines, a few ballistae and comfortable accommodation. As I stared another voller swung in from a light scattering of cloud. She was all black, and reminded me of the fliers used in the Ice Trade, where entrepreneurs bring ice down from the Mountains of the North to the warm customers of the south.

"What!" exclaimed Yavnin. We all looked in alarm as the black voller made a determined rush onto the packet. Dark agile figures swarmed over the sides and down onto the packet's deck.

"By Hlo-Hli!" yelped Tobi. "The shints are attacking her!"

"Drive on, Yavnin." My voice cracked out like the whip of a Sister of the Rose. "Fast as you can!"

Yavnin thrust the control levers hard over and *Purple Violet* surged forward like a charging vove. The air rushed past crazily as we went plunging down toward the fight.

"Oh, Yavnin!" Ahilya's voice broke into a wail. "It's dreadful!" She clung onto our pilot's arm with both hands.

I gave Tobi a hard stare, nodded to Tassie, and the ragamuffin responded instantly. Tassie took Ahilya's arm and Tobi assisted and together they brought the poor girl back and sat her down. She sobbed quietly to herself, huddled up in her magnificent white cloak.

There was no doubt that the gallant Air Service Jiktar could fly. He swerved *Purple Violet* around in a scorching curve to bring us riding just above both packet and black attacker. By that time I was perched on the rail ready to go.

Whether or not the others followed me did not matter. Some bunch of cramphs were out to murder the new nazab, or Swantram, or whoever, and they had to be stopped. I jumped. The deck came up with a smashing jolt and I staggered forward for a moment before gaining my balance. The deck seethed with action. Only a single glance was enough to sort out the combatants. Nazab Nath Verunder had, naturally, brought along a small personal bodyguard. They and the Air Service crew were hard at hand-strokes with the black clad stikitches.

A thump at my back heralded the breathless arrival of Tobi who reeled about until I grabbed his arm and steadied him. The situation was plain to him, too. In the next heartbeat we both dived into action.

Many and many a year ago I'd given up any romantic notions that sword-fighting was glamorous. Oh, yes, a straight one-to-one rapier contest has undoubted charms. But this fracas was the ugly boot in the guts, chop down, trample over and get stuck into the next one, fight. Finesse lay in not getting oneself killed.

The Krozair brand did, in fact, cut a swathe through the black-clothed assassins; but the cunning kick and the occasional head-butt served well. The noise splashed like a spouting volcano across the deck. Blood, of course, ran freely. The stikitches were here for a purpose, and that purpose, stocky, scarlet-faced, limping, struck efficiently about himself with his drexer. Nazab Nath Verunder who was a veteran of the Phalanx wouldn't be cut down without the devil of a struggle.

In the struggling mass of men striking violently in mortal combat there was no sign of the brilliant white ling-fur cloak of Nath Swantram. A pesky fellow whose black clothes were darkly stained struck viciously at my head so that I ducked and swiveled and sliced him low. He let out a screech and fell back. He was a Yoftin, a diff with jackal-features and stiff hair, all prickly and spiky, a member of that race of diffs renowned for their callous treatment of their womenfolk and their inhuman torments of their captives. So I sliced him again as he went down, for good measure and for principle.

That petty if justifiable action nearly undid me as a Croydim swung his short-hafted axe down on my back. A savage roll away followed by an immediate spring up onto my feet and a swirl of the Krozair brand saw the Croydim screech as the steel bit into his guts. He gobbled incoherently with the blood spouting from his middle and mouth, his wedge-shaped face incredulous with shock. I kicked him and leaped on.

The fight sprawling all across the deck of the packet turned into a confused Hack 'n' Slay melee. Yavnin and Nevko joined in and I caught a flashing glimpse of them tearing into the assassins. It was vitally necessary to force a way to the aft cabin where the new nazab struck about him like the true kampeon he was.

His personal guard, a brightly-attired bunch of hired paktuns, fought for their pay; but their ranks were thinning. The Air Service got stuck in in the best traditions of Vallia's airmen. All the same, the black-clad villains pressed on hard in steel and blood.

Nath Verunder was being driven back by sheer pressure which was only partially relieved by my companions' arrival. Spilled blood made the deck slippery. The racket roared on and on, a crescendo of shrieks and savage yells, as the combat swayed back and forth.

In this kind of hurly-burly struggle in the confined space of the packet's deck, the combatants swirled this way and that and became inextricably entwined. As I chopped a Fristle with a most unhealthy-looking bardische axe, I was swung about so that I found myself on the other side of the fracas. The aft cabin's door swung on its hinges to my side and there was clear space between the cabin and me.

Stopping only to swipe a Rapa with repulsive greenish feathers I was able to break clear of the melee and make a run for the cabin.

A hulking great Brokelsh staggered out of the opening. His black clothes were slashed to reveal a brass-studded jerkin. This, too, was slashed and his blood ran out glinting over his black body hair.

The ferocious form of Nazab Nath Verunder followed the Brokelsh. The nazab's correct Vallian buffs were liberally splattered with blood, he'd lost his wide-brimmed hat, and his face, like the setting sun Zim, showed the same concentrated dedication on this fight as had seen him rise through the ranks to his present exalted position. In that flashing moment it seemed to me that the chief pallan of Urn Vennar would have a trifle of bother with his new master.

Now, little time elapsed between that Brokelsh-disposing act and my arrival at the cabin. Verunder had gone back inside. I hauled up and cast a swift but thorough glance back for any rast trying to stick me from the rear. The fight was thinning out. The stikitches were trying to clamber back into their black-hulled flier and being chopped for their pains. Verunder and Swantram were safe and the assassins were defeated. I swiveled about and went into the cabin.

Nazab Nath Verunder lay face down on the threshold. A long Vallian dagger stuck up between his shoulder blades. Just beyond him a haggard-faced servitor was in the act of collapsing. There was blood on his right hand. Nath Swantram, Nath the Clis, withdrew his sword from the body of the servant and the fellow toppled slowly forward onto his face before his master. Swantram put his left hand to his cheek where bright blood dribbled down.

"The cramph tried to kill me!" He gasped it out, as though disbelieving what he was saying. "He murdered the nazab and—"

On that the chief pallan sat down abruptly. He dropped his sword. He looked sick.

Out of this shambles, then, the stikitches had their work done by a resentful servant. It is not unknown.

I thought that perhaps Nazabni Ulana Farlan wouldn't be going to Vondium just yet, after all.

Sixteen

Affairs in Princess Didi's province of Urn Vennar were going from bad to worse. A spate of unsolved murders, the nazabni dismissed, the new nazab foully murdered on his way to take over. Oh, yes, by Vox, affairs in Urn Vennar were in a pretty parlous state.

What, then, of my promise to Didi? You may well appreciate my feelings of resentful frustration. Every which way I turned brought no easy solutions. As for the chief pallan, he'd taken to his bed with his nerves shredded after the assassination attempt. That a trusted servitor of Nath Verunder could prove so base knocked the whole structure of trust between master and servant to pieces. Nath Swantram shivered between the sheets and was not available to anyone.

The traitorous servant, Nath the Pinion, as he collapsed, dying, had tried to speak. He mouthed words. All I could make out was: "No! No!" And the bright blood had dribbled down. "No. The master—I did—no!"

What one could make of that was anyone's guess.

Perforce, I took it upon myself to order that Nazabni Ulana remain in Urn Vennar and the under-pallan, Nogal Venning, would for the moment take over from Nath Swantram. Nogal Venning was the scion of an ancient and elevatedly high family. His ideals of Vallian citizenship, I thought, were above reproach. I spoke to him, shortly and hardly, whereat he nodded and said: "I pledge my loyalty to Nazabni Ulana, majister, as my family have served Vallia long before—" Then he checked himself, and finished up with: "As we have always done."

What he was about to say was something like: "Before some hairy graint of a Clansman of Segesthes stormed into Vallia and claimed the Princess Delia, Delia of the Blue Mountains, Delia of Delphond, as a bride." That was, as far as the generality of people knew, correct.

I nodded in a firm judicial manner, which I judged appropriate, and left him to it.

When they came to clean up the packet they found the stikitches strewing the deck were all corpses. No information might be come by there, then.

The packet, a neat little craft of ten varters, named *Lily*, would be thoroughly cleansed and returned to service.

I took myself off to see Swantram. The wound on his cheek was a mere trifle, as I'd seen, yet he lay propped up in bed swathed in yellow bandages. He'd taken on reinforcements to his personal guard. Since I'd dictated that Vallians should save Vallia when we struggled in the Times of Troubles, we no longer employed mercenaries in the Freedom Army. This diktat did not, however, prevent private individuals from hiring paktuns to serve as personal juruks. Swantram had taken on a little army. We passed a few pleasantries. Nothing was learned on either side, and we parted with the remberees as sweet as honey.

And the role of Nazabni Ulana in all this? She stuck out that little rounded chin of hers and in a most determined voice said that as Opaz was her witness she'd run the province until they appointed another nazabni or nazab. I can tell you, by Krun, I felt for her—felt deeply for her!

She was a lady who inside was all fire and passion, and outside was a prim little mouse-like miss. She did not possess the obvious feminine allure of Ahilya. There was no way—at least for the moment—that the gallant Air Service Jiktar could appreciate that.

The body of Nath Verunder was respectfully shipped back to Vondium, where his widow waited still in a state of shock. Had she not been attending a granddaughter about to give birth, why, she would have flown north with her husband—and, probably rather than possibly, flown to her death. I sent due respects and tried not to feel guilty over not attending the funeral.

With his usual inconspicuousness Naghan Raerdu slipped in to see me. He wore a dark green coat and gray trousers. Fashions change on Kregen slowly. Once women discover dress that is comfortable they tend to remain loyal to that style. Fashions come and go although with nothing like the frenetic dash after novelty of the salons and catwalks of Earth. Men are even more reluctant to change.

All the same, changes occurred. The traditional decent Vallian buff coat, breeches and high boots remained the most seen dress; lately trousers were making great strides—if the pun is allowable.

My personal chief spymaster told me he'd turned up a lead on the assassins. There was a meeting this night. He added: "Two things, jis. First, I would ask you to change your face a trifle. Second, what do I call you?"

Raerdu was one of a very small and select band of folk who knew of my facial contortions. "Agreed, Naghan. As to the face, a simple change ought to do." I pulled my nose. "As to the name, what do you suggest? I leave it to you."

He laughed in his near-invisible way. "I take that as an honor, jis." He ruminated, then: "Larghos Ravan."

"Right. Any nickname?"

"Oh, surely. Um—Silent. Larghos the Silent."

At that a smile touched my lips. Good old Naghan! He wanted to do the talking—rightly so. This was his show. He'd worked out the scheme and would be fishing in familiar waters. As he confided, after he'd run away from home to be a mercenary, and had done that, his grandfather, old Naghan the Barrel, in inducting him into the secrets of what being a spy meant, had set him a test.

"I had to join an assassins band. Up there in the Old Drak's City of Vondium—you know?"

"Oh, yes, I know Drak's City."

Naghan had been successful and had become a member of the Assassins' Guild. The only kitchews he'd seen off were those who, in general opinion, deserved to be shuffled off to the Ice Floes of Sicce. Now, that experience would be invaluable.

Gafarden might be a new city resplendent with splendid new buildings; already the dark underworld had set up shop. Dressed inconspicuously in dark clothes, off we sallied as The Maiden with the Many Smiles beamed down her pinkish radiance. On the corner of Cooper's Alley a girl sidled up. Her clothes were remnants of once expensive finery, now tattered past redemption. Her face, thin to emaciation, had dark purple smudges under her eyes. She looked to have been badly mistreated in her short life.

She and Naghan exchanged the words: "Sompting," and "Fraling," as passwords.

We no longer kept slaves in Vallia. As we followed this abused slip of a girl I felt my anger mounting. She might not be a slave; she was clearly treated as such. She was apim, young, and we followed her out of Cooper's Alley and into a section that, whilst not in the decrepit and unhygienic state of aracloins, was still a twisted maze of run-down alleyways. I realized that we were entering the old village around which the new city had been built. The palace towered above us, riding like a black ship against the stars.

The girl said her name was Paline—and that made her situation appear to me even worse by ironic contrast—so I kept my old black-fanged winespout shut for now. The place she led us reeked of stale ale, spilled wine, decaying scraps of food. The ceiling pressed low. All the men sitting around the table under a single mineral oil lamp wore masks.

Their clothes were normal Vallian evening wear and were richer rather than poorer, sumptuous here and there with laces of gold or silver. But for the black masks, these men could have been sitting at any respectable evening gathering of friends. Apart, also, from the room, which began to wear on me. The quicker we finished this, the better.

One of these fellows shouted at Paline to bring more wine, and clouted her around the ear as she went past. He was a Fristle with brown and white fur. I marked him, the blintz.

Naghan talked and the preliminaries were gone through rapidly. We needed a job done. We had the gold. Then, somewhat jolting me, when the assassin at the head of the table asked Naghan the name of the kitchew, my chief spymaster, very calmly, said: "The chief pallan, Nath Swantram, known as Nath the Clis."

"We cannot accommodate you on that commission."

"Good." Raerdu beamed upon them. "Very good. I trust you will not take my little finesse amiss. It is better we understand one another from the start."

The men around the table shifted on their seats. Their chief rumbled out: "It is better. We understood at once your intention." Paline came half-running in with a couple of bottles clutched to her narrow bosom. The chief waved a hand. "Tell us your kitchew."

"Nazabni Ulana Farlan."

A long pause ensued as Paline went around the table pouring. The tension in the confined room mounted. The mineral oil lamp threw exaggerated shadows. I swear the stinks increased.

The chief stikitche made a decision. "We have already made the steel bokkertu on the nazabni."

"Ah, yes," quoth Naghan with a casual gesture. "But you failed."

They didn't like that, by Krun!

"Go away." The chief finished his goblet and held it out to Paline. "Come back in two days. Remember, you will be watched."

Naghan stood up at once. "Very well. Remberee, koters."

That was a nice sarcastic touch. I doubted this bunch of murderers would appreciate it. So we went out quietly.

Along the dingy street I said to Naghan: "We'll come back in two days, all right. And, by Vox, we'll bring a bunch of the guard!"

"Oh, they won't meet at the same place twice."

"They'll keep an observation on us—they said."

Naghan let out his soft little chuckle of amusement. "They will try. That scruffy Och on the corner—he's one. There'll be another further on. We can't go back to the palace right away."

Now we were out of that pestiferous room I felt much better. I cannot honestly say I looked forward with enjoyment to what we must do; it should at least help to cleanse the blood.

"Tell me honestly, Naghan, what did you think of them as professional assassins?"

"Not much. I'm wondering if they're even affiliated to the Guild." Then, very sharply: "You have a plan in mind?"

"Not so much a plan. I'd like to knock that damned Fristle's teeth down his throat and get young Paline out of it."

"Yes. I like that. That's a good plan."

So you see, even imperturbable Naghan the Slippy had been affected by what we'd witnessed in that den of iniquity.

As for the Fristle, mask or no damned mask, I'd know him again. He had a nick out of his left ear. Naghan spotted that, too.

By this time all the stikitches would have slunk off to their dens, Paline would be away slaving in some dopa den, so we must now see about losing the spies set on us. I said to Naghan that perhaps he could do his famous disappearing act more easily if we parted company. He started to protest, saying he wasn't going to abandon me, so I simply pointed out that I'd turn my coat inside out, changing its color, and stick on a different face. He saw that at once, said: "Remberee," and slid off. I watched him go past a corner lamp and then, so smoothly there was no time to blink, he blended with the shadows and was gone.

Only partially satisfied with the night's doings, I trailed off back to the palace.

I passed a raggedy polsim who was looking about every which way, his narrow face worried. I grunted: "Moonlights," and walked on.

"Oh, moonlights," he replied, and then went on scouring the street.

"Bad cess to you, dom," I said to myself, "keep looking."

Sleep did not come with its accustomed speed that night.

Seventeen

Because my three new companions had stood shoulder to shoulder with me against the stikitches trying to murder Ulana on the canal bank, and because they'd jumped down onto the packet's deck to front the assassins trying to murder Swantram and the new nazab, these three fine bonny fellows had a vested interest in Naghan Raerdu's discoveries. Apart from that, they were well up to the challenge presented by the problem. They were all, I judged, prone to a spot of danger and excitement and adventure.

So I asked Tobi to dig them out and we foregathered in a cozy little teahouse at the hour of mid.

As I'd guessed, they were well up for it.

Naghan reassured them that the bunch of cut-throats we'd met in that dolorous room were, indeed, the same lot we'd fought off.

"Except for the ones who didn't run off," said Yavnin.

"That's how they should all be," quoth Nalgre Nevko.

"Aye," said Tobi. "This girl, this Paline. D'you trust her?"

"She just works for them as a skivvy and runs messages." Naghan put down his cup. "They tell her where to bring the clients."

"Yes," I pointed out. "And she'll be watched as we were." I had to explain that although these assassins appeared not to be a high class bunch, if they were true stikitches they would never reveal the names of their employers. The Aleygyn, the chief of stikitches, struck me as a man who'd slit your throat first and probably not bother to ask any questions after. "Until tomorrow," we said, and parted to go about our separate occasions.

Then, that very same tomorrow that at the hour of dim turned into today, everything changed. For a space life became a whirling dervish dance of frenetic activity. The letter from Drak reached me at the same time as the ruffians he informed me were flying to Gafarden.

Yes, well, I am sure you have guessed what all the commotion was about. My rip-roaring lads of the Guard Corps sailed down out of the jade and ruby dawn. Well, now! Nothing would suffice them but that we should start on a right tearaway party instanter. Many of the faces you have met in my narrative were gone and new ones replaced them. But the Guard Corps spirit thrived and continued like a bright blade down through the generations.

There was nothing I, as their Kendur, could do but join in the jollifications. I told my Chuktars that I would require the lads duly present and correct for the night's entertainment. When I said we were hunting assassins they rubbed their hands, for few if any honest folk care for cut-throat stikitches.

When my three new companions joined along with Naghan the Slippy, the pappattu was made all round. When we set off with a select company, for, clearly, not all could go along, my jurukkers became as deadly serious and determined as they would be advancing into battle.

The plan was for Naghan and I to meet Paline. I'd be away from the others, so could put on that simple face. My lads would surround the building once Paline led us there. Then we'd break in and show these unhealthy assassins what straight face-to-face fighting was with none of your treacherous black-clad rasts sticking daggers in the back.

Naturally, the guard did not go tromping along the road in a solid mass. Habit would have kept them in strict step. We went about the night's business in small bundles of three or four. And, equally naturally, every single one of my jurukkers wanted to go on the raid. Here the privileges of rank became apparent, for the senior guardsmen all chose themselves to go. I hid a smile at the sight of a grave chuktar leading on his nikaudo of a jiktar and two hikdars as the rank and file.

Naghan Raerdu led me on to the far end of the old village. The directions he'd been given by a surreptitious note thrust into his hand by a rapidly disappearing polsim earlier that day brought us to a tumbledown section. Here Didi, before she'd flown off to Zandikar to visit the memorial to her parents, had given instructions that no patching up should take place. The whole noxious area would be torn down and new decent accommodations would be built.

Under a flaring torch a little Och waited for us. He was the fellow who'd been spying on us earlier. I said to Naghan: "Where's Paline? By Krun, if she's—"

"Tsleetha-tsleethi, Ornol," advised Naghan. "We'll find out."

I clamped my lips as Naghan spoke to the Och. His raggedy cloak billowed as he gestured us to follow him. He went scuttling off along the narrow, congested alleyways. The torches became less as we went on. This venturing into unknown danger is the stuff of life to your valiant adventurer, and I admit to a quickening of the heartbeat. All the same, by Zair, I could do without it all the time!

"Why Ornol?" I said.

Naghan Raerdu, hat well over his eyes, answered: "What the Och chooses to repeat is his business. It will cast a trifle of confusion if Larghos and Ornol are attributed to one and the same."

"H'm." Here was another example of the deviousness of my chief spy master.

The rogues employed by the assassins to watch out for them were being taken out by my lads as they advanced. I'd given instructions that I desired no wanton killing, so blatterers would be thunking down on the watchers' heads. There'd be no warning given to the assassins.

My Guard Corps looked magnificent on parade and totally frightening to the foe during battle; half of the Second Regiment of EYJ had been formed from personnel hailing from Drak's City in Vondium. Born rogues, thieves, tricksters, assassins, they'd been taken up and molded in my personal juruk. So there were lads out tonight who could show these half-baked cramphs of Gafarden what real professional skullduggery was all about.

She of the Veils rose splendidly to cast down her golden and roseate light across the dingy alleys. I mentioned to Naghan that I required a few words with the Och guide. Moving ahead rapidly, I took the fellow's middle left into a conversational grip that, struggle though he might, he could not break.

"Have a care, dom!" He snarled it out, cockily confident in the backing of his rascally fellows.

"Where's the girl?"

"Paline? That's none of your business, rast—"

I shook him, gently. "Tell me."

"She's not well." He quietened down; but the whites of his eyes looked like the rinds of weeks' old cheeses. "She's sick."

At that moment the pinkish light all about us faded. Murky clouds billowed across the stars and obscured the moons. We were left groping forward in the fitful sparks from distant torches.

"Dom—my arm." He spoke half-fretfully, half-angrily. "You've a grip like a Shank's teeth."

"You've met the Shanks, then."

Now he shivered. "No, and don't want to, by Diproo the Nimble-Fingered. My cousin, Nath the Slick, has, and he told me—"

"Quite."

The night breathed about us like a savage animal of the jungle, feral, red of eye, waiting to pounce. The fanciful notion was not too far-fetched. The denizens of these miasmic alleys were far more dangerous than the ferocious yet simple-minded beasts of the jungle.

"Well, thief, what's your name?"

He jerked in my grip. Then, hoarsely: "Rampas. Known as the Silky." He jerked that oval head. "There is the place."

Naghan said: "I make out three rasts on guard."

The tumbledown house looked as though a giant had sat on it. A single torch spluttered before a low door. Shadows cloaked the walls. There were three men lounging about outside, as Naghan had said. One was a Yoftin, the second a Rapa, the third a Lliptoh. Diffs of various races can work together when their aims coincide and the pay is good.

We stood in deepest darkness, unseen by those casual-seeming sentries. A soft footfall heralded my three new companions. For a moment or two we studied the layout. I was aware of the growing presence of my jurukkers gathering like werstings eager for the chase and kill.

I was conscious of their movements through the gift of sight in darkness vouchsafed me by the Star Lords. They began to spread out to surround the building. Yavnin said: "I will take the right." Tobi said: "I'll handle the left." Nevko said: "I'll go round the back."

We spoke in hushed whispers. I said: "And don't kill yourselves."

Deldar Vamgal the Arm was making heroic attempts to breath softly so as to prevent his armor from creaking. To him I said: "Take care of this little Och thief, Vamgal. Make sure he does not run off." I shook the scrawny arm of Rampas the Silky. I am sure he had not called out in the sure conviction that had he done so a sword would have slid most silkily between his ribs. "I am sorry to put this duty on you, Vamgal. You are here and the duty must be done."

In a voice he manfully muted, Deldar Vamgal husked: "Quidang!" I placed the Och's arm in Vamgal's iron grip. The Deldar put his awesome face, congested with disappointment, into Rampas's visage.

"You come along o' me. Rampas, is it? You so much as sneeze and your tripes'll be splashing over the cobbles."

A certain delay followed as the troops moved into position. I realized my action about the Och was intemperate. He'd be necessary to enable Naghan and me to approach the sentries. I passed the word for Deldar Vamgal the Arm, who appeared like a wraith from the shadows.

"Kendur?" He had Rampas securely by the ear.

"I'll relieve you of your charge now, Vamgal. We need him."

"Very well, jis. He's been as good as gold, quiet as a woflo."

With a Deldar of my Guard Corps in charge of him, of course the thief had behaved himself.

Pale pinkish radiance sifted down as a straggle of clouds parted. Bringing up the Och thief had delayed us. Now we must move.

Naghan and I, with Rampas securely between us, started off across the cobbles into the moonslight. "Take it slowly." I spoke softly but very sharply, and Rampas jumped.

The three sentries saw us and straightened up. They were ready, I did not doubt, to escort us in or to chop us down as we stood. The latter was up to a somewhat terrified Och thief.

The tension of the moment was shattered by one hell of a racket bursting out from within the building. Shrieks of absolute terror vomited out like a volcano of sound.

The sentries twisted about and weapons appeared in their hands. Rampas stopped stock still. The hideous cacophony erupted—and stopped. Silence smashed back over the world.

The guards opened the door and rushed in. We dropped the thief and sprinted after them. I waved an arm in a gesture to my kampeons to follow. The noise their boots made on the cobbles brought noise back into that eerie silence.

Just inside the building a short corridor led to a door at the end. From this opening the three sentries appeared, running, staggering, their diff faces expressing a horror so great it gripped their guts so that as they fled they spewed up their last meals. They crashed past us and vanished screaming into the night.

Naghan's sword snouted up, the drexer held in the practiced grip of a fighting man. My Krozair brand was ready. What lay beyond that door, I felt with a shudder, would not readily be amenable to steel.

Perhaps, this time, the damned disgusting dead thing would stay and fight.

Naghan the Slippy earned his name not just because of his skills of effacement. His sleuthing skills counted too, perhaps more. He took a pace forward and to the side so that he stood in front of me. In a voice as cold as a wind from the Ice Floes, he said: "Jis. This is the work of the undead thing they call the Spectre. Best you go—"

"I have seen it, Naghan. It is—unpleasant. But I think I cannot run away from it."

I couldn't see his face; I guessed it compressed into annoyance and then resignation. He understood the gravity here.

All the same, as he turned to face me, he had to make a last effort, denying the resignation he understood to be final.

"Then we all must stand, your jurukkers and me."

By the pustular protruding eyeballs of Makki Grodno! I might have guessed so slippery a fellow would turn the argument against me. Of course I could not allow Naghan and my lads to be slaughtered in so vile a way. The virulent presence beyond that door would have no mercy on anyone.

"You—!" I started, then stopped, and sort of half-laughed. "Quidang, Naghan! Go and tell the Guard their Kendur bids them hold."

"And you, jis?"

A grisly reprise started off in my head. Before, I'd faced a door beyond which lay a horrific death. I'd been a get onker to go through. The strongest feeling told me that Naghan would not let me go through, this time, alone.

Oh yes, by Krun, the Dray Prescot who'd sailed down the River Aph in a leaf boat crewed by a giant scorpion might well have gone blustering and roaring through the doorway. In these latter days I had so many responsibilities weighing down my shoulders I felt constrained at every turn. To myself I mentioned both Makki Grodno and the Divine Madam of Belschutz. Just to be a free adventurer, owing nothing to anyone, swinging a sword, leaping headlong into action! That, by the Black Chunkrah, was the life!

To this day I cannot say what I would have decided. The trample of the Guard ceased at my back. The moment hung as it were with incandescent fires. Horror and probably certain death awaited. My fist ached around the hilt of the sword. The door moved. It swung open.

Slowly, out through the doorway and towards us walked Tobi Vingal.

Eighteen

Tobi Vingal did not walk steadily. His face, ashen, looked like a dirty kerchief crumpled up and thrown down into a corner. His hands groped before him like those of a blind man. Those hands were empty, and the scabbard that should have held his Lohvian lynxter flapped as emptily as his hands.

In the next instant a crowd of the Guard appeared at his back. These were kampeons, hard men with iron resolve, who had seen a very great deal

213

of the putrescent underbelly of life in their campaigns. Their tanned faces were set in granite lines. They had seen the pits of hell before; because they were who they were they could cope with the shambles they had seen—just.

Naghan Raerdu started forward. "Tobi! You have seen the Spectre?"

Tobi shook his head in a dazed fashion. "No." He husked his words, reliving the nightmare he had witnessed. "No. A shambles. Bodies—bits of bodies—scattered everywhere. Blood—"

Firmly, ordering without hectoring, I said: "Let us see."

The scene spread out before us in the harsh light from a mineral oil lamp was as Tobi had described. No one said anything. There'd been nine assassins. The objects scattered around among the blood numbered far more than that.

By chance a head on its side nearest me turned out to be that of the Fristle with a nick in his ear. The thought of Paline's whereabouts right now made me lift my foot. I intended to give the catman a thumping great kick to fulfill a promise. I paused and lowered my foot. Disgusting as these assassin creatures were, even here in this shambles they ought to be given the benefit of retaining a little dignity in death.

Tobi had not returned with us and over by an open door in the left wall his lynxter lay on the floor. There were doors to the right and rear. The stikitches like many bolt holes. As I went across to retrieve Tobi's sword, stepping carefully, Yavnin appeared from the right. We allowed him and the guardsmen with him time in silence to absorb the scene.

Shortly after that Nevko came in through the rear doorway, and stopped stock-still. He stood looking down and the group of jurukkers joined him. Again, no one spoke.

When I judged that enough time had elapsed, I spoke in a hard but even tone. "Brassud!" The command braced everyone up. "There is a young apim girl called Paline. Thin as morning mist. She must be found and cared for." Almost, almost, but not quite, I finished with that domineering demand: "Bratch!" My lads would jump to it because of who they were and who had given the orders.

Nevko said: "I'd have been here sooner but the back way is a maze of outbuildings. By Vox! Can you believe this?"

"It's real, Nalgre."

The jurukkers who crowded in through the rear door at first stood as silently as their comrades had done. Then they were swept up in the search for a simple, much-abused lass. It fell to Larghos the Lanky, a hikdar of 1ESW, to find her. He brought her back cradled in his arms, saying she'd been crouched down behind a bed in a stuffy backroom. She was not crying, and I wondered which explanation out of a number answered that. She was carried off to the palace with the strict message that Mistress Leonie the Pantry should take the utmost care of her.

Deldar Vamgal the Arm came up and said: "Jis. This thief—"

Rampas the Silky finished being sick. He hung in Vamgal's grip like a wilting length of wet string. "Oh, he's just a thief, I believe. We can let him go, Vamgal."

The Deldar shook the Och. "Thank your Diproo for mercy." His scowl would have terrified a leem. "And thank even more Names you weren't sick over me!"

The length of limp string straightened up. His lips shone. "Thank you, thank you—"

Vamgal took his ear betwixt finger and thumb. He only shook the Och gently. "Thank you, majister, you onker."

"Yes, yes," babbled Rampas. "Thank you, majister."

"So much," commented Naghan the Slippy, "for cunning disguises and fictitious names." I realized I wore my own face.

This byplay further relaxed the tension of the situation that the search for and discovery of Paline had begun to ease. Oh, and do not run away with the idea that I too-easily tolerated thieves. Not so. Even in our brave new Vallia, some of the old evils remained.

Anxious as I knew everyone was to leave this benighted place proper procedures had to be followed. Arrangements for the collection and disposal of the dead had to be organized. The noise, brief though it might have been, had attracted attention and the street began to fill with the curious and alarmed folk of the neighborhood. We sorted it all out eventually and then we could leave, trailing off in very subdued mood to the Guard's billets or the palace. This had been a night to remember—or, probably, not, when recollection brought back the horrific images in that room of blood.

As the news spread throughout Gafarden the next day, that was how the place of death was described—the kazzvew, room of blood.

The obsessive bloodlust of this undead thing people now referred to in hushed voices as the Spectre must have been slaked—at least temporarily. For the next few days the only murder in the city was what could euphemistically be dubbed as a normal crime. Because Lart the Butcher beat his wife, Jodie, once too often, she took his favorite knife and slipped it in between his ribs. The Spectre did not strike.

As for poor Jodie, known as the Traiky, she'd have to be run up before the chief pallan. If necessary, even in a case of this kind, she could appeal to Princess Didi, and thence to the emperor and empress. The official position of the nazabni remained in doubt.

Another long screed arrived from Drak in which he expressed himself as being entirely dissatisfied with the situation in Gafarden. He would appoint Rennel Lorving as the new nazab; but he couldn't yet be spared from his official duties in Vondium. I omit to mention the parts of the letter in which Drak allowed himself free rein on the subject of murders and, in particular, the foul assassination of Nath Verunder. He added that he had a mind to ask Inch to fly over from the Black Mountains and see what was causing all the trouble.

At that I perked up. It would be grand to see Inch again, all the long lean length of him. The times Seg and Inch and I had had together!

Before that, though, the chief pallan, Nath Swantram, got himself out of bed and donned his judicial robes and sat in judgment on Jodie, the dead butcher's wife. Well, of course, whilst I felt that the poor woman had at last been provoked beyond endurance, the case was nothing to do with me. I was strictly the ex-emperor of Vallia.

So, judge of my surprise when an under-pallan knocked and entered to say: "Majister. There is a girl asking to see you. She is in distress—" The under-pallan spread his left hand, his right grasping his rod of office. "She says it is her right."

When I had been the emperor I'd had anterooms full of people wanting to see me on all manner of urgent business. The abdication had freed me of that onerous burden. Still—right? Well, yes. If the new Vallia was to practice what it preached, then this girl had the right to see not just an ex-emperor of Vallia but the Emperor of all Paz. I nodded. "Send her in, Nath." Oh, yes, this under-pallan was another of the uncounted Naths of Kregen.

This girl, introduced as Matty, was well-built. She was, in fact, plump. Well, to be truthful, she was fat. Her round red face glistened and her eyes were set like blackcurrants in a pudding. Her bare forearms were as thick round as a pikeman's, narrowing to dainty wrists, from where her broad hands spread like, as they say in Clishdrin, two bunches of bananas. She was decently dressed in a flowery frock, and politeness and sympathy for her prevents me from mentioning marquees.

She told me that she'd been to plead with the nazabni who had simply said her position no longer gave her any authority. Ulana had suggested Matty see me. "The nazabni looked quite ill, majister. She's so thin I'm worried she's quesing away." By quesing Matty meant dwindling, shrinking, rather as a balloon shrinks when deflating.

What struck me was the fact that this girl amidst all her troubles could find time and compassion to worry about somebody else.

In addition, I realized with a degree of guilt, I'd been ignoring Ulana lately. I'd go and see her directly, I promised myself.

Matty went on to say that her father had a history of violence. She was the eldest of eleven children, and all had felt the heavy hand slapping them about the head for no apparent reasons at all. As for her mother, here a thick tear rolled down Matty's plump red cheek, she was a mass of bruises, black and blue, and bloody cuts from angry slashes with the handiest knife. "So, majister, please—"

"Very well, Matty. I shall see the chief pallan at once."

At this she used a lace-trimmed kerchief to wipe her face. She thanked me, not so much prettily, as thankfully. I warned her not to get her hopes up too high. "I no longer rule in Vallia. I can only give counsel."

When she had gone my office suddenly looked considerably larger.

Dressing in good stout Vallian buff, off I sallied to see Nath Swantram and try to sort something out about the Butcher's Murder.

The palace and fortress built on an ancient site contained the usual dungeons; but they had not been used for seasons, I was given to understand. Didi had ordered the construction of a new prison with proper facilities for felons, her humanitarian instincts modified by the unfortunate necessity of having to have people locked up. The chief pallan was visiting the prison, called the Chundrognik, so I could kill two birds with one stone.

As I might have guessed, Nath the Clis rubbed his scar reflectively, then spread his hands in that familiar gesture. The woman Jodie the Traiky had murdered her husband, there was no doubt. This was a matter of insufficient importance to be referred higher up. The Princess lay ill in a far away land, and if the emperor was badgered by cases of this kind, why, he'd have no time to rule the empire. "No, no, majister. The woman must hang."

This rogue was very sure of his authority. I was here only to observe and advise in the matter of the nazabni. What he said was true enough; but my lad Drak, in cases of this nature, would do as I had done and appoint a judge to look carefully into the whole affair. I put this point to Swantram. He stroked his scar. We sat in a high room of the prison given over to the governor's use. This individual, Nalgre Avansur, sat without speaking. I guessed Nath the Clis had him well and truly under his thumb—as he had the rest of Gafarden. The twin sunshine, red and green, shone in luster upon the far wall.

The chief pallan was working out in his ferrety head whether it would be better to put the case to the emperor himself, or let me do it and risk a charge of incompetence or dereliction of his duty of justice and care for the province.

I said to myself: "By Krun! Let the fellow sweat!"

At last he nodded abruptly, saying that out of respect for me—the insincerity rang!—he would send the papers to the emperor.

At least, poor Jodie the Traiky had a stay of execution.

Glancing at the clepsydra I saw the time for my meeting with my three new companions was almost upon me. I stood up, said the remberees and took myself off.

Now Didi in giving orders for the construction of the new capital of her province had insisted that the latest ideas in Vallian town planning should be incorporated. So it was that apart from the old village, Gafarden presented a clean and smart urban appearance. My rendezvous lay near the prison, so off I sauntered to The Silver Quill, looking forward to a leisurely lunch, not altogether unhappy over the outcome of my interview with Nath Swantram.

Thus when the Spectre struck again pure chance placed me very close to the action. The uproar at my back made me spin about, already guessing the dread reason for the screaming. People ran crazily from the next crossroads, surging down the street in blind panic.

A mytzer cart containing squishes and gregarians overturned with a smash and trampling feet crushed the ripe fruits. The rich odors of squishes and gregarians drifted across the mob, giving an odd, almost surreal feel to the scene.

There was no doubt about the cause of this panic rout. Folk screamed out the name: 'The Spectre! The Spectre!' The street boiled with desperate humanity hell-bent on running away from horror.

Now maybe I am Dray Prescot, lord of this and that, etcetera, etcetera, and all very fine and romantic that sounds. I saw no reason to get myself messily torn to bits. I'd seen what this ghastly undead creature could do. So—and right smartly too, by Krun!—I ran off.

If you have followed my narrative, then you should feel no surprise that I could thus tamely turn tail and flee. When the necessity could not be avoided, why, then, I'd stand and fight to death. I was not the Dray Prescot who'd arrived on Kregen those many seasons ago. Oh, yes, by Djan, I could still go berserk. But I controlled that impulse to instant resistance. Sometimes—maybe, after all, more times than not—I was still that young and intemperate Dray Prescot who'd sailed down the River Aph in a leaf boat.

So, like the greenest coy, like the biggest onker on Kregen, I stopped running and turned about.

The running screaming people all passed so that I stood alone in the street. I drew the Krozair brand. If this damned undead thing tore men and women to shreds, as, indeed, the monster did, then it must be material. It must be corporeal and have body. It should, then, be susceptible to the bite of cold steel.

So I, Dray Prescot, stood there in the empty street, with the great Krozair blade cocked ready for action, and I felt a veritable idiot of idiots, the most foolish of onkers this side of the Ice Floes of Sicce.

A luminescent blue radiance grew and swelled before me.

The column of blue light thickened and coalesced into the figure of a man. He'd bought himself a new turban, a confection of twining silk bands in pastel colors, with pearl drops and silver stars. That brave new turban stood up as straight as a church tower. I knew that very shortly it would more resemble that famous tower in Pisa.

"Jak!" exclaimed Deb-Lu-Quienyin. "You are well?"

"As you see, Deb-Lu." I half-smiled. "And you?"

"This Great Evil of which Khe-Hi warned. It is erratic—infuriatingly so."

Now the Capital Letters became self-evident in his spoken words. "Evil Days of Great Portent Lie in Wait. We await Disaster." Automatically he put up a hand to straighten the turban which did not need that. "Oh, me? I thrive." Then he added something that affected me profoundly, revealing the reason for this visitation. "Drak asked me to see you, make sure you haven't got yourself killed."

Even as the Wizard of Loh spoke so I saw a flutter of movement by the crossroads. I said: "That is a kind thought. Deb-Lu—if you turn about and observe you may see this Great Evil."

"Wha—!" He span about so that his robes billowed out.

Dripping, slimed, trailing shreds of flesh as well as rotting cloth, the Spectre glided towards the crossroads—and towards me.

The black hollow eyesockets abruptly flamed with the twin spots of red fire. The undead thing swirled skeletal arms. Blackened fingers like talons raked the air. I braced myself, the Krozair brand ready.

Blue light grew around the skeletal figure. The Spectre stopped stock-still at once. The naked skull twitched this way and that. From that ghastly form sparks of light flew. They splintered into the blue radiance. Fires twined and fought. Gradually the blue glow faded.

"I cannot—" said Deb-Lu in a gasp. "The thing is strong!"

Then my comrade Wizard of Loh stood up, tall, commandingly. He stretched out a hand. He pointed his finger. Brilliant yellow light spat forth coruscatingly. The weird energies of another plane of existence channeled through the sorcerer and burst blindingly upon the Spectre.

For a single heartbeat I thought Deb-Lu had conquered. Then a circular wheel of flame grew as fire broke from the Spectre to meet Deb-Lu's occult thrust. The dread Quern of Gramarye formed where the two lances of power met.

Deb-Lu managed to pant out: "Jak! Stand away!"

I knew what he meant. If the Spectre overcame my comrade's kharrna then the Quern of Gramarye would smash down on Deb-Lu utterly destroying him and anything else in its fiery path.

Nineteen

The street roared and crackled with the discharge of elemental energy. Massive gobbets and gouts of flame splashed the walls. The noise racketed on like demented giants hammering iron against granite mountains. Sound and heat and light shrouded me in suffocating coils.

"Deb-Lu!" I screamed it out as I dived for the nearest doorway. "Deb-Lu! Go home—Now!"

My sorcerer comrade might be here only as an illusion, a ghostly representation of himself; the powers unleashed here could reach through the lupal projection and kill him as surely as though he stood here in person. At least, that is what I believed. The door came up and struck me shrewdly in the back as I rolled over in the doorway. I twisted about to stare back into the street.

The coruscating disc of the Quern of Gramarye fluctuated. One moment it swayed towards the grisly shape of the Spectre, the next it surged back towards Deb-Lu-Quienyin. The occult powers displayed in so raw a fashion represented arcane knowledge old beyond time. I opened my mouth to yell at Deb-Lu to get home out of it when with a sound as though the Heavens fell into the Abyss, the Quern of Gramarye exploded.

The turban-crowned figure of Deb-Lu for a single heartbeat stood bathed in yellow flame. Instead of shouting I gasped in horror.

Deb-Lu! My cherished old comrade wizard! Was he—?

The blue radiance vanished in the next second. The onrushing billow of flame scorching from the Spectre seethed on through empty air.

My head felt as though it was held fast between two frying pans beating an insane rhythm into my skull. My eyes streamed. The whole world of Kregen gyrated about me in those fraught moments.

The flashing incandescence ceased. The fires and smoke and gouts of flame died. The street returned to some kind of normalcy. And the Spectre lowered at the crossroads, his head turning this way and that seeking his victim.

The door at my back was fast locked. I scrunched up into a ball, staring with eyes that pained like the devil at this damned Spectre.

Where the shaft of occult fire had struck the road a long black smear extended on. I could still see in my mind's eye the cobbles wrenched up under the power of that massive blast, hurled away like grapeshot. The Spectre could do all that again, and this time he'd have me in his sights.

The undead thing swayed. It started off, skull turning from left to right and back again, with those unearthly red eyes glaring from the hollow black sockets. Its skeletal fingers raised, clawlike.

The Spectre swayed again, and stopped. In those fraught moments I could only conjure up an image from Earth and not from Kregen. The skull and the insane red eyes turned from side to side exactly as a radar swings atop a warship's mast. If the ghastly thing turned all the way around like a radar dish—by Zair, that wouldn't surprise me!

The Spectre was rotting. It leaned forward, and halted, and swayed back. Its left forefinger—a mere yellowed bone—fell off to clink against the cobbles. Strips of decaying flesh trailed from its ribcage. It tottered.

In that moment it seemed to me the whole world of Kregen fell into a hush. All sound ceased. I scarcely breathed. And, in that heightened moment I saw—I saw with so great a horror that I shook like a green coy in his first battle—a little child wander out into the street.

She was a girl child, dressed in a pretty pink frock with white bows. She clutched a wooden doll in her left hand, and her right hand stretched before her, feeling the air. She was blind. She was crying in a soft sobbing way, calling: "Mummy! Mummy!"

And there I crouched in the doorway, I, the great Dray Prescot, curling up and hiding from the truth of the moment. I tell you, in that moment I knew what horror was.

The Spectre's glaring eyes in those blank orbits appeared to spark, to give off flames. It swayed there, and another finger fell off, the yellow bone tinkling eerily on the cobbles.

The undead thing half-turned. The uncanny silence persisted, broken only by the little girl sobbing and calling for her mother.

There was no time to conjure up Makki Grodno or the Divine Madam of Belschutz. I snatched out my old sailor knife and hurled the blade past the Spectre. It rang and clattered bouncing across the road.

In the next instant I forced myself to my feet and fairly hurled myself across the street. I could feel my heart going like a runaway vove. I dragged in great gasping lungfuls of air. I scooped up the little girl child in my left arm and ran dementedly on expecting to be fried into a crisp by an occult blast of searing flame.

The Spectre turned that macabre head about at the sound of the knife against the cobbles. If Opaz gave me the muscles and the time!

My body felt bloated, as though the blood was about to spurt from the veins. The girl cried out and I made some hushing sound as I ran. The Spectre swung back. His skull thrust forward. I pounded on. Only a few more paces, only a few more lunging strides, and we'd be beyond the portico of the opposite doorway...

Slewing sideways I crashed into the shadows of the portico and sat down with a thump, the child cradled protectively in my arms.

The uncanny silence out in the street persisted although the girl had quietened down to choked sobbing. I expected the creature to be hissing and slobbering away, screeching like a burst boiler. But no, that eerie hush hung over us, almost palpably crushing sound.

Dare I put my head around the corner of the portico? Dare I look out and possibly bring a lance of spitting fire to consume us both? Freeing the girl I placed her against the door at the back and then, dragging in a huge gulp of air, I put an eyeball around the stone.

The Spectre moved in a lurching fashion, going away from us towards the crossroads. It held its arms forward, out of my sight. I let my breath out with a silent whoosh. The undead thing turned right and went out of my view beyond the corner house.

"Opaz be praised!" Noise returned to the world, the chirrup of birds, the distant howl of a dog, a little breeze stirring the dust. I turned immediately to the girl. She clutched her wooden doll tightly and her sightless eyes gazed past me emptily. "It's all right now. What is your name, child?"

She took a moment or two to answer, gulping a bit and wiping the tears from those dull eyes. She was about five years old in terrestrial time measurement. "Finsi. Where is mummy?"

That was a question of great importance, to which I did not have the answer. "Oh, we'll find her soon. Where d'you live, Finsi?"

She shook her head, and I realized how stupid and insensitive the question was. "Never mind. We'll soon have you sorted out."

As events turned out, little Finsi was not sorted out at all rapidly. No one had so far ventured back here. The place was deserted. Lifting Finsi I went across to the overturned cart. The mytzer had long since disentangled himself from the harness and run off. I picked up an unsquashed gregarian and Finsi stuck her tiny white teeth into it with gusto. There was still no sign of a living person, so I'd have to wait and return later to find her mother.

With that, off I went to The Silver Quill and the delayed meeting with my new companions.

The uneasy thought occurred to me that perhaps the macabre silence engulfing the world had existed only in my feverish brain.

Three ovals of blue radiance wavered into life ahead of me. In the fashion of the weird other dimensions inhabited by wizards, they thickened and coalesced as the sorcerers used their kharrna to project themselves from wherever they were on Kregen to this single spot in Gafarden. The shapes took on tangible form. With a tremendous gust of relief I saw the familiar friendly faces of three of my comrade Wizards of Loh. Deb-Lu-Quienyin stepped forward. At his side stood Khe-Hi-Bjanching. At his other side stood Ling-Li-Lwingling.

"Jak!" cried out Deb-Lu. "You Are Safe?"

"Right as rain in the desert, Deb-Lu. The Spectre has gone."

"Yes," said Khe-Hi, speaking very grimly indeed. "We sensed that. The Great Evil has once again hidden from us."

"But," said Ling-Li, "where is the accursed of the Seven Arcades?"

I said, very firmly. "I thank you for coming to my aid. The Spectre was rotting away. It ran off."

"We must find the reasons for all this." Khe-Hi's hard face looked savage. "There must be something—"

"Which we will find," said his wife Ling-Li. "Now we must go."

"Yes." Deb-Lu's turban remained a miracle of verticality. That fact amazed me, a little break of dark humor in the perils of the moment. "We Will Strive, We Will Strive. From us all, Jak, Remberee."

Even as I replied with "Remberee," they were gone.

Dire though this whole murderous Spectre situation was, it was comforting to know that my comrade Wizards of Loh were actively working to find a solution. The problem was, could they find some way of dealing with the undead creature before it claimed more victims? The supernatural elements bore down on me with an apprehension I'd rarely felt before in my dealings with sorcerers. Why in the latter cases of the appearance of the Spectre did the damned thing turn up near me? Was I the target of its vindictive spite? Was I the next to be burned to a crisp or ripped into bloody shreds?

With Finsi perched on my shoulders and her bare legs around my neck I resumed walking towards my appointment. One big question which demanded an urgent answer might, with that answer, bring instant destruction down on the head of the unfortunate wight who found it. Simply, where in a Herrelldrin Hell did the damned Spectre go when it wasn't out and about ripping people up?

Truth to tell, I was becoming a trifle irritated—if, by Vox! that was the appropriate word—with this confounded undead creature. From Naghan Raerdu's and Tobi's investigations, it seemed clear the thing was bent on revenge. That vengeance appeared to center around the wronged lord, Tralgan Vorner. He was dead. Was the Spectre, then, this Tralgan Vorner rising from the tomb as a bloodthirsty ghost? Such an occult phenomenon was perfectly suited to the mysterious world of Kregen.

So, if that was the case, why should the Opaz-forsaken thing come slobbering after my blood?

One other interesting fact that caused puzzlement was—when my three comrade mages had gone and I'd looked along the street, there were absolutely no yellowed finger bones lying on the cobbles. The Spectre in its rotting way had shed two fingers, I'd seen that. Yet no finger bones were to be seen.

They say everybody loves a Mystery. Well, when the puzzle has peoples' lives hanging in the balance, then, by Krun, it isn't so lovely after all.

By this time the streets were resuming their normal appearance as folk ventured out. The news sped faster than the Agate-Winged Jutmen of Hodan-Set. Not a lot of noise filled the streets—the citizens spoke in hushed tones. The effect was as though they kept looking over their shoulders for the horrific figure of the Spectre to clasp its boney fingers around their necks—and tear their heads off.

The Silver Quill was not unduly crowded and I joined Tobi at a table for four set by the window. Finsi, placed on a vacant chair, finished up her gregarian and listened with a lively interest that, for the moment, superseded her fears.

Tobi raised an eyebrow at me. I told him what had happened as the ale was served. "We'll find her mother," he said in his cocky, confident way. "Put old Slippy onto it. He's a marvel."

I wondered what Naghan Raerdu would make of this casual use of his sobriquet. Mind you, it was apt!

Nalgre Nevko came in and said the lahals and sat down and looked at Finsi. He was told what had happened. He shook his head. "A bad business, and like to get worse before it gets better."

"Where's Yavnin?" said Tobi. "I'm famished. But we can't start before he gets here."

So we drank our ale down and waited for the absent airman.

I told them how the interview regarding Jodie the Traiky had gone. They nodded at my comment that the chief pallan was as slinky as a leem. "He cleared off back to the palace very quickly." I put my goblet down and reached for the jug. "He couldn't wait to climb back into that massive bed of his."

"So Swantram wasn't in the prison?" Nevko shook his head. "I'd have liked to have seen him meet up with the Spectre."

"Oh, aye. And where's Yavnin?" said Tobi again. "By Ling-Loh, my insides are fair set to shrivel to nothing!"

There was no denying that Yavnin was late and that we were famished. Around us people talked quietly, yet all their conversation was of this dread Spectre. The clepsydra dropped its water steadily. Eventually, as it were by mutual unspoken agreement, we ordered the meal for three and a half, ready to welcome Yavnin when he at last arrived. Finsi tucked in like a jurukker of the Guard.

"We should," observed Tobi, swallowing, "have ordered a full plate for young Finsi here."

We all laughed and nodded agreement. Finsi went on eating with her white teeth busy, completely absorbed. We'd have to find her mother very sharpish indeed to forestall the inevitable crying.

Naturally we discussed the undead creature and expressed ourselves as completely baffled by its unpredictability. What, for instance, was the benighted thing doing right now?

Nevko said: "Yes, indeed. What is it doing now?"

Tobi looked across the table. "You all right, Nalgre?"

"Of course. The whole affair is so—so spooky."

"If," I said, "if the Spectre is the ghost of Tralgan Vorner, then spooky is just the beginning of the business."

Young Tobi put down his knife. "Still," he said with much of his old raff-ish charm, "as San Blarnoi observes, black clouds may fill the sky, yet the twin Suns remain still shining."

As we digested this weighty pronouncement, Finsi said: "Master. Is there any more—please?" Her sightless eyes churned up the most inappropriate sentiments in a crusty old fighting man, I can tell you!

"Of course!" all three of us blurted out together. More food was immediately demanded and was instantly forthcoming. The sharp white teeth went chomping happily on.

Out of the blue, Tobi remarked: "D'you think this undead Spectre thing is really the ghost of Tralgan Vorner?"

"As to that," I said, "these things are known. Anyway, from what we've learned, poor old Vorner was basely dealt with by his cousin Lodermair. The murders fit. Could you blame the poor devil if he clawed his way back out of the tomb?"

"Are you serious, jis?" exclaimed Nalgre Nevko.

"I'm supposed to be Larghos—or is it Ornol?" I spoke sharply. Ears might well be listening.

"I think," said Tobi in a droll way, "it's Kadar the Blade."

"Nice," said Finsi. "Thank you, master." She put her spoon down. "Can we go to my mummy now—please?"

"My sincere apologies, Kadar." Nevko looked embarrassed. "I was just startled by your comment, that's all." He looked over my shoulder. "I must say I don't like the look of that fellow."

I was thinking how young blind innocence was caught up in harsh reality. We had to find Finsi's mother soon. "What?" I turned about. There was no doubt about it. Nevko was right. The polsim who'd just come in looked decidedly suspicious. He wore drab clothes and his right hand tucked into the front of his tunic clearly fastened on a dagger.

"Not long now, Finsi." I spoke gently. A short figure glided in after the polsim, a slinky figure with a hat pulled well down over the eyes, and the four upper limbs of an Och. The Och whispered in the polsim's ear.

"Time to go." I started to pick up young Finsi.

"What's amiss?" demanded Nalgre Nevko.

"Oh," said Tobi in his bright airy way, laying his hand on his sword hilt. "I believe we are in for some hack 'n' slaying."

"Not quite, Tobi." The men who crowded in through the open doorway did not wear assassin black. Their dark clothes were perfectly ordinary, if a little tatty in details. Their floppy brimmed hats drooped but did not conceal the white stare of their eyes. They drew rapiers. "Not quite. You take Finsi and get out of it."

"But—!"

"Do it!"

Without another word Tobi hoisted the blind girl up and moved rapidly across to the rear exit. Nevko said: "I'm in the mood for spitting a few rasts." He drew his rapier.

Other people in The Silver Quill, awoken to the peril of the moment, started to scream and mill about. Tobi had to skip to keep ahead of their mad rush for the back door. Now the Och—the self-same Rampas the Silky—gestured. He pointed straight at me.

The polsim shouted. He shouted a harsh order to the stikitches at his back.

"That is the kitchew! That is Dray Prescot! Kill him!"

Twenty

The would-be murderers moved forward deliberately. They spread out. They intended to take their time and be sure of me. They drew left-hand daggers. I felt my eyebrows drawing down at the flight of those daggers. The damned things were peakers, the assassin's dagger. They'd been adapted for the left hand to become main gauches. Vilely unhealthy weapon, the peaker, with grooves down the blade coated with poison.

"Watch out for their main gauches, Nalgre. Poison."

"Yes. May the Good Opaz rot their guts."

Of the seven assassins, the two in the center looked the most likely. Big, bulky fellows, one a Rapa the other a Brokelsh, they were the leaders. The others, a mix of diffs, would take their cue from the center two and no doubt seek to dart around and backstab us.

Because I'd been out in a civilized city of Vallia I'd not strapped a multiple-sheath of terchicks over my right shoulder. Perhaps, in view of the confounded Spectre thing, I should have. Not that, I supposed, a throwing knife would do it a great deal of harm. So, I could not hurl a terchick into the eye of the leading assassin and follow instantly with a second into the eye of the next cramph.

The sense of occasion here pressed down with none of the rituals of honorable combat. These yetches were out to murder. Without taking my gaze off them as they moved slowly forward, I spoke hardly to Nevko. "Nalgre. This is not your affair. Go with Tobi—"

He laughed. In that moment of imminent desperate action, Nalgre Nevko laughed. "I will not allow you to insult me. Anyway, as emperors go, you are very reasonable, very reasonable, by Vox!"

"Humph!" I said. "As emperors go, I'm likely to go soon."

Now, as you know, I, Dray Prescot, am not in the habit of waiting on enemies to stalk up on me. The Rapa looked choice. His green and yellow feathers and harsh beak that looked as though it could crunch through granite presented a target I could not—Zair forgive me—resist.

Moving fast—with all due humility I say that I moved rapidly—I hurled forward.

Before the Rapa assassin had time to know what was happening I was up to him. The Krozair brand swept slicingly down. His main gauche was brushed aside as though it were merely one of his own feathers. The Great Krozair brand sliced down on the juncture of neck and shoulder. The blow was judged. I was in full command of my emotions. His head did not fall off. That feathered head simply flopped sideways. He stood for an instant, then he collapsed. Before he hit the ground I was back alongside Nevko. It was, I must say, very sudden.

Nalgre Nevko said, on a breath: "That was—sudden—jis."

"Oh, aye." I didn't stop to say how many of my names contained Sudden as the nickname.

Mind you, in all this pompous boasting of prowess, by Krun, I saw the fatal flaw! At the moment of so suddenly striking the Rapa my next move should have been to swirl around and deal with the Brokelsh in exactly the same way. Now, that cramph gaped at me, and lifted his rapier and dagger in a gesture that was hardly threatening. That involuntary movement was a purely defensive reaction to an overwhelming threat. His bristly features corrugated into a grimace of pure hate.

A soft footfall at my back made me throw a flashing glance over my shoulder. Tobi walked up saying he'd given Finsi into the care of a respectable couple who were not petrified with fear as they ran off. He surveyed the six standing assassins. "That Rapa's had a nasty accident. They will try to shave their gobbly necks, you know." He drew his lynxter. "Two apiece, then, doms."

The would-be murderers stopped at the misfortune befalling one of their leaders. They were professionals, though, and they'd taken this commission. Perhaps they'd not been told the name of the victim. Perhaps that accounted for their slow and deliberate advance.

Beyond them, Rampas the Silky and his polsim pal scuttled out of the door. The stikitches moved cautiously forward. A muffled cry spurted up outside and moments later a countenance poked around the corner. That face, crimson as Zim, was followed by a massive body. One thick arm held the little Och by an ear and I swear Rampas's feet barely touched the floor. Deldar Vamgal the Arm took in the situation at a glance and without turning his head, he bellowed.

On the instant The Silver Quill filled with my lads of the Guard Corps.

This was just the duty squadron. I sighed. My personal protection had been the impetus to form the Emperor's Sword Watch and then the Emperor's Yellow Jackets. They suffered terribly when I went off adventuring and they were left at home. I might have known they'd have patrols following me about wherever I went in Gafarden. But, by the Blade of Kurin! What a warm feeling it was to see these splendid fellows!

Hikdar Ruben ti Drovensmot called out: "Jis! You are well?"

"Aye, my thanks, Ruben." I pointed my sword. "What will you do with these kleeshes?"

For the dumbstruck assassins were standing there with their rapiers and their poisoned daggers looking like a bunch of school kids caught scrumping. The crossbows leveled at them did not waver.

"Ask them the question." Tobi gave his opinion quite matter of factly. After all, he'd been living in Loh for some time. Hikdar Ruben stiffened. The hand brushing his moustache stopped. Now Ruben was a citizen and soldier of the New Vallia. He'd been promoted for meritorious conduct and his life was given to the Guard Corps. He said: "Torture is no longer allowed in Vallia!" His voice snapped like the jaws of a leem. "Our Kendur has ordained that!"

Tobi had the grace to say: "Of course. I have heard. I apologize." He sheathed his lynxter. "But, by Hlo-Hli, they deserve it!"

On that note the Guard shuffled off the prisoners. Rampas the Silky, ear in Chancery, went with them. Now I could think of Finsi, of Yavnin, of the Spectre—and of the hundred and one other problems.

Although this episode had undeniably ended with a kind of farce, it was no anti-climax. Oh, yes, there'd been no flashing blades in desperate action—well, by Krun, apart from the one swift attack! But the almost unbearable tension had fairly crackled on the air. That grim, methodical advance of the assassins was calculated to concentrate a fellow's mind, I can tell you!

The unsettling event had to be pushed back where it belonged, in the past. Finsi's mother was found safe and well. Her father had recently died by reason of falling off a cart going downhill. Provision was made for them in a quietly unobtrusive way.

Over the next few days the environs of Gafarden blossomed with meticulous rows of tents, jut lines, cookhouses. The Emperor of Vallia graced the city with his presence. His Guard Corps, now larger than mine as was proper, bivouacked around the city, because my lads had taken the best billets. Drak saw no reason to change that. He told me he was disturbed by the foul murders and was determined to get to the bottom of them. Then Inch flew in and Seg turned up, having managed to tear himself away from his imperial duties. You may well imagine the riotous time we spent! To cap it all, Yavnin appeared to explain his absence with many apologies. The Lady Ahilya had been taken ill—she was now recovered, thanks be to Opaz—and he had been unable to leave her side. He'd sent a message—had we not received it? We shook our heads. "I'll find out," snapped Yavnin. We felt sorry for the messenger who'd been so lax in his duty.

So, then, it fell to me to say: "Don't be too hard on him Yavnin. He probably got caught up in the panic. Everybody was running away from the Spectre."

Yavnin nodded in agreement. "Very well, jis."

Life had to go on in its usual routine and often hectic way. The Nazabni Ulana Farlan was granted an audience of the emperor, when Drak, in sympathizing with her position, left her in no doubt she would have to travel to Vondium. A new post would be found for her.

To keep the troops occupied, a great Grand Parade was ordered. On the day after tomorrow the regiments would assemble, there would be bands, flags waving, a series of march pasts—in short, a tremendous display would keep peoples' spirits up. Just what the Spectre might make of it all I didn't care to guess.

Most non-flying rapid travel in Vallia is by canal, the roads being less than perfect, to say the least. Consequently the normal Wayfarers Drinnik found outside many cities of Kregen are smaller. Our parade would be held on an expanse of flat ground just beyond the canal known as The Lesser Southern Cut. Much new building had taken place on the city side of the canal. The whole city intended to turn out for the great occasion, and amid the jollifications vast quantities of food and drink would be consumed.

Now, it is essential to understand that the parade in no way glorified militarism. Yes, of course, the people of Vallia well appreciated how the Freedom Army had liberated the country from the Times of Troubles. But the proper function of soldiers is to parade splendidly, to march with many banners, and to provide bands to play gorgeous music. Only when their country and loved ones are threatened should an army turn to sterner things. And, by Krun, that includes timely assistance when earthquakes, floods, hurricanes, strike the land.

You may well imagine the jollifications when Seg, Inch and I celebrated this happy meeting. With all the dark clouds about us—I venture to say because of the dark clouds!—our comradeship took on a brighter note. Their ladies were not with them, being about their own businesses, as Silda was away with the Sisters of the Rose, leaving Drak to conduct his investigation on his own. He did say to me, not fretfully, rather resignedly, "Y'know, the SoR have a lot to answer for."

Thinking of Delia, I completely concurred in that sentiment.

The emperor, naturally, would be fully occupied in all the events of the parade and its concurrent activities. Seg and Inch had brought their own medium-sized juruks and they, too, would take part. Despite the sense of celebration in the air, I was profoundly aware of an unease to which I could give no name. Would there be, by the pustulant proboscis of Makki Grodno, some frightful catastrophe on the Day of the Grand Parade?

These dark forebodings must be shrugged off. Seg and Inch went off to deal with their duties, so, mindful of an earlier mistake when I'd ignored new friends for the sake of old, I sent messages to my three new companions that we should attend the parade together and make a party of the occasion. Tobi would bring Tassie, Yavnin would bring the Lady Ahilya, and Nalgre Nevko dropped a hint that he might well have a choice lady in attendance.

All that was left for me to do was to tell the Chuktars of the regiments of my Guard Corps that I expected a smart turn out, and that, as usual, all the details would be handled by them. Then I could take myself off to The Crossbow and Leem, a fine new tavern, to meet my three companions and their ladies. I made up my mind to expect a jolly party and to a Herrelldrin Hell with gloomy anticipations.

Oh, yes, by Krun! That was easy to say. As you may well imagine, my mind was vastly occupied by the vexed question: who had put out a contract on me? The Suns of Scorpio shone resplendently, people bustled about in their best clothes anticipating a good time, street sellers hawked their wares and trade brisked up, entertainers attracted gawping crowds at street corners—and behind all this bright activity some damned cramph lurked in the shadows wishing to see me dead.

So, as a result of that, I did not wear my own face as I strolled along to the appointment. I wore the mail shirt out of the Dawn Lands. My clothes were Vallian buff, with trousers instead of breeches. As an old hare of Kregen I carried all my weaponry. I was not fool enough to believe that because we had caught some assassins, there would be no more brought in from another Stikitche's Guild.

The sign over the tavern, a slinking leem being transfixed by a bolt from a perilously close crossbow, shone bright and bold. It was not, unlike a famous inn sign of yesterday, rumored to be of solid gold. The building was new, tastefully decorated with all manner of fine-art sculptures and cornices and pediments. The tables bore fine yellow linen cloths and there were flowers in vases. Perfumes, artificially introduced into the air, certainly heightened the air of refinement.

Wrinkling up my nose at the somewhat powerful scents, in I went.

"Kadar the Blade!" said Yavnin, rising from his chair. The Lady Ahilya smiled in her distant, beautiful fashion. My face had slipped back to normal as I'd entered. The others greeted me, Tobi very jovial and his Tassie glowing. Nalgre Nevko gravely introduced his lady companion as Cindy Cwolanda. By her name she was from the North East of Vallia.

The light in The Crossbow and Leem faded. Shadows dropped down. A skinny Languelsh dressed in clothes too flashy for his merchanting trade called: "Landlord! By Loomel the Avaricious! Bring lamps!"

The gloom intensified and thunder cracked overhead. Nath the Flagon hurried in with lamps, followed by his serving lasses. We'd expected good weather, so this thunderstorm was an unwelcome surprise. Vivid light sparkled across the windows and the thunder followed almost at once.

Cindy Cwolanda leaned towards me, her large-featured face alarmed, her lips wet. "I cannot abide thunder and lightning—"

On her words a monstrous crash like the powder magazine of a three-decker blowing up shook the building. The whole place vibrated. The roof caved in and plaster and wood and debris plummeted down. Masses of dust obscured everything. All I could do was grab Cindy and dive under a table with her.

"Oh, majister," she stammered out. "Oh, jis!"

"Rest easy, Cindy. It's just a thunderbolt. It's all over."

People were yelling and furniture toppling, flagons and goblets smashing and ale and sazz spilling. The ominous creak aloft suggested the roof was going to collapse completely any moment.

"All out!" I yelled in the old foretop hailing voice. "All out!"

Blundering bodies cannoned into one another and the screaming went on and on. Grabbing Cindy around her waist I hoicked her up and started for the door. A fellow got in the way and about to barge past I saw with astonishment the scarred face of Nath Swantram almost thrust into mine. He started back, recovered and coughed as dust billowed.

"Pallan! I didn't see you in here." I pushed him. "Let's go!"

Somehow we stumbled outside. Rain pelted down. Thunder roared again but the sound drifted away. The light began to improve.

Swantram shook himself. "You were facing away."

More bodies poured out from The Crossbow and Leem onto the street. Cindy cried out: "There's Nalgre!"

Nevko came up and with him Yavnin and Ahilya. Moments later we found Tobi and Tassie. The rain began to ease off. We looked at the tavern—rather, we looked at what was left of it.

Small flickers of flame were trying to take hold. The smashed lamps did their best to ignite the ruins; but the rain still had sufficient quenching power to kill the flames. Considerable confusion hullabalooed in the street as people ran aimlessly, yelling. We made swift and strict enquiries and found no-one was missing. The rain stopped. The Suns of Scorpio shone out again, as they always do, ruby and jade, drenching the land with color and brightness.

Nevko took Cindy's arm. "What happened to you? I came straight across; but you weren't there."

Cindy essayed a small laugh. Truth to tell, it was a mischievous little laugh in the circumstances. "Oh, I was hiding under the table with the majister."

Tobi guffawed at this and Yavnin smiled. Then he said: "It's all over now. If we're to be in time for the parade we'd best go."

Tassie put her arm around Tobi. "I'm all wet. But we'll soon dry out. And I don't want to miss the parade."

A practical as well as a charming lady—young Tassie.

Ahilya said: "Yes—but—well—I daren't think what my hair looks like." We were all kind enough not to tell her.

Despite their words, the ladies were still recovering from the shock of their recent experiences. Maybe the parade would put them to rights, maybe it might make matters worse. The decision was not mine to make, of course. The confusion was sorting itself out now. Folk began to move down the street towards the canal bridges. So, perforce, we went with them. There was no sign of Nath Swantram.

Now do not believe I denigrated the ladies by mentioning their shock to the exclusion of the men's, far from it. Because of their professions and experiences of life, the men were better able to handle this kind of situation. The crowds began to move with more urgency. They filled the street like a human tidal wave and then—then the screams at the back burst out with a name—with the name:

"The Spectre! Run, run! The Spectre!"

The ensuing bedlam racketed to the sky. The whole mass of citizens surged along the street carrying everything away. Tobi and Tassie, fast locked together, were swept on, and Yavnin, shouting: "Stay together!" went helter-skelter away with Ahilya half-climbing up his powerful body. Nevko grasped Cindy, looking wild; but they, too, swirled away in the tide.

Minded to hang back and catch another sight of the undead monster, I struggled for only a few heartbeats against the human onrush. There was no way a fellow was going to push in the opposite direction to this rout. Panic, utter, complete and total panic, blew reason to smithereens.

A Lamnian woman was thrust bodily against me, and rebounded, and fell to her knees. She carried two small children in the crooks of her arms. In the next second she'd have been trampled. There was just time to scoop her up, set her on her feet, and clap an arm about her. We hurled on, wedged between contorting bodies. Lamnians are one of the foremost merchant races of Kregen, and this grandmother was taking charge of the infants whilst the parents saw the parade. Now all I could do was try to see that she and the kids were not harmed.

She tried to gasp out something, a word of thanks, but the surrounding hullabaloo drowned everything, almost destroying coherent thought. Onwards we hurtled, caught like a chip in a millrace. The canal came in sight and the people funneled into the bridges. The canal itself was a mere moment of glinting water and then we erupted on the other side, spewing out like champagne from a shaken bottle.

The rout did not stop. Shrieking and waving their arms madly, the good folk smashed on headlong, finding gaps between the serried regimental ranks of soldiers. I saw Seg astride a zorca. He was shouting, his words unheard by me; but the jurukkers stood fast.

Good old Seg!

Somehow the Lamnian lady and I were out of the mad mob. We fetched hard up against the front rank of Seg's First Archer Regiment. The Jiktar in command recognized me. Very quickly the Lamnian and the twins were ushered to the rear, and Seg cantered over, his eyebrows raised.

"Well you may ask!" I said, giving myself a shake to adjust the disarray of my weaponry. "That damned Spectre's chasing us."

Seg used his sword to point across the canal. "Where?"

He was right. The space between the houses and the canal lay open and empty. No Spectre stalked there.

"Did you see the damned thing, my old dom?"

"No."

"It must have chased the people at the back the other way."

As usual, Seg was right. Once panic hit the mob, they'd run blindly away and nothing was going to stop them. I opened my mouth to agree, and instead said: "Right. But here it comes now."

On the instant Seg roared in his commanding fashion words to hold his bowmen steady. There was visible a wavering motion in the ranks; but the regiment stood.

"Now we shall see what five hundred Lohvian Longbows can do." My blade comrade's tone was grave; but rippling through the words the clear jubilation of a master of his craft at the prospect of a supreme test came through like a clarion call. I nodded. At that moment the Chuktars of my regiments galloped up and rapidly we sorted out the shooting organization. Everyone was keyed up. The atmosphere between us trembled with the anticipation of what was to come.

The Spectre drooled. To my surprise he had all the fingers of his left hand present and correct. His rotting skull wobbled grotesquely as he advanced. Those twin pits of unholy crimson fire shone eerily from his eyesockets. He stopped. He moved sideways, and then back. His skeletal arms writhed above his skull. He started to charge forward.

The orders to loose rang out over the parade.

There were a lot of bowmen on parade. The air visibly darkened for a moment as the shafts sped. Timing was vital, and the regiments shot in synchronization. Hundreds of steel-tipped arrows struck all about the undead monster, hundreds smashed into it, shattering bones.

The thing danced as though in impotent fury, and staggered back. It tried to forge on against the hail of feathered death, and reeled to a halt. It stood, shaking, looking like a pincushion. Once, then twice again, it tried to advance, and failed, and fell back.

For a third time the Spectre essayed to move towards us against the sleeting arrows. It halted. It wavered and pieces of bone fell off.

"The damned thing's shrinking!" shouted Seg.

"Aye," said Inch, riding up, impossibly tall in the saddle. "I was hoping to chop it to bits. But now—" He shook his axe.

The Spectre dwindled. Rotting shreds collapsed. Smaller and smaller the thing shrank, until only the sere skull balanced atop a pile of bones. Then everything puffed into a startling display of scintillant lights and an expanding cloud of dust.

Nothing was left.

The Spectre had ceased to exist.

Tremendous cheers rose from the ranks and the lads waved their bows aloft in triumph. "Hai Jikai! Hai Jikai!"

So, then, it was all over bar the shouting—and the shouting and celebrations went on a long, long time. Drak felt the events were parade enough and the regiments were dismissed to enjoy themselves. Ever the frugal quartermaster of an army, Seg gave orders for fatigue parties to collect up all the arrows. That night Gafarden rang with the jollifications. With Drak's permission when we old comrades met that evening, my three new companions and their ladies were invited.

There was, of course, a great deal to talk about. We'd rid Gafarden of the scourge of the Spectre. There was Nazabni Ulana Farlan to be settled. There was Nath Swantram to be investigated. Yavnin would be going back on duty. Nalgre Nevko had pressing business with rich merchants. Tobi was still attached to Tassie, much to the surprise and gentle amusements of his friends.

So, all in all, a happy outcome.

"Apart," said Tassie, on a breath, "from all the poor folk who were murdered."

We agreed, subdued for the moment. Seg brisked up, saying: "By the Veiled Froyvil! Wasn't the shooting fine?"

Drak said: "Yes. It is difficult to argue with the steel bokkertu."

I agreed, and added: "First thing in the morning I'm off to find your mother, Drak, wherever she may be."

By Zair! Seeing Delia of Delphond, Delia of the Blue Mountains again, was a far finer sight than all the shooting in two worlds!

Twenty-one

And then...

Shards of glass glittered across the marble floor. Fire crystal radiance struck back in stars of light from the heaping piles of gems. Everywhere the glint of gold filled the chamber with richness. No single speck of dust marred the luxurious yet somber scene.

The nine sarcophagi stood in their ring of death. The altar at the center supported the emerald whose greenness sheened into the air with the mysterious tones of the undersea. Silence reigned.

Tralgan Vorner halted just inside the entrance and put a hand to his face. He felt the flesh and the bone structure. That face was solid, heavy, and he knew the dark blood flushed to give him that lowering appearance of the Vorner family. Strange, he said to himself, damned strange to have my own face back!

As though that were a prearranged signal, the sarcophagi moved.

The covers slid aside, the coffin lids lifted. Tralgan Vorner watched with a fascination compounded of expectancy and fear. The Thaumaturges of Sodan rose into view. Tralgan swallowed—hard.

He thought he'd conquered the eeriness of this place. He believed the Thaumaturges understood his mettle, the depths of his hatred and the all-encompassing nature of his thirst for revenge. Yet—yet he knew also he stood there transfixed with a thick terror that the sorcerers would not honor their compact with him.

The Thaumaturges of Sodan stared upon Tralgan Vorner. All of their skull faces with the blood-red floating orbs turned towards him and he felt the psychic blast like the blow of a scythe.

All the sorcerers glared on him. All of them. All eight of them.

The sarcophagus that had contained the remains of Rafan-Ymet the Ineluctor stayed fast shut. The light caught the arcane carvings and in Tralgan's heightened state the runes seemed to writhe with ominous power. Tension breathed so forcefully upon him that he closed his eyes and felt his whole body trembling.

Lights sparkled and darted about him. He felt as though a million dagger points pricked him. His brain felt as though it was being crushed between millstones. His heart raced.

The brilliance of the stabbing lights struck through his closed eyelids. All that he was, all his ib, everything that made up Tralgan Vorner sucked away in the scintillant spots of light. The Thaumaturges learned everything. They knew. They knew how Rafan-Ymet had once again died, and this time had gone beyond recall down into the Ice Floes of Sicce. So he waited for sentence to be passed on him.

Why had he returned? Why had he stolen through the secret passages guided by the mental key the sorcerers had given him? Why?

He knew only that he had to return here. There was no other course of action open to him in all of Kregen. So, as he waited for the judgment, an odd fact registered on his consciousness. Perhaps it was simply that his mind took refuge in commonplace impressions to mask the agony to come. The stench of decay did not nauseate as it had done on his first visit. Could it be he was growing used to the stink?

He did not think so—as far as he could think. There was more flesh on the sorcerers' bones and the rotting strips of skin dangled more thinly. He swallowed down—and the voice spoke.

"Tralgan Vorner, dispossessed but rightful Elten of Culvensax! Is your revenge forgotten? Is your hatred slaked? Have you lost your anger?"

"No!" Resentment flared. "No! But—" Tralgan swallowed down again, wet his lips, and, knowing his fate must come to this, spoke as firmly as he could. "I am profoundly sorry about Rafan-Ymet."

"The vaol-paol unites. His circle is closed."

Tralgan received the distinct and shocking impression that these mages cared little for their truly dead colleague, and therefore, by implication, didn't much care for one another. Were they, then, rivals?

"They shot many arrows, very many arrows."

A sound that might have been a snigger whispered around the chamber. "The arrows did not kill Rafan-Ymet."

"But—"

"When we are at your shoulder, you must stay close."

"Yes, yes. But I was swept away—"

"That we understand." The raw power of the statement shocked solidly into Tralgan's consciousness. How far did these kaotim mages extend their influence? The chamber was wide and high under the broken glass roof. Gold glittered. Gems sparkled. The crystal light beat down. Yet Tralgan Vorner felt constricted, choked, pressed in. The encompassing voice, like silk drawn across a saw, spoke with meaning.

"Remember! We draw our fresh life from you! Remember! Your ib and your blood are ours! Remember! Stay close!"

Tralgan Vorner bowed his head in mute acknowledgement.

From the sarcophagus next to the closed tomb of Rafan-Ymet a cadaver floated up, ancient vestments and rotting skin trailing like some blasphemous tail of a bird from hell. The kaotim hovered before Tralgan Vorner. Its blood red eyes glared with the light of madness.

"I am Nasan-Ydor!" The voice penetrated Tralgan's brain as a drill bites through wood. "Remember! I am Nasan-Ydor, known as the Inculcator. I speak for all—for now."

Vorner knew what would happen next. This Nasan-Ydor would take the place of Rafan-Ymet. Together, they would go out into the world of Kregen where vengeance and ambition would bring them the victory.

All his fears fell away. An overriding sense of authority nerved him for the future as the sorcerer invaded his being. The lids of the tombs closed, the sarcophagi stood silent as the grave. Even in these moments, Tralgan savored that. The eerie chamber once more lay as it had been. The gold and gems sparkled.

Oh, yes! The promise of the future beckoned alluringly.

"You, Tralgan Vorner, shall complete your revenge! And I, Nasan-Ydor the Inculcator, will have all of Vallia for the Thaumaturges of Sodan!"

Turmoil on Kregen

A note on Dray Prescot

The undead monster called the Spectre has been destroyed. Princess Didi's fine new city of Gafarden no longer suffers under the threat of the animated corpse. Didi herself lies seriously injured in Zandikar in the Eye of the World, lovingly tended by her cousin, Princess Velia. Ulana Farlan, the governor of Didi's province of Urn Vennar, has been removed from office. Now the rogue and schemer Nath Swantram, Nath the Clis, rules.

Prescot is a man above middle height with immensely broad shoulders, who moves like a hunting cat, silent and lethal. There is about him an abrasive honesty and an indomitable courage. Educated in the harsh conditions of Nelson's Navy he gained the quarterdeck; but only when he arrived on the exotic world of Kregen under Antares could his true qualities find expression.

The mysterious Star Lords need him to further their obscure plans. Pushed into trying to unite all the continents and islands of Paz by the Star Lords, Prescot recognizes the enormity of the task.

Believing the Spectre destroyed by hundreds of arrows, Prescot returns to his home of Esser Rarioch in Valka to be with the divine Delia.

Some parts of this story give details that Prescot could not have known until later. They are inserted where they aid clarity. Due to this logical presentation, we know what Prescot does not.

We know the Spectre, dead and animate, is about to terrorize Gafarden again as Tralgan Vorner, the wronged Elten of Culvensax, seeks vengeance on those who betrayed him. Within Vorner the Spectre lives.

So join Dray Prescot as he attempts to learn a new skill, there on the high balcony of Esser Rarioch, under the streaming mingled lights of the Suns of Scorpio.

Alan Burt Akers

One

Delia said: "You put one needle like this, the other needle thus and place the wool just so. Then turn—oh, no!"

Like a slippery eel a needle fell from my fumbling fingers and tinkled on the marble floor of the high balcony.

"You fambly, Dray Prescot." She reached down in a flowing motion of pure beauty and caught the needle up in her slender fingers that could wield a sword with the strength of steel. "Try again. Like this."

"Yes, my heart," I said—very meekly.

Once again the wool curled like a tentacle of a monster of myth and the needles went every which way. "Sink me!" I burst out. "I'll not be beat by confounded knitting!"

"And quite right, too," said Inch, all the seven feet length of him lounging out onto the balcony. "Anyway, I thought you could knit. Sasha taught me ages ago."

From up here on this secluded balcony of the castle palace of Esser Rarioch all the splendid panorama of the City and Bay of Valkanium lay spread out beneath us. The early morning shimmered with the promise of a wonderful day. A light perfumed zephyr stole among the brilliance of the flowers bowering this niche of beauty. This, indeed, was what it was to feel young and alive on Kregen under the Suns of Scorpio!

Well, of course, I should have known better. The world of Kregen is undeniably supremely beautiful. It is also dark and terrible and menace forever lurks not far away.

Inch sat himself down in his fashion of curling those long legs away neatly. He wore a brass chain about his neck with a simply enormous padlock dangling on his morning tunic. The end of the chain vanished into the doorway—and here came Sasha, laughing, holding the brass links like a dog's lead.

"And dear Inch made a fist of it at first, Dray—so do not despair." She shook the chain gently so that it chingled.

Neither Delia nor myself questioned the meaning of the padlocked chain. Inch was from Ng'groga where life was dominated by Taboos. He'd broken a Taboo and was now doing penance. At least he'd not been at the squish pie, which he loved inordinately, for then he'd be standing on his head.

"True," said Inch, equably. "What I wanted was—well, now that disgusting Spectre has been destroyed we have more problems."

"Surprise me."

"There are rumors up north of restlessness. The racters—"

"What!" said Delia, sitting up. "They conspired against my father. He was murdered. They disappeared. Don't say—" She did not go on. Once the most powerful political party in Vallia, the racters had vanished as a cohesive force. Totally committed to gaining their selfish ends by whatever means they could, they had sought to rule all Vallia. Rich and powerful, they had at last been overcome during the Time of Troubles. Now Vallia was liberated and the emperor Drak and the empress Silda ran the country with benign hands.

I stood up and walked to the carved marble balustrade. If true, this news was bad—very bad. There was no doubt in my mind that my lad Drak was the best for Vallia. I had to believe he would handle this crisis—if it came to that—with his usual tact and firmness.

Speaking carefully, Inch went on: "There have been meetings. Mercenaries are being recruited. It is said, and it seems likely, this is the work of the grandchildren of those racters we defeated."

The perfume of the flowers wafted sweetly all about and a little brown scorpion waddled along the balustrade towards me. "Dray Prescot!" The scorpion's voice sounded harshly metallic.

Neither Inch nor Sasha could see or hear the scorpion. I spoke to the thing and I knew they could not hear me either. "Not now!"

"Onker! Look up!"

A sensation as of an agonizing groan shocked right through me. "Not now!" I said; but I looked up.

Oh, yes, there he was, planing in tight circles above with the twin suns-light striking in gold and scarlet glory from his feathers.

One black beady eye cocked a look of great calculation as he swung about above us. Delia did not gasp. She took my arm in that firm powerful grasp and I put my hand over hers. So, together, we looked up and waited for whatever of misfortune the Gdoinye would bring.

The squawk racketed down like the rip of a rusty saw.

"Dray Prescot! Onker! Emperor of Onkers!"

My free hand curled into a fist and tightened around the hilt of the rapier buckled up over the morning lounging robe. As you know, Kregans on most occasions of social life find it prudent to carry a weapon or two—preferably three or four. I'd contented myself with a rapier and left-hand dagger. Plus, of course, my old sailor knife snugged over my right hip. The rapier hilt bit into my skin, so fierce the desperation filling me.

"You failed to complete your assigned task in the Dawn Lands."

Was there a squawking note of petty triumph in the Gdoinye's words?

Mayhap. I did not think so. He was the spy and messenger for the Star Lords and performed his duties to his own obscure satisfaction. Now he planed about with the Suns of Scorpio striking refulgently from his plumage. "The duty is urgent, onker. Urgent."

Delia looked about, expecting to see the Gdoinya, the twin sister, which called her for missions for the Everoinye. Only the single great raptor sailed against the blue brightness of the day.

"When," called up my Delia in the sweetest voice in two worlds, "when, oh great boaster, is it never most urgent?"

"Ha!" I exclaimed, both vastly amused and proud of Delia, Delia of the Blue Mountains, Delia of Delphond.

The Gdoinye swirled lower, flirting a wing as he banked in the turn. "You have the right of it, my lady. With the Everoinye it is always most urgent." His tones did not racket down in a raucous squawk. Rather, they sounded downright respectful. Marvel of marvels! But then, naturally, even so supernatural a fellow as this fell under the spell of Delia's poise and charm—and shrewdness, not to say downright cunning. "My lady, I bid you remberee." This astonished me even more. Then, in the old intemperate screech: "Be about your business, emperor of onkers, so that the Everoinye may shed their light upon you."

With that the Gdoinye winged up and away and the world filled with the pulsating blue light of the Giant Scorpion.

There was just time for me to cry out: "Delia! My heart!"

There was just time for Delia to call: "I know! My love—"

Then the sundering wash of blue radiance tore us apart.

What a tempestuous and frustrating life I led on Kregen! The damn Star Lords kept on hurling me away from all I held dear, tearing out the very roots of my being. There was no redress. No, by the disgusting diseased liver and lights of Makki Grodno! Because I possessed the yrium, that marvelous and wonderful and hateful super-charisma, the Everoinye had chosen me to be their instrument in bringing all the islands and continents of Paz together to resist the Shanks who raided from around the curve of the world.

So be it. I'd do the dirty work at the speed of light, then hightail it back to all I wanted on Kregen or Earth.

The monstrous shape of the Scorpion formed and bore me away. That dratted Phantom Giant Blue Scorpion of the Star Lords whisked me aloft into winds and bluster. The Everoinye were adept at fashioning concealments for my sudden departures as I knew from conversations with those who'd been around when I'd gone—ha! Gone! Ripped away, more like. My slippered feet hit a soft mass and I sank down thigh-deep into clinging snow.

The first thing I noticed was—it was cold! Cuttingly cold.

The next item to take my attention—and this despite Zim and Genodras shining away up there in full daylight—was a shimmering vibration in the air and a trembling vibration through the snow. A noise like a million leems coughing rumbled through the frigid air.

A voice cut like the very chill all around: "Dray Prescot!"

Turning at once I stared up slope. The mingled red and green beams of sunlight streaked the whiteness of the snow. Tiny shards of glitter spiked up from the surface. Upslope a handsome wooden chalet promised refuge from the bitterness all about. My morning robe did nothing to keep me warm.

"Dray Prescot!" The voice rose, hectoring. "Come on! Hurry!"

"I'm hurrying, confound you, Otto the Lance!"

He looked just the same as the last time I'd seen him. He wore his black leathers over a mail shirt and was girded with weapons. Oh, and, of course, seeing he was a darling of the Star Lords, he had a voluminous ponsho fleece wrapped about him. His remarkable hat, very tall-crowned, still sported its aigrette of faerling feathers.

"I've told you not to call me Otto. At the moment I'm using the name Starson." His bright angular face with that black bar of a moustache looked to be more worried than he'd admit to. He swung an arm up, pointing back. "Can't you see!"

All this had taken but a few moments. I could see all right. Up there it looked as though the whole world was falling on us in a smothering welter of snow. The noise boomed on and on, louder and louder. White billows rolled and gushed and tumbled remorselessly down.

Avalanche!

The neat chalet stood directly in the path of the roaring tide and would be swept away headlong.

As Otto—or Starson—said, there was little time. We must hurry.

The snow churned away around my legs. The damned stuff impeded the slightest movement. Plunging up and down I ploughed my way up. "And if you're Starson now, well, I'm still Jak."

Just before he turned around to fight his way up through the snow, he called: "Aye! Jak the Sudden."

Steam gushed from our mouths and nostrils. The awe-inspiring sight of the avalanche spurred us on. The thing would engulf the chalet and tear it to pieces and scatter the bits all the way down the mountainside.

No need to ask why we two kregoinyi had been catapulted here by the Star Lords. Someone crouched shivering in the chalet with the thunder of approaching doom in their ears. Probably they were far too frightened to think of running out and trying to escape. As we neared the wooden building I began to think we'd be swept away, too.

"Hurry, man, hurry!" His harsh voice rasped as the steam plumed from his mouth.

Saving my breath for fighting through the snow I quickened my pace. Stubbornness and silly puffed-up pride made me forge on and overtake this Otto, self-styled Starson. He favored me with a bitter glance as I went by so that, although I didn't smile, I gleed a trifle. In addition, I plead in mitigation of my childish behavior two points. One, we were in a hurry and the quicker I got there the better. And, second, I said absolutely nothing in the way of suggesting he follow his own precept of urgency.

The roaring snow monster bore down on us, closer and closer.

The damned white clinging stuff clung all right. I've never liked snow. Never have. As I trudged on, every step a battle to lift the leg and thrust it forward and so down and the next leg up and down, I came across a deep rutted line carved into the snow, curving away to the left. There were two lines in parallel and the crystal glitter in the runnels showed they'd been made recently.

Whether or not I felt any sensation in my feet when I stamped them on the wooden steps of the porch I cannot say. Just thankful to be out of the damned snow I bashed the double doors open and plunged on through. A comfortable residence for a mountain retreat, the place spoke eloquently of money. The furnishings all were of good taste. That, at the moment, was a matter of supreme indifference to me.

"Where are you?" I bellowed. "Come on. Hurry!"

Starson bundled up at my back, yelling: "Kov! Kov!"

He pushed past, for I'd halted as my gaze fell on the coat rack by the door. The row of pegs supported a single ponsho fleece garment. On the floor below stood a single pair of bulky felt boots.

Racegoers speak with awe of the fabled zorca Fleet-hooves. He won every race in which he was entered. He led from the starting post to the finish. Famous and fabled though he was, he'd been dead these past two centuries—his name lived on.

If Fleet-hooves had started with me as we raced for the ponsho fleece and the boots, I'd have been wearing them whilst he was still thinking about lifting those fabled hooves on the start line.

Starson went yelling about the chalet and the onrushing rumble of the avalanche battered at our senses, battling with his shouts.

He came bursting in from the inner door waving his arms.

"There's no one here!"

"Then let us depart."

The noise rolled unbearably upon us. The floor shook. The far wall broke inwards in a smothering welter of snow. The whole chalet lifted and tilted. We were thrown toppling sideways as the chalet about us flew to flinders. Everything turned white and then black.

The avalanche bore everything away to oblivion.

Two

Snow clogging my mouth. Snow blocking my ears. Snow blinding me.

Over and over I went, smothered, feeling the frightening power of the avalanche. Down the slope we hurtled, bits of wood flailing about in the white smother. With a ferocious sweep I cleared my eyes—but blackness persisted as the snow pressed in.

Gasping for air, wallowing about like a fish on land, I caught the abrupt pallor of blueness. A blue radiance glowed into life. Within that globe of light the figure of Starson, upside down, became visible.

The Star Lords were calling their kregoinye back! Starson was being rescued. Mentioning Makki Grodno to myself I made a muscle-cracking effort to stabilize my avalanche-driven antics. The blue globe began to move—began to move away from me!

Somehow I flung myself forward within the encompassing snow. A desperate lunge, a frantic grab, and I gripped Starson's ankle.

Gasping for breath proved a mistake as a slogging great slurp of snow slammed into my mouth. I spat, infuriated by that unwelcome ice cold intrusion but mostly by the callous way the Star Lords appeared prepared to abandon me to a frozen fate.

After all, they wanted me to run about Kregen pulling their chestnuts out of the fire. And, too, they required me to unite all the continents and islands of Paz to resist the Shanks who came reiving in fire and blood from over the curve of the world. To do that the Everoinye fancied I could make myself this confounded Emperor of Emperors, the Emperor of All Paz. Yet they'd not deigned to haul me out of this blasted avalanche as they pulled out their pet kregoinye, Starson.

Tumbling head over heels but with my fist firmly wrapped about Starson's ankle, I felt myself being dragged along like an ice breaker.

The speed of the Scorpion's transit exploded, as they say in Clishdrin, with force enough to rattle my back teeth.

In the next heartbeat blueness enveloped everything. The damned suffocating snow evaporated, the blackness swamped with blue, and I went hurtling headlong into an azure phantasmagoria.

I blinked. It was still cold. Snow. The dreadful white clinging muck existed everywhere about me. I was still on that Opaz-forsaken hillside smothered in snow. European languages on Earth have just the one word for snow. Eskimos have well over a hundred words for snow, describing the different kinds they contend with.

Well, bully for them. Sitting up, I clenched the ponsho fleece tightly about me. At least, the Star Lords had allowed me to retain that. My fist still gripped about Starson's ankle. I truly believe his ankle bones would have broken through before I'd have relinquished my grasp. With a welter of white he struggled up and yelled: "Jak! You idiot! Leggo!"

Spitting out an Eskimo description I said: "Blasted Star Lords! They're a definite danger to my health."

Upslope the wooden chalet stood undamaged, bright against the white glare. Beyond and further up the mountainside the first ruffles and spumings of white froth betokened the avalanche preparing to descend in all its awful majesty upon us.

"The stupid Everoinye!" I yelped, mightily incensed. "They've messed it up again!"

"Jak!" Starson sounded frightfully upset—ha! frightfully!

Let him worry about the Star Lords. All my fanciful thoughts that we'd come to a better understanding seemed to me in that freezing moment to be a mere figment of my imagination. Did the Star Lords truly require me to be the Emperor of All Paz? As you will be well aware, I didn't give a damn either way. All I wanted was to be back in Esser Rarioch with Delia. Still, when all was said and done, there was merit in uniting the lands of Paz to resist the Shanks. Then, it followed, why did it have to be me, plain Dray Prescot, to be the simple tool used by the superhuman Star Lords? Because I had the yrium? Of course!

The avalanche over our heads rumbled with menacing power.

The wind cut. The cold cut. The damned unfairness of fate cut. I shouted: "Starson! Get your fat carcass up to the chalet! There are people to be rescued."

"You! You!" he gargled, blowing snow every which way. "I know! I'm in command here and don't you forget it."

Once again we toiled up to effect the gallant rescue. I was not so much light-headed as feeling insubstantial, as though in all this fiasco, and knowing it to be real, I acted in some fantastic play.

There were no double lines cut into the snow. Under the overhang of the eaves stood a family-sized sled piled with furs. At least, by Vox, it was nice to know what we were going to do since we'd already done it.

This time I allowed Starson to precede me. Inside the chalet the warmth closed in more strongly than before. The smell of cooking lingered in the air. Starson bellowed: "Kov! Kov!"

Why was I not in the slightest surprised when the four numims appeared? We'd rescued this little noble family before, Starson and I, when he'd been calling himself Surrey. Logic followed that we were in the independent kovnate of Larnydria. Kov Randalt looked thinner than when I'd last seen him, and his powerful lion-man's face looked more shrunken than I cared for. The Kovneva Esme lay supine in a narrow carrying cot. The dread disease chivrel from which she suffered, apart from turning her hair white, weakened her daily. The two children appeared to me to be bearing up well. Lion folk, numims, are a proud and hardy race of diffs upon Kregen.

Their wonderment at seeing we two fellows again was dealt with swiftly and ruthlessly by Starson. In no time at all they were wrapped in ponsho fleeces taken from the row of pegs by the door. Now, all the pegs were empty and all the boots were gone.

As we went out I realized the ominous noise of the avalanche had become a mere part of our surroundings. The dull sky revealed not a single beam of light from Zim and Genodras. Gloom pervaded the mountainside. I tell you, that was a sad place.

My new comrade and I lifted the kovneva aboard, the children were snugged down safely, the kov instructed to climb on so that we two kregoinyi could push the sled out onto the beginning of the slide.

With quick thoughts for Zair and Opaz, I thrust hard and then swung about ready to jump aboard.

Starson slipped. His left hand grasped the rail of the sled. His body twisted as the sled began to move. In moments he'd either be dragged along helplessly—or he'd let go and be stranded.

Now, as he hadn't been about when the Everoinye first dropped us down at the wrong time, he must have scrambled aboard. I leaned over, got a grip on his wrist, snapped out: "Jump!" and hauled.

He came inboard like the proverbial sack of potatoes and landed all in a heap alongside the kov. He spluttered. Then—we were off.

Away we went, hammering down in a welter of whiteness sprouting in a huge feathering wave on each side. Up and down went the sled, roaring on in a spuming avalanche of our own. The real avalanche coruscated in a foam of whiteness, chasing us.

Which would be the swifter? Our sled—or the dread half-mountainside falling upon us?

All I could do was hang on and hope.

As you know, I am inordinately fond of the waltz music of the Strausses. However, as we went thundering down that mountain, the pulsating rhythms of the Thunder and Lightning Polka drummed into my brain. It seemed to me that thunder broke crashingly about my ears, and lightning bolts sizzled past my head. What a ride that was!

On we foamed, roaring across the damned snow, hurtling down the hill. The children huddled together, and the kov pulled his ponsho fleece about them. The poor old kovneva, terminally in decline from the remorseless ravages of the chivrel, just lay there, a supine lump.

Don't ask me how long that headlong descent lasted. As we plummeted down it seemed to me that time stood still and we went on and on for an eternity. We spewed out as the slope lessened and pine trees passed in a blur, slewing around so that we nearly toppled over. When we finally came to rest it seemed to me we'd only just started, and the mad rush down had taken only seconds.

The overcast sky lowered down on us. The trees stood all about, dark and forlorn. Starson pointed. "There. Lights."

Through the shadowy aisles of the pines lights bloomed ahead, some four hundred or so paces off. Kov Randalt heaved up.

"Where there are lights there is warmth!" Then he checked himself abruptly. I had the wry thought that lights did not necessarily indicate warmth. That was not the thought that halted the kov. He stared at Starson, and, speaking slowly and with vehemence, said: "We are not among friends here."

The last time we'd encountered this proud but shattered numim, we'd had to run off before a mob out for his blood strung him up. We'd had the assistance of the savapim Tyr Hangrol ti Ferstheim then. When Kov Randalt went on to spell out the situation, saying that all his retainers and servants had deserted him and that he and his family had hidden in the remote chalet right on the borders of the country, I knew for certain the Savanti would not send a savapim to assist us.

We were still in Larnydria. Over the mountains the neighboring kingdom of Enterdrin had the usual relationship of countries in the Dawn Lands—that was, they were usually at war. If, the kov said, we could cross Enterdrin then the next nation, the numim-ruled Felandia, would offer refuge. So—that was the task the Everoinye now set to our hands.

Now when a fellow takes up the adventuring business he has to endure cold and heat, rain and snow, success and misfortune falling impartially upon him from the heavens. By this time I had to acknowledge to myself that I was uncomfortably cold. The others were in better case for they hadn't waded through snow in a morning robe and slippers.

I said: "I will go and scout out the lights."

Starson started to say something in a hard voice, stopped, said: "Very well. Go."

Immediately, in the next heartbeat, he turned to the sled and spoke to the kov, making sure he and Esme and the children were all right. I did not smile to myself; I just hitched up my sword belts and set off.

The lights turned out to be illuminated windows from a small huddle of cabins, throwing oblongs of yellow radiance across the snow. The pines stood all about, somber and, in that setting, ominous. The folk were probably eking out an existence as fur trappers, I knew very well that, by Krun, I would not want to live here.

That thought, whilst as ever on Kregen remaining watchfully alert, made me believe they'd be friendly enough. Just in case I checked the rapier and main gauche ready for quick draws—just, you understand, to be on the safe side.

My first couple of bangs on the nearest door evoked no response.

I banged harder.

The door opened slowly and a gust of warm and pungent air wafted about me. Lamplight shone from within, turning the fellow in the doorway into a black silhouette.

"Who is it?"

His voice, hoarse, held a quavering note. "A fellow who's stranded in this confounded snow," I said. I spoke up so he could hear me, at the same time I put a down-drooping fall to the words so he'd grasp the idea I was really in need of assistance. Well, by the Black Chunkrah! I truly was!

A woman's voice called from inside the cabin. So, swiftly, I said: "I mean you no harm. My friends and I just need rest and some warmth. We are frozen."

For a space the moment hung. Then the door was pushed wider and I stepped through. The warmth was most welcome, most welcome indeed!

The place was simply furnished and yet snug. The lamp was a cheap mineral oil affair; but the fire's bright blaze seemed to me to be decidedly what was required. "Llahal," I said. "My name is Jak. I must go and fetch my friends—and I thank you most graciously." Although the sentiment was what I intended, the words somehow didn't quite match that intent.

The Opaz-forsaken cold must be addling my brains.

The smell from the stew pot hanging above the fire reminded me that my inward parts were muchly in need of sustenance. I just hoped Starson or the kov had some money, for I had none. That made me realize I mustn't tarry, so, repeating my thanks, I said I'd go now and fetch the rest of the party. I mentioned there were two children. This was not only cunning on my part but a trifle despicable, for the woman gave a little sympathetic cry. The couple were Fristles and their cat-faces expressed what I took to be genuine concern.

As I have said before, not everyone living on Kregen is a mighty warrior or an unhanged villain. The ordinary folk make that fabulous world all the better for their presence.

The trudge back through the snow found me in better spirits. We'd get ourselves warm, eat and drink, and then plan our next moves.

A fleeting dark shape under the trees swooped over my head and came to rest on a branch a few paces off. Cruel curved talons bit into the bark. The arrogant head tilted to one side. His plumage shadowed without its usual bright sheen in that miserable gloom. In the next second his wings unfolded and flapped and he soared up and away and very quickly was lost to sight.

"Now what the blazes," I said to myself, "did that bird of ill omen want?"

Pushing the Gdoinye out of my mind I stepped out stoutly.

A surprise awaited me back at the sled. Well, of course, on Kregen you expect surprises every day and twice on weekends.

The trim shape of a flier rested by the sled. The relief I felt almost overwhelmed me. This explained the Gdoinye's rapid visit. The Star Lords provided for one of their favorites so now we could fly the kov and his family clear across Enterdrin and deliver them safely to their friends in Felandia.

Ha! The Gdoinye kept on calling Dray Prescot an onker, and here, once again, Dray Prescot obliged by confirming that observation's truth.

Starson was busily assisting the children to board the voller and I was pleased to see that both of them observed the fantamyrrh. Kovneva Esme was already snugged down in her ponsho fleece. Kov Randalt, looking up, saw me trudging along towards them, and pointed. Starson swung about. Another man's head lifted up above the gunwale.

That head was crowned by a very wide-brimmed hat festooned with faerling feathers, quite unlike Starson's monstrosity of a hat.

Nimbly, this fellow, the pilot of the voller, jumped down. He wore a magnificent coat of russet furs. I knew the clothes under that desirable garment. There would be the gallant doublet and the flaring breeches and the torrents of fine white lace at his throat.

He said: "Lahal, Nath the Hammer." His lean, bronzed face with the crystal-blue eyes, the wide curled moustaches, the small pointed beard, looked just as dashingly handsome.

"Lahal, Larghos de la France."

Here was another kregoinye most highly favored by the Star Lords. Whatever function Kov Randalt and his family were destined to perform in the devious schemes of the Everoinye, they were certainly receiving right royal treatment.

A distant rumbling through the air and a beginning vibration under our feet told most eloquently that the avalanche had not finished with us. I just hoped the rotten thing would stop before reaching the cabins.

"We must hurry." Starson climbed aboard. "Come on, Larghos."

"I am with you, mon ami. Parbleu! This is no place for a civilized man!" With that the gallant dandy leaped into the voller.

Starson—Otto the Lance—looked down. "Nath the Hammer," he said with more than a trace of sarcasm. "I sensed you were mighty cutting about changing names."

"As to that," I started to say, and put my hand on the coaming ready to climb aboard.

"Ah—my apologies." Lárghos de la France spoke without any trace of apology in his tone. "This is a four place airboat and we are already overloaded with the children. My regrets."

For a moment I just stood there, hand on the coaming, feet in the damned snow.

Onker, the Gdoinye said. Well, and wasn't he right? Here were two brave kregoinyi much favored by the Star Lords. And here was I, their handyman, their Jack of All Trades, the fellow they flung in when everything else had failed. I did not mention Makki Grodno. I did not mention the Divine Madam of Belschutz. I was past that.

Yet, as I have mentioned, I fancied I was forming a better relationship with the Star Lords. Probably the presence of these other two grandees in the Everoinye's scheme of things made them overlook this fragile new relationship. Whatever—the outcome was the same.

They did have the grace to call down the remberees as the voller lifted off. She went up smartly, turned, and whistled off into the distance and vanished—just like the confounded Gdoinye vanished.

Darkness thickened among the trees. The cold stung. I lifted my arms and let them fall back to my sides. There was nothing new in Dray Prescot being abandoned to his own fate—was there?

Hoping that the avalanche wouldn't reach as far as here, I swung about and set off bashing through the snow towards the cabin and the friendly Fristles.

Three

Nath Redfern, known as Nath the Limp, heard the commotion from Little Lace Street as he patrolled his Watchman's beat along Haberdasher's Avenue. Long shadows from the rosy pinkish light of the Maiden with the Many Smiles lay across the alleys and streets of the new city of Gafarden. Nath the Limp hoisted up the lantern on its pole and hurried towards the corner. Young hellions up to no good, was his verdict on the noise, and he'd soon restore peace and quiet to the nighted city streets.

He'd picked up his injury resulting in his limp when he'd served in the Tenth Churgurs at the Battle of Bengarl's Blight. That seemed a long time ago now. He rounded the corner to see the contorted shapes of the youngsters having fun throwing empty bottles about. Mindless young idiots, he thought, and roared out an: "Oi! You! Stay where you are."

Of course, being hot-blooded youth in the full flower of undirected vigor, they shrieked with laughter and ran off as fleetly as palies, leaving Nath the Limp limping far astern.

The end of Little Lace Street gave onto Larming Street, which was the end of Nath's patrol area. He fumed in frustration. A figure turned smartly into the street and a lantern atop its pole shed lemon across the cobbles. A voice lifted. "Hai! Nath! What's all the kerfuffle?"

"Shando! Just a bunch of good-for-nothing kids having their idea of fun."

The two Watchmen approached each other. Shando, who'd served in the Fifth Zorca Bows, and thereby considered himself a cut above a mere infantryman, even if he'd been a churgur, snorted. "Damned kids!"

"Aye. A spot of service in the army'd do 'em a power of good."

The two veterans stood talking for a moment. The night breathed about them, the Maiden with the Many Smiles shone down her refulgent pinkish rays, and the scent of Moon Blooms wafted sweetly on the air.

They were just talking about the merciful relief everyone of Gafarden felt that the disgusting object known as the Spectre had at last been destroyed, when a series of hideous screaming screeching shrieks broke frighteningly on the still night.

Nath and Shando jumped about, and their lantern-topped poles thrust down and forward like spears. The shrieks culminated in a bubbling gurgle and died away in a long fading groan.

"By Vox!" said Shando.

"Opaz forfend!" said Nath.

Together, cautiously, they approached the shadowed alley off Larming Street from whence the awful noise originated.

Like the old swods they were they shone their lights in first.

The thing that lay sprawled in black blood had once been a man. The body was unrecognizable, ripped into shreds. One arm had been thrown a dozen paces away, and a leg stuck up out of a refuse container at the side of the alley. The lights and shadows wavered eerily over that nauseous scene. The two kampeons regarded the shambles stoically.

At last, Shando said: "Best call the Deldar."

"Aye." Nath rubbed his nose. "I don't like to say it; but—"

"The Opaz-forsaken creature was destroyed. It was witnessed."

"It was. Just so. But—"

Shando shook his lantern pole. "How many arrows pierced the thing? Hundreds!"

"Even so, even so," said Nath the Limp. "Devils are known to return—"

Shando, who was known as Shando the Fomentor, snorted. "Aye. And where is the Spectre now, hey?"

At that both old soldiers turned about, throwing the lights of their lanterns in the crannies and crevices of the alleyway. A blue glow took their immediate attention. It appeared to them to emanate past the mouth of the alleyway a little further along Larming Street. Together, cautiously, they went back to the street. The blue radiance died as they reached the street. The fuzzy pink moonlight washed in roseate shadows all about them.

A man walked towards them.

He was dressed in a mangy old ponsho fleece, and his feet were thrust into bulbous felt boots.

The figure stepped into the lantern light. Nath looked intently. He stiffened to rigid attention.

"Majister!"

In turn I looked at this crusty old kampeon, now a Watchman in the city of Gafarden. The baptism in the Sacred Pool of far Aphrasöe has blessed—or cursed?—me with an eidetic memory. So I could not of course know all the names of every swod in the Freedom Army of Vallia; those I did know I remembered.

I said: "Lahal, Nath Redfern. Well met."

Nath Redfern said, somewhat garblingly, and not surprising in the circumstances: "This is Shando the Fomentor, majister. There is a corpse in the alley. Cut up bad."

"Majister," spat out Shando the Fomentor, who was not known to me but who clearly accepted what Nath said. "Majister! It is the Spectre!"

If I own to a cold breeze blowing around the back of my neck I merely acknowledge any fellow's dread at the name of the Spectre.

"The Opaz-forsaken thing was destroyed. I was there. I saw it." I moved forward purposefully. "Where is the corpse?"

"Down here in Fishbone Alley, majister." With the lantern lights throwing splashes of color through the night we moved down Fishbone Alley. It was called this because at one time skilled workers who shaped and pierced fish bones to make needles lived in the alley.

A few people began to gather, alarmed at the noise. I told the two Watchmen to hold them back, and looked down on the pathetic body. This hideousness certainly looked like the work of the Spectre. But, by the pustulating proboscis and bulging belly of Makki Grodno! I'd seen the damn monster shredded by hundreds of shafts. I'd seen it melt and flow and vanish. The ghastly thing could not still be alive—could it?

We here on this Earth are only too dreadfully familiar with what are called copycat crimes. This murder could have been committed by some sick individual aping the Spectre. One precept in life is to assume the worst and hope for the best. I had to assume this was, indeed, the handiwork of the Spectre, and hope that it wasn't.

The crowd was thickening and more lights appeared. Clouds obscured the Dahemin, the twin moons forever orbiting each other as they orbited Kregen. Returning to the mouth of Fishbone Alley I, somewhat curtly, told a likely looking fellow, a Rapa whose feathers sheened darkly in the lantern light, to run and fetch the officials of the city. Everything would have to be done following the correct procedures. Gafarden had suffered far too much from the murdering Spectre to botch any fresh investigation.

Naturally, questions were asked. The two Watchmen had seen nothing, nor had anyone else. No dark shadows running from the scene of the crime featured in this investigation. When, eventually, the body was carried away and nothing else, for the moment, remained to be done, I took myself off to the palace and the rooms there set aside for my use.

The ridiculous ponsho fleece and the felt boots had served me well in the bitter cold of the mountainside; now I needed a prolonged session in the Baths of the Nine. Then a slap-up meal would put me right with the world once more.

The friendly Fristles had indeed taken me in and so saved my bacon. I just wondered if this fresh murder here in Gafarden had not taken place, would the Star Lords have plucked me from Larnydria?

As soon as my essential inner and outer requirements had been satisfied, I set about bringing myself up to date on developments in Gafarden. Tobi Vingal came bounding into my office and the door crashed to after him. Brash and happy-go-lucky, he was a welcome sight, and his heavy features flushed with pleasure as he snapped to attention.

"Majister! I mean, jis!"

"Lahal, Tobi. Sit yourself down. As you are acting as my assistant, you can tell me everything that's going on."

The chair crunched as he sat. He made a face. "Well, now—not a lot, jis, not a lot." He paused, scratched his nose, and added: "There was a murder last night—but I hear you were there."

"Aye. If this is the Spectre again—well, I just don't know."

A small silence fell. Then Tobi went on to tell me about the doings of the various people of interest to us—all of which you will hear in due course.

For his non-alcoholic drinks Tobi was partial to colored sazz rather than parclear. The necessary orders were given and very quickly a tray was brought in bearing a jug of sazz and two glasses. Tobi poured and lifted his glass.

"Shiraz!"

He quaffed and smiled and licked his lips.

"Shiraz?" I said. "What's that all about?"

"Why, jis. Just a toast. Something one says before drinking. It's all the rage in Loh where I was." He drank again, and said: "You've never heard that toast before?"

"Not in the parts of Loh I've been."

"Well, jis, it's a big place."

So I just nodded and said: "Opaz Sublime," and drank off my sazz.

Tobi went on to tell me that Jiktar Yavnin Purvun was back in Gafarden. I was surprised.

"I thought Yavnin was going to Vondium to take command of a new vessel in the Vallian Air Service?"

"That didn't come to anything. I don't know why. But there is a new Fleet Admiral now. Maybe—"

"New Fleet Admiral?" Vangar ti Valkanium had taken over the high command of the Air Service when the Lord Farris died. "What's his name?" I couldn't conceive that Drak would have dismissed Vangar.

"No idea, jis. The Presidio is different these days."

A little shiver took me. Tobi looked up. "Jis?"

"Nothing," I said. The disquieting news Inch had brought twined with the damned cold on that mountainside when the avalanche cascaded down like white Doomsday. Things were not right in Vallia.

Of my three new comrades, Tobi, Yavnin and Nalgre Nevko, there was no news of the latter. Tobi just said that he'd had to go to Vondium on merchant business. Well, by Krun, we'd had some right roaring times together when the Spectre roamed Gafarden. If the misbegotten thing was truly back, we were likely to experience more of the same.

Tobi confirmed that ugly rumors circulated in North Vallia. The descendants of the racters who'd been roundly defeated all those seasons ago, growing restless and feeling family pride and shame, intended, it was said, to take over. They'd finish the job their forebears had so signally failed to do.

Mind you, they were being clever in being active in the north. Lately, Drak had been away in the southwest. These neo racters would drum up support in many different quarters of Vallia, and flit from here to there like woflovols on a night of Notor Zan. If they managed to load the Presidio with their adherents, then Drak would have to act swiftly and very adroitly.

One of the under-chamberlains knocked and came in wearing an expression compounded of puzzlement and apprehension.

"Majister. The chief pallan, Nath Swantram, is demanding to see you." The under-chamberlain, a little Och called Quarmby, hesitated. Then: "He has guards with him, in armor, bearing swords."

In his casual, reckless way, Tobi said: "Guards usually do." But I saw how his left hand clenched around the hilt of his sword.

"Well, Quarmby," I said, very jovial, leaning back in the chair. "Show the chief pallan in."

"At once, majister." And Quarmby hurried out.

"What the devil does the fellow want?" Tobi stood up and started to prowl about the office. "And the Nazabni Ulana Farlan is still in the city. Although, of course, she is no longer the nazabni."

I felt extremely sorry for Ulana, although I'd been perhaps the chief architect in the decision to remove her from office. If only she could get over her infatuation with Yavnin Purvun she could get on with her life. There was much for her to accomplish in Vallia.

"I agree, it must be very galling for Ulana. Nath Swantram is not your most delicate kind of fellow."

Now Ochs are not tall diffs. Quarmby appeared in the doorway and opened his mouth about to shout the introduction. He went flying forward and sideways as the chief pallan strode impatiently in giving the little Och a push quite out of proportion to the need. The glitter of steel filled the passage beyond his bustling figure.

Tobi stopped pacing instantly, and swung around to stare at the chief pallan. His color was up. The scar disfiguring the left side of his face, slashed across nose and mouth, stood out vividly. Nath Swantram did not much care for his obvious nickname, Nath the Clis.

He marched up to the desk with a kind of swagger ill-suited to a quiet office. A rectangle of yellow paper between his fingers slapped down on the desk. He stood back a pace and glared at me with obvious gleeful enjoyment. For a moment complete silence reigned.

All manner of appropriate—or inappropriate—remarks rushed through my head. I looked up. "What, Swantram? No Lahal?"

He made a curt gesture. "The matter is serious. This is the warrant for your arrest."

I did not touch the yellow paper. "On what charge?"

He put a finger to his scar. Despite all his swagger he was ill at ease. "You are no longer the Emperor of Vallia. You must bow to the Law as anyone else."

In my old gravel-shifting voice I fairly snarled out: "Get on with it, man!"

He jumped.

Tobi spoke in a voice not quite as steady as he would have wished. "You can't arrest Dray Prescot! He is the Emperor of Emperors, the Emperor of All Paz!"

"Best keep your mouth closed, cramph," said Nath the Clis without turning his head to look at Tobi. He drew himself up. He opened his mouth to carry on talking and I cut in harshly.

"And best you keep a civil tongue in your head, Swantram!"

He didn't like that. Still, having got this far he intended to carry on this farce to the end.

"You ask what the charge is. I shall tell you." Now he was really enjoying this. He pointed a finger at me.

"You are under arrest and charged with the murder of Tyr Larghos Fernleigh, my chief secretary."

Four

"Who in a Herrelldrin Hell is Larghos Fernleigh?"

"My chief stylor."

"Well?"

He fingered his scar again, and this time there was calculation in that stroking finger. "There are witnesses—"

"What confounded witnesses?" I wouldn't give this rast the satisfaction of making me stand up. I sat. I stared up malevolently.

Nath the Clis stood his ground, give the rogue that. "The two watchmen who found the body. You were the only other person present. Oh, yes, you were wearing a silly disguise." He sniggered. "A ponsho fleece, I'm told. You and no one else was there. You murdered Larghos Fernleigh."

Tobi Vingal, a chavpaktun, a mercenary who wore the bronze chavonth head at his throat, a right roaring reckless fellow, drew his sword. This was his favorite lynxter, the sword of Loh. I shook my head. "Put that away, Tobi. This nonsense can be dealt with without the steel bokkertu."

Sullenly, his heavy features congested, Tobi growled out: "Aye, jis." And he shoved the blade away. Then, most truculently, he added: "By Lingloh! These shints deserve the favor of steel!"

"Oh," I said, casually. "They will. All in Opaz's good time. Tsleetha-tsleethi. The steel will be cleansed."

The good Tobi couldn't repress his feelings. He burst out: "It is perfectly clear the majister did not do this! This murder is the work of the Spectre!"

Nath the Clis sniffed contemptuously. "All Gafarden knows the Spectre was destroyed. Shot to pieces by many arrows."

"But the fashion in which this flunkey of yours was killed." Tobi was so highly incensed his face positively writhed with anger. "I'll sort this out! I'll see—"

"Tobi!" I spoke in a cutting, incisive voice. "Don't prattle on so. Shut the black-fanged winespout."

He checked, looked at me hard, nodded. "Quidang!" He understood my meaning. Any more outbursts and he, too, would be carted off to the dungeons. He had to remain free, on the outside, to carry word of my arrest.

At the chief pallan's abrupt command his guards tramped in. Well, they hauled me off to the dungeons of the old fortress under the spanking new palace Princess Didi had built atop the ancient pile. Everything happened with swiftness. In no time at all I was ensconced in a dismal cell deep underground with the water seeping from the walls and the stink of centuries of corpses in my nostrils.

This Nath Swantram, Nath the Clis, the chief pallan, was a fine rogue, to be sure. He hungered to be the nazab of Urn Vennar, ruling the province in the name of Princess Didi. Transparently, he wanted more than that. He aspired to the nobility. He wanted a province of Vallia for himself.

Well, by the stinking black body juices of Makki Grodno, I said to myself, if the shint thinks he can get away with that, quite apart from bunging me in a cell on false charges, he has a very great number of different thinks coming. Bad cess to the rogue! By the Black Chunkrah, yes!

I remained quite calm. Perfectly level-headed. By yes, I, of course, meant no. Swantram would not get away with his roguish schemes.

And—there was another black mark against the cramph. He'd had me carted off to the old dungeons which hadn't been used for seasons. Princess Didi's new more salubrious prison, the Chundrognik, was now the official place of detention. But, unofficially? Perhaps Swantram tucked his victims down here and conveniently forgot about them.

Paradoxically, because I was incarcerated in this miserable hole, what happened was by that fact made easier.

The cell door opened with only the slightest of creaks. Belkran the Gaoler walked in wearing the most remarkable expression on his hairy Brokelsh face. The keys dangling from the ring in his hand jangled as that bristly hand shook.

Three more men walked quietly into the cell. They wore simple dark clothes, were heavily armed, and each had his face swathed in an encompassing scarf. Their eyes in the reflected light of the stub of a candle glittered.

I stood up.

Not a word was spoken. The keys were taken from poor bewildered Belkran. The three masked men ushered me out and shut the door on the gaoler. The lock was clicked and the bolts shot home. In a bunch we walked steadily along the dank passage under the arching roof. Our footfalls sounded no louder than a kitten's on carpet. A Rapa guard slumbered peacefully against the wall, and just beyond him his fellow was just beginning to sit up, holding his guts, moaning.

One of the three masked men gave this unfortunate guard a clout around the ear and he fell back with a squawk.

On we went, through the dismal passageways and up the slimed stairs, passing four or five other diffs snoring away in total disregard of their wardenly duties. Not one had been killed.

The last part of the ascent into the streaming radiance of Zim and Genodras passed with a remarkable lack of incident. I'd expected trouble here and was primed to grab a weapon and fight it out. That kind of numbskull heroics proved to be unnecessary.

As I said, because the prison was not in general use, the guard rota was thin on the ground. We emerged into the suns shine and I whooped up an enormous lungful of the superb Kregan air.

Three scarves whipped away from three faces and, lo! the three masked men turned out to be my three new companions in Gafarden.

Naturally, I was not in the least surprised.

Tobi Vingal unshipped the rapier and main gauche he wore and handed them to me. He declared that he was not familiar with the disciplines required for rapier work, although I was not sure I believed him.

Jiktar Yavnin Purvun said: "What a disgusting hole!" His athletic figure which was normally clad in the uniform of the Vallian Air Service and his frank open face with that hair paler than the usual Vallian brown gave the ladies palpitations—and none more so than Ulana Farlan to her despair. "Disgusting!" he repeated.

"Oh, I've seen worse." Nalgre Nevko's hard face with those thin decisive lips gave sure indication that he knew what he was talking about. His hair, like Yavnin's, was lighter than usual. A small scar along his left cheek gave his hard professional appearance an even greater presence.

"I give you all my thanks, doms." I strode along with them buckling up the sword and dagger. "But how the devil did you manage to find me down there?"

"Experience," said Nalgre Nevko, and he spoke harshly.

"Oh, we made a few enquiries." Tobi's reckless ways did not altogether conceal the determination in him.

"Yes." Yavnin half-turned to me as we walked. "The first guard was most happy to tell us."

That I was most happy they'd not killed anyone was obvious; I had the odd feeling that if I mentioned that they would feel puzzlement and conceive I was going soft.

Chanting grew louder as we went on and soon filled the air with the strains of "OO-lie O-paz, OO-lie O-paz." Every day in Vallia was a day consecrated to Opaz, each with its name apt to the manifestation of the Invisible Twins. Today was The Day of Opaz Enthroned. The long lines of chanting devotees wound along the avenue, and passersby acknowledged the supreme authority of Opaz by respectful bows.

"Opaz certainly was with us today," quoth Yavnin. "I admit I expected trouble."

Telling him I was glad to see him, I added that I was surprised. My question about his new command was received with silence, followed by a little grunt of negation. I did not press the enquiry.

These three stout fellows, each one so different from the others, conducted me to a clean but cheap lodging house on Wainwright Street. The landlady, a high-colored Hytak with a high-colored voice, called Mistress Felima, welcomed us, and addressed me as Koter Naghan the Abstemious. I acknowledged that, and glared upon my companions. They, the hulus, had difficulty in keeping straight faces.

When we were alone in the comfortable room upstairs, I said: "And I suppose you think that's funny."

"Well, jis," they said. "It is."

As you can see, our comradeship was blooming.

Now these fine fellows did not know that I could change the appearance of my face, a trick taught me, as you know, by our comrade Wizard of

Loh Deb-Lu-Quienyin. They'd brought me to this safe house and arranged all the details so that I could remain in hiding. They did not know I could walk into the palace and not be recognized.

One of the few people who did know, Naghan Raerdu, one of my most efficient secret agents, was still in Gafarden. I asked for him to be contacted and to come to see me.

These strapping new companions of mine imagined that after they'd rescued me so bravely and brought me to a safe house I'd be content to stay mewed up, cowering away in this hidey hole. Well, our comradeship might be blooming; evidently, they were still unaware of the true nature of Dray Prescot. The true reckless, bloody-minded nature of Dray Prescot, I might add.

When they at last left, with their good wishes still ringing in my ears, I ate and drank and waited in a right paddy of frustration until Naghan Raerdu showed up.

Naghan, known as the Slippy, came in without, it seemed, disturbing the air which he displaced. I doubt if Mistress Felima even knew he'd entered her establishment.

"Well, jis," he greeted me after the Lahals, "this is a bad business."

"Aye, Naghan, it is."

"You want me to root around and see what I can find."

Nodding, I went on to tell him that besides investigating this latest murder, he should look into the disquieting rumors from the north. Public opinion is a fickle beast and, while Drak and Silda were popular and in conjunction with the Presidio ran the country well, unpleasant rumors and downright lies could undermine them. In Terrestrial terms, we were sitting on a time bomb here.

At my request Mistress Felima brought in refreshments. She looked startled to see another person in the room and said that she'd no idea anyone had come in. I put a hand to my mouth—just in case my inner smile escaped to my lips. But Naghan the Slippy knew!

Later on, just as Naghan was about to leave, the door crashed open and Tobi burst in looking wild. He was followed by Yavnin and Nalgre and they, too, looked disturbed.

"There's been another murder!" yelped Tobi.

They all started to jabber on together until I raised my hand and brought order. Gravely, Yavnin gave the news. One of the chief pallan's under stylors, a Xaffer called Frayling the Pen, had been discovered in a yard at the back of The Gardenia Bower where he habitually took parclear and cakes. He was scattered about the yard.

The Slippy said: "You were here, jis, so that proves you could not—"

Harshly, Nalgre Nevko broke in. "You were rescued, jis, and on the outside, free. Nath Swantram will still blame you."

"That's of small moment." My old gravel-shifting voice made them stiffen up. "What is important is that these murders must be the work of the Spectre. The damn monstrous thing isn't dead. It's back here in Gafarden. There's an unholy time ahead, doms."

Five

They'd brought along a decent set of Vallian buffs with the tall black boots and so as I strode along in the mingled lights of the Suns no one paid me particular attention. My companions had cleared off so as not to attract too much unwelcome interest in the lodgers at Mistress Felima's house. Naghan the Slippy had vanished in his silent way to carry out his fresh investigations.

Although the thoughts remained unspoken, it was perfectly clear they expected me to stay in the lodging house in hiding. Ha! With a face that did not sting too much and which I could hold for a considerable time, I was off out into the streets sharpish.

By Krun, yes!

The fellows had also brought a fine drexer, the straight cut-and-thruster which was now in general service in Vallia. As for the knife, the weapon I habitually refer to as 'my old sailor knife', well, by Vox, even though I'd had enough new ones and lost so many of them, the comforting feel of the knife snugged over my hip remained constant.

In the top of the left hand boot a neat sheath integral with the leather afforded a snug haven for a smaller version of the knife, rather after the fashion of a Bowie knife.

At the intersection of two streets where a little kyro opened the vista my onward progress was stopped by a large and noisy crowd. There were all manner of folk there, many kinds of diffs, and the vendors were selling their wares as fast as a leem pounces. The center of the attraction stood on an upturned barrel and gesticulated and shouted, haranguing the mob.

This fellow took my interest. He wore ordinary buff, had rapier and main gauche strapped to his waist, wore a hat with a sweeping feather around the brim. The feather was black and white.

He was apim, Homo sapiens sapiens like me, with a face like a walnut and dark eyes under heavy eyebrows. His nose, large, round, looked more like a squashed tomato than a nose.

Perforce, I stopped to listen. The crowd were clearly restless. Some laughed and jeered; some stood silently listening; the majority were taking in the fellow's word seriously.

I will make no attempt to transcribe his speech word for word. What it all boiled down to, in a nutshell, was that now was the time for change in the island empire, that the emperor and empress were no longer fit to rule, and that the quicker they were got rid of, the better.

So I, Dray Prescot, the father of that same contumed emperor, stood listening in grim silence.

The servitors of Vallia—for we keep no slaves—wear banded sleeves of various colors. Each color combination signifies the allegiance, which lord or house or business or political party the wearer serves. Placed at strategic points in the crowd stood men wearing banded sleeves of black and white.

I felt an itch down my spine. Black and white. Damned Racters.

Gyps ran about excitedly among the legs of the crowd. Children, bored out of their skulls, tugged at their parents, wanting to go home. Slender trees outside a hostelry, The Scented Bower, cast their perfumes upon the air. And over all the streaming mingled radiances of the Suns of Scorpio brought color and light to the world.

Then this rabble-rouser carried on vehemently to say that the dreadful Spectre murders were the fault of the emperor. If Drak looked after the people of Vallia properly then these awful crimes would not occur. This struck a chord in the listening crowd and they ceased to prattle amongst themselves and listened intently.

A man standing next to me, a hulking Brokelsh with a drayman's apron and wisps of straw in his black bristle hair, called out in support. Politely, I asked him the name of the orator.

"Why, dom! He's the famous Tyr Prangman ti Volden. He's the right of it when it comes to running the country, by Vox!"

There was no doubt about it that now this Prangman fellow had the ears of the crowd. People were yelling agreement, urging the rabble-rouser on. Gently, I began to ease myself through the pressing crowds towards Prangman and his upturned barrel.

Anybody who thinks that running a nation is easy needs his head examining. I'd had my fill, and so had my divine Delia, and we'd both abdicated. Drak, of course, was born of a line of emperors. In Silda, my comrade Seg Segutorio's daughter, Drak had the perfect partner.

In my view the disgusting Makki Grodno himself could not find fault with Drak or Silda. These confounded neo-Racters were out for the same selfish ends as their ancestors—power for themselves and a Herrelldrin Hell for anyone else.

"Excuse me, dom," and "Your pardon, mistress," I said as I continued to ease my way towards the front, allowing nobody to take offence. I was genteel politeness itself. Gradually, I moved through the throng towards the upturned barrel and the spouting Tyr Prangman ti Volden. By this time he'd worked himself up into a right old paddy and was declaiming facts and figures that, in more measured moments, would instantly be seen to be false.

Then—ah, then! This Prangman cramph started on about how the Empress Silda was a known courtesan, harboring many lovers, and how the Emperor Drak took no notice, besotted in drink.

Well, now! By the bulging thighs and mammoth stomach of the Divine Madam of Belschutz! I couldn't have that. No, by Zim-Zair!

Almost at the front of the crowd I came across a Hytak of the tailed variety clad in homespun and waving a short thick stick. His powerful face was congested with blood. "You rast!" he bellowed. "As sure as my name's Vanner the Downright, you lie!" He caught a glimpse of an approaching Rapa out of the corner of his eye. The Rapa wore the black and white schturval. In a twinkling the short thick stick laid a thwack across the Rapa's beak. "You, Prangman, are an unhanged rogue, a liar and an abomination in the sight of Opaz!"

Incontinently, the Rapa fell down. It was nicely done. I stepped over his fallen body to stand beside this Hytak Vanner the Downright. "Take care, dom," I said from the corner of my mouth. "There are too damned many black and whites about."

Without waiting for an answer I surged forward, took this Tyr Prangman ti Volden in a cunning grip and so tossed him head over heels off his barrel and into the dirt.

What made my despatch of the fellow the more urgent were the despicable words he'd spoken about Princess Didi, whose province of Urn Vennar this was. Didi remained in Zandikar, still not well and slowly recovering from a most horrendous wound. She remained in my thoughts and as soon as this troublesome business with the Spectre was finished I'd be off to the Eye of the World to see her. As it was, not only my duty but the fiat of the Star Lords kept me here.

Pandemonium broke out. Everybody, it seemed, had a grudge against everybody else. The black and whites started to lash out and they were met by lusty blows in return. The whole kyro erupted into a howling pell-melling mob. The noise boiled to the sky.

This proved to me in stark emphasis the unhealthy state of not only this city of Gafarden but the whole of Vallia.

The Hytak Vanner the Downright grabbed my arm. "Well done, dom. But I think we'd best be off."

"Aye."

So I, Dray Prescot, etcetera, etcetera, ran off.

Now a most curious thought had come to me. A troublesome thought. This rabble-rouser Prangman in spouting his anti-imperial message was, in fact, asserting his rights to a political viewpoint.

A political dialogue should have ensued. Instead, I'd demonstrated the overwhelming force wielded by the government—admittedly, in this case at second-hand. I'd simply used bully-boy tactics instead of a reasoned democratic discussion. I felt, and by Krun I admit it, I felt downright ashamed of my actions.

Drak and Silda would not have approved. They did not try to govern Vallia wielding the big stick.

Mind you, this shint Prangman shouldn't have ladled out the slanderous and totally untrue filthy accusations of Silda and Didi.

On that score alone he deserved to be upended off his barrel. Silda and Didi, Sisters of the Rose, were unsullied ladies of Vallia. I took in a deep breath as I ran after Vanner. Leaving the murky world of politics aside, maybe, after all, Prangman deserved to be upended off his barrel on the simple score of gallantry to ladies.

Vanner and I were not to be let off lightly by the neo-Racters.

We'd been marked. Four hulking great fellows spread out in front of us. Their swords remained sheathed; but they wielded most knobbly and unhealthy-looking clubs.

There was no need for their leader, a Rapa whose violet-colored feathers clashed with his tunic, to call out: "Blatter 'em!" But he did.

Vanner was up to the mark. He fairly hurled himself at the nearest thug and his short thick stick went up and down in a blur.

Two heartbeats later, using an old Krozair technique, I took the next one's knobbly cudgel away from him, kicked him, and swirled to meet the third's attack. A ducking dive under the bludgeon, a swift twist, a short jab, and he reeled away, screeching, holding his guts. What of Vanner?

The Hytak was in the act of using his stick to parry a blow and swinging his tail around. The tail stiffened, jabbed into his adversary's throat. I winced. The fellow, another Rapa, tried to scream and made only a garbling noise.

Vanner carefully struck him a clean blow on the beak and he toppled away, lax and limp.

"Well, now," quoth Vanner the Downright.

His tail coiled neatly around his waist. Between the time he'd parried the blow to when he'd whirled half round and his tail struck, barely a heartbeat and a half had passed. He was quick!

Of course, this being Kregen, we weren't out of the woods yet.

The melee in the square rioted on. Probably the folk were using their pent up angers and fears over the Spectre to knock one another about. How long the city guard would take to appear depended on the mettle of the Deldar in charge that shift. From the edge of the scrum, spinning out, as it were, like sparks from a Catherine Wheel, three men charged for us.

These were an entirely different proposition from the four groaning on the ground.

For a start, they wore fringed leathers. The black and white schturvals showed bravely at the front of their shoulders.

They were all apim and their faces carried that lean and hungry look of the fighting man about to earn his hire. Finally, all three carried swords, glinting in the suns' rays, pointing at Vanner and me.

"Run!" yelped Vanner the Downright. He started off with all the speed exemplified in the classical description—he ran like a startled ferret.

As he'd just said, I repeated: "Well, now."

I'd run off thinking that to be the best course. Now these three swordsmen who were far more than mere thugs, expected me to run off again. If I didn't, then they confidently expected to spit me.

You do get a bit tired of continually running off in the face of danger. That, by the Blade of Kurin, is true!

The weapons in the fists of these men were rapiers. Well, that would make it more interesting. Even before I'd met Mefto the Kazzur, I always knew that one day I'd bump into a swordsman who had my measure. I never, as you know, claim to be the best swordsman of two worlds. That is childish boasting.

Perhaps, in this scrappy encounter on the edge of a riot, I would meet another sword fighter who could take me.

Vanner's shout was just audible above the crowd's hullabaloo.

"Come on, dom! Run! They've got swords!"

Giving the Downright no reply I faced the oncomers.

Now, as you know, I'd been trying to be the calm and controlled Dray Prescot who thought before he acted. I abhor violence, as, again, you know. Trouble is, people keep offering violence towards me. Here, I should have run off with Vanner. Clearly, I ought.

"C'mere, you cramph!" shouted the nearest fellow in a most coarse way. "We'll teach you not to manhandle Tyr Prangman!"

They held their rapiers and left hand daggers in a competent fashion. They were not coys, novices. They knew their business—and they meant business, by Vox.

Slowly, without show, I drew my rapier and main gauche.

Holding the weapons down, pointing at the ground, I called: "Listen, doms. I've no desire to fight you. Why don't—"

The answering roar sounded like a hungry chunkrah. He just made an incoherent bellow and shook his sword violently.

So, that was that. No point in hanging about waiting, then. Snouting the rapier and dagger up I charged headlong at them.

They say that as you grow older you grow more tolerant. Well, after my dip in the Sacred Pool of far Aphrasöe I was still young. These Racters deserved the tolerance meted out to folk who wish to dominate and subjugate everyone to their own selfish ends. Oh, yes, of course, these bully boys were paid by the high muck-a-mucks in the Racter hegemony to terrorize anyone who sought to stand against them. If they were earning their hire, then, by Vox, I had to earn mine as this so-called Emperor of All Paz.

So, in a somewhat ugly mood brought on by the intransigence of these three hired killers, I went headlong slap-bang into them.

Well, we fought. They knew the tricks of their trade and their swordsmanship proved interesting. The harsh scrape of steel on steel, the tramp and slither of feet seeking purchases, the panting grunts of these three as they fought, sullied the bright air of Kregen.

My first onslaught sent one reeling back, dragging his shoulder from my blade. He dropped his dagger, and cursed vilely. The other two sought to flank me so that I darted back and then, instantly, leaped forward again like a leem. The rapier flashed once, twice, the main gauche twitched to flick away a seeking sword. All that attack accomplished was to keep my hide unpunctured and to drive them back onto the defensive. Well, by Vox, the first result was damned important!

Moving forward again with the blades gently weaving so they'd not guess my intentions, I pressed on them.

"You rast!" shouted the fellow with the pierced shoulder. "Give up now or it'll go worse for you."

Without wasting breath on vainglorious and useless boasting I lunged to the right, flicked my blade around and under his dagger and sent it flying. Without stopping I plunged on, turned instantly, and my straightened rapier blade went clean through his comrade's throat. This one looked astonished. He'd jumped to attack me the moment I'd half-turned my back on him to deal with his comrade. Now, suddenly, a length of steel stuck clean through his throat. No wonder he was surprised.

A little hiatus ensued. The fellow who's Adam's Apple had been so summarily de-cored fell down. Bubbles and froth dribbled from his lips. This was not a pretty sight. And I'd done it.

That it was all their damn fault was true; all the same...

The unwounded swordsman hovered. In a kind of dance he hopped up and down on the balls of his feet, clearly unsure of what the hell to do next.

Holding his shoulder where a small dribble of blood seeped over the leather, that fighter, apparently the leader, yelled out in a vicious snarl. "Stick him, Samdo! Get stuck in!"

Samdo hopped up and down and swished his sword about.

All the time the crowd noise from the riot smashed in waves across the square. Fresh shouts lifted. "City Guard!"

Samdo screeched: "It's no good, Lart!"

This fellow Lart had the most impressive set of black eyebrows. His nose, a thin and dyspeptic affair, flared as he dragged in a huge breath. "I've marked you, you cramph! We'll be back, as Slem is my witness!"

With that he bellowed to Samdo to leave Nath the Fulleron—presumably the man on the ground with a mangled throat—where he was and to run as though the Iron Riders of Hodan Set were after him.

Both swordsmen swung about. They ran swiftly away into a side street and were lost to view.

Not being altogether the onker I am so often called, I followed suit and sprinted off into the welcoming shadows.

Six

Murky clouds began to spread across the brightness of Zim and Genodras. A light rain started, drifting with the gentle breeze, casting a misty indefiniteness over the streets and houses. Pavement cobbles glistened like neatly stacked rows of apples. Although the Suns would be a bur or two before they vanished over the horizon, the streets began to clear of people.

A man and woman scuttled into a doorway as I approached. The door slammed with a bang. As I passed the sound of a heavy beam being slotted into place at the back of the door slapped out clearly.

Not because of the approach of evening. Not because of the rain. Oh no! The good folk of Gafarden shut up shop early before nightfall because of the Spectre. No doubt existed in my mind that the damn monster had returned to haunt us. I'd seen it killed, shot to pieces by hundreds of arrows. Yet—it was back alive.

My face now felt as though I'd stuck it into a beehive.

The face-changing effect was hurting not because of the time I'd worn this new face; but because of the fight. Time, then, to return to Mistress Felima's. So, perforce, I turned about and retraced my steps.

The kyro where the riot had erupted around the agitator Prangman stood deserted. No lights shone from any of the windows in the buildings surrounding the square. I doubted if The Scented Bower would do much business this night.

The matter of this Prangman fellow would have to be looked into. Clearly, he'd come down from the north where the Racters festered. Here in Urn Vennar we were nearer the north of the island than the south and the obvious thought occurred to me that this province would be the neo-Racters' next target for lies and subversion.

Mistress Felima welcomed me back and fussed and insisted on taking my buff coat to be dried in the kitchen. She brought in a capital meal which cheered me up a trifle. Alone in my room, just popping the first of the palines from their pottery dish, I became aware of the blue glow in the corner. Alert, I sat up, chewing.

The oval of blue light radiated magic, no doubt of that!

The light thickened and condensed and turned into the familiar form and features of Ling-Li-Lwingling.

"Lahal, Dray. You are well?"

"Lahal, Ling-Li—aye, as well as can be expected. You? And Khe-Hi? And Deb-Lu?"

"Busy, busy, as ever." Her handsome face betrayed concern beneath the smile she put on. "There is news."

"Ah."

She went on to tell me the latest news from Vondium. As a most powerful Witch of Loh, she had simply gone into lupu and sent this image of herself to see me here in Gafarden. Wizards and Witches of Loh do not usually serve others, they take on those people of whom they approve as clients for their thaumaturgy.

She, her husband Khe-Hi-Bjanching, and dear old Deb-Lu-Quienyin, all adepts of the highest order, had taken on Vallia. They'd proved of immense value in the past—and, by Krun, would do so again.

As she spoke I could feel the aura of power and strength flowing from the blue radiance. What she said made me sigh in annoyance and frustration. Down south in the island of Pandahem the Bloody Menaham had once again broken out from their borders and gone with fire and steel invading their neighbors in North Pandahem. Seg Segutorio, the Emperor of the federation of South Pandahem, was already gathering an army for defense. Drak had immediately responded to the entreaties of Queen Lushfymi of Lome—who was still around and still as beautiful as ever—and in turn was putting an expeditionary force together. After her troubles, we all had a soft spot for Queen Lush.

Now the army of Freedom Fighters which had saved the island from the hordes of pillagers and reivers and Flutsmen and Aragorn and all the rest had been much reduced of late. In a busy empire men and women are required as farmers and craftsmen and traders, to carry out the multifarious tasks required to keep the empire prosperous. You don't want masses of people wasting their time drilling and marching and being soldiers. Until an emergency strikes...

"So your son is taking everything he can scrape up and—"

"I understand, Ling-Li. Of course. He can take my Guard."

Her smile this time was genuine. "We all knew you'd agree."

Apart from the fact that there was little else I could do, if Drak considered the situation dangerous, then it was.

She wanted to know if I intended to go to Pandahem.

"No, Ling-Li. There's unfinished business up here."

After I'd given her polite remembrances to various people, we said the remberees, the blue glow faded and she was gone.

This news was most unwelcome. We'd had trouble with the Bloody Menahem before, as you who have followed my narrative will know only too well. We had friends in Pandahem. The old animosity between the two islands now resided, defunct, in the past. Except for these bloody-minded and blood-thirsty folk of Menaham.

And, again as you who have followed my narrative will know, the Mystique of Paz still had the spirit to inspire. Oh, yes, the schemes of the Star Lords demanded of me that I make myself the Emperor of Emperors, the Emperor of All Paz. Well, the Everoinye demanded and perhaps, possibly, one day, that might transpire. As it was, the people of Paz just had to see that their destiny lay in helping one another instead of fighting. The damned fish-head Shanks from over the curve of the world had still to be reckoned with.

The frisson one felt at the name of Paz strengthened the sinews and summoned up the blood. Under the beneficent gaze of Opaz we of Paz must unite. Anything else would allow the Shanks in—and disaster.

The next morning Tobi came in looking positively mournful. He slammed the door, naturally; but he lacked his usual bounce.

Diplomatically, I did not comment on his hang-dog look.

He told me the news. There had not been another murder at the decomposing talons of the Spectre, although a ruffler had died in a brawl. Again, diplomatically, I felt it unnecessary to comment on my part in that unfortunate affair. "A damned black and white, he was, jis. By Lohvanna of the Grotto! The Racter shints are stirring up trouble all round the city."

After that little outburst, he fell back into this unusual melancholy.

Then, slouched moodily at the table, he told me that his lady love, Tassie, the light of his life, had been swept off her feet by a Hikdar in the Vallian Air Service. He went on to complain bitterly that he could never seem able to maintain a steady relationship with a girl. "They all ditch me in the end!"

Diplomacy once more was required. I wasn't about to tell Tobi that Tassie was a sensible, practical girl to whom—perhaps—Tobi was just too much of a rackety, restless, unsteady character. Tassie had impressed me when she and the others of these new companions of mine had gone through some hairy experiences.

Then Tobi surprised me.

"Could you, jis—would you—have a word with her—please?"

"Well." I spoke hesitantly. "I suppose I could. If you think it would do any good. But Tassie struck me as a girl who knew her own mind."

"Oh, aye, she does that to be sure."

So, with understandable reluctance, I agreed and a secret meeting was arranged. The murder warrant was still out for Dray Prescot, and they'd added the second Spectre murder in, too.

Now the famous Vallian buff clothes with the curly-brimmed hats look much alike from man to man. Minor differences of tailoring can be detected, of course; but folk see what they expect to see and unless there was a particular reason for studying a man's clothes, why, one fellow looked like a pea in a pod to his neighbor.

This suited me, by Krun! I could change my face well enough; clothes had to be planned more carefully.

Anyway, by the pendulous bosom and cellulite thighs of The Divine Madam of Belschutz! What in a Herrelldrin Hell was I dreaming about in interfering in Tobi's private life? In his love life, to boot. I'd be not so much embarrassed as feeling redundant when I spoke to young Tassie. For, make no mistake about it, having given my word to Tobi I'd keep that promise.

So, clad in anonymous Vallian buff, wearing a diffident face, I sallied forth that evening as Zim and Genodras slipped down the western sky.

Once again the streets cleared early and lay deserted as I passed along. The meeting took place in a small house along Cortilinden Wharf bordering the canal. I resumed my own face and knocked. The door opened to reveal a small plump apim lady, wearing a floury apron which she rapidly discarded, a flush across her cheeks.

Tassie appeared and made the pappattu. The plump lady was Nessi Thindan. Her husband, Larghos Thindan, a tallish, black-eyebrowed fellow, shook hands. Tassie introduced me as Nath the Introspective, whereat I essayed a smile. These were her friends from the Records Office where she worked. They could not, she told me, when we were privately alone, be brought into danger by harboring a fugitive from justice. "Although, of course, jis—Nath—I do not believe you could do these terrible things." Her oval face and heavy-lidded eyes regarded me frankly. "And only because you are the emperor would I agree to meet you when Tobi asked." She heaved up a sigh. "Poor Tobi!"

"Aye, Tassie. Poor Tobi indeed. Still, you know why I am here. Clearly, I cannot interfere in your life. If you have found someone else and nature sways all, then what message do I carry back?"

She shook her head in despair, as I judged, at the pitfalls of fate. "Poor Tobi! You must, jis, tell him I love Logan Verlan."

"A Hikdar in the VAS."

"For the moment. His father, old Strom Ornol, will soon be finding his way through the mists past the Grey Ones. Then Logan will be the Strom and will leave the Air Service and—"

My interruption was automatic. Even as I spoke I tried to mollify my tone. "So you will become the Stromni—" It came out crudely enough, Opaz forfend.

Tassie flushed up. "Yes, majister! But that is not the reason. I truly love Logan Verlan!"

"I believe you, Tassie."

"Logan is meeting me here and taking me home. He'll—"

Her words were interrupted by the knock on the door.

She put a quick finger to her lips. Moving rapidly she showed me to a side door and ushered me out onto the alley between houses. "Thank you, jis. Tell Tobi—tell him—I'm sorry." I could not be sure if there was a glisten in her eyes. The door closed softly.

Walking quietly back to the wharf I decided to have a look at this fellow Logan Verlan.

Standing in the shadows at the corner of the house I watched as Tassie came out of the front door. The lantern shone full on the pair of them as they kissed in greeting.

The VAS airman wore civilian buff. He carried rapier and left hand dagger. The brim of his hat curled extravagantly. The lantern light illuminated that hat, and the feathers sprouting from the band.

Those gallant feathers were all black and white.

Seven

Instantly, I knew what had to be done.

Since the Time of Troubles in this new liberated Vallia a number of political parties had been formed, flourished, and withered. Nowadays anybody could belong to any political party they wished; there was no crime in that. The Racter Party was perfectly legal.

What they wanted was, in my view, totally illegal.

The lantern light fell across this fellow Logan Verlan. The hatbrim shaded the upper portion of his face revealing the thin mouth beneath what looked like two knitting needles. I recalled in a flash my bungled attempts at knitting there on the high balcony of Esser Rarioch and I sighed. Was that so long ago? Still, when the Star Lords call, up you go, my friend.

This habit of beeswaxing moustaches so that they resemble needles is looked upon in most circles as highly reprehensible. It is scarcely manly, as they say. Personally, I don't give a fig. Although not caring for the vanity of the thing, I am prepared to allow any other fellow the right to beeswax his moustache. Still, by Zair, it wouldn't do for the Krozairs of the Eye of the World!

And, of course, standing there in the shadows spying on the two lovers, that reminded me of the fearsome brushed-up moustaches of Hikdar

Frazan ti Relzana. And, so, that reminded me of Princess Didi whose province of Urn Vennar this was. The wound she had taken had proved far more serious even than we'd suspected at the time. She was slow to mend. Some time yet must elapse before Princess Velia would feel her niece and friend was capable of sustaining the journey back from Zandikar to Vallia.

A number of aphorisms rushed through my mind. Boldness be my friend. Strike while the iron is hot. Take the bull by the horns. Well, by the gross flabbiness and ponderous pendulousness of Makki Grodno! I'd strike right enough, and shrewdly, praise Opaz!

So, on the instant, I staggered around the corner. I put on my simple face, one I could hold for a very considerable time. I laughed. Lurching from loo'ard to starboard, I cannoned into Logan Verlan as he relinquished his loving grasp of Tassie. I giggled.

"Why, dom, I crave your pardon." My hat sported no feathers. I peered owlishly. "Black and white. A friend!"

"You oaf!" Logan Verlan drew away. His hand gripped his rapier hilt. "I'll teach you manners—"

"No, no, dom. I mean no harm. But," here I put intense meaning into my words. "We Racters— It's not safe to show your colors around here."

Well, he huffed and puffed; but he took my meaning. He accepted me as a Racter who, although a trifle merry, was anxious to care for the well-being of a member of the party. Tassie looked on and had not the slightest idea that this befuddled black and white was the very same emperor to whom she had been speaking so recently. The anonymity of the buff clothes proves my point.

Tassie gripped onto the Air Service man's arm. "Oh, Logan. What this koter says is true. You must take care!"

Whipping off my hat and making a creditable bow, I said: "Llahal and Lahal. I am Tyr Kadar ti Vernonsmot." I hoped Delia wouldn't object too much, for Vernonsmot was a neat little place in her province of Delphond. And, by Vox, I'd sooner be with Delia in Delphond than here, playing skullduggery with a nice young lady and a fellow who could be a right deep-dyed villain.

The sound of trotting hooves made us turn back to look. The zorcas were of high quality and metal, their harnesses liberally bedecked with silver riding ornaments, their spiral horns gilded so that they glinted in the rays of the newly-risen twins. This was a bunch of young gallants, twenty or so of them, probably returning from a jaunt, possibly out for a night's entertainment. The Spectre had put a damper on much of Gafarden's night life; but it still went on.

They were chatting in a subdued fashion and the hands that did not hold the reins hovered close to the hilts of their weapons.

As they passed we stood aside and exchanged polite: 'Mellow

Moonlights.' They trotted on, jingling splendidly, and turned off from the wharf to be lost to our view.

"Ah," said Logan, "that's the life!"

About to make some noncommittal reply I checked. Half in shadows and half in the feeble rays of a lantern hitched to a house corner, two men stood close together a dozen or so paces ahead of us.

Now all manner of rogues plied their trade in this new clean city of Didi's. Barely above a whisper I said: "Logan. Up ahead. Be ready."

His reply was to draw his sword and step a pace before Tassie.

A fine-spirited young Racter, then, by Krun!

We walked on as though nothing on Kregen concerned us. The two men were arguing. They spoke in fierce hushed whispers; but I caught the words: "You'll never win her over," and "You're making a fool of yourself." A third man hove into the lantern light. "That's right, you great fambly." He spoke in the incisive tones of a commander.

Mind you, how could you blame young Tobi? He must have been waiting with his blood pressure about to burst from his arteries. He couldn't hang about waiting any longer, so he'd come on down here after me. And the other two had followed him with the best intentions for his own good and were as likely to move him as a new-born baby can wield a Great Krozair Longsword.

The three of them, arguing vehemently, moved into the light.

To my surprise the third, who had used so commanding a voice, was not Jiktar Yavnin Purvun of the VAS but Nalgre Nevko.

The night breathed softly about us. Since the advent of the Spectre, Gafarden's night life had considerably abated. As we moved on I heard a distant confused noise, like the shushing sound made by waves on shingle. Tobi stepped out boldly, his heavy features wrought up into a lop-sided grimace and his fists cocked up. "Tassie! He's no good for you! Come with me—"

His voice was drowned out by the ferocious bellow as Logan Verlan jumped forward, swishing his sword. "Leave the lady alone, you cramph! Or I'll blatter your liver into sausage meat!"

In the little silence that followed that outburst Yavnin with exquisite politeness said: "Surely you mean liver pâté?"

With equal courtesy but with great meaning, Nalgre said: "And I think you would be seriously prevented."

Half my attention was taken up by this pretty little scene. The other half tried to decipher the distant confused uproar.

Give this sparky Racter his due, he was fast. He moved abruptly. He leaped forward; his rapier lifted into the air and the hilt crashed down on Nalgre's head. Nalgre Nevko toppled forward without a sound and lay prostrate and unmoving.

"You shint!" roared Tobi. He would have smashed full into Verlan but for Yavnin's sudden and detaining grasp on his arm.

The ugly passions churning in these people could almost be smelled on the air. The furious beat of galloping hooves took my attention away. Round the corner hurtled the troop of zorca riders. They were beating their mounts to make them gallop faster which no zorcaman would ever do unless the emergency was indeed dire.

"The Spectre!" they yelled as they rushed past. "The Spectre! Run, doms, for your lives!"

Their eyes were white with terror. Their zorcas scattered flecks of foam as they strained on. The whole situation here changed. The petty squabble was instantly put aside. Yavnin released Tobi, bent, seized up Nalgre. "Come on!" he shouted, and began to run towards the nearest bridge over the canal.

Logan Verlan slapped his rapier away. He took hold of Tassie and with a quick: "Come on, Tyr Kadar!" hurried her away.

Perforce, I followed, and in a helter-skelter scramble we sprinted towards the bridge and crossed the canal whose dark waters glinting with a few stray lights were not as dark as the feelings in me. Zair rot the Opaz-forsaken Spectre!

Eight

"But I want to *see!*" Thus spoke Tassie.

We'd paused for breath in the lee of warehouses with the welcome shadows all about us. Now young Tassie was a most determined lass, as was self-evident. She'd not screamed when the dread name of the Spectre had been shouted at her from a troop of terrified zorcamen. She'd run fleetly with Logan Verlan across the bridge.

"But, Tassie—" started the immediate protest from Verlan.

"I've heard that the horrible thing cannot cross water."

"We-ell—"

"Anyway, it can't see us here."

Tobi said that he thought we ought to push on and I knew he was thinking of his lady love and not himself. Yavnin, still carrying Nalgre, agreed.

They did not all look at me as they would usually have done when I was in the role of emperor. For that little addition to my disguise I was grateful. Logan Verlan, in a most doubtful way, said that well perhaps as we were in good cover and unlikely to be seen we might stay to watch what transpired.

Tobi fumed at this but managed to restrain himself. He said nothing; but if looks could kill, as they say in Clishdrin, Verlan would have dropped dead on the spot. Tassie swung round to face me like a female zhantil ready to spring. "What do you think, Tyr Kadar?"

"This is a most foolhardy idea, young lady. But if you stay then, quite clearly—"

"Yes, yes," snapped Verlan. "We'll all stay."

Yavnin said that Nalgre should be taken at once to a doctor. Blood seeped from the crack on his head. The argument seemed a long time ago now. We all agreed on that and so the VAS Jiktar carried Nalgre Nevko away. I just hoped the sword hilt had not done him any serious injury.

The distant confused noise had died after the zorca riders fled and we'd crossed the bridge. I did not doubt that every front door along the street was barricaded with any and everything the folk could wedge against them. Tassie felt her friends Kotera and Koter Thindan were quite safe in their neat little house along the canalside.

A light rain began to fall, wisping gently across the cobbles and roofs. The light from the Twins faded; but The Maiden with the Many Smiles rose above the city buildings. The light slanting in with the raindrops shining through gave an eerie look to the street. An uncanny silence dropped about us.

Round the corner and walking steadily on, the undead thing threw a blasphemous shadow in the light of the Moon.

"What a revolting beast!" exclaimed Tassie. Her face shone, her eyes were wide, the corner of her lower lip caught up by white teeth as she finished that automatic gasp of disgust.

"Ssh!" Verlan's whisper cut. "We don't want the obnoxious thing to hear us."

The Spectre had clearly once been a human. The thing resembled the Spectre we'd seen shot to ribbons; yet there were differences. When it first came into view substantial amounts of skin and flesh clothed its yellow bones. It quickened its pace. We all stared in a fascination that sickened us. It held its arms high in the air, skeletal hands crooked, waving like an orangutan. The purulent undead corpse began to shed strips of skin. A finger broke off and tumbled across the canalside with a rattling clatter distinctly audible in the eerie brooding silence.

Pus dribbled down its rotting legs. Its mouth widened to reveal blackened stumps of teeth. Its lower jaw broke away and dangled momentarily and then tumbled down to be kicked into the canal.

And all the time that dread silence held us in stasis.

The Spectre made for the bridge. Tassie put a hand to her mouth. Whether the ambulatory corpse could cross water or could not, she was about to discover for herself.

Slowly now, slower and slower, the Spectre staggered forward.

More chunks of its hideous corpse fell off. It began to deliquesce. The rib cage showed for an instant and then collapsed like a crushed barrel. No blood poured out, only pus and greenly-black ooze. The Spectre's eyes, luridly red within their orbits, seemed to flash sparks. I could swear a halo-like circle of diamond bright lights flowed from them, to vanish almost in the instant they were born.

"What in a Herrelldrin Hell was that?" demanded Tobi, staring fixedly at the grotesque mass of rotting, collapsing flesh and bones.

"More damned magic," said Verlan, and his arm around Tassie tightened. Even if the Spectre heard us now there looked little prospect of it crossing the bridge before it fell to pieces completely. So we wouldn't find out if it could cross water or not.

With parts falling off at every lurch the thing reeled to the edge of the canal by the bridge abutments. For a moment it stood there, swaying. Then its right leg fell off, collapsing under it, and the Opaz-forsaken Spectre fell in the water.

Tassie moved forward impulsively to get a better look down. Logan Verlan held her arm and she shook it and rapped out: "It's dead now, anyway, Logan."

Tobi said: "All the bits and pieces that fell off—look!"

Spirals of black smoke lifted from the discarded arms, the leg and various other bits. In moments they shriveled and dissipated.

No sign of the Spectre showed in the water. Nothing remained of the unholy creature.

All praise to Opaz, the monstrous creature was gone. A somber thought struck through me with profound anguish. Oh, yes, the Spectre was gone, dead again, dead twice over—but would another Spectre appear in its place to continue its murderous career?

Not mentioning that unwelcome idea to the others, I waited to see if Tobi and Verlan would continue their quarrel. If they did, why, then, I'd have to act, and not relish it, either, by Krun!

The drama so brutally unfolded before us put a damper on spirits. We were all subdued. Tobi gave the VAS airman a dirty look, gazed forlornly at Tassie, shook his head, and announced in a choky voice that he was off to see how Nalgre fared, and remberee all.

We gave him the remberees and he went off at a fair old clip. No surprise touched me that they made no further reference to the Spectre. In pursuance of my plan—ha! That old chestnut, the Plan called the Plan!—I must now cuddle up with Logan Verlan and gain his confidence.

The horrific nature of what we had just witnessed, of course, gave a first class, if macabre, introduction. The experience lay between us like a demonic calling card.

We walked along, Verlan with his arm around Tassie, talking in low tones about generalities. The fellow was a damned Racter; but all the same he'd acted up in a sprightly fashion and, given the situation, in a responsible way, too. This pseudo-companionship continued as we agreed to meet up again on the morrow, when, without doubt, we'd discuss this night's events.

As we parted, Tassie, leaning against Verlan, said: "Thank you, Tyr Kadar. It's all been so-so—"

"Remberee. Until tomorrow."

With that we went our separate ways. I didn't bother to follow them so wended off to bed. Logan Verlan would keep until the morning.

Gold everywhere. Gems scattered in prodigal profusion. An arching glass roof high above, at one place broken into a hole, with the fire-crystals shining through. The effulgent light, limning the nine sarcophagi in their circle about the altar, caused the runes to writhe in apparent movement. Nothing had changed in the chamber of death since Tralgan Vorner had last taken his leave here.

Standing just inside the hidden entrance from the maze of tunnels and caverns at his back, Tralgan Vorner stared upon the scene.

Yes; something had changed here. The smell of rot and decay did not hang as heavily upon the air. And—here Vorner allowed himself a small self-satisfied smile—there were obvious gaps in the piles of gems.

Those jewels gave him his fortune, his position and the means of exacting his revenge. This place still cast a chill upon him; but the stark terror dropped away. Some of that ib-cringing fear returned at the unwelcome thought that some of his revenge had been accomplished but the revenge and dreams of conquest of those who resided here had not.

He stared upon the nine sarcophagi ranked in their circle. There were nine sarcophagi; but only eight Thaumaturges of Sodan since the final death of Rafan-Ymet the Ineluctor. Now there were only seven Thaumaturges of Sodan since the final death of Nasan-Ydor the Inculcator.

When the sarcophagi rotated to bring their heads facing the central altar and the lids moved gratingly open and the coffins rose into view, Vorner knew that only seven corpses would sit up to gaze upon him with their blood-red eyes floating free in their boney sockets. Another Thaumaturge had gone down into the grey mists to seek passage through the Ice Floes of Sicce. Fear did touch Tralgan Vorner then. How could he not be blamed?

The monstrous voice crashed out to ring in reverberating echoes about the sumptuous chamber.

"Tralgan Vorner! Rightful but dispossessed Elten of Culvensax! You return to us empty-handed!"

He had to conquer this fear. He had to speak up boldly in this ghastly place of terror and death. He licked his lips.

"The fault was not mine—I am sorry that Nasan-Ydor—"

The blood-red eyes glared upon him with the intensity of madness.

"We are aware."

The feeling that these undead creatures did not care for what happened to their fellows and sisters once again made him believe they didn't care, either, for one another at all.

They had told him much of their history, how King Rikto the All-Glorious by wiles and trickery had incarcerated them here so long ago that all memory and record of him and them was lost in Vallia. They had waited for century after century until Tralgan Vorner fell through the glass roof over this tomb of silence and death.

Tralgan Vorner's hatred fuelled their pseudo-life.

His heavy, sullen features flooded with the dark blood of the Vorners. A corpse floated into the air from its coffin. It trailed rotting strips of flesh; but Vorner was again struck by the amount of flesh and skin clothing the sere bones. Was his hatred, then, fuelling these ghastly things' resurrection?

The corpse hovered over him. Sparks of light flashed. He knew what was happening. This was the replacement Thaumaturge for the dead and gone Nasan-Ydor the Inculcator.

The voice speaking in his head keened from hoarseness to a lighter whisper. "I am Lazan-Yvon, known as the Inconducive. Once I was called Semtilla the Fair." Was that a sigh echoing in his head? "But that was before—" Again that suggestion of regret. "My fame eclipsed others. Where these two who were once men have failed, I, Lazan-Yvon the Inconducive, will succeed!"

Vorner shivered. Yes, he believed her. The Thaumaturges of Sodan wished to hold power over all Vallia. They had failed in the task when they were alive. Now they would succeed as undead creatures.

Oh, yes, Tralgan Vorner believed these animated corpses would succeed. He believed that fervently.

The corpses returned to their coffins, the sarcophagi lids closed. Silence hung eternally in the chamber. His hands trembled only slightly as he scooped up gems and filled his sack. The voice in his head said: "Yes. We shall have need of wealth. I have a plan that cannot fail." The whispering tones sharpened. "Now let us go and claim Vallia for the Thaumaturges of Sodan!"

Nine

The black feathers had once beaten strongly in the wing of a rippasch. The white feathers had once beaten strongly in the wing of a perept. The feathers adorned my hat and looked brave in the light of the Suns. The feathers disgusted me—yet for the sake of Vallia they must be worn with panache.

Oh, yes, you who listen as the tape whispers through the heads, you will know just how much these black and white feathers displeased me. But when one comes to the Fluttrell's vane, as they say in Havilfar, one must accept the needle, as they say all over Paz.

I'd had to restrain myself and keep a very straight face when the hatter, expertly fitting the feathers, said: "Yes, dom. The Racters have the right of it." His needle and thread went in and out sewing the black and white abominations firmly into place. "This Emperor Drak is a disgrace to his grandfather. As for this Empress Silda, well—" Here he bent forward confidentially. "What Tyr Prangman says of her is all true, and, by Vox, I'll wager only half the story." His needle shone. My hands were curled tightly into fists down at my sides. I said nothing.

So, here was I, the great Dray Prescot, prancing about in the streaming mingled radiance of the Suns of Scorpio, flaunting the colors of the gang who wanted to destroy my lad and his lady wife, the daughter of my blade comrade, Seg Segutorio. The farcical situation was enough to drive a fellow to drink, by Krun!

Going into the palace atop its hill I removed the hat from my head and tucked it under my arm where the Racter feathers were covered.

The place appeared to be as busy as ever, with folk hurrying about their tasks. The general air of bustle pervaded these working sections of Didi's palace with a sense of purpose.

Four men with their heads close together talked in a side-corridor as I passed in the main passage. I did not break my stride. A moment later I wheeled about and marched back, taking a good look at these four as I went.

One was a red-whiskered Khibil, at his side stood a tailed Hytak, and next to him an orange-feathered Rapa. They were all paktuns, that was very evident, wearing swords and with the glint of silver at their throats. Mortpaktuns, wearing the silver pakmort, they listened intently as the fourth man spoke.

Turning about again I went on and past. I was wearing my own face so it would have been inconvenient to have been seen eavesdropping. Although, of course, that wasn't the right word; I had not heard what they were talking about.

The fourth fellow, the one giving instructions, was Naghan Raerdu, known as Naghan the Slippy.

When he came into my office later I said nothing of what I'd seen. When the Slippy felt the time was right, he'd let me know.

"Lahal, jis. One or two items to report."

"Lahal, Naghan. Excellent."

The poor devil who'd been ripped up and tossed about in the Spectre's usual bloodthirsty fashion had been Liflan Somanch, known as the Disputer. He was a Fristle. As a lawyer he'd enjoyed a high reputation for litigation involving convoluted arguments.

"And, jis, he was a lawyer retained exclusively by the chief pallan, Nath Swantram the Clis."

This information did not surprise me.

"How many more people are there to be murdered to slake the vengeance of Tralgan Vorner's spectral ghost?"

"If the Spectre was Tralgan Vorner."

"Aye, Naghan, true, true. We don't know for sure."

"I expect more from Tobi out of the records, jis. He may look rather a heavy lump and he is, undoubtedly, reckless and careless; but he has the makings of a fine agent in him."

"Agreed." Then, as this was Kregen, I added: "If he lives."

"As Opaz wills."

Then we got on with the various necessary tasks to hand which did not affect the Spectre business. Yavnin had gone off to Vondium in further quest of an aerial command. In addition, he'd call on the Lady Ahilya Vorona. Poor Ulana Farlan! I said to myself. Chucked out of her position as the nazabni, ruling Urn Vennar for Didi, she had to bear the additional heartbreak of pining for Yavnin. Yavnin had eyes only for Ahilya. The disconsolate Ulana must pine in vain.

Nalgre Nevko, still with a bandage around his head, had gone off to Evir over the Mountains of the North. He'd said that he hoped to do profitable business in connection with furs. I didn't envy him the cold and the icy winds and the snow in the bad season.

So, my three new companions being absent and Naghan Raerdu about his spying business, I was left to attend to the black and whites.

Also, I'd not failed to notice that the two Vallian Air Servicemen, Jiktar Yavnin Purvun and Hikdar Logan Verlan, didn't know each other.

Although the VAS, like the army, was much curtailed in these piping times of peace, the organizations were still large enough so that everyone couldn't know everyone else. And, anyway, by Vox, how could these days be called peaceful when the army was down there in Pandahem trying to contain the onslaughts of the Bloody Menahem?

Letters from Drak and Seg told me that there had so far only been skirmishes. The big battles lay ahead. Even so, in the most minor of skirmishes good men could get themselves killed.

Judge of my pain when I read that Jiktar Nath the Steadfast, an old comrade and a man to fight alongside, had been stupidly slain in just such a petty skirmish. This was Vallia's life blood being poured out in sacrifice for the ideal of Paz. More and more I was aware of how profound my hatred of war was. Yes, on Kregen you have to take up arms from time to time. That is the tragedy and the pity of it all.

Ornol Havening, one of the under-chamberlains, came in to say that a man wished to speak with me. Ornol said he wore strange dress. He had a monstrous sword strapped to him.

"His name, Ornol?"

"He calls himself by some outlandish name—Pur Zygon Farzena, I think it was, of Zandikar."

"Send him in."

The fellow with the outlandish names was ushered in. He had a pair of magnificent upswept moustaches and a mop of curly hair. His face bore the marks of travel, yet he was alert and brisk. He wore a white tunic and to his belt was scabbarded a Great Krozair Longsword.

I stood up as he entered.

"Lahal, Pur Zygon."

"Lahal, Pur Dray."

I didn't know him. He was not a Krozair of Zy, belonging to the Krozairs of Zimuzz; but he was a brother Krozair. I pointed at the chair across from the desk and sat down. "You are welcome, Pur Zygon. Ornol—arrange some refreshment, please, at once." Ornol bowed and went off. I added: "Pur Zygon. Your news?"

He did not spread his hands; but he leaned back in the chair. He looked tired. "King Zeg charged me to waste no time. Princess Didi has taken a turn for the worse—"

I snapped bolt upright at this.

I felt quite distinctly the throb of blood at wrist and temple. "Go on." My voice growled out in the old gravel-shifting way so that Zygon blinked, wet his lips, and went on quickly: "The needlemen saved her. She is weak. Princess Velia will not have her moved from Zandikar. But I have to tell you, Pur Dray, Princess Didi will not be coming to Urn Vennar for a long time."

With a discreet rap on the door, a pretty Fristle fifi came in with a tray of sazz and parclear and miscils. I said: "Wait."

Then, to Zygon: "You travelled by voller—by airboat."

"Yes, majister."

"You'll want real food, then." To the Fristle maiden: "This is very nice, Selena; but the koter needs a real meal. Can you arrange that for me?"

"At once, majister," she said, all aflutter.

When she'd taken her pert pink-ribboned tail out, I asked Zygon how his flight over the Stratemsk and the Hostile Territories had gone, and then quizzed him about doings in the inner sea, the Eye of the World.

"The Stratemsk was awe-inspiring, flying between those colossal mountains. I had no trouble in the Hostile Territories, although being warned beforehand about the Ullars."

At this I nodded, and said: "Ah, yes, them!"

Zygon continued: "The worst part of the whole trip was crossing the Klackadrin. My head was spinning, I didn't know what was happening. Then I remembered King Zeg had said to fly as high as possible over the Klackadrin."

"Those Zair-forsaken gases from the cleft in the world are not only noxious, they're hallucinogenic. You flew well."

He drank comfortably. He told me the incursions of the Green Grodnims continued and that all the cities of Zairia were preparing. Then, not as comfortably as before, he said that the dread news of the Spectre had upset both the princesses when it reached Zandikar. Didi had more or less to be tied down to prevent her flying at once back to Gafarden. He finished up by saying that everyone was mightily relieved that after the rotting collapse and disappearance of the Spectre it was perfectly plain that the Spectre had committed the murders and not Dray Prescot. "I imagine, Pur Dray, this fellow Nath the Clis was duly apologetic and repentant."

"Hardly." The dryness of my tone told Zygon as much as the words.

Nath Swantram had not apologized. He'd grudgingly admitted that I had not been the murderer, although he pointed out that all the evidence led directly to me. He did say that he'd not had time to refer the matter to the emperor. "One does not bother the emperor if it can be avoided." He sounded both pious and unctuous.

I favored him with a look that, had it been steel, would have sliced him in half. "I quite understand."

His scar abruptly shone out, slick against his skin. He realized just what he'd said. He licked his lips, spread his hands. Before he could start on some mumbled explanation I cut in with: "The emperor is fully engaged in Pandahem. As this stupid affair has ended without real trouble, let's leave it at that."

You see—how calm and dignified and temperate this latter-day Dray Prescot! My Val! If I hadn't changed then I never would!

Nath Swantram visibly relaxed. He didn't attempt an explanation nor did I expect him to. The moment appeared opportune for further enquiries. I asked him what was the latest situation on what had come to be called The Butcher's Murder.

"The emperor has not replied to my letter—as you say, he is engaged in Pandahem. The woman is in as comfortable a cell as possible."

I nodded. "I shall follow the case with interest."

He went off and I imagine he went off with relief. So, now, I could speak calmly of the incident to Pur Zygon, Krzi. He might be a Krzi and I a Krzy—we both stood together when others threatened.

Making sure Zygon was looked after properly and expressing my thanks for his arduous journey, I said I would prepare letters for him to take back to Zandikar. He stood up. "I can tell you, Pur Dray, that, by Zim-Zair, I miss the Eye of the World!"

That struck through to me. I didn't think he was prodding or trying to make a point. He was just expressing a heartfelt emotion.

"Were I at liberty to return to Zandikar, I would fly back with you, Pur Zygon. I would relish the journey." I made what was an empty gesture. "By Zair! I, too, miss the Eye of the World!"

So, that evening, I went about one of the two spots of business that kept me here in Gafarden. At our meeting on the morrow after the Spectre had been destroyed, we'd got along fine, although Logan Verlan did say that he wore the black and white schturval and he was fully prepared to stick anyone who challenged him.

That, therefore, was why I'd bought the black and white feathers. We met up at the Scented Bower, had a jar or two, and then went along to a modest house a couple of streets away where the meeting was scheduled to take place.

Verlan gave the password to a couple of heavies on the door: "Teract!" He introduced me as Tyr Kadar ti Vernonsmot, and we were ushered through.

The room was low-ceiled but spacious, with ranked chairs. A podium at the end raised the speakers above our heads. I fancied this Prangman fellow would relish that. The windows were shuttered. A couple of tables along the side wall bore jugs and glasses and light refreshments. On the wall at the back of the podium a massive jar on a shelf sprouted a whole aviary of black and white feathers. The black and white schturvals of the men and women waiting here oppressed me with a sense of foreboding.

I remembered with a pang the Black Feathers of the Great Chyyan.

When Prangman marched in and mounted the podium he held up a hand for silence and the welcoming 'Lahals' died down. He stared down on us, all hanging on his words.

The fustian poured out, a downright pack of lies in which everything for which Drak and Silda stood for was twisted and turned into a grotesque parody. I sat there, lips compressed, silent.

A hubbub broke out beyond the door. We all turned to look. On entering I'd automatically taken note of the room's arrangement and the two further doors along the side walls. Now the main door burst in. Armed men broke into the room, yelling: "Down with the Racters!"

In the forefront of the attack three men leaped on, bold, active, confident. One was a Khibil, the second a Hytak, the third a Rapa.

I recognized them.

By Krun! So this was what Naghan Raerdu had been planning. And his little scheme to blatter the Racters was like to get me killed!

Ten

The meeting divided into two halves. One half shouted: "Fight! Fight for the Racters!" They hurled themselves forward into a headlong charge on the attackers breaking into the room.

The other lot screamed: "Run! Run!" They scrambled in a panic rout towards the side doors. These were frailer men and women. They screamed and clawed forward in a terrified mass of bodies.

There were women in those who shouted fight and ripped out swords. These were Jikai Vuvushis, tough battle maidens. And I hung about completely undecided. I could not fight those who wished to assist the cause of the emperor, could I? Yet I couldn't run off as that would have totally blown my persona with Logan as a stout adherent of the Racters. The quandary flared stark and brutal.

Logan Verlan, sword out, flung himself at the newcomers. For a moment I saw him; then he was engulfed in the struggle as steel scraped on steel and the room broke into the insane turmoil of battle.

No one took any notice of me. For a moment I stood alone. Everyone was totally engrossed in the passions possessing them. Fight or run! The mob howling to get out of the side door rushed crazily on and in their blind panic a woman fell. Uncaring feet trampled over her.

She was a respectable Kotera of Vallia. Her clothes spoke of some wealth and position. She rolled like a rag doll under the trampling boots. She wore the black and white schturval. She was a woman. So, by the stinking bodily effluences of Makki Grodno! What else could I do?

Cursing the humanity that denied inhumanity, I lunged forward, elbowed a screaming fellow out of the way, knocked down a fat man who screeched like a ponsho trapped in the jaws of a leem, and grabbed the woman. She was a fat bundle and I hoisted her up, spun about, kicked a black and white who wouldn't get out of the way fast enough, and so dragged her out of the press.

Standing her up on her feet and still holding her, I said with a viciousness I really did not feel: "Go out! And don't fall down!"

The uproar of the fight across the room drowned her reply. She tottered and I pulled her upright. "Go on!"

Then it was vitally necessary to spin about to check if any of Naghan Raerdu's bully boys were about to blatter me.

At once the situation became apparent to me. Naghan the Slippy had not sent quite enough fighting men to overpower the Racters in the meeting. The conflict swayed. The noise battered prodigiously. Already the stink of spilled blood filled the air with nausea.

There was no sign of Logan Verlan. There was time for me to swing back to the fat lady and spit out: "Kotera—get yourself out of it! Run—but take care. Do not fall over again."

She drew herself up. Her bosom presented a most impressive sight. "I give you my thanks, Koter. I would have—"

"Go, lady. May Opaz go with you."

Why on Kregen I was being so punctilious with a damned Racter I couldn't comprehend. If she hadn't been a confounded black and white she'd have been a nice rotund lady with a happy family, I dare say. As it was, I acknowledged my emotions were befuddled.

Now because these fine fellows sent by Naghan the Slippy shouted: "Down with the Racters!" and not: "Kill the Racters!" I judged he'd given them instructions to be harsh but not to slay anyone. They were professional enough not to get themselves seriously wounded in tangling with these plotters. By the same token I fancied no one had gone round the back to catch people running away. The rotund lady should escape safely.

Most of the Racters at this meeting looked to be civilians and so the task handed out by Naghan proved not too difficult. Logan Verlan was not a civilian. He'd told me what he'd do in a situation like this, and here he was, going about his task with gusto.

Naghan's men were forced to take Verlan seriously. I caught a glimpse of him foining off a couple of Rapas and managing to stick one through the arm. The other Rapa screeched at this, flicked this way and then that and so stuck Logan through the thigh. This, then, was my cue.

Without drawing a weapon I sprinted across to the edge of the fray where Verlan was trying to hobble off. Once he left the fight no one tried to attack him further. I grabbed him by the arm.

"You're wounded, Logan. Come on out of it."

Swinging around and bending down I hoisted him up in a fireman's lift. His arm dangled. He tried to speak, and coughed. The last of the fugitives bunched through the side door. Hardly any time at all had passed since I'd picked up the rotund lady. He tried to wriggle, and I told him to keep still. "Kadar—" he said, mushily. I began to harbor the nasty suspicion that he'd taken an earlier wound before the pink in his thigh brought him down.

A couple of exceedingly fat men were the last through the door as I came up with them. Bustling on outside I turned my upper body so that I could look back at the fracas.

Only because not enough fighting men had been sent were the Racters gaining the upper hand. They were not reluctant to kill. The professionals fought on grimly; they made no headway.

So I, Dray Prescot, had to quell my instinctive desire to hurl this damned black and white to the floor and hurtle back to assist the men battling against the Racters.

Verlan had to be got to a needleman. Most thigh wounds are serious and if the artery is cut, fatal. Outside, the Maiden with the Many Smiles did, indeed, smile down on the city. Pinkish light illuminated the street and the shadows lay in fuzzy vagueness.

The fleeing members from the meeting simply disappeared in all directions. The noise of the combat barely reached the street. The best place to take Verlan I could think of right at the moment was The Unhanged Drikinger, a shady hostelry in a cul-de-sac known as Flint Alley. This lay within the old village, or town, really, around which Didi had built her new city of Gafarden. There Doctor Lomax the Potion practiced his healing arts on all manner of cut-throats and pick-pockets and other rogues of the night.

Naghan Raerdu had quickly sniffed the place out and reported its location to me—which right now was mightily handy, by Krun!

The Spectre might be dead once more; the good folk still refused to venture out too far abroad at night and so few people were about to stare at me as I hurried along.

The tavern presented a dog-eared appearance, with thick vines clothing the old walls and obscuring the small windows. A few lights glowed and a rusty lantern outside the front door shed radiance enough to let me see where to go.

The smell of ales and wines puffed up in a miasma as I went in. Thankfully, unlike Earth, no tobacco fumes sullied the air. Lomax the Potion was instantly recognizable. A wretch lay flat on a table with a gag stuffed into his mouth and four of his cronies holding him down. Lomax worked industriously with needle and thread sewing up a gash across the man's belly. This, I judged, would be a typical scene in The Unhanged Drikinger.

Doctor Lomax finished off the last stitch, bit the thread and turned to regard me and my burden. On Earth he would have peered over the tops of steel-rimmed glasses. He was a sprightly figure, his yellow apron stained with blood, and blood shone on his beak and feathers. He was not a Rapa but a Relt; diffs of a gentle nature, Relts, quite the opposite of their Rapa cousins. He waved a hand.

The four men lifted the groaning fellow off the table. Lomax gestured to me and I stepped forward and deposited Verlan on the bare blood-stained boards.

"Thank you, doctor," was all I said, and all I had need to say.

Some pointedly enquiring looks took stock of me. Verlan and I were dressed in buff and were obviously koters. We were, I suspected, being sized up as marks by the devotees of Diproo the Nimble-fingered. Also, we both wore the black and white. Still, bringing Verlan here had appeared the best option. I hitched up my sword belt.

They took the hint, and eyes were averted.

Looking back at the operating table I saw Lomax busy at his work. I wondered why he was not using the ubiquitous acupuncture needles. He was dubbed the Potion and I wondered if that explained the riddle.

I labored under no misapprehension that Doctor Lomax operated for free. He charged gold for his services. He, too, had seen we were koters and, therefore, had gold in our purses. No doubt he had cronies who would enforce his surgical demands for payment.

Some time had elapsed since the golden nectar had flowed past my tonsils, so—and I appreciated the incongruousness of the act—I called for the barman to set up a jar of ale. An Olumai, fat and knowing, he slapped the jar down and snapped up the silver piece I slid across the counter. I waited for the change. It was not forthcoming. By the stupendous charms of the Divine Madam of Belschutz! Should I force the issue?

This whole ridiculous nonsense brought on by Naghan Raerdu's eagerness to serve, by Logan Verlan's headlong desire to stick those who did not share his beliefs, and my own innate responsibilities, brought me to this pass. I quaffed down the ale and went back to the operating table. The Olumai barman, wiping his hands, smirked.

In a voice I tried to modulate, I said: "Doctor Lomax. My friend is being stitched up. Why do you not ease his pain with your needles?"

Lomax went on with his work diligently. He did not look round. "The pain is a trifle. Your friend is fit. Needles don't come cheap."

"So that's it! All right, doctor. Here is gold." I showed him two gold talens, glinting silkily in the light of the lamps. "Now use your needles to soothe away the pain being endured by my friend."

The two gold pieces went like eels through a weir into his pouch. He opened his bag and produced his needles and used them with a needleman's skill. Immediately Verlan stopped the moaning even he, a seasoned VAS officer, could not suppress. He gave a deep sigh, and relaxed, flat on the bare tavern table.

"Gold," said Doctor Lomax, "always works wonders."

I did not reply—that's a cheap philosophy that is not always applicable—instead I put a hand on Verlan's forehead. He was hot; but I judged not dangerously so. Lomax nodded and confirmed that. Even I could see that Verlan had taken a nasty wound which had jagged into a gash larger than the width of the rapier blade.

"Your friend was fortunate. Beng Sbodine the Mender of Men undoubtedly smiled on him."

"Oh?"

"Oh, yes. The thrust missed both the femoral artery and the femur. I've seen rapier blades snapped and left in the thigh when they hit the bone. As for the artery—"

"Yes." I looked down on Logan Verlan. "Five-handed Eos-Bakchi most certainly rolled the dice in your favor, Logan."

He managed a twist of his lips I took to be a smile.

The next problem would be the clientele of The Unhanged Drikinger. Conscious of the covert looks, the suggestive winks from one to another, the general air of impending mayhem, I rather fancied my little ploy with the sword belt had passed its sell-by date—as they say in Clishdrin.

Swinging around with the jar in my left hand I quaffed a draught and my right hand fumbled out half a dozen gold pieces. The talens winked mightily prettily in the mineral oil lamps' glow. A few paces took me to the bar and the scowling barman. I slapped the money down.

In a loud but not commanding voice, I said: "Drinks all round!"

Without waiting for the result of that I whistled across to the table. Verlan came up into my grip like a fork of corn into the baler. He spluttered out that, by Vox! he could walk. My arm around him and holding onto him, he started off.

By this time the clientele of The Unhanged Drikinger were clamoring at the barman. They yelled out their orders for their favorite and most expensive drinks. Whilst I cannot be totally sure of this statement, I do not believe a single one called a 'Thank you.'

Well, you didn't really expect them to, did you?

The door appeared to be as far away as the Mountains of the North from Vondium as we crossed the floor. The pandemonium as drinks were called for and set up and the continuing pandemonium formed a macabre backdrop to our progress. Verlan tried manfully to walk; but he gasped and sagged against me. His face looked green.

Taking him up again, this time in a cradle grip, I crossed the final few paces to the door.

The fresh air hit us like a cold wet cloth after a sweaty bout of sword practice. Firmly, deliberately, I walked off along the street. Perhaps there had been no need for that extravagant gesture. Perhaps, by Zair, there had!

What I did think pertinent in the situation, what was important, was my exultant feeling that my actions must place me in a very favorable light with Logan Verlan and thus with his contacts in the Racters. They say if you can't beat 'em, join 'em.

Well, by Krun, I'd joined 'em and I'd beat 'em, too!

Eleven

Thus exulting childishly in my own cleverness and bold intentions, I became aware that, indeed, Pride does go before a Fall. We were not out of the woods yet.

Of course, any onker, any fambly, would know instantly that a tavern full of rogues and cut-throats contained more perils than might be deflected by a handful of gold. The very sight of the gold inflamed greed. Where that had come from, there'd be more.

My guess was the four shadowy figures padding along after us would be the cream of the cream of the tavern society. They must be in a very strong position to prevent everyone in The Unhanged Drikinger from running out after our money. Whether they'd share the loot out with anyone else was a moot point. They slunk along, gaining on us.

Oh, well, by the Blade of Kurin! I'd just run off from a fight to my displeasure, so these four would reap the benefit of that.

With Logan Verlan placed safely on a handy doorstep, leaning his back against the wooden door, I straightened up and faced those who sought to part us from our gold. If they had to, they'd part us from our lives and not care overmuch about that, thankyou!

They saw me turn to face them and they stopped. I said nothing.

"Give us your gold and you can go." Thus spoke the one who stepped out boldly before the others. He was a Tikur, a member of a race of diffs whose mores were lamentable, whose social graces were unpolished, to whom an honest day's work was anathema and who seldom if ever observed the Fantamyrrh.

He swished his sword, a clanxer, the old cutlass-like blade of Vallia. His face was remarkable for the array of brown teeth biting into the lower lip. He did not look like an apim, having copious amounts of black fur distributed over his body. His damned eyes were bright enough, though, by Krun!

Of the other three, one was a green-feathered Rapa, the remaining two were apims of distinctly villainous appearance. All carried swords.

This situation was entirely unwelcome and unwanted. Well, these four footpads welcomed and wanted what they imagined was going to happen. Without show I unlimbered the rapier and main gauche.

Just how these unhanged rogues intended to go about the business I neither knew nor cared. I'd not wait around for them. Silently, blades held just so, I hurtled headlong into the attack.

The light proved tricky with sliding pinkish shadows alternating with the radiance of the Moons as the clouds passed along. The savagery of the onslaught caught the four of them totally by surprise. The rapier went slickly into the Tikur, parting his black hair for him. He reeled away dropping the clanxer, cursing in a sort of wailing scream.

Before the blade hit the ground the main gauche drove with a precision I felt appropriate to the occasion into the guts of the Rapa.

His green feathers wilted, as it were, and he let out a gurgle. Writhing like a beetle on a pin he staggered back and the cramph dragged the dagger away with him.

No time to leap forward to retrieve the dagger; time only to whirl like a dervish to meet the onslaught of the two apims.

They'd seen their comrades thrust through; but they came on bravely enough. They were breathing with loud rasping breaths, their mouths open revealing brown snaggly teeth. Their eyes in the streaming light looked like those of feral cats. They swished their swords. They came on in a rush, snarling, without a scrap of pity in their black hearts.

Without having to think what to do I went through the actions as detailed in San Loren ti Vandiyar's ancient and famous treatise on rapier and dagger work against multiple opponents. Checking those swift and automatic reactions, I did think I didn't want to slay these rogues, richly though many folk of Gafarden would say they deserved that fate.

Instead of, therefore, in the next instant having two dead men on the ground, there were two screaming fellows running for their lives, streaming blood. Short though the encounter had been, I gained the distinct impression these two were far more used to bludgeons than swords. No doubt they were trying to move up in the world.

The Tikur cursed thickly, stood for a moment, then he, too, ran off streaming blood. The Rapa reeled about like a willow tossed by the wind. A couple of strides took me to him. The dagger came out with a pull. I gave him a push. He didn't run off; he staggered. I hoped, strangely enough, he'd make it back to Doctor Lomax.

In the nature of these encounters, all had passed swiftly.

The oiled cloth came out of its pouch and the two blades were wiped clean and shining in the Moonslight.

On the way back to Verlan I stared about narrowly. No one else I could see was about.

Verlan was not visible as I walked back smartly. He'd slumped sideways and slid down the door. His eyes were closed. No blood seeped through the yellow bandage around his thigh so I judged nothing serious had occurred. I said: "Logan. Time to go."

He stirred and opened his eyes. His face looked drawn.

"Kadar." He spoke in a slurred voice. "I'm tired."

Well, he would be, naturally enough, after his exertions and loss of blood. He hadn't seen that brisk little fight. Still in that mumbly voice, he said: "What happened?"

"Oh, some watchmen turned up and the thieves ran off."

His eyes closed again. "Good."

Only now did I do what I should have done before. I took his feathers and mine off our hats and stuffed them away under my coat. Now we were just anonymous respectable koters and not damned racters.

The strong and pleasant scent of Moonblooms touched the air as a reminder that all life was not fighting and strife. The fight was over and my reactions were under control. The thing just had to be pushed aside. What a rackety old life I did lead on Kregen, to be sure!

Remembering the care and skill with which the hatter had sewn the feathers into place, I suppose I regretted my brutal tearing away. Skill in any trade or profession is always a pleasure to watch. It affirms one's faith in the destiny of humankind. Still, by Krun, as far as I was concerned there was no destiny, no future, for these confounded neo-Racters.

Mind you, I must correct that generalization about professional skill. There's precious little pleasure watching the technique employed by an executioner as he goes about his grisly task.

As I hoisted Verlan up with a quick word to reassure him, I reflected that, yes indeed, my life on Kregen was extraordinarily rackety and prone to sudden outbreaks of violence. These, as you know, were not of my choosing. My very calmness after a fight—was that proof that I was growing calloused, uncaring? I sincerely hoped not, in the good graces of Opaz.

We went off at a fair pace through the moonlit streets. Verlan belonged to a squadron based on the field just outside Gafarden. As the ship-hikdar he held a responsible position and was clearly on the lookout for promotion to Jiktar and his own command. Sink me! Didn't I know his feelings? Hadn't I been in just that position back on Earth? He'd expressed himself very forcefully in our conversation how disappointed, angered and generally depressed he was at not going with the VAS contingent to Pandahem to fight the Bloody Menahem.

The task now was to get him back to his base without attracting the unwelcome attentions of his superiors.

Well, with the timely assistance of Opaz—and Zair and Djan, too, I daresay—that trick was accomplished without too much fuss.

Riding back on the hired zorca with the empty saddle on the zorca on his leading rope, I felt the strong pang of desire that the rest of my problems could be dealt with as easily.

Of course, not just because this was Kregen but because that was the way of the world, I knew those problems would be just as intractable as ever. As I say, what a rackety old life I led!

How Verlan explained his wound was up to him. That wasn't my concern. Anyway, by Vox, he was a doubly-damned Racter, wasn't he?

The hostler at the livery stables turned out somewhat surlily at my knocking on the door. An Och with his hair disheveled and his leather apron all tied up lopsidedly, he blinked like an owl as I led the two zorcas into the stables. He gave me back the deposit and then I could turn my steps towards my rooms and my waiting bed.

A gust of amusement made me shake my head. Poor damned Black and White Logan Verlan! His magnificently-engineered moustache, thoroughly messed up by the scrapes he'd gone through, resembled the blunt ends of stencil brushes when I'd dumped him into his quarters.

So—off to bed. Ha! The Guard Commander who'd caught night duty turned out to be Deldar Nath the Rumphious. "Majister!" Even at night a busy palace is never silent; but sounds were muted. Deldar Nath's bellow shook the tapestries.

I gave him a look. He went on: "Three koters to see you, majister. Been waiting a long time. Pur Zygon Farzena, Koter Tobi Vingal and Koter Naghan Raerdu. Waiting in your office."

"Thank you, Nath," I spoke a trifle heavily. He bashed his right fist across his breastplate in salute.

So—not off to bed.

I trundled along to my office knowing there'd be news, and, by the massive bosom and obese nether parts of the Divine Madam of Belschutz!—the news was bound to be bad.

Twelve

The news brought by Tobi and Naghan Raerdu, while not bad, was not necessarily good—it was interesting.

Saying that I'd deal with Pur Zygon first, I sat down, leaned back in the chair and for an instant closed my eyes. Of course, that was a sin. When affairs of state are concerned you cannot afford to let yourself be tired.

Zygon asked for the letters I'd said I'd write. He was itching to fly back to Zandikar. I told him I'd write them soonest. He could fly later on today. He nodded, saluted gravely and went off—off to bed, of course. Some people didn't know their own luck.

They'd been quietly drinking wine, an evening red of good vintage, and I poured myself a full glass. When I rang the bell the little Fristle fifi Selena entered pertly. I asked for food and she ducked her pretty head and went off—as always with a saucy flirt of her pink-ribboned tail. They get away with murder, these beautiful Fristle fifis!

"Now, what's your interesting news?"

They looked at each other. I knew their characters. I knew Naghan would be cautious. I knew Tobi would jump straight in as his reckless nature dictated. I was right. Tobi spoke at once.

"Well, jis. It does seem as though we do have a conspiracy on our hands." He went on to elaborate on the affair of Tralgan Vorner. "The records of the trial have gone missing." Here he put a finger to his nose, his heavy features flushed. "If, that is, there ever was a proper trial at all."

"Well," I said. "He was condemned to death and was executed. There should be records." I sipped wine. "If there was a trial."

Naghan said: "Probably not. That ties in with what I've been finding out. Also, if this Spectre is the ghost of Tralgan Vorner then that explains why Nath the Clis's lawyer and his stylors are being ripped up."

Tobi, in his eager way, said: "We're beginning to piece this together."

"Unlike," I replied dryly, "the Spectre's victims."

They digested that, nodded; they didn't laugh.

Naghan went on to say that the people of Gafarden knew that the Spectre had been destroyed and had reappeared. Now the new monster was supposedly dead, the people believed he'd come again. "That's why the streets still empty early."

Selena brought the food in and we ate companionably. We had to solve the mystery surrounding this fellow Vorner. I recalled how reluctant the chief pallan had been to worry the emperor over my murder charge. Tralgan Vorner had been the rightful Elten of Culvensax and would most certainly have appealed to the chief pallan, and to Princess Didi and the emperor. Common sense indicated that. Had he done so?

The door opened and Selena came in again, carrying a terracotta bowl covered by a yellow cloth. She inclined her head to us and then went on with her task. She was on duty through this part of the night and would perform her duties even if high-level discussions were taking place where she had to clear up—or, in this case, feed the flick-flick plant on the windowsill.

The flick-flick plant sensed what lay in the bowl. The six-feet long tendrils uncurled. The orange cones opened. Selena put the bowl down, took off the cloth and then retired smartly.

Bright green tendrils swooped. The sticky pads flicked one after the other into the bowl. Each tendril retracted carrying a large glistening bluebottle fly. The flies went down the maw of the orange cones. Although there was no noise, you'd swear there were satisfying chomping sounds of a good meal being ingested.

The people of Gafarden kept their new city clean at the command of Princess Didi. So few flies contaminated the place that the flick-flick plants had to be fed specially reared flies for their meals.

When Selena went out I yawned. Covering that gross dereliction of duty

I said: "It seems I must speak with Ulana Farlan. She was, at the time of the execution of Tralgan Vorner, the nazabni of Urn Vennar."

"So," said Naghan, "she should know if any appeal was sent." He told me that pending a fresh appointment Ulana was staying at a small hostelry on Velia Avenue. She was on what was effectively half pay. Velia Avenue was one of the smartest and most expensive places in the new city. Small the hostelry might be; luxurious it most certainly would be. So Ulana was being looked after.

Tobi scratched his nose. "Jis." He stopped, and rubbed his nose. "Jis. The Spectre fell to pieces. D'you really think the fiendish thing will return?"

I stared in what was an empty fashion on Tobi. All I could see was a glorious vision of bed. So I was not as diplomatic as perhaps I might have been.

"Return, Tobi? Of course the Opaz-forsaken thing will return. I imagine it'll do that until we find out where the blasted monster comes from and blow that up."

Tobi swallowed down. "Yes. But, jis, what do you mean by blow up?"

What, indeed? I was on Kregen, where gunpowder was unknown and where I'd been through tortuous trials to keep that secret intact. I stood up. I looked resolute. "Blow up, Tobi, means we must find what lies behind the Spectre and Tralgan Vorner, and deal with those problems in such a way so that they do not recur. Dernun?"

Tobi and Naghan stood up.

"Ye-es," said Naghan.

"Oh, aye, Jis," said Tobi.

Mind you, I might have lived a long life on Kregen; I still carried the roots of my upbringing in Nelson's Navy always with me.

So, at last, at long long last, I could find that enticing bed and, with my last thought always the same, go to blessed sleep.

Not all that early the following day I set off for Velia Avenue. I'd missed the first and second breakfasts and so stoked up at the fore-mid meal. After the rain the streets shone and the trees along the avenue looked particularly attractive. Folk went about their business; but the constrained feeling of impending doom kept faces unsmiling.

Strange how quickly the populace pick up on what the government does not tell them—well, some of the time, at least. The damned Spectre would be back. No one doubted that fell prophecy.

You needed gold on Velia Avenue rather than silver. The shops looked as though you'd have to put on your best clothes to enter their august premises. The hostelries were as far removed from the taverns of the town as imagination would have it, as Paz is from Schan.

Either side of the entrance stood a huge pot of Cwofan ware, bearing sweet-smelling violet and pink flowers. The scent came at me in a great gust. That was as much over the top as the rest of the place. Inside the front hall the reception area sparkled. I went on in towards the cubicle with its slatted blind where the porter reigned.

Ulana Farlan might no longer be the nazabni of Urn Vennar; here in The Zorca's Horn she lived in style and comfort.

Two things struck me as odd as I approached.

Just visible on the floor inside the door to the cubicle lay a pair of feet. The shoes were highly polished. The rest of the body was not visible within the cubicle.

The porter was a woman, a Rapa woman. She wore a plain yellow apron and her feathers were neatly trimmed—by Krun, they were cropped close to her head with a savagery owing nothing to fashion.

Her high-beaked face regarded me impassively. Politely I gave her the Llahal and asked for Ulana's room.

For a moment she did not reply. She looked past my shoulder.

Without thought I lunged sideways and swiveled.

Two Rapa women with upraised swords bore down with murderous intent. They wore scale armor over their feathers. They were big. They rushed upon me, hissing in their excitement.

The rapier and dagger came out smartly. Two swift parries gave me the chance to skip back. My sideways plunge enabled me to avoid them along the front of the cubicle. Had I remained rooted to the spot in abrupt terror, as clearly they expected, the Rapa acting as the porter would have stuck me from the back.

Halting in their mad rush, they swung about to face me.

"By Rhapapolana the Stitcher of Skulls!" The nearest woman shook her sword as though that would settle the issue. "Apim! Man! Give up now!"

"Or you are dead!" amplified the second.

"Dead and meat for rippasch!" finished the porter.

I knew about these Mothers of Carnage. They were dangerous. The strict way Rapas treat their women is a byword on Kregen and even their courting rituals are marked by savagery and violence. Some Rapa women revolted, went wild, shook off constraints and formed their own sororities in defiance of their menfolk. They were not quite like apim sisterhoods nor the sororities of Hytak ladies. They were for hire. Assassinations, kidnaps, arson, any act of terrorism imaginable, they would carry out—for pay.

Once Ulana Farlan had been sacked as the nazabni I'd understood the attempts on her life had ceased. Evidently, that assumption was wrong.

The Mothers of Carnage circled me and the porter came out of the cubicle. Her yellow apron concealed her scale armor. Their swords were the serviceable drexers of Vallia. Now I muchly dislike fighting women and abhor having to slay them when necessary.

With Ulana's life in danger there was precious little option.

Also—I guessed there was precious little time left.

The blades flickered, steel scraped against steel. They were hissing and screeching and flecks of foam flew. The sword techniques here were practical in the extreme. Clean thrust, withdraw, on guard, parry and lunge. One Mother of Carnage went down and the second tried to be clever and her drexer dragged too slowly to parry the lunge.

The porter danced back, seething with rage.

"Man! You will surely die!"

Quickly flurrying the rapier before me I dodged back and around the cubicle and ducked inside. The register lay open. Ulana had booked in a few days ago and I flicked through the coarse pages until I found her entry. The Chemzite Room.

The damned porter nearly had me as I whistled out of the cubicle. The drexer passed close by my ribs. The rapier did not pass by her ribs; it passed through.

Well, by the Blade of Kurin, that had not been a pretty day's work and whilst I was in nowise proud of the deeds, I damned-well was not ashamed, either.

Where women are held in thrall and subjection to obnoxious men, once they can break out they become far more vicious in their actions than the men who have for so long held them down. This is known on Earth, to the torment and death of captured unfortunates.

Up the stairs in four-step leaps, along the first corridor searching for the Chemzite Room—nothing—up the stairs again, running, fast, fast! I raced along like a maniac.

Bloody Mothers of Carnage! I knew what my Delia and the Sisters of the Rose would say about them! Mind you, by Holy Tokai, how could you blame them for their excesses having broken free of the chains that bound them from birth? All the same, when they hired out their mercenary gangs for assassination—wasn't that carrying the cry for freedom and equality a trifle too far?

Of course, they would answer, then it's perfectly correct for men to be stikitches and hire out to assassinate folk. I tell, you, it's devilishly difficult to get straight answers in this life, by Krun!

Chemzite is a precious stone of great value. I tended to doubt any genuine chemzite stones were within a hundred dwaburs of this room in The Zorca's Horn. The name was blazoned elegantly on the door as I skidded along the corridor on the third floor. I was not at all elegant. I should have waited and listened. I did not.

In fact, I did neither. I just booted the door open and barged through.

They'd stripped Ulana of all her clothes. They'd tied her in a hard-backed chair. They hadn't gagged her, for they wanted her to talk. Three of the gruesome Mothers of Carnage were about to do unspeakable things to Ulana. Standing a little back, as though this was no business of his, a ferret-faced polsim put a lace kerchief to his twitcher of a nose. He was dressed in buff yet I sensed this was not his usual mode of attire.

"You will say exactly what I have told you—dernun!"

He had time to finish his sentence before I burst into the room.

Over to one side of this luxurious room, and spoiling its elegance, lay a couple of dead bodies. They were Chuliks. Their oily yellow skins looked even more sallow, their fearsomely upthrust tusks just pathetic. A single glance confirmed that each had been stabbed in the back. This, then, was what had happened to Ulana's guards.

A ceramic bowl of brackenberries had been overturned and in the brief, treacherous, struggle, they'd been trampled underfoot. The pungent smell of brackenberries filled the air of this refined room and twined in a macabre fashion with the raw stink of spilled blood.

Halting on the threshold, I said: "Ladies. If you leave quietly now, no harm will come to you." The blood glistened thickly upon the rapier and dagger blades.

"You," I pointed at the polsim. "I would have words with you."

When I'd dodged so rapidly into the cubicle in the lobby to find Ulana's room I'd had to step over the dead body of the real porter.

He was—rather, he had been—an Och. He was probably as harmless as a fluffy summer cotton-wool cloud. The Mothers of Carnage had simply chopped him down. His head was caved in and blood and brains spattered the floor. This was their usual mode of conduct.

What, then of Ulana's plight now? What of my polite invitation to them to leave quietly? Ha!

These three harpies looked much the same and much like the three below. The fact was they could all have been stamped from the same die. They wore fancy insigne denoting rank within their sisterhood so the gold rippasch brooch fastened to the shoulder of the Rapa who stepped forward probably meant she was of the highest grade here.

"Man! Put away your Jiktar and Hikdar. You will leave, not us."

The one at her left side said: "And harm will come to you."

The one on her right side said: "You will leave—horizontally."

By the use of the terms Jiktar and Hikdar for the rapier and left hand dagger she revealed they probably understood swords. The slang terms were in common use among the sword-wielding classes.

Poor Ulana, all white, her flesh dinted in by the bonds—she gave a gasping cry. Tears glistened on her cheeks. She wasn't white all over, for her eyes were red. "Help! Hel—"

The nearest Mother of Carnage casually backhanded her across that pallid face. I hurtled forward headlong, blades out-thrust.

Difficult to keep the old temper in control. Difficult not just to go bald-headed at them, yelling. Sword-work must come first.

They drew smartly enough and we set to. Circling around, they tried the usual tricks. These three proved superior blade-women to the first three. Oh, they weren't in the same class as some Jikai Vuvushis I knew; but their very ferocity would, in normal circumstances, serve to give them the edge of terror.

After I'd pinked one in the arm above the leather armband and just missed with a lunge that should have gone clean through a throat but instead merely mangled an ear, they drew off a pace. They swirled their blades in circles trying to reflect the light into my eyes. They did not attack; instead they stared loweringly upon me.

The polsim screeched out: "Stick the rast!"

I cocked an eyebrow at the women. I do not usually talk as some fighters do during combats of this nature. Still, it would be useful to sow a seed.

"Why, ladies, don't you ask *him* to stick me?"

By the distended belly and gargantuan thighs of the Divine Madam of Belschutz! How clever I thought myself! How diabolically Machiavellian I was! Ha! My words galvanized the polsim.

He drew a throwing knife from over his shoulder and flung.

Like any green coy, caught completely off guard, I moved far too late. The terchick thunked high into my left shoulder.

The Mothers of Carnage screeched and hurtled forward, their blades darting for my hide.

Thirteen

Slow, Dray Prescot, I said to myself in biting condemnation. Too damn slow!

I jumped back. For a moment I could avoid that onslaught and sidle around. The pain had not yet struck. Rather, the shock numbed my shoulder. The left hand dagger hadn't fallen to the floor and I tightened my fingers experimentally. My fingers moved and gripped. So nothing vital had been severed.

How long I'd be able to use the main gauche remained open to serious question. As long as it took to deal with these harpies, by Krun!

Moving now with the speed I'd singularly failed to use before, I plunged back into the fight. The confounded knife stuck in my shoulder waggled like a harpoon in a fish. When the pain hit, it would hit!

These Mothers of Carnage rushed on as though, as they say in Clishdrin, they were hell-bent on their own destruction.

In the swift circling and stamping, the savage lunging and steely riposte, the ducking away, the Polsim hovered at the far end of the room beyond Ulana. Now I did not want him to escape. So I tried to keep near the door to catch the ferret-faced fellow if he made a run for it.

The Rapa whose ear had been ruined for the wearing of an earring succumbed to a quick up and under. These bladeswomen wore scale armor—I, of course, had none—so I didn't even bother to attempt a body thrust. The next one took the rapier through the throat and this time the lunge was true.

A high-pitched wailing continued all the time we fought. Poor Ulana, tied up all naked, howled to the heavens.

The remaining Mother of Carnage, the one wearing the golden rippasch badge, had no intention of giving up. She continued to bore in with a determination which, in another cause, would have been admirable. The pain began to bite with tearing fangs into my shoulder. Greasy wetness on my wrist and hand told how the blood trickled down.

So we clashed blades and thrust and parried and the main gauche could not fulfill the task for which the weapon had been built. With a contemptuous flick of her blade, the Rapa knocked the dagger aside. I could feel the absence of strength in my fist, like a void, empty and dull.

By this time the polsim had had enough. He tried to wriggle past and I swirled rapidly away from the woman and gave him a trifle of a tickler. The point of the rapier drew a spot of blood from his cheek. He squawked as though he'd been run through and scuttled back to hide behind Ulana.

"Don't forget, polsim," I said, somewhat thickly. "I want you alive!"

Boasting in the middle of a fight! What depths you've sunk to, Dray Prescot, I said to myself. The Rapa took advantage of that stupidity and flung herself at me in a clever passage. Her blade darted every which way and the rapier matched and held the drexer.

The pain in my shoulder was becoming intolerable. Still, pain is an occupational hazard for a paktun and must be pushed aside.

That furious rush and the resultant encounter gave the polsim the opportunity to slip past. He called out in triumph: "You're a dead man, apim!"

The Mother of Carnage's sword began to whistle rather too closely about my midriff. My rapier still held the blade out; I wondered how long that would continue.

A final effort must be made. The trick turned out to be a rather nice variation of the rotation and flick that would disarm an opponent. The routine was totally extemporized. The passage finished with my blade through the Rapa's throat.

As I withdrew I heard a thunk—a juicy thunk—at my back. In the same movement I sprang to the side and turned abruptly.

The polsim came flying through the open doorway into the room. He lay there like a washing up cloth. He was not dead.

A bright voice said: "He's alive, Pur Dray, as you wished."

Here came Zygon, striding into the room, balancing his Great Krozair Longsword across his left forearm. He was beaming. Then he saw the throwing knife.

"Pur Dray! You're wounded!"

"Lahal, Pur Zygon. Oh, aye. Thank you for the polsim."

"Lahal. But—"

"The lady in the chair is the Lady Ulana Farlan. Would you please take care of her." That was not a question. Zygon knew Pur Dray Prescot as the greatest Krozair in the Eye of the World—admittedly a long time ago and quite possibly before he'd been born. To him, this was a command. He jumped forward, ripping off his cape.

In all the excitement there'd been no time to take stock of Ulana. I'd noticed the way the ropes cut into her flesh. She'd stopped crying and screaming. Her hair which usually was tied into an excruciatingly tight bun at the back of her head had been freed. That hair framed her face in a most pretty fashion. As to her figure, well, gentleman or not, these things if glimpsed in a passing second, are noted. I'd always thought of her as a little mousey creature. With her hair free and the curve of her body—I really wondered if our gallant Jiktar Yavnin of the Vallian Air Service could find as much beauty and warmth from Ulana as he'd ever find from the cold blonde Ahilya. Ah, well, not for me to interfere there.

The confounded throwing knife was now plaguing me. Zygon used his dagger to free Ulana from her bonds and swept his cape about her nakedness. He was perfectly matter of fact. He turned to face me, supporting Ulana.

"A needleman for you, majister, and a Puncture Lady for Lady Ulana." He started purposefully towards the door. He nodded at the blood-fouled blade in my fist. "These little stickers they use around here. Rapiers, I believe. Useful—h'm—useful. Still—"

"Oh, aye." I wasn't light-headed from loss of blood just yet. "But the Krozair brand would—"

"Quite," said Pur Zygon.

"Anyway, how in a Herrelldrin Hell did you happen by?"

"The letters. I saw you leave and so followed. I lost a bit of the way. When I saw the corpses in the lobby I assumed danger."

Here was an example of the old Krozair nose for peril!

"Those blasted letters. I'll write them as soon as possible."

He gave me a funny look and I shook my head. He wanted to know what should be done with the polsim. No one from the hostelry had put in an appearance after the noise of the fight, so we had to assume the Mothers of Carnage had dealt with them as they had the porter.

Telling Zygon I could walk—which was barely true—with the knife still in situ, I suggested we clear off sharpish. The Krozair of Zimuzz was well up to the challenge. "I'll carry the damned polsim over my shoulder." He turned in the exquisitely polite fashion of a true Krozair. "Lady Ulana. If I support you, can you walk?"

She drew the cape more tightly around her nakedness. "Yes. I thank you—" Her voice betrayed the depths of the terror through which she had just gone. She endured well, did our Lady Ulana.

So, a sorry little procession, we trailed off out of the room and down the stairs. We met no one.

Feeling The Unhanged Drikinger to be an inappropriate place to take my wound and Ulana's need for attention, we headed for the palace. One of the doctors there, Lornrod the Poultice, could be trusted. A dry old stick of an apim, with a wart the size of a walnut on his cheek, he would attend to our several injuries.

As for the polsim, a thwack from a Krozair would keep him in deepest slumber for some time yet. His time for questioning remained.

The odd thing was—and yet, given the unrest in Gafarden, not so odd after all—was the total lack of interest in the folk we passed along the streets. They gave us a glance, lowered their heads, and went on.

I had to admit that, by the lustrous lips and bright eyes of the Maiden Katie of the Lake, it was passing strange for a fellow with a knife stuck in his arm, an unconscious polsim slung over the shoulder of a man wearing outlandish garb, and a naked woman half-covered by a cape, to walk abroad in daylight without so much as a comment from the populace. Mighty strange, by Krun!

Because I'd been the Emperor of Vallia and was now supposed to be the Emperor of Emperors, the Emperor of All Paz, we were able to march straight through into the palace. Deldar Nath Feringhim, very punctilious, guard commander on duty, insisted on assisting us. We all went through to my office where Zygon dumped the polsim on the floor and then very solicitously placed Ulana on the couch.

"Nath," I said sharply to the guard commander. "Doctor Lornrod the Poultice, and quickly now."

"Quidang, majister!" Nath Feringhim took himself off as smartly as his acknowledgement of my order. Shortly the doctor came in, tut-tutted, and started on my knife. At least, that was what the confounded thing seemed to be to me now. "No, no," I said, exasperated. "See to the lady."

"But, majister—"

"The lady. Now!"

Ulana sat up, grasping the cape about her. "Majister—you are wounded—"

Very patiently I told her to let the doctor make sure she was all right. Seeing I was in earnest she lay back and the doctor checked her eyes and her pulse. He stuck a few acupuncture needles in here and there and stood up. "The lady will be fine now, majister."

Then he started on the damned throwing knife. Amid all the blood and the salves and the bandages he strapped me up. I felt a trifle better. His needles dispelled the pain. There was work to be done and the quicker I started the quicker it would be done.

"Ulana. What was it that this miserable polsim wanted you to say?"

She gave me a long look. Her eyes were remarkably attractive, a fact I felt sure Yavnin had never noticed.

"That Nath Swantram had asked me to refer the matter of Tralgan Vorner to Princess Didi and to the emperor."

"And he had not?"

"Most decidedly not. He was adamant that we should not."

I nodded.

The pieces were falling into place in the jigsaw. The doctor and a couple of hastily summoned handmaids took Ulana off to my quarters. I trusted she would sleep well. As for me, there was more to be done. The summons was speedily answered by Naghan Raerdu. He frowned. "Yes, jis. It is coming together."

Telling him what Ulana's last words were before they carried her off, I felt a chill of impending catastrophe. "She said, Naghan, she'd have her vengeance on those who had done this to her."

The Slippy rubbed his chin. "Yes, jis. She is a most determined lady. If she finds out—oh, yes, by Vox, I believe her."

The polsim stirred and mumbled. "Naghan. Perhaps you'd care to take him off and find out what he knows. Someone hired him and those ghastly Mothers of Carnage."

Zygon said: "I'll tell you all about it, Koter Naghan." He glared at me. "And you, Pur Dray, are for bed instanter!"

"Absolutely." Naghan brisked up. He hauled the polsim off the floor. "We will ask the necessary questions. You, jis, need to rest."

"It's not yet evening!" I protested.

These good folk did not know of the Sacred Pool in far Aphrasöe. They didn't know how my baptism there enabled me to recover from wounds with magical rapidity. All the same, by Krun, I did feel the effects of the wound. Perhaps a few burs rest would work wonders.

"All right," I said in a disgruntled tone. "I'll get some rest." I looked at Zygon sorrowfully. "I'll write those letters as soon as I get up."

He gave me the raffish smile of the Krozair enjoying himself. "That is perfectly all right, Pur Dray." He brushed up his ferocious moustache. "All this mayhem and blattering is vastly amusing, by Zair!"

This bright spark of a Krozair saw my face which, I suppose, must have looked somewhat lowering. At any rate, he drew himself up. "Ah, what I mean, majister—these events are distressing when one considers the Lady Ulana. But to be a part of exhilarating mysteries, why that is—ah—well, exhilarating. If you understand."

"Hmph." I used the old stock word that covers a multitude of meanings. "Mellow Moonlights—even if it is nowhere near night."

With that I took myself off. Then, of course, my own bed was occupied by Ulana Farlan. The couch was ample enough. I stretched out. There was just time for me to think the last thought I always have before sleep before I swept away enfolded in a cloud of slumber as opaque as a night of Notor Zan.

The intention was to have a short period of shut eye and then be up and about the multifarious tasks under my hand. Well, as they say in Zairia, Man sows but Zair reaps.

My eyes opened to see Doctor Lornrod the Poultice standing over me. I blinked and felt the grittiness at the corners of my eyes. The good doctor's face was half-illuminated by lamplight. Shadows clustered in the corners of the room. I sat up and felt the pull of the wound in my shoulder.

"Keep still, majister." The Poultice's wart threw a shadow across his cheek as he bent. He gave me a check and then straightened up. "Ye-es, well—h'm."

"What in a Herrel—ah—what does that mean, doctor?"

He said my sleep had served me well. No few burs had passed since I'd settled down to rest on the couch. Now it was the middle of the night and the hour of dim was upon us.

Absolute disgust with my conduct made my lips curve down.

The doctor gave it as his opinion that he'd never seen a wound healing so rapidly before. I just grunted and asked him to send out for food. I was famished.

With the meal came in Tobi and Naghan the Slippy. The questioning of the polsim had proceeded in a civilized fashion. His name was Ornol the Slim—well, to be sure, there wasn't a lot of him—and he expressed himself as entirely sorrowful that he'd accepted the commission.

"Those Mothers of Carnage are strictly bad news. This Ornol the Slim says he has used them before for various nefarious purposes. He has promised not to do so again."

Tobi added: "If you can believe him."

No doubts remained that the villain of the piece was, indeed, the chief pallan, Nath Swantram the Clis. When Ulana was still the nazabni he'd given out a contract for her assassination. The attempts on her life had been foiled. Swantram yearned to be the nazab. That had not happened. Remembering how the newly appointed nazab had been murdered, ostensibly by his servant, I suspected Swantram's hand had plunged the dagger in. After that treacherous act he'd callously murdered the servitor.

Now the chief pallan did not want Ulana killed. He needed her to lie for him. He must be aware that we were growing warm on his trail of villainy. Oh, yes, you can quite see why he did what he did; but personal ambition driven by greed and cleverness does not excuse betrayal and murder.

So Tralgan Vorner was innocent. The schemes of Nath the Clis had originated the rest of the tragedy. Vorner's alleged murder of the judge and the cadade was just that. He hadn't killed them. Yet he'd had no trial. No wonder he came back as the avenging Spectre!

Using the Mothers of Carnage to put pressure on Ulana was a clever, and devilishly repulsive, move. There was little doubt that Ulana, with the threat of those gruesome Rapa women hanging over her would have lied for Swantram with the fervor and conviction of a seasoned swod in the ranks.

Mind you, having sorted all that out, there could well be further ramifications to the plot we must yet uncover.

"You'll have the cadade arrest the shint at once, jis!" Thus the good Tobi, filled with fire and indignation.

Very quickly, Naghan Raerdu snapped out: "I think not, Tobi."

"What! Why not? The cramph needs—"

Raising a calming hand, I reminded Tobi that the khibil Captain of the Guard, Jik Pranton the Faranto, had been sacked by the chief pallan. The newly-appointed nazab, Rennel Lorving, had not yet arrived in Urn Vennar, held up by unfinished business in Vondium. So that left Nath Swantram running the province. He'd appointed a new Captain of the Guard, Rendo Froison, known as the Blatter. Rendo the Blatter was a Rapa.

"Oh," said Tobi, comprehending.

"Tsleetha-tsleethi," cautioned Naghan the Slippy.

The thing would have to be done nip and tuck and, at the same time, circumspectly. We'd have to plan the strike very carefully. There were some members of the palace guard I fancied I could trust, like the hytak Del Nath the Rumphious and the apim Del Nath Feringhim. Of course, my other two new companions would thirst to get in on the act. In addition, I rather thought Pur Zygon would delay flying back to Zandikar. Anyway, I still hadn't written the confounded letters.

The under chamberlain knocked and came in to say that Koters Purvun and Nevko wished to see me at this hour. He looked outraged. When I told him, very brightly, to show them in instanter, he nodded and lost his disgruntled look. He was beginning to understand my ways.

"And, Quarmby, bring more wine, please!" I called after him.

These two fine fellows came in and the wine followed on their heels. After the lahals we supped the evening red and then I said: "Suppose you tell 'em the news, Tobi. You'll burst with it else!"

"Absolutely, jis!" Tobi tore into the information we'd had and our deductions and assumptions. When he'd reached the point where we intended to arrest the chief pallan, Yavnin nodded gravely. Nalgre Nevko spilled his wine. The red stain glistened on the cloth like blood.

Ignoring that, for one does not draw attention to little mishaps of that nature, I said: "Poor old Tralgan Vorner! I always felt he didn't have a fair chance. Somehow, all these revelations do not come as much of a surprise to me." I sipped and finished: "Anyway, if Tralgan Vorner's ghost is the Spectre, which seems likely, it is extraordinarily difficult to put blame on him, by Vox!"

"Yes, majister." Nalgre spoke heavily. "I recall you saying as much when—when all these murders began."

"Aye," said Yavnin. "I remember."

He and Nalgre had just arrived in Gafarden and had already contracted for a massive party tomorrow night. The ladies Ahilya Vorona and Cindy Cwolanda would attend. They wanted us to join them.

"That could be difficult," burst out Tobi, jumping in with both feet as usual. "We have this shint to take up."

Again my new calm manner amazed me as I spoke. I cautioned them to remain silent about these developments. We would not tell a soul of the information we'd gathered until the time came to strike. Naghan Raerdu was aware of the chief pallan's movements. He ventured out more often now, having got over his fright at the attempt, as he thought, on his life. "So, we can all have a jolly time tomorrow night. It will be good cover. Oh, and, I think Pur Zygon would like to go to the party before he flies off to the Eye of the World."

After a few moments' discussion, all this was agreed to.

Nalgre Nevko, who had remained silent, looked up. "Yes. It will be—interesting."

"The party or the arrest?" said Tobi, incorrigible as ever.

"Both." Nalgre Nevko's voice was as dry as the Ochre Limits.

Tobi smiled in his easy fashion. "Right. All the same, Nalgre, you look a bit off color. What have you eaten?"

Nevko heaved himself up. He certainly had changed from the man who'd come in full of the scheme for the party. "Yes. Yes, I do not feel myself. Not at all. If you'll forgive me I'll give you all the remberees."

Amid a chorus of remberees and Mellow Moonlights, Nalgre Nevko left. Yavnin shook his head. "These days the uncertainty bothers everyone." Then he spoke more openly about his hopes of a command than he'd done before. "Everything's in turmoil in Vondium. Half the fleet officers have been suspended or discharged. I've just about given up all hope of advancement."

We made sympathetic murmurs. I couldn't understand why a gallant and efficient officer like Yavnin should be without employment in our modern VAS. Merit got you on these days; not gold or to what high muck-a-muck you were related.

Yavnin went on to say he'd caught the tiresome duty of conducting an investigation into why an officer had been stabbed in a street brawl. "Silly fellow won't own up. If it was a duel and he's covering up, it'll go the worse for him. Feller by the name of Hikdar Logan Verlan."

At once I felt guilty. I'd been so wrapped up in the business of the Spectre I hadn't gone to see Verlan. If I wanted to maintain my schemes with the Racters I must trot along today as Tyr Kadar.

After they'd all gone off to bed I sat up and was able to write my letters. One was to Drak asking about the latest state of the VAS, without, naturally, mentioning any names.

Zygon came into the office to collect the letters. He said he'd checked his airboat, loaded provisions, and was all ready to fly.

I told him the news on the chief pallan and what we proposed to do.

"Didn't I say, Pur Dray, that I'd be delighted to assist in these schemes of yours? I did. So, if it is all right, I'll go along."

That was what I'd expected him to say, of course. Then he rocked me back a trifle.

"You will not go naked?"

Well, apart from a scarlet breechclout I'd been through some hair-raising scrapes almost naked. Zygon didn't mean that. He touched the hilt of his Krozair brand. Yes, to go anywhere without his Krozair sword would make a Krozair feel naked, yes, by Zim-Zair!

"I will take my sword, Pur Zygon. Thank you."

By Zair! Already I felt better! Much better!

Fourteen

Ulana Farlan decided she really did not feel well enough to go to the party. She expressed her regrets and asked me to apologize to my friends and to thank them for their kind invitation. She sat up in my bed with a violet shawl draped about her shoulders. Her hair fell freely about her head and, again, I wondered if Yavnin might not reconsider his affection for Ahilya.

Telling her that I understood and that she should stay in my quarters for as long as she wished, I started to take my leave. She held out a hand. "Majister. I must ask you—my Chuliks?"

I shook my head. She put a lace handkerchief to her mouth. Her lips, newly to me, were full and red. "I am so sorry."

She went on to say that Princess Velia had, on the request of Princess Didi, instructed her bankers to provide funds for Ulana's upkeep. So Didi had paid for The Chemzite Room in The Zorca's Horn on Velia Avenue. Well, that was like my girls. I just hoped Didi felt no guilt that Ulana had been removed from her post as nazabni.

Then, in an entirely different tone of voice, all spikes and spitting hatred, Ulana said: "I have never felt so much hatred for anyone as I do for that rast Nath Swantram. I could throttle him!"

"Ah, yes," I said, warily.

"He's still after me, you know. Those awful Mothers of Carnage—I've told you the truth, majister. You will protect me?"

There was no hesitation as I assured her I would. Whatever happened to Ulana, I knew that I could never allow her to become the victim of those harpies. Anyway, Swantram was due for the chop.

She lay back and closed her eyes. She looked a totally different person from the prim little mouse I'd seen before—who Yavnin had seen before.

"When I see Nath Swantram," her voice held all the chilling menace of the Ice Floes of Sicce. "Oh, yes, when I get him—when I get him—oh, yes, that heap of manure will rue the day he was born! By Vox! I mean it!"

I believed her.

Taking my leave of this mousey little lady who had been transformed by horrific experience into a spitfire, I went along the busy corridors of the palace. Deldar Nath the Rumphious, on duty, looked remarkably pleased with himself. "Hai, Nath," I said, cordially. "Have you won a fortune at Jikaida?"

"Ah, majister! Would it be, would it be to the praise of Opaz. No, no. I've just signed up four Chuliks, hefty lads, for the guard."

After the expected Shank invasion of the Chulik Islands had not transpired, the Chulik mercenaries were returning to take up their various positions. I congratulated the Rumphious. Being new, the four Chuliks should be untainted by Swantram's corruption. They'd come in mighty useful in our arrest of the chief pallan.

Mind you, Nath the Clis, the unhanged scoundrel, must be wondering what had happened to his agent, the polsim Ornol the Slim. So my first port of call directed my footsteps to The Zorca's Horn.

From a discreet vantage point across the way I surveyed the luxurious hostelry. Wearing the famous anonymous buff and not my own face, I was merely an idle onlooker.

"Terrible business, koter. Terrible business—and in Velia Avenue, too. I wonder what Gafarden is coming to."

He was an apim, like me, clad in high quality buff. His face, plump and well-fed, his hands, soft and unused to hard work, and his jewelry proclaimed a man of substance. He shook his head. "Dreadful business, dreadful."

"How was it discovered, koter?"

He wore a rapier and main gauche but I'd be pulverized if he had much skill judging from the way they hung on their belts.

"Cleaners. Bunch of screaming women running out. It really is not good enough for Velia Avenue. All the same, the chief pallan himself, in person, came to superintend. So that proves he, at least, appreciates how much class we of Velia Avenue give to the city."

"I'm sure."

There was no more to be seen here now. Nath the Clis had moved rapidly once the corpses had been discovered. He was, indeed, a highly competent administrator. The tragedy was that corruption had claimed him. I wondered, not without a tinge of sorrow, if he still retained some vestige of honor and honesty.

Politely taking my farewell, I sauntered off as though my curiosity with this murderous tragedy had been slaked. The small crowd of onlookers still gawped. This was not the work of the Spectre, so the folk speculated and hung on events. They weren't ghouls, they merely shared a common—and, I suppose, regrettable—fascination with bloody murders.

Still trying to decide what the chief pallan would do next, now he'd seen the shambles at The Zorca's Horn, I took myself along to the livery stables to hire a zorca. Another Och led the beautiful animal out. He looked just like the Och who'd been surly the other night, so this was a family concern. I paid over the deposit, had a look at the zorca, then mounted up.

Yes, the problem facing Nath Swantram now would be to digest the meaning of what had happened to his agent. Where, he was no doubt cursing away, where has Ornol the Slim got himself to? Where was Ulana Farlan? Who'd done for the Mothers of Carnage?

From what I judged of his character he was a bold fellow with all his cunning. He'd been a soldier, made his money, and now wanted a title and real power. Probably taking him up would not be as easy as Tobi suggested.

The change in that raffish young man represented a miracle. After his rejection by Tassie he'd been like a thundercloud—and now he floated about as chipper as a skylark. So—he had found himself a new young lady. Had to have done, by Vox! Because he'd said nothing I assumed the romance—if that wasn't too strong a word—had not progressed beyond the first stages. Well, good old Tobi! Good luck!

So, of course, as I trotted gently along, my thoughts turned from my new friends to my old blade comrades. As ever, wouldn't it be grand if Seg and Inch and Turko and Old Hack 'n' Slay and all the others were here!

If Drak wasn't swanning around in Pandahem, at my suggestion, he'd be up here in Gafarden like a shot. That made me wonder if, when Zygon dropped my letters off on his way to Zandikar, Drak would even have time to read them let alone act on them.

The Deldar on duty was not at all keen to let me in to see Logan Verlan. With forethought I'd brought a basket of fruit. Using the power of the yrium which completely captivated the Deldar, I talked my way in. I made no attempt to bribe him. His bronzed, open face and the cut of his jib told me that he was your dedicated VAS man.

So, here at last was Verlan, sitting disconsolately on the edge of his bed, idly fiddling with his rapier. We exchanged greetings, the fruit was passed across, and then: "I'm in something of a pickle, Tyr Kadar." He hesitated. Just like Tobi and his request about Tassie the situation became very clear. "Look, Kadar, would you speak up for me?"

With very little hesitation, I said: "Yes."

"Tell the truth about being set upon. We were. But I took the wound in the street, not at the meeting."

"Very well."

He took up a gregarian and held it in his palm. "You're not much of a sworder?" He nodded before I could speak. "I guessed so."

Let him think that. That belief had served me well before.

He hadn't seen the fight, slumped in his doorway. And, at the enquiry, I would not have to lie. Well, not overmuch, by Krun!

He asked after his black and white feathers and I told him they were perfectly safe. They were. They were secreted in a chest under the very bed upon which Ulana Farlan rested. Mine rested there, too.

The room in which the enquiry was held turned out to be spartan and functional. Wooden chairs and a table, a stylor, pens and ink, and the great flag of Vallia hanging on the wall at the back of the enquiry board. There was some discussion as to my admission. Still, Yavnin had always struck me as a fair man, and now he proved it.

"If Tyr Kadar ti Vernonsmot, as a witness, can vouch for your story, then he shall be admitted."

So that was that. Devilish strange, though, to be sitting only a few paces away from Yavnin and to make no sign of recognition!

He took me for a koter of Vallia—which I was as well as a few other pretty and empty baubles of titles—and so worthy of trust.

We told the story. And, by Krun, it rang true!

"Your evidence will be studied and a verdict given." Yavnin put on his command face. "Brawling is expressly forbidden by the emperor. In this case you appear to have had no other recourse."

Yavnin's face lost that harsh look. "You'll probably hear tomorrow, Hikdar Verlan." He leaned forward. "Do not fret too much tonight."

As I say, Yavnin Purvun was a true gentleman of Vallia.

We all rose and the proceedings were over. Verlan tried not to limp as we went out. My own wound didn't trouble me at all now. Doctor Lornrod the Poultice had stuffed the bloody opening with turmeric. Turmeric stops the bleeding very effectively and also acts as an antiseptic. He came well by his nickname, did the good needleman.

Outside, Verlan thanked me fervently. He'd thought his career had gone like the ashes of last night's fire. "We Racters have to help one another, Logan." Even as I spoke I hoped the hollowness of the words did not carry through. Sarcasm was there, too, and a smidgen of self-contempt.

Then—then, by Vox, I shook that daft notion off. What I did, I did for the good of Vallia.

Mounting up, I looked down. Verlan appeared far less strained and under pressure from the haunted man he'd been before the enquiry. He wasn't cleared yet. Yavnin, I felt sure, would honor his hint.

The remberees were spoken and again I jogged slowly back relishing the warmth of the Suns and the freshness of the air. High over the splendid new city the palace appeared to soar above the old citadel. Underneath crouched the confounded dungeons where, for a brief time, I'd been incarcerated by the rast whom we wished to take by the heels.

The Slippy said the chief pallan did venture out more now. Probably our best chance would be to arrest him on the outside. To take him within his quarters in the palace would, by Krun, be tricky, like trying to catch a silver shining sliptinger with your bare hands.

Thus cogitating on the problems facing us I became aware of the circling shape above. I looked up. Yes, there he was, the scarlet and gold raptor, arrogantly flirting his wings, cocking his head on one side so a black beady eye could fasten on me.

The Gdoinye cut the bright air with his blunt-headed and stubby-winged outline sharp against the sky. His primary feathers fingered the wind as he turned in superb control.

A shivery sensation took me. Oh, yes, I'd become accustomed to the damned bird squawking mocking insults. I'd recognized his powers as the messenger and spy of the Star Lords. All the same, by Krun, no mortal fellow could contemplate these supernatural goings-on without a frisson up his backbone.

No mocking squawk emanated from the Gdoinye. He circled, keeping his baleful eye on me. There was much to be done here; I did not doubt that there was also much to be done over there in the Dawn Lands. I had the strongest conviction that I'd not finished with the numim family or with Otto the Lance. Not, by Vox, by a long chalk!

As though satisfied with his scrutiny the Gdoinye soared aloft and winged strongly away. He turned into a black dot and then vanished past the windmills of the miller's section. One thing remained true: I muchly doubted whether the bird of ill-omen would ever be satisfied with the reprobate Dray Prescot.

The hired zorca returned, I decided to take a meal in The Dandelion Triumphant, a middling-order establishment that aspired to greater things. The proprietor, a Languelsh who'd forsaken trade for catering, probably envisioned himself set up along Velia Avenue. His food was good and his ales and wines acceptable, so I said good luck to him in his dreams of grandeur. His aspirations differed so markedly from those of Nath Swantram they inhabited two different worlds.

Eventually, after the hour of mid, I wandered off back to my quarters wearing my own face and went along to see how Ulana fared.

Quarmby met me, looking worried. He handed me a note. So I guessed what had happened at once, and sighed.

Ulana wrote that she was utterly bored with being mewed up. She again turned down the invitation to the party. That was because Yavnin would be there. She finished by writing no one would recognize her as she had adopted a truly cunning disguise.

In those words I had a sudden flash of the young Ulana, up to all a schoolgirl's tricks. When her father the nazab died she'd taken on the gravitas she felt necessary for the position of nazabni. If only she could let her hair down in both senses, well, then she might be in with a racing chance for the dashing Vallian Air Service Jiktar.

Dressing for the entertainment I felt as always the absence of Delia. Ling-Li had said Delia was off with the Sisters of the Rose. Anyway, if I'd tried to rush off to Esser Rarioch and take up the skill of knitting again, the confounded Star Lords would have enveloped me in the ghostly blue radiance of the Great Blue Scorpion and summarily dragged me back to Gafarden.

The color blue was not favored in Vallia and this always saddened me. Even after all these seasons green remained a color I'd wear only if the situation demanded it. The evening robe, therefore, was of russet hue. For the evening, red, I fancied, would be just a little too flash.

I did don the brave old scarlet breechclout, though. In addition to rapier, dagger and knife, I strapped on a quiver of terchicks over my shoulder. The black velvet mazilla, very smart, very fashionable, jutting up at the back of my head, served to conceal the throwing knives.

A cape, of the same russet color, hung down in neat folds.

So, dressed up in not too dandified a state and properly equipped, off I went to the rendezvous.

The Skylark Bank thronged with people in evening clothes taking their places in the pleasure craft readily for hire. The canal reflected long streaks of red and green. Most of these folk would finish their dinners early and be off home before—just in case—the Spectre put in an appearance. All the same, they were Vallians and they meant to enjoy themselves, Spectre or no.

Our party spotted me and waved, so I was a trifle late. They were all there. The Lady Ahilya wore—or half-wore—her gown with the elegance of a great lady. Cindy Cwolanda glowed, very happy with Nalgre Nevko, who seemed to have forsaken his moodiness. Tobi, all smiles and appearing to dance whilst standing still, introduced Medi Milva. She was quite small and beautifully formed with a fresh young face from which her two brown Vallian eyes regarded me coolly. Her gown, lilac with embroidered poppies, suited her. The lahals were spoken.

Naghan Raerdu had brought Nelana Lishmey. I knew her as one of his trusted agents. Her face, rather square with a generous mouth, and the strength of her body, told of a woman not to be trifled with.

That left Pur Zygon and me as the remaining couple. I did not relish the thought and, for that matter, nor did Zygon. Still, were we incompatible, the evening would be a disaster. As it was, we two Krozairs got along famously. As, by Zair, Krozairs should.

Whilst laughter rang out from the crowds, and happy chatter, the jollifications seemed, at least to me, to lack the full-bodied enjoyment a holiday afternoon like this should bring. One indication of the state of mind of Gafarden under the potential continuing threat of the Spectre lay in this—no flower petals strewed the water with color. Perfumes there were in plenty from the blossoms along the banks. Let Makki Grodno take the confounded Spectre! We all ought to enjoy ourselves whilst we could.

We boarded the canal boat, a roomy cruising craft. Plush seats, polished tables, much gleaming brasswork, all told of the owner's pride in his vessel. The galley did not smell of cooking. Flowers in ceramic pots added that necessary touch of informal luxury.

Now, as you know, the canalfolk of Vallia form a class apart. The vens and venas maintain their own culture and traditions. The root cause of their distinctive nature is the canal water. This is poisonous. If you swallow canalwater you'll become seriously ill, and you may well die. So—no one fell in.

The six oarsmen took up their sweeps, the cabin boy pushed off and Master Abso steered out among the other craft.

This hire of pleasure boats proved a highly profitable venture to the canalfolk in addition to their freighting trade. The Spectre had seriously cut down their revenues. Well, everybody suffered.

Chatting away we were pulled along the cut. Dinner was served. The Suns of Scorpio still blazed in splendid ruby and emerald and it did not rain.

Zygon was a bit of a puzzler for a Krozair. For one thing, he could fly a voller. He said in his grave way that his ambition was to become a Bold and then an Archbold. I said, only half teasingly: "And then the Grand Master of the Krozairs of Zimuzz?"

Perfectly seriously, he said: "In Zair's good time, Pur Dray."

I regarded him more closely. "Yes, Pur Zygon. I believe you will. You have my heartiest good wishes."

The afternoon wore on. The meal finished, we drank moderately and talked and enjoyed the occasion. Medi wanted to know all about the inner sea and Zygon spoke somewhat of conditions there. When I said Medi was beautifully formed, that could be construed as a mere male's pig-ignorant reaction to her. She was far more than that as her first cool appraisal of me showed. Tobi was in the highest of spirits. Perhaps, this time, he had found his true lady love?

Master Abso came forward to say that we should turn back.

We had, in truth, ventured a goodly distance along the canal and most of the other craft had already turned. The canal was well wide enough for these pleasure craft to turn about without needing a winding hole.

Yavnin, laughing, said: "Yes, Master Abso. A hundred and eighty degrees, then." He used Kregish figures; that was his meaning.

Only one other boat kept company with us as we pulled back.

Shadows lengthened and the water darkened on the west bank. Still, it had not rained. This business about the poisonous nature of canalwater had vexed me when I'd been emperor. After all, I'd fallen in and might well have died, save the baptism in the Sacred Pool of far Aphrasöe had mitigated the water's effects. Deliberations with the Pallan of the Canals, Mantig Roben ti Vindlesheim, confirmed the difficulty in changing the water. Pure river water flowing into the canals was changed by this unknown agency. If we could find that cause something might be done. Of course, the vens and venas might well oppose any such move, cherishing their culture.

Mind you, if the wise men could discover why the canalfolk were not poisoned by the water, the whole populace might benefit.

Water rippling past our bows made a soothing sound. We pulled along smoothly, the oarsmen in perfect unison. Up ahead a bridge crossed the canal. Each bank rose in solid masonry and brick from the water. The path didn't exist along this stretch of the cut so the haulers would have to make their way along on the other side of the buildings. The boatmen would haul out their sweeps and pull their vessels until the haulers could rejoin them.

The Lady Ahilya was trying to be condescending to Medi and, as I saw with inner amusement, failing lamentably. We were really a happy party on an afternoon's holiday; all the same, Ahilya sometimes soured the occasion. Of course, she was totally unaware of this.

As for Yavnin, either he was oblivious or totally forgiving.

So as the twin shadows of the bridge fell across the boat I was looking at Ahilya and Medi. I was not looking up.

Master Abso was. He let out a yell: "Vaosh! No—!"

Credit where credit is due—Zygon was the first out of the cabin onto the little afterdeck. The next instant a crashing smashing bashing ravaged the boat. Everything shook. The boat rocked as though caught in a rashoon of the inner sea. Some of the folk screamed.

"A damned great rock!" bellowed Zygon.

Water began to gush up in the hole punched by the rock.

Master Abso screamed out: "Don't drink the water! Keep your mouths tightly shut." He looked pretty desperate. "By Vaosh, if I find the cramphs who did this—!" He needn't have warned us for all of us knew only too well the deadly danger of the canalwater.

The place chosen for the attack meant we could not paddle to the bank and alight. The walls rose sheer. We were trapped in a boat sinking into water that could kill.

Fifteen

Both Cindy and Medi screamed at me as I leaped up onto the gunwale.

"Jis! No—Majister—No! No!"

Yavnin bellowed out: "Jis—the water—you'll—"

I heard no more as I took off in a racing dive. That damned treacherous water came up and hit me and splashed away and I started a powerful crawl, cutting along as though in the final of a swimming gala. Everything depended on speed. My new friends might all die if I didn't do this exactly right.

The other pleasure boat was pulling away ahead. The folk aboard appeared totally oblivious to what was tragically happening to our craft. I powered my arms and feet, fairly cutting through the damned, condemned, disgusting water. The thought struck me as I lunged on that Drak and Manrig Roben must find a solution to the canal water poison.

Faintly to my ears the sound of yelling from the boat reached me. I guessed they were all shouting at the tops of their voices.

Each time my head came up I glared at the boat ahead. At last the helmsman turned to look aft. At last?—at long damned last!

The next time my head came up he was still staring aft.

No time to feel rage at the fellow's obtuseness. Time only to smash forward for the last two strokes, heave up and grasp the rail and so tumble inboard. Water drops flew in a wide spray as I leaped up and started a charging dash for the tiller.

The happy people enjoying the last of their afternoon picnic shrieked and cowered away from this maniac who'd boarded and scattered poisonous water across them. I didn't blame 'em, by Krun!

A single savage yell at the oarsmen: "Backwater! Now!" and I barged into the helmsman, knocked him sprawling. "Backwater!" There just wasn't time to turn around. We'd have to pull stern first.

The ugly side of the yrium burst out full strength. That super-charisma stiffened the oarsmen as though they'd been lashed by ol' snake. In the next instant, and not without a slight tangle of their oars, they were frantically pulling backwards.

I stared apprehensively at our boat. She was low in the water, too damned low, by Vox!

"Come on, you lollygagging layabouts! Pull! Pull!"

To my heightened senses we appeared to crawl along agonizingly slowly. The sinking vessel did not seem to me to come one whit closer. Steering backwards is a tricky business to the uninitiated; I gave all my attention to our boat, so dreadfully low in the water, and to bawling encouragements to the oarsmen. The steering was quite automatic, a product of my youthful service in Nelson's Navy.

The gap between the two pleasure boats began, thankfully, to narrow. Now, we were appreciably closer. I went on bawling and raving at the oarsmen like the veritable maniac I suppose I truly was.

True or not, maniac or not, my vehemence drove the oarsmen to redouble their exertions. The shining blades pulled strongly and not one single crab occurred, thank Opaz.

The last few paces before our boats came alongside seemed to me to be the longest and most drawn-out yet. Then the boats bumped together. "Hold her fast!" Hands in the boat reached out to grasp the sinking craft, surprising me, another testimony to the yrium.

No surprise touched me when Ahilya proved to be the first to step across. Yavnin thrust her on. Medi and Cindy followed.

They'd stopped yelling. They looked unhealthily pale and their eyes looked hollow. Nelana stepped aboard without assistance.

The men did not step aboard at once. There was an argument going on over there. By Vox! I knew what that was all about!

"Come on, you bunch of famblys! The nearest ones first!"

Yavnin leaped and landed on the deck with the balance of an airman. Again, I knew he'd gone first because to argue further would have been madness in the perilous situation. Tobi stepped across, then Nalgre, then Naghan. Again, completely without surprise I saw my Krozair brother had contrived to be last.

The canalfolk came aboard last, and Master Abso last of all. He regarded me glumly and then turned to watch as his fine boat disappeared beneath the surface.

We were all, thanks to Opaz, accounted for.

Naturally, a great deal of excited jabbering ensued.

Letting them get on with it, I went over to the helmsman I'd so impolitely dislodged from his tiller. I said: "I give you thanks. Had your lads not obeyed promptly and backwatered skillfully, why, by Vox, I don't think my friends would have survived."

He'd heard all the jis's and majister's floating about. He stared hard, then nodded. "Lahal, majister. I am Master Sonylo. I saw you with the nazabni—as she was then—before."

"Lahal, Master Sonylo. Yes, that was a day on the canals not to be lightly forgotten."

Naghan Raerdu came over. "The reaction will start hitting them soon, jis. But I'd like to—"

"I wonder why I am still standing here jabbering away, Naghan. I'll go—now!"

With that I stepped up and dived overboard.

What a hullabaloo must have ensued! Swimming towards the buildings whose sheer sides made it impractical to attempt to scale them without proper equipment, I edged along towards their end. Here the towpath began again, or ended, depending which way you were travelling. I hauled myself out and cast a swift glance at the boat.

A hullabaloo surely had ensued, without a doubt. They were standing along the side all looking at me. The boat sank alarmingly under this unbalanced weight and I waved to them to step back.

The last I saw of them as I ran around the buildings to reach the road they were still all gawping away.

Now, I did not expect any simple clues. There most certainly would not be discarded cartridge cases a detective might look for on Earth at the scene of a crime. There might be footprints if the ground hadn't dried too much, for we'd not had rain this day.

No one was about and the Suns were declining with indecent rapidity to folk who wanted to get home and bolt their doors before dark.

On the bridge I cast about for clues. Eventually I had to give up and admit there was nothing. Only the place from which the stone had been dislodged was plain. A gap in the coping told that story. Enquiries would have to be made in the morning of people who lived hereabouts. There was the slimmest of chances they'd seen something. In the nature of things, I doubted anyone would have.

The Slippy turned up at that moment. He'd been running. From the bridge I saw that the boat had pulled into the bank. People clustered on deck; there was no sign of my new friends so I assumed they were running along after Naghan.

"Anything, jis?"

I shook my head and then said: "Still, have a look."

"Aye."

By the time the others arrived still nothing had been found.

The Twins began their eternal orbiting above, occasionally obscured by clouds. The rain would probably start soon—too late for us to find footprints.

We called it a day and trailed back to the boat where we arranged passage with Master Sonylo. Gold changed hands. In somewhat of a depressed state, the enormity of what had happened sinking in, as it were, afresh each time we thought about it, we went our separate ways. All those who could not tolerate canalwater had had a close shave and the vividness and horror of those moments would live in their minds for a very considerable time.

The fellow—or woman, for that matter—who had instigated their bully boys into hurling a chunk of stone down onto us would be safely tucked up at home, calm and innocent as a summer dove. Their alibi would be as rock solid as the Mountains of The Stratemsk.

They'd have loyal friends in for the afternoon who'd vouch absolutely they'd spent all the time together—as, indeed, they had. Even if we knew who the rast was, we could prove nothing.

Could the culprit be the chief pallan, Nath Swantram, Nath the Clis? Had he somehow caught wind of our scheme to take him up?

I shook my head as I prepared for sleep. We were like a gang of blindfolded boxers, striking out at unseen foes.

Even more pertinently, we, blindfold, were attempting to parry the knocks aimed at us with ruthless ferocity. If that last pleasure boat had pulled away earlier, well, then, by Vox, my new friends would have drunk of Vallia's oh so sweet canal water and shortly thereafter might be dead and on the way to the Ice Floes of Sicce.

Not on that thought, as by now you know, I closed my eyes.

When a guilty conscience pricks a fellow he tends to rise early in the morning. I was up before the first breakfast was served. I might have kicked my heels waiting impatiently, or ordered up a special breakfast, as was common practice. Instead I busied myself with papers, writing letters, reading reports, generally keeping abreast of the state of Vallia. These tasks are essential.

After breakfast—and not, I might add, still munching a handful of palines as I went—I walked smartly off to see Belkion Clander. Belkion was a banker, a shrewd Lamnian whose cognomen spoke eloquently of the respect he enjoyed. He was called Belkion the Trusty. Enevon Ob-Eye, my chief stylor, at the moment in Valka, regularly sent up payments. I had no doubts that Belkion's accounts would tally every single last copper ob.

The house and banking office were strongly constructed, as was prudent; but they were modest. Vulgar ostentation was not for Lamnians as a rule. Belkion greeted me with a smile and a handshake and sent for sazz and parclear. He wanted to show me the current account. I waved it away. "I've far too much to do than pore over figures, Belkion."

Then, ruefully realizing I could have hurt his feelings, I added quickly: "I'm sure they're all in order."

"I understand, jis. It is this awful Spectre."

"Aye."

The gold was counted over and I stuffed it away. Now, so many of the plays and stories feature the mighty hero charging about righting wrongs and rescuing fair damsels and generally being heroic. He is never short of the wherewithal to take lodgings for the night, or buy a gourmet's meal, or acquire new trappings or weapons when he's lost those he bought last time. He's so busy rushing about wielding his sword that he cannot have time to earn much. As he is your mighty honorable hero he never, of course, accepts payments from those he succors.

So how does he come by all this wealth? The groundlings gawping away never seem to ask this pertinent question.

Because of all my fancy titles and broad lands owing allegiance to me, there was plenty of cash coming in. Enevon Ob-Eye could send gold far afield. All the same, by Krun, more than once I'd been stranded without a single coin when the Star Lords whisked me off.

Belkion the Trusty employed Pachaks as guards. That spoke volumes of the respect in which he was held. After the polite remberees I walked off, heavier than when I'd entered.

The quicker I went to see Logan Verlan the quicker I'd get over the guilt feelings that had woken me early. There were enquiries to be made regarding his wound and the result of the court of enquiry. Also, and most importantly, by Vox, there were enquiries to be made regarding these Opaz-forsaken Racters.

Striding along and sniffing the glorious Kregan air, I wondered how Naghan the Slippy was proceeding with his investigation. I had no real faith that anything would be discovered about the cramphs who'd chucked a damned great coping stone down into our boat. If the culprit was really Nath the Clis, why, then, we'd take him by the heels tonight. That was a prospect that, whilst not pleasing me overmuch, certainly did not displease me. Oh, no, by Krun!

The soberly-clad polsim who'd followed me from Belkion the Trusty's premises made up his mind to move in when I was crossing a bridge over the canal.

He proved to be an excellent devotee of Diproo the Nimble-fingered. Excellent; but not quite sharp enough...

He let out a startled yelp. "My arm! Dom—you'll break it off." I eased the pressure of my grip. I regarded him sorrowfully. This was the way he earned his living under the Suns and precious little would cause him to change. Anyway, I just did not have the time to carry this on any further.

Giving him another squeeze—whereat he yelped again—I said: "Think yourself lucky, dom. I'm in a hurry." Then I cast him off.

He scuttled off as though the Agate-winged Jutmen of Hodan-Set were pursuing him in full cry.

There was a task to be done before Logan Verlan was attended to. Returning to the palace and resignedly acknowledging the plethora of 'majisters' thundering about my ears, I went to my bedroom and knocked.

Ulana called: "Come in!" and in I went.

She was sitting on the couch, partaking of a light meal from a tray balanced on her lap. She wore a voluminous robe. She looked very much refreshed and her cheeks bloomed with a healthy flush. Her eyes regarded me with a bright glance very different from the normal retiring look she had. Now I had to get her out of the room.

Talking of this and that she finished the snack and put the tray down. She expressed herself as alarmed at our accident—as she phrased it—and said she was thankful to Opaz we had escaped.

"Now, majister, if you will excuse me, I have to—"

"Of course." I stood up as she left the bedroom. The instant the door closed I dived under the bed like a ferret, hauled out the chest, ripped out the feathers, slammed the lid and kicked the chest back out of view.

When Ulana returned I stood up from the chair, and said I had to take my leave. She gave me a very peculiar look. Then she said: "Maybe whoever cast down the stone will repent of his actions."

I shook my head. "We can but hope." Fat chance of that!

All the same, I thought, as I left the palace and headed for the livery stable, there'd been something mighty odd about Ulana. Naturally I'd not brought Yavnin into the conversation. Perhaps she'd heard from him.

Changing myself into Tyr Kadar at a convenient shady doorway, I hired a zorca, and gently rode off to see Logan Verlan.

Things of import were going on all around me, and they were lurking in the background. Skullduggery of a most villainous nature was being practiced. Well, by Vox, for the sake of Vallia I'd practice a spot of skullduggery myself.

Riding out from the cover of the last grove of trees, I looked towards the field. A column of black smoke rose high and as I urged the zorca into a gallop flames broke up in red and orange spurts of fire from the buildings. The place burned fiercely and soon the evil crackle of the conflagration sounded clearly. I dug my spurless heels in and the zorca responded magnificently. We bounded towards the fire.

Logan Verlan was there; but far more importantly, Yavnin was there to finish up the findings of the enquiry. If he got himself burned to death I'd miss him. I surely would miss him, Opaz knew!

The zorca flew over the grass and the flames roared louder and more fiercely.

Sixteen

The voice of Lazan-Yvon the Inconducive spoke with chilling meaning in Tralgan Vorner's head. The woman who had once been Semtilla the Fair, dead for millennia, yet living again through Vorner's hate, resurrected into an animate Spectre, drove her words into Vorner's brain. He felt the power, the hate, the condemnation, the passion.

"You are remiss in your duty, man! You swore your hatred would endure and yet you accomplish nothing for me."

"The matter has taken a different turn." Vorner spoke up bravely, despite the screaming fear eating into his guts. "My vengeance—"

"Your vengeance!" The spitting contempt seared. "You prate of your revenge, yet you hesitate and do nothing. You were told to do my bidding yesterday. And today what have you done? Nothing!"

"I am saving Nath Swantram for the end. Let him suffer agonies of anticipation—"

"He is nothing now. You were told to let me slay Dray Prescot. You had the opportunity, yet you did nothing. Today, I shall surely slay Dray Prescot. Surely!"

"But why? He is not the emperor, he can make no difference to your schemes for Vallia."

Expecting an answer loaded with biting sarcasm, Tralgan Vorner cringed in his ib. The whispering voice in his head remained silent.

He licked his lips and swallowed down, hard. The night air wafted gently, filled with scent of Moonblooms. Many stars twinkled. The waters of the canal beneath the bridge glimmered darkly. Yes, a fine night, and a fine night on which to die. What would this female Thaumaturge of Sodan do to him in punishment for his disobedience?

The silence continued, and for Vorner that silence echoed and shouted and bellowed in the vacant spaces of his brain.

At last the voice said: "There is merit in your words, man, astonishing though that be. The emperor and his family must return to Vallia soon. I shall leave Dray Prescot to the last, as you with Nath Swantram."

"But—but you will kill him?"

"Oh, yes, never fear!"

Tralgan Vorner swallowed down again. "There is an under-chamberlain of the palace, Larghos Vanka the Smooth. He sups with friends tonight. He assisted in my betrayal—"

"Yes, mortal man! We will destroy him!"

The vicious feeling of satisfaction in the words broke over Vorner as though a bath of acid had been poured on his head. He recognized those feelings, for he had shared them for a long time.

"Let me go, Kyr Tralgan Vorner!"

Vorner opened his mind. The string of brilliant lights gyrated from his head and circled him like a blasphemous halo. The lights coalesced. The Spectre appeared. Again Tralgan noticed how much more skin and flesh clothed the yellow bones. The red eyes glared madly. Without sound the Spectre glided towards the house where Larghos Vanka the Smooth, who had helped in the plot to destroy the rightful Elten of Culvensax, enjoyed a pleasant gathering among friends.

The appearance of the Spectre continued to give Vorner the shivers, no matter how long he'd seen the disgusting thing. It vanished round the back of the building. Another ghastly murder was about to be committed. Again, Tralgan Vorner licked his lips.

His emotions jumbled together like a fruit cake mixture in the mixing bowl. The way ahead was not clear; but he remembered the man he'd been before returning home to disaster. Honor meant everything.

Firmly, not running but at a rapid pace, he began to walk away from the house, over the bridge, into the city.

One of the most uncanny elements of the Spectre's appearance outside was its silence. In deathly quiet it struck and slew.

A shrilling began at his back. The air seemed to tremble. Vorner began to run, mouth wide open, eyes glaring, arms pumping. Absolute panic thrilled through him. He felt—oh, he felt as though the world of Kregen was spinning faster and faster and he was trying to run against that omnipotent force.

The shrieking shattered the silence of the night. It shrilled higher and higher and slobbered into a wail.

Abruptly, chopped short, the wail ceased.

The silence fell back like a thunderclap.

Sweat covered Tralgan Vorner. He could not stop running. Had he really disposed of the Spectre?

In this fashion the previous Thaumaturges of Sodan had perished, when he'd been unable to keep close to them. Was Lazan-Yvon the Inconducive really dead again, finally dead and on the way through the grey mists to the Ice Floes of Sicce?

He devoutly wished so. "Praise to Opaz!" he panted out, running, running.

When flames chuckle and dance in friendly warmth from a log fire on a cold winter's evening, fire proves itself the friend of mankind.

When flames roar and crackle from a burning house, when the windows shatter and the walls totter, when the roof collapses, then fire is the deadly enemy of mankind.

The zorca galloped on nobly. The blaze spread vividly into the sky and the black smoke writhed like contorted demons. Leaping off and sprinting across to the ring of onlookers, I saw Yavnin staggering from the fire. His clothes still smoldered. People were yelling orders and counter orders; but a water-bucket chain formed. Fat lot of good that would do!

A couple of airmen grabbed Yavnin, tripped him up, rolled him over and over. He reared up, furiously angry; but they'd smothered the smoldering in his clothes. He clutched a blackened parcel. His face looked as though he'd been applying all black camo-cream with a paintbrush.

"Yavnin!" In all the excitement I had not forgotten to become myself again. "Yavnin! Are you burnt?"

He swung about like a burnt offering. "No—no, jis." Then, with a surprised stare: "What are you doing here?"

"Oh, thought we could sink a jug or two together and then I saw the smoke."

The uproar continued about us. There was no doubt the fire would have to be left to burn itself out. A drawn-faced needleman came over to examine Yavnin, but the Jiktar waved him away with: "I am perfectly all right. See to the others."

"As you wish, Jik," and the doctor hurried off.

Yavnin nodded to me and walked off a little way. He took the partially-burned parcel out and showed me. "Opaz-forsaken Hikdar!"

The whites were mostly black now. But, undeniably, these were black and white feathers, Racter colors.

"The enquiry fined him fifty gold pieces and he went mad. I tell you, jis, he was lucky. They wanted to fine him a hundred but I talked them down." Yavnin shook his head at the folly. "He was raving about injustice and how he would punish us all." He shook the sooty remnants of the feathers. "This is all I could find of him."

"You mean—he set the place alight? Out of revenge?"

"Aye."

"This is the Hikdar you told me about—got himself wounded in a brawl. And now he's all burned up in the fire he started."

By the disgusting diseased liver and lights of Makki-Grodno! Just when I was so skillfully insinuating myself into the Racter's confidence, all my schemes were dashed to the ground. What a waste of time! My investment in skullduggery had damned well not paid off.

Those were my first reactions. Naturally, I felt a stab of pity for Logan Verlan. My greater sorrow, of course, was for young Tassie. This tragedy would come as a hard blow to her.

The confusion was being sorted out. Work parties were detailed to clear up the mess. Yavnin at the moment was unemployed and was here only for the enquiry. I started to say: "Come on, Yavnin. Let's—"

He was staring at the Vallian Air Service fliers parked out on the field. The hunger in his gaze glared out clearly. Yet these were smallish vollers. Yavnin was due a first line voller. I knew he'd jump at the chance of commanding one of these until something better came along. Drak must look into the condition of the VAS—soon!

He swung back to me. "Jis—ah—yes, of course. I was just—"

"Aye. Your zorca's handy?"

We went across to the lines where the riding animals were tethered and Yavnin brought his zorca out and mounted up. Seeing him so needful of a fresh command was painful to me. I knew exactly what he was suffering. We cantered off with the stink of burning in our nostrils. The fiasco over Logan Verlan just had to be pushed aside.

All the same—what a hulu! Because he'd expected to get off altogether, when they fined him fifty golds he set the place alight. That he contrived to have himself burned up too probably had not entered into his calculations. Such is blind revengeful anger.

We had a couple of jars at a small quiet tavern where the Moonblooms arched over the door, petals closed for the day. The Larynx and Whistle served quality ales and charged accordingly and was patronized by a small and discerning clientele. The place was quiet and we were not disturbed. We discussed tonight's raid and trusted Opaz was with us.

Yavnin said he was contracted to see Ahilya at the hour of mid. So we parted on the promise of tonight's little fracas. A letter awaited me back at my quarters. The merker had flown off and Quarmby, very officious, produced the letter like a rabbit from a conjuror's hat.

Nath Javed, known as Old Hack 'n' Slay, also known as Nath the Impenitent, wrote that he had not been assigned a command in the Vallian Expeditionary Force off to Pandahem. He said he was disappointed, dejected, desperate. At this my mouth twitched. With my permission, he went on, the writing ragged and uneven, he would travel to Gafarden where the news said some scoundrelly Spectre caused trouble. There was a post scriptum. Old Hack 'n' Slay wrote he would start for Urn Vennar instanter. If I didn't want him, I could send him away.

Nath Javed had proved a blade comrade and was an exceedingly tough individual. There were no tear stains on the paper. Had there been that would be entirely appropriate, judging from his mood of dejection. Well, by Krun, I'd soon cheer him up!

Quarmby said the Lady Farlan wished to see me.

Ulana stood amid a confusion of boxes and chests. Four handmaids were packing up dresses and tunics, cosmetics and jewelry. All the paraphernalia of a lady about to travel choked my bedroom.

"Majister," she started without preamble. "I wished to thank you for all your kindness to me in my hour of misfortune." The air of brightness about her persisted, and this pleased me. "I do not know how long I shall be away. Friends in the North have welcomed me."

"Take plenty of furs, Ulana." I spoke laconically, and she smiled. By Vox! She did look different from the little mouse, crushed by her dismissal from her position of nazabni, she had been.

"Yes." We talked for a few moments. As I took my leave, wishing her a safe journey, she said, firmly: "Again, majister, thank you. I shall never forget your kindness to me."

So that was that.

During the afternoon I spent some time making sure all my equipment was in apple-pie order. Your wily old fighting man likes to go into action fully prepared. Tobi came in, ready primed for tonight.

A noise outside and a knock on the door heralded Quarmby. He started to speak and a burly figure pushed past quite politely.

"Hai, Jak! Lahal and Lahal! Oh—I mean, majister!"

His scarlet face, his level brown eyes, the compact toughness of him—oh, yes, he was just the same.

"Lahal, Nath." I turned, gesturing. "Tobi, this is Chuktar Nath Javed. I think he will joy to go with us tonight."

"What, Jak?" bellowed Old Hack 'n' Slay. "A fight? Will there be skelebones?" He thumped his chest. "I'm just in the mood to blatter the unholy. Indubitably, yes!"

Seventeen

The whetstone hissed smoothly and sweetly along the blade. The stone was Devron Obni, a high quality product something like terrestrial Turkish stone. The color, as the name suggests, was a deep red. The sword, a drexer, would cut cleanly by the time I'd finished.

Tobi was fiddling with his armor, not happy with the straps. Naghan Raerdu sat poring intently over the map of the palace. His guile and my gold had obtained the map—well, they were really architect's plans. Nath Javed came in just then carrying some of his kit and instantly my quiet room filled with noise and bustle.

There was absolutely not a shred of doubt that I was happy to see Old Hack 'n' Slay. He called me Jak most of the time, remembering our first meeting and our perilous adventures thereafter. Yes, indeed, highly conducive to have a blade comrade like Old Hack 'n' Slay along!

An under chamberlain knocked and came in to say a koter wished to see me on a matter of the utmost urgency. Quarmby had long gone off duty and I looked at Frewill, a spritely Fristle, and shook my head.

"Far too busy. Plead my excuses, Frewill, please."

The Fristle licked his lips. "Ah, majister. He says his name is Kyr Nath Feslon. He wishes to talk about Kyr Tralgan Vorner."

"Does he, by Vox! Wheel him in, please, Frewill."

"Aye, majister."

The moment the Fristle closed the door, Naghan the Slippy said: "Shall we stay, jis, or I could—"

"We'll all hear what this Nath Feslon has to say."

Nath Javed looked across. He held a rapier. "I say, Jak—I mean, jis—I've been getting the hang of rapier and dagger work more particularly lately. But, tonight—?"

"Fighting swords, Nath."

He grunted at this and slid the rapier back into its scabbard. All the same, knowing Nath the Impenitent, I guessed he'd take the rapier and main gauche, the jiktar and the hikdar, along with him.

Frewill returned and announced our unexpected visitor. We all stared with frank curiosity.

Kyr Nath Feslon walked in with a steady step. Dressed in a plum-colored evening robe, he still contrived to look robust, a man of gravitas. His heavy-featured face with full lips and nostrils curled somewhat, appeared flushed. He wore rapier and main-gauche.

He marched straight up to me, halted, and said: "Jis. I have much to tell you."

I stared at him. Now, I admit, I stared in a fashion some would call haughty, although, as Opaz knows, I reck little of titles.

Feslon saw that look. He nodded. "Majister—forgive me. But the matter is pressing."

"Lahal, Kyr Nath Feslon." I spoke coolly. In a way, I was smoothing out this awkward encounter. "You have something to tell me touching on Kyr Tralgan Vorner."

He nodded again, this time much more decidedly. "Aye, jis—I mean, majister. Kyr Tralgan Vorner was betrayed and destroyed by enemies who lusted after his estates."

I stopped sharpening the drexer and laid the weapon aside. "This I know, Kyr Nath. He has my fullest sympathy. Were he alive now I would—still. Tonight we're attempting to—"

"That I know. I would go with you."

Naghan Raerdu popped up at this. "What do you know—?" he began in a most truculent fashion. I raised a hand and Naghan fell silent.

"Go on."

This Kyr Nath Feslon began to tell the story. You have already heard it as it has been inserted into my narrative at the appropriate place. How Vorner returned home on his father's death, how he was falsely accused of murder, how his cousin Lodermair seized the Eltenate, and how Nath Swantram tricked Vorner into signing the Eltenate over to the chief pallan. And, then, how Vorner was consigned to an oubliette where he was expected to die and moulder away—only he contrived an escape. We all listened, enthralled.

Then the story told how Tralgan Vorner, with so much hate boiling in him, made his compact with the Nine Thaumaturges of Sodan.

We all sat silently, listening, trying to grasp what was being said.

"So Tralgan Vorner did not die? He loosed the Spectre?"

"Aye."

I thought I saw it now. Slowly, I said: "So he was given a different face. He wore the face of Nalgre Nevko. And you, Nath Feslon, are Nalgre Nevko—and, also, you are in truth Kyr Tralgan Vorner."

"Yes."

My friends did not all start talking at once. The room fell into a deep silence. I picked up the sword and began to sharpen it. The whetstone made a soft hissing into the quietness.

Presently I said: "Well, it seems Nalgre you have much to answer for. You were wronged, yes, and you have my sympathy. You slew your betrayers. But you also killed—in a most terrible way—innocent people. What have you to say to that?"

He did not spread his hands. The dark blood mounted in his cheeks. That was the black blood of the Vorners. "I wished only to revenge myself on my enemies. The Thaumaturges slew the innocents."

Again I sat in silence, sharpening the sword. The whole story hung together. I wanted to believe him. The Spectres had a pseudo-life of their own. Once out of their host and on the rampage, they would kill anyone who stood in their way.

He coughed. "You do not seem surprised my face was changed." Telling him that wizards could perform marvels in that connection, I added that I also believed he'd had no wish to murder innocent people.

"Thank you, majister."

"But there is more?"

"Oh, yes." He brisked up, looking relieved and also triumphant.

Now this whole scene had progressed in, what was to me, a most strange way. There was an air of déjà vu, as though I expected what Nalgre Nevko—or Tralgan Vorner—said. My friends' faces expressed complete surprise at these revelations which they found astonishing. Still, they had not had the experiences of mages and the Star Lords I'd had. Only Naghan the Slippy knew I could change my face and, in fact, he'd given a knowing nod when Tralgan Vorner said his face had changed.

All the time we'd been chasing the confounded Spectre, Nalgre Nevko had been our comrade, bringing the disgusting thing along with him!

The Spectre had fallen to pieces not because of our hundreds of arrows: but because Nalgre had been rushed off in the panicking mob. When we'd watched the second Spectre deliquesce and fall into the canal, that had happened because Nalgre was wounded and carried off by Yavnin Purvun. Truly, we had been as blind as babies!

Now, in his triumphant way, Tralgan went on speaking. He told me the Spectre demanded that he be let loose to destroy Dray Prescot. Everyone tensed up at this. I waved Tralgan on. "Because you had expressed your feelings about me, jis, I could not acquiesce. I was, I admit, in mortal fear. But—" He stopped and put a hand to his lips.

"I was sickened by the unnecessary murders. Only Nath Swantram remained. I'd been reserving him, and I hoped the cramph suffered from anticipation."

Tralgan went on to say he'd at last made up his mind. He'd let the Spectre loose—and then he'd run off as fast as he could. "I expected the thing to let loose his powers at me, shooting lances of fire to burn me to a crisp."

"H'mm. As far as I know wizards can only shoot these monstrous bolts of psychic energy that burn against one another. I could be wrong."

Thinking of Deb-Lu and his contest with the Spectre when the Quern of Gramarye had swayed so perilously back and forth, I just hoped that assumption was correct.

Tralgan went on talking rapidly, excitedly, wrought up. "Don't you see! I ran off and left the Spectre. I heard it screaming. Usually it is silent. It screeched and wailed." He looked around on us, hugely enjoying the moment of victory. "Then it stopped. It didn't screech any more. I was too far away. It rotted to pieces!"

"Thank Opaz!" exclaimed Tobi.

"So the thing is finally dead," said Naghan Raerdu.

"So I've missed cutting the rast up!" quoth Old Hack 'n' Slay. "Well, at least I'm here."

I looked hardly at Tralgan Vorner. "I give you my thanks for your concern for my life—and for your courage. The whole experience was obviously dreadful for you." I extended my hand. "Shake on it, Tralgan. Welcome back to life."

So, solemnly, we shook hands.

Tralgan sat down and Tobi brought over a jar. The hand that lifted the wine was not, quite, steady. Tralgan drank and said: "Can any of you conceive of the terror I felt? Only rage and hatred and the sweet prospect of my revenge sustained me. Oh, how I hugged my vengeance to myself!"

"Um," said Yavnin, shifting in his chair. "That's a pretty negative way of going on. Still, one can understand it."

"I'll tell you the worst of it. The loneliness really dragged me down. I felt empty, wasted. The fear of the Thaumaturges stayed with me all the time. I've never felt more alone in all my life."

Another of those meaningful silences fell, broken only by the hissing of the whetstones. There was a single-minded deliberateness in the sharpening noises as we prepared. Then Tralgan Vorner said:

"I felt cut off from the world, completely alone. Then I met you, Tobi, and you, Yavnin, and you, jis." He lifted a hand. "I cannot tell you what your friendship meant to me. I'm sure it kept me sane."

Again, no one said anything. Well, for the sweet sake of Opaz, there was very little that could be said, was there?

In the end, feeling a trifle pompous, I said: "That's all over now, Tralgan. Smoke blown with the wind."

After that the tension was broken, more wine was brought in and we went on with our meticulous preparations for the night's nefarious business.

Now, in situations like this, where fighting men gird themselves for battle, many and various are the customs in which they indulge.

In my time in the Eye of the World I'd met zazzers who drank themselves into a fighting frenzy. I'd known men who prayed non-stop to their particular deity. Some paktuns played simple games wagering their worldly possessions on the outcome of the fight.

Some warriors sang before the battle.

Old Hack 'n' Slay started it. He began softly to hum a regretful little melody and gradually we all joined in and soon we were singing 'She left me on the bridge'. A soldier's life is full of partings. After that we had 'She kissed the mortilhead', and then 'Only two Moons saw our goodbyes'.

I began to fret. All this doom and gloom was no good, was no damn good at all, by Vox!

So I started up with the raucous and hilarious song which ends with the immortal lines: "He had no idea at all, at all, no idea at all."

This changed the mood completely. We laughed as every swod who sings that song laughs. Then a jumble of sprightly ditties followed until the clepsydra dropped the last drop and it was time to go.

If you think I was being mightily arbitrary in this decision about the fate of Vorner, I acknowledge there is merit in that point of view. Perhaps, you think, I should have run him up in front of the magistrates and demanded hideous punishment for his hideous crimes.

Yes, that was a viewpoint. Just because we understood his motives in vengeful reaction to the injustices heaped upon him, did not necessarily mean he should be forgiven.

Well, deem me soft, an' you will, I was not prepared to cast the first stone.

What would be done, I vowed, was to make recompense to the families of the innocents who had been slain. Of course, that could never return their loved ones to life. But it would be better than nothing.

Well, all that would be attended to. In addition, I'd have to replace Master Abso's fine pleasure cruiser. His boat had been sunk because of me, so therefore in justice alone I must make amends.

A sudden and idiotic indecision hit me. Should I take some of the black and white feathers with us? Perhaps Swantram was tied in with the Racters. That was not an impossible idea. Poor old Logan Verlan's feathers reposed once more in the chest under the bed. Those Yavnin had brought out, all smoked and blackened, had been Verlan's second set of feathers. Without very much thought I brushed the idea aside. Swantram's private juruk we must overcome to get at him were not involved with Vallian politics. They just earned their hire as guards. Well, this night they—and us—would prove their mettle.

As far as I knew, everyone here was a follower of Opaz.

Without any self-consciousness, Yavnin took it upon himself to say for us a few brief words commending our ibs to Opaz the Restorer.

My last act before we left to join the Deldars and their swods held a special significance. Pur Zygon looked on in approval.

Feeling the same old tremble of excitement I took up the Great Krozair Longsword. With fingers that did not tremble I buckled on the superb blade. Now we were ready.

Closing the door at our backs, I moved up ahead and led off.

Eighteen

"I'll be three blinks of a leem's eyes." Naghan Raerdu spoke softly. Without further ado he went, and, being the Slippy, was gone like smoke.

Tobi had extinguished a lamp burning on its bracket against the wall so we stood half in shadow in the little alcove at the foot of the staircase. Those stairs led aloft to Nath the Clis's apartments. Our decision to lay him by the heels within the palace had been forced on us by Naghan's intelligence that the chief pallan once again feared for his life. He remained mewed up.

The two Deldars were not on duty but were kitted out for duty. Nath the Rumphious and Nath Feringhim brought the number of Naths in our party to three. Well, that is a familiar situation on Kregen.

The four Chuliks were—well, they were Chuliks. With time one can begin to distinguish one Yellow Tusker from another. Some of the good folk who'd previously employed Chuliks were, these days, a tad reluctant to take them on again. They'd all run off to their islands when the Shanks threatened invasion, so their erstwhile employers wondered if they could be trusted not to desert again.

These four were pleased to be taken on by the Rumphious and my gold served to increase their enthusiasm for tonight's venture. We were, after all, engaged in a nefarious undertaking. What? Go up and arrest the chief pallan? Wasn't that treason? A few words of explanation—and the gold!—settled that disquiet.

Now just because these fellows were hired mercenaries, and members of a race of diffs looked on askance by others, did not mean they were not human beings. They all had names. They were not cardboard figures to be shot down out of hand. Tranter, Storon, Chemki and Tarach—those were their names.

Soundlessly, the Slippy appeared with us again. With him he brought a Sylvie. Well, the quite outrageous pulchritude of Sylvies is relished by some; others, including myself, find it far too overpowering for true beauty.

Once again, good Vallian gold produced results.

This Sylvie, Sinkie the Earrings, worked within Swantram's apartments. She said he'd recently abused her. She did not say what she'd done to deserve punishment, and we did not ask. Gold and the desire for revenge sparked her motives with passion.

As we stood there at the foot of the stairs with the shadows dropping down about us and the remote noises of the palace barely heard, the sense of occasion undeniably caught us all. We were aware of the enormity of what we proposed. No doubt there were dry throats, and hearts beating faster than normal. I started up the stairs.

"Jis." Naghan's whisper just reached me. "It would be better if the guards went first with Sinkie. They will give us an advantage."

No time at all was needed to see that was sensible.

I stood aside and waved the guards and Sinkie on. As she passed on up the stairs her perfume wafted like a physical wave and my nostrils wrinkled up.

Still, she'd come out of this business well. No doubt she'd set up a little shop in a fashionable arcade. She knew what she was doing, and she knew the prize.

Treading like leems across a lava flow we climbed the stairs.

We were venturing into the private quarters reserved for the nazab, the justicar who ran the province for Princess Didi. We expected luxury and ornateness, and were not disappointed.

The carpets, whilst not of Walfarg weave, were thick enough to lose a shoe. The tapestries glowed with patient handiwork of many skilled people proud to display their art. The lamps—all of Samphron oil—shed their mellow light and the shadows fell warmly. There were pictures. As I passed along the gallery I saw the people represented in those massively-framed portraits. Well, now! Of course, what did you expect?

When I saw the portrait of Velia, I own I swallowed down. This was not the Velia who now so jealously nursed Didi in Zandikar. This was Velia, Didi's mother. She had died in my arms in the far away lands of the Green Grodnims. I looked away. The next picture showed Gafard, Didi's father. With pleasure I saw the artist had transformed the Sea Zhantil's clothing and accoutrements from green to red. He looked the bright merry man I remembered with joy. So I walked on, recalling blustery days on the inner sea and in Green Magdag.

Thus bound up in memories both joysome and sad, I almost missed the thump from up ahead.

A Rapa lay sprawled on the carpet with his beak most decidedly bent. His three-grained staff lay where it had fallen from his lax hand. He was not dead. I'd given instructions that we should slay only if there was no other recourse.

Just above him two pale rectangles on the walls showed where two portraits had recently been removed. It did not take a genius to guess whose faces had looked down from those pictures. Nath Swantram had removed the portraits of the nazab and his daughter Ulana, the nazabni, with indecent haste when he took over control.

The guard we were up against was the private juruk of the chief pallan. They were mostly Rapas and Brokelsh, with a sprinkling of other diffs. Mercenaries all, they'd fight until they considered it expedient to discontinue such an unprofitable activity.

There I went again, boasting to myself. I took a grip on my sword hilt and pressed on after our Deldars and Chuliks.

The corridor ended in an anteroom. Three Rapas stood before the door with its bronze representations of mythical beasts.

They'd have to be rushed. There was no way they wouldn't see us as we advanced.

They saw us. The Deldar in command shouted: "Llanitch! Stand still!" The three halberds came down in line. "You have no business here." He shook the halberd. "Get back down below where you belong, you bunch of festering cramphs."

No need for me to shout: "Charge!" like some posturing idiot. We all surged forward and the fight was brief, exceedingly so.

Three Rapas slumbered on the luxurious carpets.

Sinkie the Earrings walked over and stood looking down on the Rapas with an interesting contemplative expression on her face.

"Good. Never did like them. They smell awful."

There was no answer to that.

So far we had come along splendidly in this venture. We'd successfully reached into Swantram's quarters without raising the alarm and without anyone being killed. There remained the most difficult obstacle to our final success, an obstacle that could thwart all our plans.

Any prudent lord or lady having a castle or palace built for them will instruct the architect to provide a bolt hole, an escape route, a secret passage leading from their private chambers out beyond the confines of the walls. Didi, being a prudent lady as well as a glamorous princess, would of a surety have had such a secret way built.

Equally surely, that cramph Swantram would know of the escape route. We must reach into his more private rooms and apprehend him before he could scuttle off.

Eyeing the door and the bronze beasts writhing upon its surface, I abruptly felt the pressure of what we were doing crush down.

All of Makki Grodno's pendulous parts collided, as it were, in my brain. For the simple sake of justice we had to succeed.

I pushed the door open.

The room beyond lay completely deserted. This was clearly a reception area. The table was positioned so that anyone entering would find themselves facing the stylor with his pens and papers. The chair was turned halfway around as though the stylor had just stood up. A massive pot of Cwofan ware held yellow and pink flowers. To the right stood a set of four doors, another led off towards the back and on the left a blackwood stair ascended to a door at the top.

Sinkie said: "Servants. Guards." She pointed to the doors. "We must go upstairs. That's the master's chambers."

Without further ado the two Deldars stepped forward. "I'll go up first." The Rumphious stepped on the first tread.

"And I'll go at your side." Feringhim shoved up alongside the Rumphious.

The Chuliks followed. Tobi growled out: "Let me get up there." Pur Zygon glanced at me and then studiously avoided my gaze. Well, we had to work this sensibly. The Deldars and the Chuliks had already given us an advantage. Stupid of us not to continue with a good thing.

The door at the top of the stairs opened to show a corridor softly carpeted and illuminated by Samphron oil lamps. Tapestries glinted with gold and silver thread. There were no windows.

We prowled on as Sinkie said: "They live beyond that door."

"Oh?" said Yavnin. "Who?"

"Why, the Mothers of Carnage, of course."

At this I felt a distinct sinking of the heart. Bad enough to have to fight Rapas and the others, yes; fighting women, even creatures like these harpies, did not sit well.

The Rumphious halted, turning to me. "Jis. These—women—"

Feringhim nodded. "Aye, jis."

"They'll attack anyone without authority coming through that door."

Tobi spoke with immense reckless satisfaction. "Excellent!" He pushed to the front, his lynxter ready. "So now I can go first."

Looking quickly about I saw the enraged faces, the opening mouths. These merry men were about to start a ferocious argument over who went first. I said: "I shall go first. Queyd-arn-tung!"

Tobi started to say something, despite my injunction that there was no more to be said. I gave him a look and stepped up front.

The need for haste in what was to come beyond the door made me slide the drexer back into the scabbard and draw the Krozair brand.

A little murmur from Zygon: "Zair with us!" and I kicked the door in.

Absolute silence greeted us after the smash of the door faded. The place lay in darkness. You could see as much as you can see on a night of Notor Zan. In a whisper as ferocious as a leem spitting, I said: "Lights!"

Somebody struck flint and steel. The puff as the tump blew into flame sounded loudly in my ears.

Even before the torch illuminated the room the smell told me what we would see.

The torch light flickered across the walls in a way that, to our heightened senses, appeared downright eerie. The room led through an opening where the curtain had been dragged from its rail into an office. Blood splattered the walls. Blood ran into pools on the floor. The raw stink filled the air with a choking miasma.

We'd found the Mothers of Courage all right. They were scattered around. Also, we had found Nath Swantram, the chief pallan.

At least, we'd found his head. That lay isolated on the desk as though positioned there on purpose.

The rest of his various parts must be mingled with the detritus of the Mothers of Carnage.

Tobi choked out: "The Spectre! It has to be! The bloody Spectre!"

In that weird flickering torchlight everyone turned to stare at Tralgan Vorner, who'd been Nalgre Nevko.

All those eyes bore down on him in condemning accusation.

Nineteen

"I swear! I swear on my father's grave!" Tralgan Vorner glared at us in that eerie flickering light. "For the love of Opaz—the Spectre! I heard it—I heard the thing die! I swear!"

Those accusing eyes bore in on him. How could they believe what he said with this ghastly evidence before us?

The words fell to Naghan Raerdu. Heavily, he said: "Look about you, Tralgan Vorner. Is this the work of human hands?"

Vorner shook his sword. "I tell you! No-no—no human could wreak this. But—but—"

Practically, speaking harshly, Yavnin bit out: "You said you heard the Spectre shrieking, then wailing, then—"

"Then nothing! It wailed to silence. I was away—away! The Thaumaturge must have rotted. It could not survive without me."

The tenseness held us all. The air smoked evilly with blood and passion. If Tralgan Vorner spoke the truth, then how could this hecatomb be? If he lied—then why?

Tralgan Vorner walked steadily to the table. He picked up the bloody head of Nath Swantram and held it aloft. "I wanted this man dead. Aye! I wanted to slay him for the evil he did me. But that is all." He shook the ghastly object. "I swear I believed the Spectre truly dead."

Again in that harsh practical voice Yavnin said: "But it is clear he is not."

Reckless and feckless Tobi might be. He possessed a shrewd streak in his makeup.

So now, slowly, he said: "Could it be—is it possible—could this Thaumaturge have found a new host?"

On that a silence fell.

Presently, hesitantly, Tralgan Vorner said: "I suppose it is possible. If the thing found someone who hated enough."

Well, as to that, no doubt we'd find out in Opaz's good time.

This whole fraught situation with these gallant fellows all primed and ready to go would descend into a meaningless wrangle if a firm hand was not taken instanter. I looked about in that erratic illumination where eyes glittered and teeth glistened whitely. "We'll discover the truth before long, by Vox. Now—" I pointed to the back wall. A tapestry hung askew. "There is a doorway." I started off purposefully.

This must be the escape route, the secret way out. The others followed. The door led onto a stone stairway, spiraling down into darkness. "Torches!" I bellowed and without waiting started on down.

In the dust, as the torchlight flashed down, footmarks were plain to see. They were quite small; but they were blurred. We went on towards the bottom of the spiral staircase where a door opened out into a boathouse buttressed by brick and columned in stone.

The water glimmered blackly. A single boat rode beside the quay. The silence brooded about us. "The Opaz-forsaken rast came this way, that's for sure," said Yavnin. His voice echoed weirdly.

"And he brought his own boat." Naghan Raerdu looked about, as usual looking for clues. There was nothing to be found.

I spoke hardly. "We shall take this boat. We shall get well out of this. Later on we will be able to think more of what this all means and the best ways of proceeding. Wenda!"

Chuliks are not the handiest of seamen, so they sat huddled in the center of the boat. The Deldars, and Tobi and Yavnin, took up the looms of the oars. "Sinkie," I snapped. "Sit you here by me."

She flopped down beside me in the sternsheets as I laid hands on the tiller. The others boarded smartly and Naghan shoved off.

Tralgan Vorner, a humped shape in the shadows, bent close.

"Jis. I swear by all I hold sacred. The Spectre did stop wailing. It did! How this happened—I don't know—"

"Leave it until the Suns shine down on us again, Tralgan."

The sight I held in my mind's eye continued to burn a horrific picture into my brain. Nath Swantram's head, severed from his body, positioned neatly on the table, remained a sight I'd see for a long time. The scar across his face appeared to be more powerfully incised even than in life. He'd been a rogue and he'd met a ghastly end. Justice, some would say, had been done. Was that the kind of justice we needed in the new Vallia?

"Give way!" The command barked harshly, echoing from the stone vault. The oars dipped and pulled and we glided out onto the canal.

Clouds obscured the light of the Twins and our torches glimmered across the water. The opening to the secret boathouse was well hidden. You could pull past it a dozen times and never know it was there.

No one spoke. The blades dipped and pulled and the water swirled past as the boat surged on. The water sounds appeared swallowed up by the night.

No one sailed abroad on the canal so we had absolutely no problems in pulling around to the branch leading into the lower levels of the palace. Here we'd been attacked by assassins, here Ulana's life had been attempted, here Tobi Vingal had joined our merry party.

The boat bumped the stone and we alighted—all except the Slippy. He said he'd dispose of this floating incriminating evidence. This being agreed on, the Deldars and Chuliks went to their quarters and the rest of us trailed off to mine.

The two Naths with their Yellow Tuskers had fabricated an alibi—should that be necessary—in the best traditions of conspirators.

We, of course, had been sitting quietly in my rooms all the time, whatever it was went on wherever it was went on.

Of course, common sense would tell the investigators that no human hand had ripped the Mothers of Carnage to pieces. No man or woman had torn Nath Swantram's head from his shoulders.

Of course not—these ghastly murders were the work of the Spectre, that was abundantly plain.

And that, naturally, left us with the unpalatable fact that if Tralgan did not lie, the Spectre was once more at large in Gafarden.

In this unwholesome situation it was quite useless to mention dear old Makki Grodno or the Divine Madam of Belschutz, for we faced stark reality. Some person was walking serenely about the city with the Thaumaturge of Sodan pent within them and ready to burst forth.

The targets of Lazan-Yvon the Inconducive had been revealed to us by Tralgan. Who, then, harbored this undead creature?

With a heavy heart and a feeling of sorrowful despair I thought I might truly guess the identity of this unfortunate person.

On these black thoughts, as though we were merely a merry party who'd spent an enjoyable evening in my snug, we parted to seek our beds. The remberees were spoken in somber tones. The future for Gafarden looked bleak in the extreme.

We contracted to meet up at The Larynx and Whistle just before the hour of mid. The place was, thankfully, quiet. We sat with our jars and, by Krun, we did look a most miserable lot!

Tralgan shifted in his seat, very uncomfortable, not drinking. He kept trying to speak, and stopping, and so relapsing into a moody silence. I guessed he labored under feelings of guilt. At last Yavnin said in his forthright way: "Stop it, Tralgan! You did the right thing. It was just unfortunate that—"

"Aye!" Tralgan heaved up a sigh. "Aye."

"We'll just have to keep watch and try to catch the benighted monster." Tobi drained his jar and rose. "Another?"

I shook my head as the others quaffed off.

"No, thank you, Tobi. I have an errand."

Taking myself off, not in the most mellow of moods, I found I was not just unhappy about what I must do next, I was most profoundly depressed about the task. The Records Office hummed with the news. Everyone could not stop talking about the terrible massacre at the palace. The chief pallan! Dead! Torn to shreds!

I found Tassie on her own, sitting with a pile of papers on the desk before her. She gave me a wan smile and stood up. "Lahal, Tyr Kadar. You have heard about—" She could not go on. Her eyes were red, she was wan, and I felt a great gush of sympathy for her.

She did not refer to the death of the chief pallan. I said what I could, a few words which I felt appropriate—but, what in a Herrelldrin Hell could you say to the poor girl?

There was no bringing Logan Verlan back for a happy wedding.

The anonymous Vallian buff would serve again. Also, I had to put myself through this intolerably sad scene again. Giving a couple of murs to the praise of Opaz, I went back into the Records Office. Tassie was just leaving to take her break, so I asked her if she would care to take a bite with me. She nodded, trying to hold her head up, a scrap of yellow lace to her mouth. "Thank you, jis."

We went to a respectable establishment where ladies were welcome and I'm sure she had no idea of what she ate. She did manage to ask after Tobi and I said he was surviving. I did not mention Medi and turned the conversation so when I escorted her back to the Records Office I fancied she was perhaps not quite as miserable.

Ha! That was just a fancy. She was suffering badly, and trying to bear up with courage.

Having to go through that emotional ordeal for a second time was the price I paid for prancing around as two different people with two different faces. That gift from Deb-Lu is not all clever skullduggery and fooling the unholy, not by a long shot!

Feeling in no need for company, for as you know I am your true loner, I spent the rest of the day brooding and trying to work out a plan. The Suns of Scorpio floated across the sky, it rained, I ate and drank, I swished a few weapons about for some exercise, and then it was time for my friends to gather in my chambers. I greeted them, wine was poured, and I said: "Tralgan, you told us of the death chamber where the Thaumaturges of Sodan lie in aeons long death."

"Aye, jis."

"Then we shall take an expedition down there and destroy the lot for a second time. And this time they'll be truly dead!"

Twenty

Naturally, they all started shouting at once. The gist of what they were saying in their excitement was that they were all going.

Well, of course! What else could you expect? This irrational desire to go off adventuring into dire perils exhibited by my comrades just because I was going was a phenomenon noted before.

This time, their presence would be more than welcome, by Krun!

The consensus of opinion was that we must plan carefully and leave as little to chance as possible. The expedition couldn't be mounted overnight. We were going up against dark forces whose powers could shrivel a fellow's backbone if he thought too much about it.

The obvious requirement was voiced by Tobi in his casual, off-hand way that masked, I felt sure, much more profound thoughts.

"Any venture like this needs a mage."

They all nodded soberly. The Slippy rubbed his ear. "There is a likely candidate—I've asked him to help once or twice before."

"Go on."

Naghan Raerdu told us this mage, a Wizard of Fruningen called San Wunbigen, had magicked him out of a spot of trouble. He did not specify the trouble or the magick. I digested this. In the normal way of things I'd prefer to have a Wizard of Loh along. My comrade Wizards and Witch of Loh were about their business, a law unto themselves, assuredly, but caring for Vallia. They just were not available. And—it was true—we needed a mage with us.

The island of Fruningen lies northwest of the island of Tezpor north of Rahartdrin, a large island off the south west coast of Vallia. A swift flier could be there and back in no time.

"Very well. Contact this San Wunbigen, please, Naghan. Mind you, he might decline to go with us."

"He is a wizard. But he cannot make gold."

San Wunbigen's location turned out, as Naghan explained, to be in Vondium where he was carrying out some research he did not care to discuss. I told Naghan that his remark about wizards and gold was most profound, whereat he smiled acknowledging the sally and said he'd fly off straight away.

Yavnin declared we would need a quartermaster and he was volunteering himself for the job. There was no need for a specialist armorer. We'd all see to our personal weapons with the exactness any fighting man of experience gives knowing his life depends on the reliability of the tools of his trade.

Time was running along. "In the morning, koters." I spoke firmly, to ensure they understood. So the little meeting broke up.

Once more we were acting as conspirators, although this time we were about to embark on an altogether more fraught enterprise.

In the morning I was up early and off to the first breakfast. Quarmby was on duty again and he caught up with me and said Pur Zygon was here. Telling Quarmby to bring him along to the breakfast room I went in. I was sharp set. When Zygon was ushered in I waved him over and we selected our provender and sat down companionably.

We talked of this and that, for clearly it would not be prudent to discuss our intentions. That the Spectre once more threatened the citizens of Gafarden dominated all conversations. A loud and hectoring voice over in the direction of the door took my attention. A man entered very briskly, speaking to a little Xaffer at his side in a bullying way. This fellow was tall—not as tall as dear old Inch, of course, for he was apim. He wore very fashionable clothes. Instead of the usual buff his outfit consisted of trousers in the fashion of Hamal, a tunic very tightly buttoned, with an atrociously short cape at his back. The idea of wearing trousers was penetrating Vallia; I wore them myself, so that part of his attire passed muster. The color was a silver grey.

Since we'd banished slavery in Vallia, the old slave grey was no longer seen, and the color was becoming acceptable. This grey was extremely—well, one can only say—show-offish.

Gesticulating in a grand way the grey clad charmer barged on without looking where he was going and collided with a serving girl.

She was an Ennschafften, one of that race of diffs with simple, naive faces. The men are very strong and are employed as servants, in the stables, performing manual tasks. The women are prettiness personified, gentle, sweet ladies, employed as house servants. These simple folk are generally called Syblians.

The girl staggered and tried to recover her balance, and fell. Her tray of drinks flew up and cascaded down over the beautiful silver-grey suit of this tall fellow.

He swung about. His face was as thin as a hatchet. His eyes under black brows caught the light and glittered, it seemed to me, with malevolent fury.

"You stupid, clumsy animal!"

The girl lay on the floor at his feet. He drew back one foot and gave her a thumping great kick in the ribs. She let out a moan and rolled over.

I stood up. But Zygon was before me. The room fell silent and his chair went over with an almighty crash. He saw he would not reach this disgusting scene in time to prevent a second kick, so he let rip with a true Krozair roar.

"You! Kicker! Let the girl alone!"

The tall man stood still for a moment. Then, with exaggerated slowness, he turned about. He looked Zygon up and down in that deliberate disdainful way some nobles have of asserting their own power. I did not like this at all. I started to move across. The kicker put a finger to his chin. "You said something?"

"Yes." Zygon spoke calmly. "Let the girl alone."

"I think you are out of your depth—stranger." He could see the clothes Zygon wore. "You do not know who I am—cramph."

Now I stood at Zygon's side. My Krozair brother half-turned. "D'you know this fellow?" He sounded as though he was enjoying this.

"Never seen him in my life."

Undoubtedly, Zygon was enjoying himself. Now all Krozairs, like the Kroveres of Iztar, are dedicated to protecting the helpless. There was absolutely no way on all of Kregen Zygon could act other than he did. Mind you, he relished it, for it cleared the lungs and sent the blood around and generally toned a fellow up.

"I'm not surprised," said Pur Zygon, Krozair of Zimuzz. "I doubt if anyone would care to know the—ah—koter."

In the appalled silence that followed the little Syblian girl stood up shakily, gathered her skirts and ran off. She was Tanzy, Tanzy the Smile, always willing and helpful with her tray of drinks.

The black brows drew down. He stiffened. His right hand crossed to clasp the rapier hilt. In a strangled voice he rapped out: "Xervan—tell these two doomed rasts who I am." Then, before the Xaffer could open his mouth, the bullyboy yelled out: "Guards! To me!"

Well now! Zygon began: "You stupid great onker—this is—"

I caught his arm and said: "Save it."

Zygon gave me a swift look. Then his hard, generous mouth curved into a smile. "Aye." So, Zimuzz and Zy waited for the comedy to continue. With the heavy tread of armored men, the guard detail on duty at the doors entered the breakfast room.

The Xaffer took a huge breath. In his piping voice he said: "You have the honor to be in the presence of Rendil Overnon, the nazab of Urn Vennar."

I couldn't help it. "What?" I yelped. "What happened to Nazab Rennel Lorving? He's the new nazab."

The Xaffer shook his head. "Nazab Lorving is dead."

The guard approached; but I stared narrowly at this kicker fellow, the new nazab. Dark schemes were afoot here, that was sure.

This Rendil Overnon—this creature—bellowed out: "Deldar, take these two rasts and throw them into the deepest dungeon in all Gafarden. Keep 'em there until I send for 'em. Dernun?"

A familiar voice said: "Jen. Are you sure?"

The new nazab fairly blew up. He started yelling and cursing in terms totally inappropriate for a genteel breakfast room. "Deldar! Drag 'em off at once! Or you'll cool your heels in the dungeon!"

"I don't think, jen, that is wise," said Nath the Rumphious.

There appeared every chance this new nazab would have an attack of apoplexy. Raving on he ordered the guards to strip the Rumphious of his authority. "Throw the mutinous dog into the dungeons along with these two rasts. By Vox! I'll show you how to run Urn Vennar!"

Quietly, I said: "I think, Zygon, you'll have another letter to carry to Drak when you fly to Pandahem."

"Assuredly, Pur Dray. After you know what."

"Quite."

Then, in my old gravel-shifting voice: "Nath! Stand fast!"

For a moment the tableau hung, as though this Rendil Overnon did not quite grasp what was going on. He half-drew his rapier. He began his ravings again. This farce had gone on quite long enough. I felt the guilt that I'd allowed the scene to deteriorate like this. The glare I gave Overnon must have been what folk call the old Dray Prescot Devil's Look, for he flinched back.

Now, as you know, I have little truck with honor when it gets good folk killed. All the same, honor is important in some situations. There was no faulting the actions of Zygon. Perhaps he need not have taken so much relish in it all. But protecting the weak is always of paramount importance to a Krozair brother.

So now, in the same hard cold voice, I said: "This has gone on long enough." Overnon tried to say something but I bore him down. "You, Rendil Overnon, knocked the girl down. It was your fault. Your actions are despicable and not worthy of a koter of Vallia."

He fairly snarled at this, his lips writhing. "I am the nazab of Urn Vennar! I have been appointed by the Presidio. I'll have your hide flayed and—"

I admit, I was uncouth. I roared at him: "Shut it!"

He'd been appointed by the Presidio in Vondium, had he? Well, by Vox, I was beginning to think this Presidio was not the one I'd known. Clearly, Overnon had been appointed nazab and the power had gone to his head. He'd come stomping into his new province without the slightest idea of how a governor should behave. Power had certainly corrupted him all right!

Unless, of course, the blintz, this was how he usually behaved.

And, too, in the light of Opaz, was not my behavior a petty exhibition of power? Quarmby walked in at that moment when Overnon stepped back, his hatchet face abruptly pale. "Quarmby!" I made it brisk and businesslike. "Send for a Puncture Lady to attend Tanzy the Smile. She has sore ribs."

"Aye, jis." Quarmby kept a completely blank expression on his face. "Koters Purvun and—" I held up a hand.

"Send 'em in, please, Quarmby."

"Aye, jis."

Rendil Overnon drew himself up, a habit I fancied he liked. His tallness overtopped me. He looked down that blade of a nose with haughty contempt. "Jis, is it?" You could see he felt himself back in command of the situation. "So now I know who you are." There was a feeling of total authority in the fellow now. "You may be Dray Prescot, fake hero of cheap books and plays; you have no powers in Vallia." His sneer became pronounced. "I am the nazab. I have the power."

Well, in a very real way, that was true, by Krun!

Not bothering to reply I glanced around the room. The morning gathering always was a fine beginning to the day, where people could talk freely. Now everyone sat or stood as though in stasis. More folk entered. This stupid incident had to be stopped, right now.

Yavnin and Tobi and Tralgan appeared in the doorway. In a mild voice, I said: "Zygon, we are leaving now. Nath, you had best come with us. And those of your lads who wish to join."

"Quidang!"

The new nazab let me finish what I had to say. He licked his lips. I found that movement theatrical. His lips were too red, anyway. "You realize you are finished in Gafarden, Prescot?" He drew himself up again in that habitual movement, so I suppose his shoulders must have slumped, otherwise he'd draw himself up through the ceiling. "This is rebellion." He bellowed, an explosion of authority: "Cadade! To me!"

Of course, the damned Rapa cadade would obey orders.

Then Rendil Overnon compounded his mistakes. He drew his rapier. Zygon let fall a little grunt through closed lips.

In what I felt to be an over-dramatical gesture, I touched the hilt of my rapier. "If you wish to settle this by the steel-bokkertu, then you're a bigger fool than you look. You know I have expressly forbidden dueling in Vallia."

With that I pushed past, brushing his sword blade aside, and made for the door. My friends moved out in front. I suppose you could say I swept out. Anyway, I took a deep breath outside the breakfast room. What a stupid imbroglio, just when we had schemes afoot!

Expecting my friends to chatter away, I found they remained very quiet. Zygon did say: "He'll be after us, now."

"Then we must make ourselves scarce until Naghan gets back with San Wunbigen. After that, Overnon can roast in the Furnace Fires of Inshurfraz. We have far more important affairs than that shint."

So, together with my comrades, we walked out into the morning blaze of the Suns of Scorpio.

Twenty-one

Tralgan Vorner frowned. He put up his hand to shade his eyes from the Suns. We stared down the declivity into the narrow valley where thorn ivy bushes grew luxuriantly. To the left masses of yellow Cyanthinum blooms formed as pretty a picture as you'd find in anyone's cultivated garden. To the right the valley flattened and broadened and water glimmered among reeds.

The quietness was disturbed only by the creak of the cart being pulled up the slope at our backs. The Quoffa, like a perambulating woolly hearth-rug, made little sound as his pads plodded on. The rest of the party gathered along the lip of the valley.

And still Tralgan Vorner frowned.

Waiting for him to speak, I glanced at San Wunbigen. A slender fellow, almost fragile, with the most delicate way about him and dainty move-ments, he wasn't at all what I'd expected of a Wizard of Fruningen. He, too, stared down into the valley intently. There was about his face a sharpness in odd contrast to his delicacy of body. Naghan had brought him and his wife, the Lady Polifa, because she insisted on going with her husband. She made an almost comical contrast to Wunbigen, being buxom, full-blooded, roving of eye. They were both apims.

I'd had to put my foot down and say that we could not take a lady where we were going. Polifa had started to create a scene; but we managed to pacify her. Naghan expressed the opinion that she had a more voracious appetite for gold even than her husband.

Thus waiting for Tralgan and Wunbigen to speak, I looked the other way to our newest recruit. This was Cleito ti Lavven, a high-spirited young fellow who proved a bit of a joker. Yavnin was a friend of Cleito's father, and one thing leading to another, Yavnin was asked to prepare the lad for entrance to the Vallian Air Service. Also, I gathered, the father, Nalgre, was a trifle grim and wanted the lad off his hands until he'd grown a more seri-ous attitude to life.

The creaking of the cart stopped. Into that silence a puffing grunt was followed by: "And if I'd been there, I'd have—"

"Yes, Nath." He gave me a look. Old Hack 'n' Slay kept on bemoaning the fact he'd not been in the breakfast room when Overnon kicked Tanzy the Smile. "I'd have given *him* a kick—indubitably!"

My honest reaction to that dire promise was to shudder. Old Hack 'n' Slay had gone through hell before, when he'd saved his niece from the dis-gusting Lemmites. Now he fell silent and we all waited to find out what troubled Tralgan and the wizard.

At our backs the last summit we'd climbed hid Gafarden from view. This section of Urn Vennar was badly cut up by gullies and ridges and as a con-sequence agriculture was absent together with people.

Tralgan pointed at the opposite side of the valley. A number of dark patches that must be holes broke the vegetation. "It's different." He shook his head doubtfully. "I think I can see the entrance. But the bushes have been cut away and I'm certain the hole is larger."

As we were digesting this, Wunbigen gave his opinion that whilst there was a certain residual magic about, the level was so low that only a mage of skill could even detect it.

Well, the Wizards of Fruningen really did have thaumaturgical powers, no denying that. All the same, my lips twisted a trifle at this example's display of professional pride. I fancied the prodding to prove himself stemmed from his wife, the pushy Lady Polifa.

"Let's find out, then, by Hlo-Hli!" and down went Tobi, plunging into the valley with a whoop. Hard on his heels young Cleito hurtled on, yelling to Tobi to wait for him.

"A spot of mazingle is what them two want." Nath Javed knew all about discipline, by Vox, he did!

Somewhat less precipitously we all descended and Nando driving the cart let the Quoffa find his own way. Besides the four Chuliks, the two Deldars had drummed up another half-dozen likely lads who were ripe for adventure, smelling gold and gems.

Tralgan's surmise about the tunnel entrance proved correct.

"It goes on and on," quoth Tobi, exhilarated.

Torches were lit and we peered inside. Well, it was just a tunnel. At first it looked as though it was a natural opening; but Cleito pressed on until his torch revealed man-made tunneling. I yelled at him to come back, and somewhat reluctantly he did so.

"Get ourselves organized first, Cleito."

The gear from the cart, unloaded and humped on our backs, was all practical necessities. We were now delvers, ten-foot polers, and certain precautions were absolutely vital. These were spelled out by Old Hack 'n' Slay in incisive tones. They were the familiar guidelines that must be observed by any party of delvers, and Nath Javed knew what he was talking about. He finished: "And no skylarking, you young imps. Acting the silly fool will get you killed down there."

There was no need for me, or anyone, to echo Nath's words.

Tralgan Vorner said: "Y'know, I understand all these precautions. I've spoken to men who've explored ancient tombs. But here—oh, no, not the same." He gestured at the tunnel. "I just walked out and in without any trouble at all."

San Wunbigen looked carefully down the jaggedly-illuminated tunnel. "I pray you are right."

Master Tremiso the Deft, our shal-needleman, blew out his sallow cheeks. "In that, San Wunbigen, I heartily concur."

An important addition to an expedition, the doctor, although Tremiso the Deft was not a fully-qualified needleman. He was a shal-needleman, a deputy, the name coming from the word for shadow. Still, he could ease our aches and pains, and patch us up. If Tralgan was right, then we would not have need of his services.

As a simple matter of course I strode up ahead and started down the tunnel. Torches threw scattered radiance ahead.

Carefully, looking up, down and around, I walked steadily on.

Now this confounded yrium I possess, to my advantage and sorrow, works in different directions. Here it served to spur my comrades into demanding that I should not take the lead. There ensued some debate on the subject, a debate that, I regret to report, became heated.

In the event, Deldar Nath Feringhim and a group of his lads took the lead and we all followed the wavering lights of their torches.

Tralgan had said he walked in and out as though taking an evening promenade on the fashionable avenues of Vondium. Nothing untoward occurred to him. So, there was nothing to fear. Ha! The Nine Thaumaturges of Sodan were tricky in their wizardry. Their aeons-long sleep had been disturbed and this they had turned to their advantage through hatred and the desire for vengeance. Now their continuing malevolence manifested itself in the preparations they'd made for intruders into their gem-filled chamber of death.

The people acting as point changed regularly. Still, I found myself stuck near the tail of the procession. The tunnel remained just a tunnel, with no remarkable features. A sudden uproar began up ahead, the noise booming down between the rocky walls. Everybody halted except me, so I was able to push past and so come on what had happened at the front of our expedition.

Cleito was just in the act of standing up. Tobi, a little to the side, was not helping the youngster. A damned great triple-bladed spear on a long haft extended from the side of the tunnel. It barred Cleito off from Tobi.

"Well?"

The Rumphious, looking more anxious than anything, who was in command up front for the moment said: "Young Cleito playing the fool. This Opaz-forsaken spear sprang out and Koter Tobi just managed to push Cleito out of the way." He put a hand on the shaft, ready to snap it off. "Nearly got himself punctured too."

If nobody was injured then this incident could remain as a lesson to us all. Far more importantly—far, far more importantly!—what did this do for Tralgan Vorner's credibility?

He walked up and stood looking at the triple-bladed spear.

The Rumphious exerted strength and the wood snapped off cleanly.

"There were no traps when I walked by." Tralgan spoke up. The sincerity in his voice was palpable; all the same...

Cleito and Tobi stood talking closely. I imagined Cleito was saying his thanks for saving his life. Old Hack 'n' Slay would have a few very serious words for Cleito, by Krun!

Yavnin, thoughtfully, observed that the obvious explanation for the trap was that the Nine Thaumaturges of Sodan knew Tralgan had deserted their cause. He would tell of the treasure chamber. So they were protecting their gems—and themselves.

No one ventured a different explanation—that Tralgan lied and was deliberately leading us all to our doom.

Tralgan Vorner let rip with a laugh that echoed oddly in the confined space. He held up a hand. "No, Yavnin. Not the Nine any longer. Seven undead Thaumaturges—seven only."

"Aye." I looked around, ready to give the word to press on. "And one of the perambulating monsters is out there—somewhere."

On that somber note we started off again. Now we all knew we faced traps along the way. This spear sticking out of the wall was a very low order trap indeed. Clearly, it was intended as a warning.

Well, as Makki Grodno was my witness, I wasn't turning back!

As for the others, so far no one suggested we retire.

The next set of traps we negotiated circumspectly. A paper-covered drop was punctured by the first pole. At the bottom rows of spikes looked mighty unwelcoming. We moved on safely.

I will not relate what Nath the Impenitent, Old Hack 'n' Slay, said to Cleito. The youngster's cheeks turned red. He bit his lip.

The folk up at point changed regularly. We came to a place where the opening ahead led onto a cavern. Spears and poles dislodged a mass of a grey jelly-like substance over the entrance. The stuff stank.

Pressing on to the far side of the cavern out of the smell range of the gunk, we halted for a rest. We ate and drank. So far we'd made good progress. The strongest feeling possessed me that the Thaumaturges of Sodan had far worse terrors waiting for us.

When Tralgan had gone out and in before, the fire crystal lighting within the main chamber persisted, illuminating his way. No lights existed here for us except for our torches. From the comments of the members of the party, I knew they were conscious of the menace lurking within the shadows. Torches were kept thrust up, throwing their shards of radiance into every corner.

This confounded unwanted uneasy feeling troubling me continued. We were making rapid progress. Yes, there were traps; but everything we encountered was dealt with smartly and without casualties. I just felt we were being toyed with. In effect, the Thaumaturges of Sodan were saying to us: "Come on and take our gems, and destroy us—if you can!"

So far we had not been challenged by monsters. A hardened delver expects all manner of diabolical traps. In addition, he knows if he wants to reach his goal he will have to meet and fight the most hideous monsters—creatures of nightmare, undead, skeletons—a whole menagerie of horror.

The Thaumaturges of Sodan did not disappoint us.

From what Tralgan had told us, King Rikto the All-Glorious had incarcerated the adherents of Sodan down here a very, very long time ago. Like any prudent adventurer, I would have wished to research this ancient king. The wise men and the mages might well have discovered vital facts about him and his time. As it was, the stupid run-in with the new nazab, Rendil Overnon, precluded that. We'd had to start our expedition prematurely.

Nath the Impenitent hoved up alongside me as we followed along in the erratic light of the torches. "Y'know, Jak, there's something almighty strange about all this. I mean—" he gestured with his sword naked in his fist. "Where are all the skelebones? The monsters? The traps wouldn't catch the greenest coy."

"Aye, Nath. You are right. So?"

He grumped at this. "There's something going on we don't know."

At that moment the party halted. Together with Nath the Impenitent I shoved up to take stock of what had been discovered now. The overarching rock soared away high above our heads. The tunnel split into two. One branch went straight on, the other descended steps.

"We have to go down to reach the chamber." Tralgan pointed.

"Steps," I said. "Oh, yes, steps. Very nasty, stairs in a situation like this." Then, sharply: "Prod every last one!"

The Thaumaturges of Sodan must have laughed like drains. They set the most simple of traps, and despite all our care, we fell for it.

Fell, of course, by the gross appendages and wobbling anatomy of the Divine Madam of Belschutz, being the operative word.

Halfway down the staircase the treads abruptly flattened. We were all there, all together like a bunch of onkers. The steps turned into a steep slide. Yelling, plummeting down, helpless to stop ourselves, we all hurtled headlong into utter blackness.

What an infantile way to be caught out!

Twenty-two

We hammered on down the slope in a tangle of arms and legs. Tobi, for one, kept a grim clutch on his torch. Other torches shot shards of light against the stony roof sliding past above. Expecting all kinds of highly unpleasant spikes at the foot of the descent, I was both surprised and relieved when we cascaded out onto a smooth marble floor.

Everyone was yelling and struggling to get up. My Val! The scene must have given outrageous enjoyment to those cramphs of Sodan!

"Shastum!" I bellowed. "Quiet! Sort yourselves out, now!"

Well, by Krun, we only just made it. We were still struggling to find our feet and bring the torches forward to light up what lay ahead when this fresh tunnel filled with leaping grey forms.

Pricked of ear, lean of flank, lethal, with jaws stuffed with bone-crunching fangs, the reemins howled in blood-lusting fury upon us.

Poor old Rubin the Merry screeched as a reemin seized him, twirling him about like a rag doll. Nath the Impenitent slashed a cunning blow and the reemin fell away. "Hack 'n' Slay!" yelled Nath the Impenitent. "Hack 'n' Slay!" As good as his word he was in there, slashing about, striping the grey hides with welting stripes of blood. Zygon's Krozair brand simply tore into the reemins, chopping them left and right. The rest of the party gathered their wits about them and tore into the grey furred horrors.

The noise blossomed into the tunnel, booming in exaggerated echoes from the rocky walls. The struggle proved a desperate affair. Everybody pitched in, shouting and striking. Reemins are a nasty breed of feral hunters, totally determined to bring down their quarry.

A last glance showed me Tobi using his lynxter to deadly effect. After that there was no time to gawp about on what was happening. There was time only to bring my Krozair brand into action and slice up the grey furry horrors before their jagged fangs ripped us to pieces.

Fighting elusive adversaries in these circumstances with the lighting so erratic that one might strike blows at mere shadows, proved almost suicidal. Tobi held a torch in his left hand and used his lynxter in his right. Our shal-needleman, Tremiso the Deft, waved his torch about, keeping well back of the affray. Others grasped torches and fought with the desperation engendered by the stark knowledge that death was the only alternative.

So, now, concentrating on fronting and dispatching the reemins who attacked within the immediate vagrant lighting, I became aware that I could see the benighted things much clearer. A pallid lemon-yellow radiance washed down over that macabre scene of carnage.

Giving a reemin who leaped at me a slash that sent his head one way and his body the other, I swirled about, sword snouting.

San Wunbigen at the back of the fight stood with his head held high, his palms pressed together in the act of prayer, and his face rapt in intense concentration. The pallid radiance spread over us.

Good old San Wunbigen! He was conjuring light for us. We could see to go about our purgative work. After that the reemins ceased to be a cohesive hostile force. A lone grey furred creature howling piteously slunk away along the tunnel, his shadow going long before him.

We stood, gathering our breath, looking about with white eyes, still uneasy, tensed up with the passions of murderous combat. Then, as though consciously breaking the tension, Yavnin produced his oily rag and went methodically about cleaning his sword.

That simple act broke the bubble. Everyone began to clean their weapons. The eeriness of this place could be overcome by adhering to common, everyday tasks. And, too, by Krun, by keeping an alert lookout and using sharp weapons!

Tremiso the Deft straightened up from bending over Rubin the Merry. The doctor shook his head sorrowfully. "There was nothing to be done. The fangs bit too deeply. He is gone down to the Ice Floes."

This, then, was our first casualty. Rubin the Merry had signed up for adventure and gold and gems. He had found death.

Was he just the first of many—perhaps of all of us?

The proper rites were said over Rubin the Merry. He would have to be left here, this stony tunnel his burial plot. His quest for gold and gems brought to finality.

Now we must press on.

A youngster had once asked why Nath had three names. Nath Javed, Nath the Impenitent, Old Hack 'n' Slay, came over to me: "Y'know, Jak, it would indubitably be grand if Seg the Horkandur was with us now."

"Aye, Nath. Indubitably."

Had Seg Segutorio been in that little fracas, the damned grey furry horrors would have been shafted before they'd the chance to leap. Oh, well, he was doing what he must in Pandahem to uphold the ideal of Paz. Yes, and wouldn't it be grand if Inch, and Turko, and many others of my blade comrades were here. Well, by the Black Chunkrah, they weren't. We must go forward as best we could to rid the world of the obscene presence of the undead Thaumaturges of Sodan.

Our navigator, logically, was Tralgan. He came over to the Impenitent and me and cocked his eye aloft. We all looked up.

"By my calculations we must be under Provender Avenue. There was a little seepage under the canal. Not much. So—"

"So," growled Old Hack 'n' Slay, "don't stop for a drink."

On that stark note we pressed on under the city of Gafarden. The trickling sounds of water reached us as Wunbigen's light glowed ahead. I took notice of the plants lying wilted along the edges of little runnels. "You see, they're dying because the light's gone."

Tralgan moved on with what I imagined to be a gesture of impatience. He wanted this thing over with. We all did. But impatience equals disaster when you're adventuring below ground.

The wizard's magical light began to fade. We would have to wait until his kharrna renewed itself, the power regenerating through the arcane arts practiced by the sorcerers of Fruningen. So we were back to the torches to see our way.

This proved unfortunate.

Zygon, up front, yelled. Torches threw patches of light on the walls and floor, reflecting from the roof, and leaving far too many areas of darkness. The streaming orange hair of the torches showed what next ghastly lot of horrors descended on us.

Like flying octopi, they were, translucent, writhing long tendrils about beneath them, yellow beaks glinting ready to seize and rip and tear and devour.

If one of these fearsome things wrapped itself around your head, your life blood, your very essence, would be sucked away to leave you an empty, dry husk.

We flailed away, sword blades cleaving overhead. Tentacles tumbled to the floor. Torches thrust up and the stink of burning flesh added another dimension of horror to the macabre scene.

"Chiniluns!" screamed Wunbigen, slashing his torch wildly about over his head. "Chiniluns!"

Zygon spared a breath to yell: "I don't care what they're called! Keep 'em off!"

Stamping about, ducking, dodging, our swords continually hacking overhead, we fought. Perhaps the torches turned the trick. Grasping tentacles writhed away as the flames bit. The things emitted shrill whistles, fluttering about, trying to dive down and envelop us. Swords and torches at last prevailed. Whistling mournfully, the last few chiniluns soared up, fluttered for a moment—as though regretful—and then flew away to be lost in the darkness.

Young Cleito sustained a gash along his cheek. Apart from that we were not injured and had suffered no casualties.

Once more we resumed our advance. The tunnel levels changed as we went deeper. We were, by Krun, damned deep underground!

A cavern opened out and we all stepped through very carefully. Columns supported the roof. Our lights showed a narrow opening in the far wall, an opening blocked by a simple wooden door.

"There!" Tralgan spoke triumphantly.

Well, yes, he deserved that. He'd brought us here as he'd said he would. We all stood looking at the door. Tralgan marched over to it and laid his hand on the latch and pushed.

Brilliant light flooded across the cavern as the door swung open.

A musty, fusty smell as of centuries of decay wafted out.

There was no holding the lads now. I didn't see who was first in; but in no time at all there we were, striding into the great chamber under the glittering glass roof. The hole where Tralgan had first fallen through gaped. We all stared about—and fell silent. Absolute silence reigned in that chamber of death.

With the subtle increase of tension we'd all experienced as we progressed towards our goal, with the suspense gnawing at our nerves as we expected fresh horrors at every dark corner, with these pressures on us—here in the chamber they should all have been released. We had succeeded in reaching the lych hall where King Rikto had incarcerated the Nine Thaumaturges of Sodan.

Was my imagination playing tricks on me? Was there the faint sound of mocking laughter drifting from the glass roof?

Blanko the Arm, a hairy Brokelsh festooned with weapons, was the first to break that dead silence.

He waved an arm about, gesticulating at the chamber.

"Is this it?" he raved. "This?"

The Rumphious, sternly, barked out: "Steady now, Blanko! There must be an explanation."

"Oh, yes, Del. I've had my fill of explanations."

Tobi, in a flat voice so unlike him, said: "No explanations—"

Then everyone was shouting at once. The noise boomed to the glass roof. Enraged faces, waving fists—yes, pent up emotions burst forth there in that dread chamber so long buried from the gaze of the world.

So, I looked about.

There were the nine plinths, arranged in a circle, just as Tralgan had said. There was the glass roof. There was the chamber itself, all as Tralgan Vorner had promised.

And that was all.

The plinths stood bare, empty. There were no nine sarcophagi. There was no altar. There were no luxurious furnishings. There was no great jewel upon the altar.

Dust gritted underfoot.

If there had been heaps and piles and cascades of gems, as Tralgan had said, if there had been jewels beyond the ransom of a whole nation—not a single precious stone sparkled in the brilliant light.

We had been duped.

Our assumption had been wrong. The Thaumaturges of Sodan had not been protecting their jewels and themselves.

Oh, no! We'd had an easy journey here, the traps and monsters just enough to persuade us that treasure lay at the end of our journey. We'd gone on in hope—and now all was dust and ashes.

People started rummaging about. Perhaps—just perhaps, the odd jewel might be found among the fresh dust.

All too soon it was obvious—the place had been stripped bare.

Tralgan took it harder even than the likely lads out for wealth. He sat slumped on the floor, head hanging.

If anyone tried to blame him for this catastrophe, I'd have to step in and sort the argument. I did not relish that.

Presently the aimless hunt for non-existent gems ceased.

Yavnin expressed it perfectly. "We've been fooled, doms. Now we must go back. We'll find these damned Thaumaturges in the end!"

He started for the wooden door.

The Nine Thaumaturges of Sodan had not finished with us yet.

A creaking screech, growing louder and louder, was followed by a crash like an avalanche. A block of black stone smashed down from the architrave above the little wooden door. The slab bit deeply into the gutter at the foot. It shuddered and dust flew.

That slab looked suddenly like a gravestone.

Without even having to think about it, I knew we wouldn't get past that devilish obstacle.

We were trapped.

The Nine Thaumaturges of Sodan had lured us in here. They were far gone with their coffins and their gems and their altar. Now they played their trump card. They sealed us in their wonderful chamber and they laughed at our foolishness.

Trapped.

Oh, yes, we were trapped here in a chamber reeking of death. We could die here and rot and for century after century not a living soul would even know that once we existed and were flesh and blood men like themselves.

We were trapped. Yes—but by the foul intestines and swag belly of Makki Grodno, we were not doomed!

We were not doomed. Not while the Suns of Scorpio flooded the world of Kregen with light, not when Delia waited for me.

Oh no, oh no!

A Glossary to the Spectre Cycle

Compiled by Els Withers

References to the books of the cycle are given as:

SHK: Shadows over Kregen
MOK: Murder on Kregen
TOK: Turmoil on Kregen

NB: Previous glossaries covering items not included here can be found in Volume 5: *Prince of Scorpio*, Volume 7: *Arena of Antares*, Volume 11: *Armada of Antares*, Volume 14: *Krozair of Kregen*, Volume 18: *Golden Scorpio*, Volume 22: *A Victory for Kregen*, Volume 26: *Allies of Antares*, Volume 32: *Seg the Bowman*, Volume 37: *Warlord of Antares*, Volume 43: *Scorpio Triumph*, and Volume 49: *Wrath of Antares*.

Abso: Master of an ill-fated canal boat ridden by Prescot. TOK
Ahilya Vorona, Lady: enamored of Yavnin Purvun. MOK, TOK
Aleygyn: leader of a band of assassins in Gafarden. MOK
Alten Schongar: a Vallian airboat commander. SHK
"An even more prudent man does not even think of venturing out into the snow": San Blarnoi's rejoinder to the old Kregan saying, "A prudent man will put on two coats when venturing out into the snow."
Ancidoins: a desert tribe of South Turismond.
ankster: sword with a double-curved blade.

Banko the Swarthy: apim jurukker in the personal guard of Nath the Clis. MOK
basich: Shank term for the inhabitants of Paz.
Belkion Clander: a Lamnian banker of Gafarden. TOK
Belkran the Gaoler: Brokelsh jailer of Gafarden. TOK
bishter: disparaging Shank term for a weyver.
Blanko the Arm: Brokelsh soldier of Vallia who accompanied Prescot into the death-chamber of the Thaumaturges of Sodan.

brackenberry: pungent variety of berry.

Chakarj Effect: physical effect responsible for floating islands.

Chemzite Room: room in The Zorca's Horn where Ulana Farlan stayed.

chinilun: a yellow-beaked creature like a flying octopus.

Chundrognik: a prison in Gafarden.

Chunformo the Shatterer of Chains, by: oath used by Tralgan Vorner.

Cindy Cwolanda: lady companion of Nalgre Nevko. MOK, TOK

Clandi: a Hytak slave of the Shanks. SHK

Claydoin Ma-Le: Pachak cadade in the guard of Culvensax. MOK

Cleito ti Lavven: a high-spirited young recruit to the Vallian Air Service. TOK

Clikroit: orange-scaled beast, with a wide flat body which bends upwards, six legs on the ground and two clawed arms, capable of wielding weapons. The head is triangular, with a mouth that goes back almost to the level of the crown, choked with yellow chompers.

Cooper's Alley: a street in Gafarden.

Culvensax: an Eltenate of Urn Vennar.

Cwofan ware: a variety of porcelain.

Dandelion Triumphant, The: a middling tavern in Gafarden that aspires to better things.

Darham: new name of Dahram the Bold.

Darjad, Kov of Ronaline Hill: alias used by Prescot in Schan.

Devron Obni: a high-quality variety of whetstone, similar to terrestrial Turkish stone.

Disabled Duck, The: a tavern in Larnydlad.

Djasra: island where the Kroveres of Iztar fought a band of Kataki slavers.

Engar Valmin: a member of the Kroveres of Iztar who helped pursue a band of Katakis from Djasra Island. SHK

Enterdrin: kingdom neighboring Larnydria in the Dawn Lands.

Erinor Farlan: former nazab of Urn Vennar, father of Ulana Farlan.

Esme: kovneva of Larnydria. MOK, TOK

faerling: a kind of bird.

Felandia: numim-ruled kingdom neighboring Enterdrin in the Dawn Lands.

Felima: landlady of a lodging house in Gafarden. TOK

Fenrio: a Fristle guard in the palace of Urn Vennar, killed by the Spectre. MOK

Finsi: a blind child rescued by Prescot in Gafarden. MOK

Fishbone Alley: a street in Gafarden, where once workers made needles from fish bones.

Fleet-Hooves: famous zorca who never lost a race.

Flint Alley: a street in Gafarden.

flistis: an epithet used by Shanks.

Flostan: Och serving lady in the palace of Gafarden. MOK

flutkamp: flying ace.

flutkapt: air marshal.

Franco: escaped Fristle slave of the Shanks. SHK

Frayling the Pen: a Xaffer under-stylor of Nath Swantram. TOK

Frazan ti Relzana: Hikdar in the army of King Zeg. MOK

Frewill: a Fristle under-chamberlain in the palace of Urn Vennar.

Frolicsome Nit, The: a tavern in Gafarden.

Gafarden: new capital city of Urn Vennar, named by Princess Didi in honor of her father Gafard.

Gaji's Bowels, by: an oath used by Prescot.

Garan the Stick: Gon under-chamberlain in the palace of Gafarden, killed by the Spectre. MOK

Gardenia Bower, The: a dining establishment in Gafarden.

Haberdasher's Avenue: a street in Gafarden.

Hangrol ti Ferstheim, Tyr: Savapim sent to rescue the kov and kovneva of Larnydria. MOK

Holy Tokai, by: oath used by Prescot.

Honim: a race of diffs.

"If you cannot understand the pain, it is torture. If you understand the pain, it is not torture": Saying attributed to San Blarnoi.

Ilkenesk, Mountains of: mountains to the west of the Eye of the World.

Ismelda: slave girl belonging to Nath Arovan, impregnated by him and sold away by his wife the Queen. SHK

Jodie the Traiky: wife and killer of Lart the Butcher.

Kadar ti Vernonsmot: alias used by Prescot in Gafarden.

kazzvew: "room of blood", site of a horrific murder scene.

Kaofaril: suicide squad.

Kolsh of the Tusks, by: a Chulik oath.

Lamki the Quick: escaped polsim slave of the Shanks. SHK

Landi the Harness: Deldar in the army of King Zeg, concerning whose sobriquet there is a scurrilous nickname. MOK

Languelsh: a race of diffs.

Larghos Fernleigh: chief stylor of Nath Swantram, murdered in Gafarden.

Larghos de la France: flamboyant Kregoinye who evacuated Ismelda from Schan. SHK, TOK

Larghos Ravan: alias used by Prescot when meeting Naghan Raerdu.

Larghos Thindan: worker in the Records Office of Urn Vennar, husband of Nessi Thindan. TOK

Larghos Vanka: known as the Smooth; an under-chamberlain in the palace of Urn Vennar.

Laringen Cut: Vallian canal which joins the Great Northern Canal.

Larming Street: a street in Gafarden.

Larnydlad: city in the Kovnate of Larnydria.

Larnydria: independent kovnate located in the Dawn Lands.

Lart: a ruffian adherent of the Racters, with impressive black eyebrows. TOK

Lart the Butcher: wife-beating butcher of Gafarden.

larver: epithet used by Shanks.

Larynx and Whistle, The: a small, quiet tavern in Gafarden.

Lazan-Yvon: known as the Inconducive, one of the Nine Thaumaturges of Sodan. TOK

Leonie the Pantry: a cook in the palace of Urn Vennar. MOK

Lesser Southern Cut: a canal passing through Gafarden.

Lexarm the Black Bastard: spirit of evil who enjoys piling misery upon misery.

Liflan Somanch: known as the Disputer, a Fristle lawyer of Gafarden, killed by the Spectre.

Lily: airboat hijacked by a band of assassins.

Little Lace Street: a street in Gafarden.

Logan Verlan: a Hikdar in the Vallian Air Service, son of Strom Ornol.

Lohvanna of the Grotto, by: oath used by Tobi.

Lokushi the Cranstemer: escaped Chulik slave of the Shanks. SHK

"Lola's Sweet Armpits": title of a song.

Lomax the Potion: a physician of Gafarden.

lompa: an edible fat white tuber.

Loomel the Avaricious: a Languelsh oath.

Loren ti Vandiyar, San: author of an ancient and famous treatise on rapier-and-dagger work against multiple opponents.

Lorgon ti Thrandor: Pallan of Canals in Urn Vennar. MOK

Lornrod the Poultice: physician in the palace of Urn Vennar. TOK

lustrous lips and bright eyes of the Maiden Katie of the Lake, by the: oath used by Prescot.

Maksting: a large raptor, black in color, with metallic gold beak and claws, which sometimes spies on Prescot on behalf of forces unknown.

Mantig Roben ti Vindlesheim: Vallian Pallan of canals.

Martine the Cheeks, for the sweet sake of: oath used by Prescot.

Matty: daughter of Jodie the Traiky. MOK

Medi Milva: a lady friend of Tobi Vingal. TOK

Mother Phrutil, by: oath used by Prescot.

Mothers of Carnage: fierce sisterhood of Rapa women rebelling against male brutality.

Muldaur: a kingdom of Kregen.

Naghan the Slippy: nickname of Naghan Raerdu, grandson of Naghan the Barrel. MOK, TOK

Nalgre Avansur: a judge of Urn Vennar. MOK

Nalgre the Fornstetter: guardsman killed in a conflict with Schnarlers. MOK

Nalgre Nevko: comrade of Prescot in Gafarden.

Nalgre the Punctilious: nickname of Rango Nalgre na Voilarmin.

Nalgre na Voilarmin, Rango: pallan of the Vallian Presidio appointed to look after Prescot on the trip to Urn Vennar. MOK

Nalgre Vorner, Lord: father of Tralgan Vorner.

Nal-Hi-Munting: wizard of Loh introduced to Prescot by Khe-Hi-Bjanching.

Nasan-Ydor: known as the Inculcator, one of the Nine Thaumaturges of Sodan. MOK, TOK

Nath Arovan: Ling of Muldaur.

Nath Arumsted ti Volsover: a new and enthusiastic member of the Kroveres of Iztar, killed in an engagement with a band of Katakis. SHK

Nath the Ale: a barrel master in the palace of Urn Vennar, killed by the Spectre. MOK

Nath the Clepper: acquaintance of Darham the Bold who was a talented voller pilot.

Nath the Clis: nickname for Nath Swantram.

Nath Feringhim, Deldar: punctilious guard in the palace of Urn Vennar. TOK

Nath Feslon: identity assumed by Tralgan Vorner when talking to Prescot.

Nath the Hides: owner of a warehouse at the junction of the Laringen Cut and Great Northern Canal.

Nath the Pinion: servitor who assassinated Nath Verunder. MOK

Nath the Quill: Och slave working as a scribe for the Shanks.

Nath Redfern: known as Nath the Limp, a watchman of Gafarden. TOK

Nath the Righteous: a judge of Urn Vennar.

Nath the Rumphious, Deldar: Hytak member of the Gafarden palace guard. MOK, TOK

Nath Swantram: chief pallan of Urn Vennar. MOK, TOK

Nath Verunder: justicar sent to take over the province of Urn Vennar. MOK

nawish: beast with a hide like goatskin.

nazab/nazabni: governor/governess of an Imperial province.

Nelana Lishmey: a trusted agent of Naghan Raerdu. TOK

Nessi Thindan: worker in the Records Office of Urn Vennar, wife of Larghos Thindan. TOK

Nine Arcades of Sodan, by the: oath used by Rafan-Ymet.

Nine Thaumaturges of Sodan: nine wizards who in the long ago had tried to usurp all power and rule Vallia.

Nogal Venning: under-pallan of Urn Vennar.

Norgad the Sweeps, Ven: boatman who betrayed Nath the Clis. MOK

Nose of Zogo: promontory which projects into the Inner Sea between Zamu to the east and Zandikar to the west.

N'sharg: Neesharg.

Onko: Och slave working as a scribe for the Shanks.

Ornol the Books: scribe in the palace of Urn Vennar. MOK

Ornol the Firm: a member of the Kroveres of Iztar, killed in an engagement with a band of Katakis. SHK

Ornol Havening: an under-chamberlain in the palace of Urn Vennar. TOK

Ornol Lodermair: a cousin of Tralgan Vorner, named Elten of Culvensax. MOK

Otlora Song, the: a new song in Vallia, a chirrupy little tune that runs around like a puppy chasing its tail. The words are a rigmarole of nonsense that can be interpreted as one wishes.

Otto the Lance: kregoinye whom Prescot assisted in the Dawn Lands. MOK, TOK

Paline: girl acting as a go-between for assassins in Gafarden. MOK

Panral, Kov: former employer of Tralgan Vorner in Pandahem.

peaker: dagger with grooves down the blade coated with poison.

Pilotus: range of mountains.

Pink Lily: flier used by the Kroveres of Iztar to pursue a band of Katakis from Djasra Island.

Polifa, Lady: wife of San Wunbigen. TOK

Potion and Quill, The: a tavern in Gafarden.

Prangman ti Volden, Tyr: a prominent member of the resurgent Racter party. TOK

Pranton the Faranto: new Khibil cadade of Nath the Clis's guard. MOK

Provender Avenue: a street in Gafarden.

Pundalad: powerful and wealthy city in the southwest tip of Pandahem.

Purple Violet: voller used by Prescot to fly to Urn Vennar.

Quarmby: an Och under-chamberlain of Urn Vennar.

Rafan-Ymet: known as the Ineluctor, one of the Nine Thaumaturges of Sodan.

Rampas the Silky: a thief of Gafarden. MOK

Randalt: kov of Larnydria. MOK, TOK

Razinye: a Star Lord. SHK

Rendo Froison: known as the Blatter, Rapa captain of the palace guard in Urn Vennar. TOK

Rikto the All-Glorious: king who long ago imprisoned the Nine Thaumaturges of Sodan by trickery.

Reemin: a grey-furred fanged beast.

Rendil Overnon: nazab of Urn Vennar following Rennel Lorving. TOK

Rennel Lorving: new nazab of Urn Vennar.

Rhapapolana the Stitcher of Skulls, by: a Rapa oath.

Rikto the All-Glorious, King: king of ages past who entombed the Nine Thaumaturges of Sodan by wiles and trickery.

Ringald the Iarvin: Rapa captain of Nath the Clis's personal guard. MOK

Roildon and Renang, The: a better-class tavern in Gafarden.

Rokveil and Aeilssa: a tavern in Gafarden.

Rolan Ledwidge: a spry, useful old Vallian sailor. SHK

ronaline: strawberry.

roz: term used in the Inner Sea equivalent to kov (duke).

roznate: duchy.

Ruben ti Drovensmot: Hikdar in Prescot's guard corps. MOK

Rubin the Merry: soldier of Vallia, killed by a reemin.

Samdo: a ruffian adherent of the Racters. TOK

San Belshui of the Steaming Pot, by: oath used by Prescot.

sand-leem: desert-dwelling version of the Kregan predator used as half-tamed hunting beasts by the Ancidoins.

Schanake: a Shank succored by Prescot. SHK

Schandler: a deity of Schan.

Schannish: language spoken in Schan, the grouping of continents and islands in the hemisphere opposite to Paz.

Schnarler: swamp-dwelling, squamous, toad-like race of diffs, who typically emerge from their swamps to prey on passing caravans.

Scompeto: beast which crawls on a number of scaly legs, four jaws gaping into a cross of yellow fangs, dripping slime, waving tendrils, and hide glistening greenish gray.

Selena: a Fristle serving-maiden in the palace of Urn Vennar. TOK

Semtilla the Fair: one-time name of Lazan-Yvon the Inconducive.

Sereblind: a Shank deity.

Shalaam river folk: red-hut-dwellers of a muddy river delta.

Shando the Fomenter: a watchman in Gafarden. TOK

Sharg: nickname for Shargs.

"She Lived by the Lily Canal": title of a song.

Shiraz!: a toast popular in Loh.

shrimpa: variety of tree which can be tapped for a sweet drink.

Silver Quill, The: a tavern in Gafarden.

Sinkie the Earrings: a Sylvie serving-maid working in Nath Swantram's apartments. TOK

Skoll and Durkon, The: a cheap, rowdy tavern in Gafarden.

Skylark Bank: a canal waterfront district in Gafarden.

Sodan, Temple of: ancient temple where evil rites were performed.

Sonylo, Master: helmsman of a canal boat ridden by Prescot. TOK

Starson: name used by Otto the Lance.

Stasia: Shank lady rescued by Schanake. SHK

Stinshish: a slave camp in Schan.

Storori of Lights: Shank friend of Schanake. SHK

Surrey: name used by Otto the Lance.

Tanzy the Smile: a Syblian serving girl in the palace of Urn Vennar. TOK

Tassie: girlfriend of Tobi Vingal.

Terzul: a large coastal Shank city.

Thisi: even plumper wife of Lorgon ti Thrandor. MOK

Thoth Tower: a tower in the castle of Vornerhold.

three blinks of a leem's eyes: a very short time period.

Tikur: race of diffs whose mores are lamentable, whose social graces are unpolished, to whom an honest day's work is anathema and who seldom if ever observe the Fantamyrrh.

Tobi Vingal: Vallian reveler who helped fight off a party of assassins. MOK, TOK

Tovah the Tempestuous: Queen of Muldaur.

Tralgan Vorner: rightful Elten of Culvensax, sentenced to death in a trial of dubious fairness. MOK, TOK

Tremiso the Deft: shal-needleman who accompanied Prescot into the death-chamber of the Thaumaturges of Sodan. TOK

Ulana Farlan: nazabni of Urn Vennar.

Unhanged Drikinger, The: a shady hostelry in Gafarden.
Urn Vennar: a Vallian province.

Vamgal the Arm: a Deldar in Prescot's Guard Corps. MOK
Vanner the Downright: a Hytak imperial loyalist of Gafarden. TOK
vanxter: name given impartially to any of the various patterns of
fighting swords newly developed in Vallia.
Velia Avenue: a street in Gafarden.
voinsh: happy.
Vorner: an old Vallian family with a dark reputation.
Vornerhold: ancestral castle of the Vorner family.

Wainwright Street: a street in Gafarden.
Wantry: a pale yellow wine from the spice islands of Donengil.
weyver: a barge-like voller with tremendous carrying capacity.
Wunbigen, San: a Wizard of Fruningen who accompanied Prescot
into the death chamber of the Thaumaturges of Sodan. TOK

Xervan: a servitor of Rendil Overnon. TOK

yallom: fruit almost identical to a banana.
Yavnin Purvun: a Jiktar in the Vallian Air Corps. MOK, TOK
Yinfitter: a people fond of drums and bagpipes.
Yoftin: race of diffs with jackal-features and stiff hair, all prickly and
spiky, renowned for their callous treatment of their womenfolk
and their inhuman torments of their captives.

Zairfaril: voller used by King Zeg to fly to the aid of Prescot and Didi's
party in south Zairia.
Zinkara: river running from the Mountains of Ilkenesk to the Eye of
the World.
Zorca's Horn, The: an expensive inn in Gafarden.
Zoronsh: a Shank noble enamored of the Lady Stasia.
Zumbaya: a Kregan country.
Zygon Farzena, Pur: a Krozair of Zimuzz who visited Prescot in
Gafarden. TOK

About the author

Alan Burt Akers was a pen name of the prolific British author Kenneth Bulmer, who died in December 2005 aged eighty-four.

Bulmer wrote over 160 novels and countless short stories, predominantly science fiction, both under his real name and numerous pseudonyms, including Alan Burt Akers, Frank Brandon, Rupert Clinton, Ernest Corley, Peter Green, Adam Hardy, Philip Kent, Bruno Krauss, Karl Maras, Manning Norvil, Chesman Scot, Nelson Sherwood, Richard Silver, H. Philip Stratford, and Tully Zetford. Kenneth Johns was a collective pseudonym used for a collaboration with author John Newman. Some of Bulmer's works were published along with the works of other authors under "house names" (collective pseudonyms) such as Ken Blake (for a series of tie-ins with the 1970s television programme The Professionals), Arthur Frazier, Neil Langholm, Charles R. Pike, and Andrew Quiller.

Bulmer was also active in science fiction fandom, and in the 1970s he edited nine issues of the New Writings in Science Fiction anthology series in succession to John Carnell, who originated the series.